continued . . .

"Beautiful, earthy, and completely accessible prose . . . classic historical fiction at its best."   —Historical Novel Society

"An immersive, enlightening epic . . . intrigue, romance, and strong, willful heroines."   —*Booklist*

Daughter of the Gods

"Stephanie Thornton's heroines are bold, brave, and powerful."
                        —Kate Quinn, author of *Lady of the Eternal City*

"A wonderfully intimate and dramatic evocation of ancient Egypt, where one headstrong young woman dares to become pharaoh. Stephanie Thornton vividly portrays the heat and the danger, the passion and the heartbreak, of Hatshepsut's struggle as she defies even the gods to ensure success on the throne of Egypt. A touching love story combines with a thrilling tale of death, courage, and political intrigue to produce a superbly researched and powerfully written novel. This is the kind of book that grabs you by the throat and doesn't let go. A remarkable story, remarkably told."
                        —Kate Furnivall, national bestselling author of
                        The Russian Concubine and *Shadows on the Nile*

"An epic saga that brings ancient Egypt to life with vivid imagery and lovely prose. Stephanie Thornton is a rising star!"
                        —Stephanie Dray, bestselling author of *Daughters of the Nile*

The Secret History

"What a heroine! Stephanie Thornton's Theodora is tough and intelligent, spitting defiance against the cruel world of the Byzantine Empire. Her rise from street urchin to emperor's consort made me want to stand up and cheer. Her later years as empress are great fun to read, but it was her early struggle as actress and courtesan that really had me roaring: either with rage at the misfortunes heaped on this poor girl or with delight as she once more picked herself up with a steely glint in her eye and kept on going." —Kate Quinn

THE CONQUEROR'S WIFE

A Novel of Alexander the Great

STEPHANIE THORNTON

 NEW AMERICAN LIBRARY

NEW AMERICAN LIBRARY
Published by New American Library,
an imprint of Penguin Random House LLC
375 Hudson Street, New York, New York 10014

This book is an original publication of New American Library.

First Printing, December 2015

For more information about Penguin Random House, visit penguin.com.

LIBRARY OF CONGRESS CATALOGING-IN-PUBLICATION DATA:

Thornton, Stephanie, 1980–
The conqueror's wife: a novel of Alexander the Great / Stephanie Thornton.
pages cm
ISBN 978-0-451-47200-7 (softcover)
1. Alexander, the Great, 356 B.C.–323 B.C.—Fiction.   2. Greece—History—Macedonian
Expansion, 359–323 B.C.—Fiction.   3. Roxana, consort of Alexander the Great, approximately
310 B.C.—Fiction.   4. Macedonia—History—To 168 B.C.—Fiction.   I. Title.
PS3620.H7847C66 2015
813'.6—dc23   2015019747

Printed in the United States of America
10 9 8 7 6 5 4 3 2 1

Designed by Laura K. Corless

Penguin
Random
House

To Tim and Daine Crowley
for being as tough as Alexander to champion all my writing

THE CONQUEROR'S WIFE

Alexander deemed himself a god, the mythic descendant of Achilles and the son of Zeus, and entire nations fell to their knees in ecstatic worship of him. But he was no god any more than we were nymphs and dryads, benevolent four-hoofed centaurs or vengeful three-headed chimeras.

He called himself Alexander the Great and claimed that he conquered the world. But he would have been lucky to conquer a stinking midden heap populated by swarms of biting flies had it not been for our cunning and daring.

Alexander founded cities of culture and learning, and named them after himself in a fit of hubris. But he razed more cities than there are stars in the sky, slaughtered their men, and burned their ancient palaces so that the four winds carried the gray ashes to rain down upon lands more distant than Alexandria-the-Farthest.

He claimed that the earth trembled, mountains quivered, and oceans overflowed their shores at his approach, but without us, Alexander would never have mounted a single golden throne or worn the coveted eagle diadem of Persia, much less the combined crowns of Greece, Egypt, and India.

Like Achilles, he sought glory and everlasting fame, and beseeched the gods that his name would echo throughout history. Yet so many of his baser deeds have been forgotten, or retold to forge him into a hero worthy of epic ballads.

But that is only part of the story.

It was because of him, and for him, that we did great, and also terrible, things.

Just as Zeus sat in his throne room atop Olympus, surrounded by the gods of violence and light, the goddesses of desire and the hearth, so too was Alexander surrounded by us.

His lover.

His sister.

His wife.

His soldier.

We were murderers and poisoners, innocents and warriors. And without us, Alexander would have been only a man.

Instead, he was a god.

❋ · CHAPTER 1 · ❋

336 BCE
Aigai, Macedon

THESSALONIKE

I thought the wedding feast a threefold gift from Olympus: We celebrated our newly made political alliances, dined on more Delian honey cakes than I could stuff in my cheeks, and witnessed the return of my golden brother from his scandalous exile. Yet in the days to come I would wonder if we had offended the gods or if perhaps the Olympians merely found our petty lives tiresome after the extravagance of the marriage ceremony. Regardless of the cause, the three old crones of Fate set their rusty shears to cutting countless lifestrings after that terrible day.

The morning began with a banquet of dried apricots, flat *staititas* topped with sesame seeds and goat cheese, and crusty loaves of olive bread meant to symbolize the fertility of the recently deflowered bride—one of my barely known half sisters—wed today to a dour client king of Molossia.

"You have honey on your cheek, Thessalonike." The youngest of my father's seven wives and his current favorite, Eurydice, pursed her cinnabar-stained lips at me from across the women's table. "And I think you've had quite enough apricots, lest they make you plumper than you already are."

I rubbed my sleep-heavy eyes and licked away the sticky sweetness with my tongue, earning stern glares from all my father's wives and a lopsided grin from my half brother Arrhidaeus.

"Like a frog, Nike," he said, bouncing in his seat and clapping his fat hands before him. The son of a common Illyrian dancing girl, Arrhidaeus was twice my ten summers, but his mind remained that of a child. Despite his towering height and broad shoulders, he was allowed to sit on the women's side of the hall because none of the men would have him.

"Or a salamander." I laughed, letting my tongue flick between my teeth until Eurydice kicked my foot beneath the table. I scowled, wishing my pretty stepmother were still confined to her chambers with her infant son, where she couldn't nag me.

The last apricot drizzled with honey beckoned, so I shoved it into my mouth before Eurydice could swat my hand. This afternoon would include endless recitations of Homer's moth-eaten poems and prizes of gold bullion for the finest sculpture celebrating the marriage alliance between Epirus and Macedon, but I was hoping to sneak away to watch the javelin throwers and *pankration* matches. If I was lucky, maybe the *pankratiasts* would break the rules and try to gouge out each other's eyes.

If I were ever a naked and oiled *pankratiast*—which I never would be because I had the misfortune of being born both a girl *and* royal—the first thing I would do was go for the eyes.

In fact, Arrhidaeus had long ago shortened my name to Nike—the rest of my name proving too cumbersome—and it suited me to share the name with the winged goddess of victory, for like Nike I loved to win above all things.

"Come," Eurydice said, standing and smoothing the elaborate pleats of her woolen *peplos*. "We shall continue our weaving until the men return from the arena. Then Philip has granted us permission to listen to the poets."

I stabbed my finger inside an olive, wishing I could do the same to my ears when it came time for the recitation. I dropped the pit to the ground, then winked at Arrhidaeus before I crushed the salty green flesh between my teeth. My half brother didn't notice, being too busy digging with a tiny silver spoon into a pomegranate. Eurydice swept off in a cloud of violet perfume. No one noticed—or perhaps cared— when I didn't follow. My father's youngest wife had pretensions of being a dutiful matron, but Eurydice was better suited to gossiping about the latest fashion of beaded girdles or how much her recent treatment of foul-smelling ceruse had whitened her skin.

"Follow me," I whispered to Arrhidaeus, casting a furtive glance around the hall.

"Where?" he asked. His thick lips drooped into a frown as he gave up on the spoon and used his fingers to fish the last juicy red seeds from the pomegranate's husk.

"To the arena," I said, pulling him from the table even as he licked his scarlet-stained palms. "I'd rather pluck my eyes out than spend the day weaving."

"No," he said, shaking his head. "Don't hurt your eyes."

"I won't, my Titan, at least not if you hurry."

My half brother grinned at my name for him. The Titans were immortal giants with tremendous strength (although they'd been overthrown by the Olympians, which I chose to ignore). Regardless, the nickname was kinder than the others my father's court called Arrhidaeus: "donkey face," "walnut brain," and "half-wit." Several of the nobles' foulmouthed sons had felt the sting of my slingshot in response, so now they held their tongues when I was nearby.

I glanced at the courtyard's columned entrance, the wilted olive branch that announced the birth of Eurydice's son still tied to the plinths, and saw that my eldest half brother, Alexander, and his boyhood companion Hephaestion had arrived, their hair damp and complexions ruddy from the baths. Their heads were bent in deep conversation—one the color of a lion's mane in summer sunshine and the other with curls as dark as a crow's wing in winter. Their claim on each other's affections was well-known throughout the palace and they'd walked in each other's shadows since Alexander's recent return to Aigai following his exile. Despite that, most of the women—and some of the men—now swiveled in the direction of my beautiful, scandal-laden brother, several holding chunks of bread suspended in midair as he and his friend passed.

Hephaestion's chiseled features softened as he stooped to whisper in my brother's ear before striding toward the table on the men's side of the courtyard, its walls decorated with a fresco of a griffin attacking a stag. Alexander arranged himself stiffly on a dining couch, his tawny hair parted in a severe line down the middle, and his lips curved into a frown as he glanced at our father's empty dais. My brother's return had inspired continuing whispers that Eurydice's newly delivered infant son would supplant him as our father's heir.

Life had been simple until my father married Eurydice of Macedon, her belly already swollen with a boy child, or so she had crowed to anyone who would listen. Perhaps it was a result of the wine or the summer's heat, but at their wedding ceremony Alexander's blood had almost been shed after Eurydice's father had offered a public prayer to Zeus to grant my father a new, full-blooded heir. Alexander, born of Philip's Macedonian and Olympias' Epirean blood, had leapt from his seat in a rage and thrown his cup of wine at Eurydice's father, causing my father to draw his sword. There was a collective gasp of shock as my father lunged forward, presumably to stab his own son, but instead he tripped on the edge of his couch and fell face-first to the ground. In the outrage that followed, Alexander and his mother were forced to flee from Aigai, leaving me bereft of both a brother and the woman who had raised me after my own mother died giving me life.

Alexander had been ordered home for the wedding, though our father utterly ignored him now that Eurydice had birthed his fully

Macedonian son. Olympias remained in exile, abandoned in Epirus with only her devotions to Dionysus, her famed pet snakes (which I adored, especially the spotted leopard snake I'd taught to tickle my feet with its tongue), and her hopes of one day seeing Alexander on the throne to keep her content. And that meant Eurydice remained in control of my father's household.

And in control of me, at least when she was paying attention.

We were almost to the doorway when a strong hand encircled my wrist. "Sneaking off again, Thessalonike?" Hephaestion's voice held an undercurrent of laughter. "I should return you to Eurydice," he said, popping a stray date into his mouth and chewing it thoughtfully. "I heard her mention an important tapestry, something about a design of Athena's defeat of Enceladus involving thousands of very complicated and extremely tiny knots."

I groaned and fell to my knees on the hall's black-and-white checkered mosaic. "Please, no. I'd rather you killed me first."

"No, Nike," Arrhidaeus said with an emphatic shake of his head. "No killing."

"Is my sister threatening another dramatic death?" Alexander asked as he stepped forward, his shadow falling on me. "What is it this time, Thessalonike? Impaled by Persian swords? Ripped apart by lions? Drowned by Scylla and Charybdis?"

"Nothing so glorious," I muttered. "Death by weaving."

Alexander, my golden half brother and descendant of both Heracles and Achilles, shared a grin with Hephaestion and laughed, leaving me scowling and Arrhidaeus' brows knit together in consternation so I had to pat his arm to reassure him that all was right in the world.

"Are you two going to release me or return me to my doom?" I asked, folding my arms in front of me.

Hephaestion tapped his chin. "She's a demanding little thing, isn't she?"

"Always has been," Alexander said. "When her mouth isn't full of sweetmeats or honey rolls, that is."

I stuck out my tongue at him. Some people stuttered in Alexander's presence, fearing his mercurial temper and the aura of the gods that clung to him, but I'd spent the full ten years of my life in his mother's household and knew that the man before me had recently been a boy who drooled in his sleep and kept a tattered copy of Homer's *Song of Ilium* under his pillow, believing it would imbue him with the power of Achilles.

"If you're going to continue insulting me," I said, "then Arrhidaeus and I are leaving for the arena."

"I'm sure that will go over well," Hephaestion said, glancing heavenward. "Surely no one will notice Philip's daughter at the men's games."

I narrowed my eyes in speculation. "They won't care if I'm accompanied by my father's son and heir."

A dark cloud passed over Alexander's features. I'd forgotten for a moment the talk of Eurydice's son supplanting him, but the storm passed as Hephaestion threw his arm around Alexander's broad shoulders. "You," he said to my brother, "must accompany your father into the stadium, but perhaps Arrhidaeus and I can escort young Thessalonike."

Alexander didn't answer, but he looked past us to where my father entered the courtyard, every guest lifting a terra-cotta *skyphos* of wine in his honor. Before my birth, the poets claimed that the birds sang of Philip's beauty, but now a livid pink scar ruined one side of his face, a battle wound from the siege of Methone that had also claimed his left eye as a spoil of war.

"If you go to the arena, go quickly." Alexander's own eyes—one the pale blue of a spring sky and the other the darker hue of an oncoming storm—remained shuttered as he tugged my blond curls, identical to his own. "Your secrets are safe with me, little sister."

I shrieked with glee, then grabbed Arrhidaeus' and Hephaestion's hands and dragged them from the hall, my blue *himation* flapping behind me while Arrhidaeus' chortles of laughter chased us on. Through the palace courtyard with its potted quince trees and then the apricot and pomegranate orchards, beyond the southern Sun Gate and the shuttered *agora*—its stalls closed in preparation for the glorious spectacle awaiting us—and then to the amphitheater nestled into the base of one of Aigai's rolling hills, its autumn grasses muted to a dull gold. Crowds of men swathed in furs already jostled for the best view of the naked wrestlers and javelin throwers, but we found seats near the bottom row. My eyes bulged to see my eldest half sister, Cynnane, seated nearby with her husband, Amyntas, a lone woman among a sea of men, her crinkly curls somewhat tamed by a sheen of olive oil and her body dressed not in her customary short *chiton* but in a refined *peplos* that flowed all the way to her sturdy ankles. I hadn't seen her since the birth of her daughter a few months ago, and women weren't allowed in the arena, but Cynnane wasn't a proper woman; she'd been instructed by her Illyrian mother in the ways of war, traditions passed down by the chieftains of their family for generations.

I ducked behind Arrhidaeus, glad for the shield of his hulking shoulders, for although being near Alexander never tied my tongue, I never failed to garble my words in Cynnane's imposing presence. The meager autumn sun had scarcely climbed over the horizon when the music of lyres and horns proclaimed the arrival of the twelve gods of Olympus.

Before the athletics could begin, priests dressed in white *chitons* strained beneath the weight of a sedan chair carrying a life-sized statue of Zeus. The great god of thunder scowled above his marble beard of curls and massive bare chest, poised as if to attack us with the mighty spear clutched forever in his hand. Behind the gods and goddesses of the sun and oceans, death and love, wisdom and war, came a thirteenth statue, bearing a striking likeness to the ruined man of flesh and blood who entered the earthen floor of the arena. The spectators cheered wildly at the sight of my bearlike father despite his lame left leg, dressed in his customary greaves and boiled leather armor, his black beard trimmed to the sharpness of a spearpoint. I shrank back as his good eye scanned the arena, my heart thudding in my chest.

And, like the gods that surrounded him, my father decided he need not rely on mortals for protection. He raised a hand beneath his white *chlamys*, dismissing his seven Royal Bodyguards and leaving himself flanked by only Alexander and today's bridegroom, two princes taking their places behind the battle-scarred warrior who had conquered Macedon and united all the Peloponnese people under his rule.

My father limped toward the center of the arena, lifting his arms and preparing to speak.

But a single guard doubled back from the entrance as the others exited, a black-haired man in a scarlet cape whom I recognized as Pausanius, my favorite of my father's Royal Bodyguards. Pausanius had spent much of his time guarding Alexander's mother, Olympias, before her exile and had often used his knife incised with spirals and concentric circles to cut my honeyed dates into bite-sized pieces. Now I thought that perhaps he carried some sort of urgent message. He came close to my startled father and embraced him. Then silver flashed in his hand like one of Zeus' lightning bolts thrown to earth.

A dagger.

Philip of Macedon, my indomitable father with a face ruined from battle and a body riddled with sword wounds, gave a deafening roar as he clutched his ribs. Pausanius stumbled back, then ran across the open ground and through the doors of the stadium, the same entrance through which my father had just strode, ready to be enthroned as a god.

No one moved as crimson stained the ground. It wasn't until an

ocean of red spread from the vulnerable spot in my father's cuirass
and down his chest that the crowd began to scream and my mind
made sense of what I'd seen.

My father had been stabbed and now his lifeblood lured Hades
to drag his shade to the underworld.

In one terrible slow moment he fell to his knees in the dirt, clasping his ribs, as Alexander ran to him and shouts rang out across the
arena.

I screamed, the never-ending sound coming like water from
behind a broken dyke, and Hephaestion vaulted the short wall onto
the arena floor. "Arrhidaeus," he commanded over his shoulder, "take
Thessalonike back to the palace. Keep her safe." He called to my
half sister with her wild hair even as her husband followed Alexander. "Cynnane, accompany them!"

I stood, transfixed as my father's lifeblood poured in a torrent
from his chest. I'd watched spotted goats and pristine white calves
being sacrificed in the names of our gods, but never before had I seen
a man die. Arrhidaeus slung me over his shoulder, but I twisted and
strained for a glimpse of my father as the remainder of his bodyguards surrounded him. Alexander stood over our father, clasping
the hilt of the decorated knife that had once cut my sweetmeats and
now gleamed with our father's blood. The air seemed to shift above
Philip of Macedon and I knew he was dead then, his *psyche* released
from his body like a tremulous gust of wind.

"This dagger shall usher one more shade to Hades before the day
is done," Alexander yelled. "Find Pausanius and drag the filthy assassin here so I might bury this blade into his belly as he did my father!"

He said something more, but I couldn't hear—the crowd swallowed the sight of my brother, and my ribs slammed into Arrhidaeus'
shoulder as he bounded out of the amphitheater and over the cobbles, dodging children playing with hoops and sticks, gossiping slave
girls carrying baskets and drop spindles, and donkeys pulling carts

of unglazed pottery. Hot tears clouded my vision, but Cynnane loped after us, a drawn dagger in her hand.

"Let me go," I yelled, banging my feeble fists into Arrhidaeus' back, but he ran on. It wasn't until we were almost to the city's Sun Gate that he paused, bent double and his chest heaving. I scrambled down, ready to lambaste him despite my tears, when a flash of color caught my eye.

A scarlet cape—my father's Royal Bodyguard. I ignored Arrhidaeus' bellowed protests as I darted down a side street toward the shrine of Aphrodite, Cynnane yelling behind me.

The sight of Pausanius' dark shock of hair made me run faster than I'd ever run before. Ahead at the gate, another man astride a yellow mare held the reins of a second horse while hollering and beckoning wildly for my father's murderer.

"Pausanius!" I screamed. I had no sword or spear, but I bent and heaved at his head a handful of pebbles from a potted orange tree, wishing for my slingshot and hoping to blind him if he turned at just the right moment. He turned, but only leered as the worthless stones showered the ground at his feet.

Yet whatever he saw behind me catapulted his expression into one of sheer terror.

He ran faster then, arms pumping as the waiting man kicked hard the ribs of the yellow mare and galloped out of the gate. Perhaps Artemis, goddess of the hunt, and Dike, goddess of righteousness, joined together to see justice done that day, for silver flashed from behind me and embedded itself in Pausanius' thigh. He crashed into the cobbles with a howl of rage, clutching his skewered leg. And then Cynnane was beside me, her hair in ever wilder disarray and her dagger hilt empty.

"Blades are more effective than stones, little one," she said with a tweak of my nose. "Remember that."

A larger flash of scarlet and silver emerged from the main street and the remainder of my father's guards hurtled toward Pausanius with their swords.

"Stop!" I shouted. The men hesitated, blades poised to strike, the bloodlust in their eyes making me recoil in fear. Pausanius cowered at their feet, the trembling mongrel curled into himself. "My brother Alexander commanded you to bring this criminal to him," I said, gasping for breath even as I raised a hand to halt them. "He, not you, should punish Pausanius."

A crowd had gathered, but Cynnane stepped into the fray then, bent, and pulled her dagger from Pausanius' thigh. She wiped its blood on her *peplos* and resheathed the blade in her leather belt. "Do as the child says," she commanded. "Pausanius of Orestis doesn't deserve a quick dispatch to Hades."

"We don't take orders from a woman," one of the men growled. "Or a girl."

"Then I'll slit you open from your eyeballs to your asshole," Cynnane said, grasping the hilt of her dagger once again. "After which Hades himself can give you orders."

"You'll do as Alexander commanded," I said. "For he is our brother, and your new *basileus*."

No one moved for a long moment, but then the fury in the guards' eyes banked, albeit grudgingly. "Do as she says," the commander barked.

"Drag him through the gutters and hit his head against as many curbs as you can," Cynnane said. "This one deserves a painful and creative death."

Arrhidaeus broke through the crowd then and jogged to us, cringing and covering his eyes as the guards grabbed hold of Pausanius' ankles and hauled our father's murderer over the cobbles, leaving a sluice of crimson to mark their path back to the arena. I waited until they were gone, then sank to my knees in the street.

"Home, Nike," Arrhidaeus said, shaking my shoulder none too gently. "Hephaestion said to go home."

"Give her a moment," Cynnane said, but her voice was kind. "It takes more than a breath to recover after you've first seen men's blood spilled."

Not just any men's blood. My father's blood. And his murderer's.

I wanted nothing more in that instant than to be in my bed, with my shaggy goat, Pan, curled at my feet and my fat orange tomcat purring on my lap, a plate of honeyed apricots at my elbow and all of this a bad dream already fading into nothingness. Instead, I started to shiver, my teeth chattering as if an icy blanket had been wrapped around my shoulders.

"Take me home, Arrhidaeus," I whispered even as he crouched down so I could climb onto his back. "Please just take me home."

The gods granted Cynnane's wish for Pausanius' painful and creative death.

Tenfold.

Pausanius had been dragged back to the arena for Alexander to mete out the sentence mandated for a king-killer. Buckets of chilled water were thrown to revive him so he might see himself stripped naked while five iron clamps fixed him to a rough-hewn plank at his ankles, wrists, and neck. The dagger he'd used to stab my father was tied around his neck, both as a reminder of his crime and also to taunt him as he was left to slowly starve to death, unable to seek solace in suicide. Children threw rotten onions at him and wild dogs nipped his bound heels, but he remained on exhibition outside the palace gates, shivering by night and mired in his own urine and feces as the days passed. I did my best to avoid the rotting heap of flesh, staying in my rooms and playing with my goat, my lazy orange cat, and the three-legged tortoise I'd recently rescued. Even still, I heard my slaves whisper that Pausanius lingered so he might greet the woman who ordered his assassin's act. Yet not even Pausanius could hide from Hades forever. The moldering god of death finally claimed my father's murderer as dawn streaked the sky with orange on the same morning that Olympias arrived in Aigai.

The return of Alexander and his mother had each ushered a man's soul to the river Styx, so that superstitious minds might have wondered if perhaps my brother and Olympias had made a pact with the god of the underworld. My naive child's mind was foolish enough to believe we'd seen the end of the bloodshed.

Ignoring the pike that still held Pausanius' body, I ran to greet Olympias as her procession approached the palace walls, but she scarcely looked at me as she took Alexander's hand and alighted from her ebony litter. The pleats of her *peplos* brushed her polished leather sandals, and her burnished copper hair was coiled into flawless ringlets and threaded to frame her face.

"There is much to talk about, my son," I heard her murmur in Alexander's ear, even as her eyes strayed to where Pausanius remained, the crows that had been startled away by her arrival daring to flutter closer. "You must speak to Antipater, convince your father's general to throw his weight behind you to ensure the army's support for your claim—"

"First we carry my father to his tomb," Alexander reminded her. "Come dawn, I shall speak to Antipater and any other man you suggest."

"Of course. And now I would pay my respects to the dead."

I thought she meant she'd like to stand vigil with my father, but instead she flicked a wrist and a slave appeared at her side bearing a thin golden diadem on a cushion dyed with precious Tyrian purple. She placed the crown upon Pausanius' rotting head and bowed over her hands. "I dedicate the blade you used against Philip to Apollo," she said to the dead assassin, cutting the dagger free from his blackened neck. "Your praises shall be sung to eternity."

I stared openmouthed at her, my mind churning to realize that Olympias approved of her husband's murder. Even worse, the slaves might be correct in thinking she'd ordered Pausanius to kill my father. "Did you want my father to die?" I blurted out.

Olympias leveled an iron stare at me and I shrank back, wishing I could catch the words and swallow them.

"The poor dear is overcome with grief, isn't she?" Olympias murmured to Alexander. "No, little Nike, I didn't seek Philip's death. But his tyrant's blood has watered the earth. Life must continue."

To the handful of gathered courtiers she offered a widow's watery eyes. "The Delphic oracle once proclaimed to Philip of Macedon that the end was near, the sacrificer at hand. My husband believed this meant the war against Persia would soon be won, but such hubris challenged the gods, and thus, Pausanius merely meted out their justice."

But she had praised Pausanius' corpse. Olympias was the only mother I knew, yet my father's words after her exile floated to my mind, that she was as slippery as the snakes that she cultivated. And even a venomous adder might sometimes be mistaken for a common grass snake.

But Olympias was the woman who had gifted me with tiny iron cages for my own menagerie of lizards, toads, and broken-winged sparrows. Surely she mourned my father's death.

She slipped her arm through Alexander's and drew him toward the palace's main entrance, the rest of us following close behind. "There is still the matter of Amyntas, Eurydice, and her son."

"You needn't worry about Cynnane's husband," Alexander said. "But I shall not allow harm to befall a mother and her infant."

Olympias' lips thinned into a tight smile. "How benevolent of you."

"I forbid it, Mother."

"Of course, my son," Olympias said. "I shall do whatever you

deem necessary, yet surely it is far from wise to allow your closest
rival and his mother to prosper under your roof."

"There is no need to harm a child and his mother, her breasts
still heavy with milk," Alexander said, his voice hard as stone. "That
is my final decision in the matter, Mother."

I shuddered, chilled to the marrow of my bones at Olympias' suggestion. I wondered then what she would have done had I been born
a boy, a threat to Alexander's place as Macedon's heir. Would my name
have been whispered along with insinuations of murder before I was
old enough to toddle and talk?

For once, I was glad I was merely the worthless daughter of my
father's third wife.

I stood behind Arrhidaeus in the funeral *ekphora* as my father's
court gathered in the main courtyard that night. Slaves bearing
golden spears and arrows, ivory-studded armor, and silver shields
emblazoned with Macedon's star would carry my father's final treasures to surround his golden *larnax* before his bones and ashes were
forever locked in his tomb, its frescoes of Hades' abduction of Perse-
phone still damp to the touch. My father's wives were draped in
linens dyed with black oak apple and carried an assortment of golden
urns, bronze pouring *kraters*, and a gilded Medusa head to protect
the grave goods from robbers. It was only later that I realized two
of the wives were missing from the flock of perfumed black women
honking their noses into their sleeves.

Alexander lit a torch that illuminated our father's body, wrapped
in fine linen and crowned with a golden diadem of acorns and laurel
leaves. My father had been gruff and sometimes even cruel in life,
but my throat felt raw as I tried to swallow, remembering the man
who had gifted me with a pony and a wooden sword, reenacted the

battle of Thessaly from the day of my birth, and taught me to parry his blows with Alexander's cast-off toy shield. I'd failed with the sword and shield, but the pony and I had become inseparable, the first in my little menagerie.

Next to me, Arrhidaeus began to whimper and the sounds quickly turned to ragged sobs. "I don't want Father to be dead," he whined. "And I don't want him in the fire or alone in the dark."

Alexander glanced back at us with irritation, but it was Hephaestion who approached, carrying a torch to cast us in light stolen from the sun.

"How are you faring, Arrhidaeus?" he asked.

"It's dark and our father is about to be burned and buried," I muttered under my breath. "How do you think he fares?"

Arrhidaeus cried louder, like a puppy being whipped.

"He should remain here," I said. "I'll stay with him."

Hephaestion shook his head. "Philip was your father too. You follow Alexander and I'll take care of Arrhidaeus. Maybe you can beat me at the discus again, eh, Arrhidaeus?"

If there was anyone who could best Hephaestion at discus throwing, it was Arrhidaeus, but even that didn't soothe my brother's sobs.

"You go," I said to Hephaestion, then tugged on Arrhidaeus' hand. "Let's see if we can teach my goat, Pan, to carry our new tortoise on her head like a helmet."

"A tortoise helmet?" Arrhidaeus said, rubbing his nose and leaving behind a trail of glistening snot. "That's silly, Nike."

Hephaestion winked at me. "If it works, perhaps I'll ask Alexander to commission tortoise helmets for the entire army."

Arrhidaeus' crying eased enough for me to lead him away from the entourage with its flaming torches that would soon light my father's *pyra*, but my cheeks flushed as I glanced back in time to see Hephaestion offer me a little bow.

Arrhidaeus and I had scarcely entered the palace corridors,

freshly scrubbed with seawater and hyssop to purify them of my father's death, when I plunged my brother into a hell worse than any tomb.

It started with a baby's cry and a woman's unceasing scream.

And the smell of fire.

Lit by the sickle moon, a burgeoning flag of colorless smoke billowed from above the nursery roof. Still holding my brother's hand, I ran toward the nursery, but the plumes now swelled skyward from the children's small tiled courtyard, with the fountain I loved to run through and the wicker cages of doves that pecked delicately at the sesame seeds I brought them. I reared back to see a *pyra* burning amid the juniper bushes and potted lemon trees.

And within the *pyra*, a woman I knew, in a blue *peplos* I knew, bound arms curved around a bundle I knew. Only now her violet perfume was gone in a cloud of embers as she writhed and screamed.

Bile rose in my throat as the breeze tossed the scent of burning flesh and cedar into the wine-dark heavens. The heat of the fire pushed me back and Eurydice's screams and her son's cries fell silent, replaced by the greedy crackle of flames and Arrhidaeus' renewed howls.

Olympias stood before the conflagration, wearing an expression of ecstasy as shadow-flames danced on her face and her golden snake bracelets seemed to writhe up her arms. I choked and clamped my eyes closed, wishing I could unsee the image seared into my mind.

And I knew then that my father was right, that Olympias was worse than any viper.

"No," Arrhidaeus shouted. "No, no, no!"

"Remove Arrhidaeus to his rooms," Olympias commanded. I opened my eyes as guards stepped from the shadows and pulled Arrhidaeus back from the makeshift *pyra* even as he reached out as if to rescue the bodies from the flames. I ducked my head and turned to follow, my lungs screaming as I tried not to breathe, but Olympias' voice stopped me cold. "You shall stay by my side, Thessalonike." I cringed, my every muscle trembling as if Poseidon shook the ground beneath my feet. "One day you may be queen of Thessaly or Illyria or even Sparta, and this"—she gestured toward the *pyra*—"is a lesson all queens must learn."

I had no choice but to obey, yet I set my gaze beyond the fire with its hisses and smell of Hades' brimstone and desolation, trying desperately to ignore the blackened silhouettes—one tall and one so very tiny—in the middle of the flames. I'd harbored no love for Eurydice, but surely she hadn't deserved to die. And her tiny son . . .

"Eurydice was a traitor," Olympias said, as if reading my thoughts. "And traitors must die terrible deaths. Remember that, if ever you are tempted toward leniency for your enemies."

"But Eurydice only wanted what you wanted," I choked out, shocked at my own daring and stupidity. "To put her son on the throne."

"Perhaps," Olympias said. "And for that, I gave her the mercy of dousing the wood with olive oil."

I was saved from having to speak, or perhaps from having my tongue chopped out, as Alexander barreled into the courtyard behind me, the disbelief on his face warped first by shock and then by rage. His wild eyes scanned the fire and he recoiled; then he drew his sword and pointed its tip at Olympias' throat. "You've overstepped yourself, Mother!"

"You are supposed to be at your father's tomb," Olympias said. She tilted her chin back as if daring him to slit her pale throat. "This was to be done and the ashes swept away before you returned."

"I forbade this!" he yelled, motioning at the *pyra*. "Eurydice and her son were as harmless as Arrhidaeus!"

My mouth went dry and it became impossible to swallow around what might have been shards of glass embedded in my throat. Arrhidaeus shared my father's blood, but he was simple *and* illegitimate, surely no threat to Olympias or Alexander.

"You're too soft, son of mine." She spoke calmly, her voice almost drowned out by the crackling flames. "Eurydice was an ambitious bitch, and would have used her son to garner support against you and steal your father's throne. This is my gift to you, Alexander. It is my name that shall be blackened with their deaths, not yours."

Alexander seemed to hesitate, then growled deep in his throat and lowered his sword so fast that it clanged against the tiles. "If you dare touch Arrhidaeus, I swear I'll build your *pyra* with my own hands."

Olympias gave an elegant shrug, her copper hair still catching the light of the dying fire. "His mind and his bastard birth preclude his being a competitor for your throne. Keep him alive if you will." I sagged with relief, but her next words stopped my heart. "My brother, Alexander of Molossia, has turned tail and run back to Epirus, but what shall you do with Amyntas? As Cynnane's husband, he might set his sights on your throne. You still have the army to persuade—"

"The army is mine, for Antipater has sworn to throw his weight behind me. The men will do as their general commands."

Olympias thrummed her fingers against her arm. "Antipater was always your father's dog. I'm glad to see he shall be yours to command now. And Amyntas?"

"He fell on his sword this night," Alexander said.

"At your request?"

"Yes."

The world went cold then, that my golden brother had widowed brave, beautiful Cynnane with a mere command. My fear and revulsion ripened, expanding in the night air until I thought I would choke on it.

Olympias smiled, an expression more fearful than if she'd ranted or raged. "Good boy. You learn quickly."

But Alexander only glowered at his mother. "I'll have your word right now that neither Cynnane nor her daughter shall share Eurydice's fate."

"Of course," Olympias answered, as if granting a trinket. "Cynnane was a lucky woman to marry such a wise man as Amyntas. We must assure that she and her daughter are provided for."

A strangled cry of outrage escaped from my throat and drew Alexander's and Olympias' attention. "Thessalonike," Olympias said, in a voice I knew too well from all the times she'd caught me in the cellars, my cheeks stuffed with dried figs. "Return to the nursery. You shall not speak of what you've seen here."

I nodded and turned to run as fast as my feet would carry me, but Alexander caught me by the hand. "Don't touch me," I hissed. I withdrew my hand in disgust and then I ran—away from them and the heat of the fire, from Eurydice's shade and that of her son, back to my goat and my tortoise and my gentle brother, whose sobs still echoed down the hallways.

And I swore a solemn vow to myself that if Olympias was right and this was what it meant to be queen, I'd never allow the golden diadem to touch my head.

Lest I become a monster like her.

A letter came a few days later, on the morning my brother took control of the army. A dust-laden messenger launched himself from his nut-brown horse with a flourish, but it seemed only I noticed him, what with all eyes fixed on my brother and the aging general at his side. I still felt nauseated every time I looked at Alexander or Olympias and had set my eyes on everything except them to avoid the remembrance of the fire in the courtyard, the smell of roasting flesh, and the treachery that had shattered my innocence.

Antipater of Macedon, my father's dog and a general whose many

years and battles meant that his unfashionable beard was more frost
than ash, had just finished a speech urging the army to love Alexander
as they had our father. Alexander stood before them dressed in full
battle armor: a leather cuirass on his chest, his fair hair hidden
beneath a bronze helmet topped with eagle feathers and crowned by
a gold sphinx, and his shoulders draped with a lion skin as his ancestor Heracles had once worn. It was Olympias who stepped forward
to relieve the rider of his message as Alexander spoke to his men,
something about spreading our father's legacy and the might of Macedon across the craggy mountains and beyond the churning seas. I
listened with half an ear while Olympias scanned the paper. A slight
smile tugged at her lips as she took her place among the women and
children once again.

And then she beckoned to me.

I hesitated before wading past Arrhidaeus and the remainder of
my father's wives (all of whom sat as far from Olympias as decorum
allowed), ignoring their pinched lips and pale faces.

"The homeland of your mother revolts again," Olympias said.
"Its armies move against my son."

I wiped my suddenly sweaty palms on my *chiton*. Surely Olympias wouldn't hold me responsible for a rebellion in a land I'd never
seen, even if I did share its name. My mother had looked upon me
in my cradle from her deathbed and claimed that I was as strong as
the Aegean waves that crashed on the rocks below her childhood
home in Thessaly. Yet I was born on the day my father's men conquered her homeland at the Battle of Crocus Field, and so he had
decreed my name should be Thessalonike: *Victory in Thessaly*. Now
the Thessalians revolted again, and I wished I knew some good
words to curse them with. Too bad I refused to speak to Alexander
or he might have taught me some.

Then Olympias smiled, a gesture that might have frozen the sun.

She didn't offer any explanation, only watched as Alexander led his men in the ceremonial march between the two severed halves of a recently sacrificed dog, its red and purple entrails spilling from the furry brown body. I looked away, recognizing the poor beast as one my orange tom had often taunted, my eyes stinging at the thought that the poor animal had been wagging its tail and eating a fine feast of minced liver only this morning. The army would be purified once the cavalry and infantry had passed between the sanctified dog as decreed by the oracles, and Alexander would officially take his place as their commander.

And then I knew why Olympias smiled so.

"Alexander will lead the army against Thessaly, won't he?" I asked.

She didn't glance at me, only nodded. "And he will rout them."

I'd sought to curse the Thessalians mere moments ago, but I felt only one thing for them as the army raised swords, banging on their glaring sun shields and cheering their acceptance of my brother.

Pity.

Regret and relief roiled deep in my belly as I watched Alexander leave our city, a golden lion at the front of a long line of shield bearers and foot companions, all dressed in greaves and leather breastplates, carrying lances and Macedonian *sarissas*, those deadly pikes made of sturdy cornel wood and tipped with iron that could pierce through the strongest cuirass. Their shields were freshly stamped with my brother's newly claimed symbol: a sixteen-pointed star, one spoke for each of the twelve gods of Olympus and the four seasons, as if Alexander planned to harness all of those mighty powers. Alexander rode his black horse, Bucephalus, an untamed beast whelped in Hephaestus' fiery forges that he'd broken as a young man and since taught to kneel in full armor, and the crowds threw fragrant jasmine petals into the air and chanted his name. And my golden brother threw back his head and laughed, a glorious sound that made the crowd cheer louder.

"I love Alexander," Arrhidaeus said next to me, grinning his lopsided grin. He'd lost weight since the night in the courtyard and I'd had to give him my three-legged tortoise to coax a smile out of him, but now the parade distracted him and he clapped his hands. "Everyone else does too."

I watched as Alexander threw his fist into the air, prompting a deafening cheer. It seemed Arrhidaeus was right; the army cared little for the recent murders and not even Achilles and Heracles could have looked more glorious as they strode into battle. A shudder passed through my bones as I remembered the way those brave heroes had perished. Only the gods knew whether my brother would follow in their footsteps, and I was ashamed to feel myself softening toward him, knowing as I did what horrors he'd sanctioned for his throne.

I longed to leave Aigai, to climb Egypt's ancient pyramids and gape at Persia's renowned Ishtar Gate, as Alexander claimed he would on this conquest, yet I could never leave Arrhidaeus. And a girl could never travel with the army, although I'd heard stories that King Darius of Persia kept his entire family with him when campaigning.

Alexander met my gaze and grinned, then beckoned to his newly appointed bodyguard: Hephaestion. My brother riffled in his saddlebags and pressed something into his friend's hand, winking at me before turning away. Hephaestion guided his horse toward the shaded dais where I sat with the royal family.

"A gift for Thessalonike," Hephaestion said. His slow smile was the one I'd seen prompt giggles from both the kitchen slaves and the stableboys, but I sensed he was laughing at me as he pressed the bulky package into my hands.

I looked down to see my eldest brother's dog-eared copy of Homer's *Song of Ilium*. I wrinkled my nose, prompting a laugh from Hephaestion.

"Surely my brother cannot bear to part with his precious book," I said, holding the thing like a dead rat. I much preferred *The Odyssey*, with its tales of adventure and exploration.

"Alexander sleeps with that poem. It's dearer to him than almost anything." Hephaestion winked at me. "Except me, of course. Your brother bids you keep it safe for him; he shall order Aristotle to send him another copy," Hephaestion continued. "He wishes you well versed in the accomplishments of the great heroes, for he claims he will one day rival even Achilles."

"Something about animals would have been more interesting," I grumbled. Maybe something on snakes or dogs. I'd already read Aristotle's ideas in the *History of Animals*. I'd taken to heart his suggestion to crack open chicken eggs at regular intervals in order to observe the generation of organs like the lungs and the brain, a practice that had earned me a round scolding from the cook and a lecture about how only uncivilized *barbaroi* would keep fertilized eggs in their kitchens. I wondered if perhaps Aristotle had penned a manual on spear throwing or how to wield a sword, both skills that seemed suddenly practical in this upside-down world I now lived in.

"I had a feeling you'd turn your nose up at Homer, so I brought something else." Hephaestion laughed again and tweaked my ear, revealing a lumpy burlap bag in his palm. I tore it open greedily, my bruised heart expanding at the honey cakes inside. "And you, little lioness, shall be full-grown when we see you again. Shall you honor Aphrodite with your beauty then or Athena with your wisdom? Perhaps Artemis, lover of animals?"

"All three," I chirped proudly.

Olympias cleared her throat, bringing me back to reality. "That's enough, Hephaestion," she said sternly. "You shall dine on Alexander's dust if you don't follow now."

And thus, Hephaestion bowed to us, kicked his horse in the ribs, and charged off, toward Alexander, Thessaly, and the victories yet to come.

I didn't know it then, but it would be many years before I'd see Alexander again, at yet another funeral that would set the shears of the three Fates into a deadly flurry once more.

❋ · CHAPTER 2 · ❋

Thebes, Greece

HEPHAESTION

"Smile, Alexander," I said, as he reined in his demon-horse Bucephalus amid the city's death throes. "You craved a good fight since we left Aigai, and today you had it."

Alexander glowered at Thebes' stone citadel, looking far older than his twenty years. "Thebes underestimated me. I shall not halt the slaughter until the city's blood stains Bucephalus' knees."

"That's the last thing Ox-Head needs." I wrinkled my nose even as Bucephalus snorted at me, baring huge yellow teeth beneath a ridiculous helmet of golden horns that made him look like a misshapen bull.

Artemis' tits, but I hated that horse.

"The oceans could turn red with Theban blood and it still wouldn't be enough," Alexander said, nudging Bucephalus' ribs and pushing forward into the city.

I looked to the heavens before I urged my horse to follow, for Alexander had a flair for the dramatic when he didn't get his way. Thebes had dared revolt against Alexander after Thessaly had so kindly capitulated, quaking in their greaves as they watched Alexander cut steps into the supposedly insurmountable cliff face of Mount Ossa and lead his troops over the top, surrounding the Thessalians and prompting their generous surrender. They'd hailed Alexander as their *basileus* and heralded him as a hero descended from Achilles, which put him in a kinder mood when it came to sparing their people. Alexander had drunk his fill of Thessalian wine and boasted that there would be easy victories all the way down the peninsula.

That was before he ran headlong into Thebes and its Sacred Band, the elite military unit who'd snubbed their noses at him and called him an upstart barbarian. Of course, that same unit's warriors now lay rotting beneath the uncaring sun.

Not that I was going to mention that to Alexander. The Sacred Band was past saving, but its city still stood.

Thebes was an unwashed whore of a city, but I didn't care to see the ancient stone *polis* razed as Alexander threatened just because they'd put up a good and honorable fight. This, the City of Seven Gates, had birthed my favorite poet, Pindar, yet I doubted whether I'd have time to sightsee at his former home or seek out his urn of ashes amid the looting and pillaging.

I reined in, waiting as Alexander barked orders at his generals, motioning with succinct gestures where to deploy the cavalry, shield bearers, and foot soldiers to finish securing the city. The sun gleamed off his hair and his golden soldier's belt, earned when he'd killed his first man in the earlier battle of Thebes with his father. Alexander roared in triumph from Bucephalus' back, the leopard skin he sat upon gleaming gold and his lion helmet seeming to preen in the sunlight. "Put the city to the sword," Alexander yelled. "Thebes shall be scourged from the earth today, a warning to those who would declare against me!"

I might have pointed out then that these were *Greeks*, not cowardly Persians or stinking Latins, but being Alexander's bodyguard meant keeping my mouth shut and perhaps impaling a few Thebans with a *sarissa* to keep them from stabbing him through his cuirass.

I cursed the Thebans under my breath; the stupid bastards

should have surrendered when they had the chance and left me to my crates of wine and my copy of Plato's *Republic*.

The cavalry and foot soldiers moved to the various districts they intended to plunder, black flags of dark smoke unfurling in the city's western sections and making me shudder at the thought of what treasures the ravenous flames might be destroying. Alexander and I continued through to a newer neighborhood with less graffiti on the walls and fewer stray dogs lurking in the alleys, its wide avenues laden with twisting cypress trees and the polished marble facades of the well-to-do, similar to my father's home in Macedon. A second of Alexander's guards joined us: Ptolemy, officially the son of Lagus of Macedon but rumored to be one of Philip's illegitimate sons, and a man with an appetite for women to rival even that of Zeus.

My sword aimed in front of me, I pushed through the open gates of a particularly graceful estate. An overturned basket of peas lay near the kitchen entrance and my horse sidestepped a dead slave sprawled facedown in a pool of scarlet. My ear picked up something different here, the angry barkings of what might have passed as raving fishwives.

"See what that's about," Alexander said with a wince. "Before my ears begin to bleed."

I gave an exaggerated salute and dismounted, leaving Ptolemy with Alexander as I entered the courtyard.

"Throw her in with him!" a man yelled, standing next to two other mercenaries, thickheaded Thracians from the looks of their discarded crescent shields. The first gestured wildly toward a well situated at the corner of a tidy garden. The *kyria* of the house stood across from him, her lovely face an affectation of calm, yet the delicate matron clutched her ruined *peplos* at her shoulders, and two girls like miniatures of their mother cowered nearby. A trickle of blood from the corner of the mother's mouth was already growing dark and her pale hair had fallen loose. The largest of the three Thracian brutes finished binding her wrists with a leather thong, then shoved her toward the well while the other two hefted thick paving stones into their arms.

"I don't recall there being time for any unscheduled swimming, not while there's an entire city to be sacked," I said, lowering my sword as I strode into the garden. "It appears some explanation is warranted."

Six heads swiveled toward me, and I'd swear relief flashed over the woman's face. "This foul bitch murdered our captain," the first man said, his eyes widening as he snapped to attention at the lion emblem of Alexander's bodyguard on my golden helmet. His face was smeared with sweat and pockmarks, and his breath might have killed us all. "We've arranged for her to greet Charon the boatman on her way to the river Styx."

Thracians were famed for being stubborn as mules and slightly less intelligent. A well-trained dog might have found a way to kill their captain and leave the world a better place.

I waved his boast away. "What I don't understand is how a mere woman murdered one of your bravest commanders," I said.

The man's lips turned into a sneer as I removed my helmet and ran a hand through my sweat-matted hair. "You're Hephaestion, right? Shouldn't you be off protecting Alexander's manhood?"

A second Thracian leered at me. "Protecting it by letting Alexander hide it up your arse? We hear he succumbs to your thighs every night."

The slur wasn't the worst I'd heard, but it made me want to bash some mercenary heads together. Apparently this one needed to learn that I didn't take kindly to insults.

My sword was at his neck before he could blink. Men revered Alexander for his royal blood, but I still had to prove myself. I didn't begrudge these Thracians their right to learn who I was the hard way.

"I have a better idea," I said, keeping my voice low. "How about I hide this blade in your throat and save the rest of us from having to listen to your flapping tongue. A mealymouthed Thracian mercenary doesn't get to insult Alexander," I continued, reveling in his quick transformation from leering bastard to terrorized foot soldier as my sword tip nicked his neck. I leaned in close. "Would you like to take back what you said?"

Of course, the cowardly ass nodded, fairly pissing himself in the process.

"Perhaps the *kyria* . . ." I paused, waiting for her name.

"Timoclea," she provided.

"Could better explain how she sent the Thracian commander to his death?" I asked. Timoclea's brown eyes strayed to the well, and a slow smile spread across my face, although I kept the point of my sword cozy with the Thracian's throat. "Let me guess. . . . Their captain never learned to swim?"

She lifted her shoulders in an elegant shrug. "The brute killed my slaves and cornered me in the house. . . ." Her voice trailed off, and I could well imagine what spoils the Thracian commander had availed himself of once he had her alone. Her chin jutted in defiance. "When he demanded the silver, coins, and jewels, I told him I'd dumped them into the well when you Macedonians arrived outside the city."

"And then you accompanied him here?" I leaned forward so I could see down the well. It was wide and deep, but there was enough sunlight to make out a jumble of paving stones and, beneath them, what appeared to be a man's leg, pale and fat like a dead trout. I grimaced and glanced back at Timoclea. "I believe you may need to dig another well."

"What she needs is a grave," the first soldier growled.

Gods, but these Thracians were thick-skulled and dim-witted. I wished I had a second sword to scratch this one's throat. Where was Apollo with his plague arrows when you needed him?

Timoclea shrugged. "He leaned too close to the edge to catch a glimpse of my emeralds and pearls."

Yet the paving stones atop his body were the work of a crafty matron. No doubt Hades was cursing the arrival of an ugly lout who only ever had a woman when he forced himself upon her. "The gods may yet smile on you, Timoclea of Thebes," I said, lowering my sword to cut the thongs that bound her wrists. "I take you under my protection, for Alexander himself may wish to meet a woman of such rare courage."

The Thracian idiots opened their mouths to protest, but I silenced them with a glare.

"And my children?" Timoclea asked.

"The girls too," I said. The eldest reminded me of a younger version of Thessalonike, although I suspected if that were the case, she'd have helped to push the commander into the well and then celebrated with a plate of Delian honey cakes. "My sincerest apologies for the ill treatment you received. War is a grim business."

Timoclea rubbed her wrists and beckoned for her children, nodding toward the angry black plumes billowing into the sky above the rooftops. "You soldiers destroy all you touch."

"We've acquired the souls of butchers," I admitted, trying to recall where I'd read that line of poetry. It really was quite good.

I sheathed my sword as we approached her gate, glancing at the mounds of corpses littering the streets. I swallowed a wave of revulsion. This was no fair fight of soldiers eager for Macedonian blood, but the slaughter of women and children.

"Close your eyes," I commanded the girls.

They looked to their mother, their brown eyes dark with confusion. "Do as he says," Timoclea ordered.

They did and I lifted them up, one in each arm. "Don't look until I tell you to, all right?"

They nodded and squeezed their eyes tight. Alexander, resplendent in his purple *chlamys* and gleaming helmet atop Bucephalus, saw us then. Of course, old Ox-Head with his golden horns appeared unperturbed by the slaughter spread before him.

"Spare only the priests," I heard Alexander order, his generals scattering like ants to do his bidding. The girls in my arms tensed as I set them down, their backs to the carnage.

"You can look now," I said, then saluted.

Alexander gave a wry smile as his eyes flicked over Timoclea and her girls. "Lovely, but a bit too old and too young for me, Hephaestion. And I already have a mistress."

Brilliant and handsome, charismatic, and courageous though he was, Alexander sometimes lacked a rather key trait: tact.

Ptolemy, mounted beside him, stroked his chin, looking over Timoclea like she was on the slave block. "I'd be happy to take her off your hands."

"We travel the world not only to conquer," I said, ignoring Ptolemy and giving Alexander a pointed look.

"You are correct," Alexander answered offhand. "I travel and conquer so the world will never forget my name."

"And so you will be remembered as just and fair," I retorted, even as Thebes writhed around us in its death throes. "Before you stands a matchless Theban treasure."

Alexander glanced about the citadel, but he must have determined that the killing, raping, and pillaging could go on without him for a few moments, so he dismounted, keeping Bucephalus' reins loose in his hand while Ptolemy hovered nearby. "And who are you, *kyria*, that you have so captured Hephaestion's attention?"

Timoclea clasped her hands before her as if welcoming him to a banquet. "I am Timoclea, the sister of Theagenes, who fought the Battle of Chaeronea with your father, Philip, and died there in command for the liberation of Greece. My husband died in that battle as well, leaving me to fend for myself these past three years."

"She killed one of your Thracian captains," I said, sensing Alexander's growing impatience. "Lured him to her well with promises of buried treasure and pushed him in."

Alexander cocked an eyebrow at me. "I assume he deserved it?"

"He did," I answered.

"Rare courage for a woman," he mused, rubbing his fingernails against the leather of his kilt. Crusted with filth and blood, they were in need of a good soak. War was a dirty business.

"Reminds me of a certain sister of yours," I said. "Two actually."

Alexander chuckled. "Cynnane has the courage of an Amazon."

"And Thessalonike is a little beast. It seems a shame to see such courage put to the sword."

"I agree, and I shall reward your bravery." He nodded to Timoclea. "I grant you and your children your freedom, as a gift to my sisters."

Somehow I doubted this Theban's freedom was a fair trade for Cynnane's dead husband, but it was too late to save Amyntas. The poor, doomed fool had been in the wrong place at the wrong time, married into the wrong family. Amyntas was lost, but the entire city of Thebes trembled with fear as she waited for the rest of Alexander's swords to fall.

"It seems to me," I said, halting Alexander's departure, "that other Thebans might possess similar courage. The city is taken and the Sacred Band of Thebes is no more. Perhaps the inhabitants would serve you better alive than rotting in the streets."

"Your heart is too tender, Hephaestion," Alexander said, but his face softened. He surveyed the terra-cotta roofs spread before us, occasional screams making Timoclea's daughters cower like mice. "I am victorious," he said. "And thus I can afford to be merciful." He beckoned to an approaching guard as he remounted Bucephalus. "Cease the slaughter," he said. "The remainder of the city shall be taken as slaves. Spare the priests and the house of Timoclea."

Tears welled in Timoclea's eyes, the blatant gratitude shining there making me turn away. "Alexander," I called. "One more thing?"

"I do have a battle to manage, Hephaestion," he said, but he smiled at me from atop his horse. "What is it?"

"Spare the family of Pindar?"

"You and your precious Pindar." He sighed, but his eyes sparkled with mirth. "I'll save them, on one condition."

"And what might that be?"

"That they promise to produce no more bad poetry."

"Pindar's poetry rivals Homer's and you well know it."

"Sacrilege!" Alexander shouted over his shoulder, laughing as he nudged Bucephalus' ribs and galloped toward the citadel. Ptolemy followed behind him, but not before casting a lingering look at Timoclea, dark as a shadow and just as fast.

I watched them go, satisfied that I'd done all I could. Alexander was a man of extremes, burning bright as the sun over the rest of us mere mortals so that it often fell to me to rein him in, as pleasant a task as curbing Zeus' temper. I'd been scorched by his changeable moods, but I was pleased enough with today's outcome to promise myself a cask of my favorite burgundy Lesbos wine before falling onto my bedroll tonight.

And speaking of my bedroll . . .

I turned to Timoclea. "Now what shall you do?"

She rubbed her eyes, the first sign of weakness I'd seen from her. The vulnerability there made me want to cup her delicate cheekbone in my hand.

"Encourage my city to cooperate with your men."

"To send us on our way as soon as possible, you mean."

She offered me a wan smile. "Is it not one and the same? You seem a decent man, Hephaestion of Macedon, despite the company you keep."

Beneath her ragged hair and ruined attire, there was beauty there, a touch of Aphrodite if the goddess ever found herself past the first flush of youth. After a day of killing and saving Thebes from being only a memory sung in the song of bards, I wouldn't mind sharing that cask of burgundy wine, and perhaps more, with a woman like Timoclea.

I gave her the grin that never failed to make kitchen slaves eager to shed their *chitons*. "I'm so far from decent that I'd offer you more than just temporary protection, Timoclea of Thebes. A woman alone, needing a strong arm to protect her?"

"And you, a man in need of a woman in his bed?"

"Well, when you say it like that . . ."

But Timoclea of Thebes was no kitchen slave, and a piece of me would have been disappointed if she'd giggled and batted her lashes. Instead, she studied me. "And here I believed—as I think all of Greece does—that Alexander held the key to your affections."

"Alexander and I learned the pleasures of the flesh together," I admitted. This was a common practice, although typically it was an older man who would teach his *eromenos* about love. At seventeen, we had been deemed men, but like Achilles and Patroclus, our affection for each other remained constant even as we discovered the wonders of women as well. Alexander once claimed that only sex and sleep reminded him that he was mortal; add wine and books to that list and my vision of Elysium was complete. "We're closer than brothers, but we've large appetites and neither of us wishes to eat from the same dish night after night."

"I see." Timoclea smiled. "While I don't doubt that you could show an old widow like me a new trick or two, I have my daughters to care for."

I'd expected her rejection, yet it still stung. However, I could have my pick of pretty chariot drivers and camp women eager for a roll in my tent, one of each even. Or perhaps I'd seek out Alexander tonight.

"Thank you," Timoclea said. Then she stood on tiptoes and brushed her lips to my temple. "May the gods protect you, Hephaestion of Macedon."

I gave her a cheeky grin, then mounted my waiting horse to follow Alexander. "Actually, I don't think the gods know quite what to do with me."

Her laughter followed behind me. Timoclea would return to her estate and raise her girls to sass their future husbands. And I would follow Alexander, as I'd always done.

We continued on our way after Thebes to Delphi to consult the oracle of Apollo before heading for fabled Troy and, beyond that, Persia, where Alexander hoped to lure Darius, King of Kings, into open combat.

We arrived at Delphi on one of the season's unlucky days, at odds with the stunning vault of winter blue sky overhead and the crisp smell of cypress in the air. Yet Alexander had been in a foul mood even before we started marching.

"I don't care for prophecies," he said, approaching the famed Temple of Apollo, nestled like a hidden treasure at the base of rocky Mount Parnassus. The rest of his guards craned their necks to catch a glimpse of the fabled mountaintop. "I'd gallop right past Delphi if I could."

"Prophecies are just words," I said. "They can be twisted to suit your liking."

"Tell that to Oedipus," Alexander muttered. "Or my father."

He was right of course; the power of words had ruined—and saved—many a man.

One glance at the homely woman waiting on the steps of Apollo's temple and I was certain Alexander would have whatever prophecy he wished from her dry, cracked lips.

I, of course, was wrong.

"We've just marched from conquering Thebes." Alexander wore his famous smile as he approached her after dismounting, the one that made everyone—even me—eager to do his bidding just for a chance to bask in its warmth.

"It matters not if you marched from Egypt itself," the priestess said, crossing her arms over her board-flat chest. There was no doubt that we were addressing the Pythia, Apollo's oracle, draped and veiled in sumptuous cloth of gold to honor the god of the sun, although surely even Apollo would have shuddered to behold her face. "There shall be no divining on so unfortunate a day."

"Ah, well," I said to Alexander, wrinkling my nose against the temple's otherworldly, sulfurous scent. "You'll have to wait until tomorrow for your prophecy."

Alexander scowled at the Pythia. "You would refuse to scry for Alexander of Macedon?"

"That's exactly what she said," I answered for her. The priestess looked down her hooked nose at us, the effect marred by her pock-marked face and misshapen lips. It would have cost a fortune to muster the dowry to make up for her lack of Aphrodite's graces, so it was likely that her family had married her to Apollo instead. Still, the cold fire that burned in her blue irises might have shriveled the manhood of any potential bridegroom.

"I command you to divine for me," Alexander said, his hand on the hilt of his sword.

"There shall be no divining on the unlucky days," the priestess said. "So Apollo has decreed and so it shall be."

But Alexander was accustomed to both men and gods scraping to do his bidding, Apollo and his sun chariot be damned.

"You dare refuse the descendant of both Heracles and Achilles?" Alexander asked, his eyes narrowing dangerously.

"No man can command the oracle at Delphi," the priestess said. "Lest he wish to incur the wrath of the twelve Olympians."

And with those words, the Pythia instead incurred Alexander's wrath. Deflecting Zeus' lightning bolts would have been less painful.

"The gods favor me," Alexander said, grabbing the priestess by an arm and dragging her into the temple. "And you *will* prophesize for me today."

I heaved a sigh. "Bar the entrance," I ordered Ptolemy, the lone guard not gaping over his shield. It wouldn't do for word to get out that Alexander had manhandled the most famed priestess in all of Greece.

Of course, the Pythia realized this.

"Unhand the oracle," she cried, her voice reverberating off the ancient temple walls. I hurried after them, cursing the heavy armor I wore, and found the priestess on her knees before Alexander, his sword pointed at her moon-pale neck. Assorted offerings lay piled against the walls: golden coins and yellowing knucklebones, ivory flutes and bronze figurines in an assortment of animal and human shapes, all given to the god of light, music, and oracles. Somehow I doubted whether Apollo would approve a sacrifice of his priestess' blood.

"I will have a prophecy of victory against Persia," Alexander threatened. The cool light from the entrance mingled with that of the flaming orange torches on the walls, the smell of sulfur stronger here. "If I have to carve it from your throat."

I wanted to drag Alexander from the temple as he'd done the priestess and knock some sense into his thick skull, yet I recognized his tone and knew that his words were no jest. Only the night before, our two heads on the same pillow and our bodies slick with sweat, he'd murmured his dream to me.

"I shall surpass even my father, Hephaestion," he'd said, staring up at the canvas ceiling of his traveling tent. "He only conquered Macedon and the Peloponnese, but I shall vanquish Persia, and beyond to the endless sea. Even the gods shall sing my praises into eternity."

It was an improbable dream, but if any man could do it, it was Alexander.

Although murdering Greece's most famous oracle might hinder those plans.

I gestured to the Pythia's cedar and ivory throne, an ancient gift from the renowned King Midas, elevated over a crack in the ground that seeped foul-smelling vapors. Bug-eyed male figurines guarded the relic, their stone hands resting on the heads of tamed lions. "Might the oracle of Delphi make an exception for Alexander, descended as he is from the great Heracles and Achilles?" I asked. "Do we not head to Troy in the morn, Alexander, to vanquish the Persian king and offer his riches to Apollo and all our gods?"

"We do, and we require a fortunate prophecy to rally our men for our long campaign there." Alexander's sword didn't move, and the oracle swallowed hard, raw hatred in her eyes. Then she turned and walked to her elevated chair, regal as a queen approaching her throne. She took her time arranging the folds of her golden *peplos*. With a final venomous stare at Alexander, she closed her eyes and breathed deeply, as if trying to gather Apollo's wisdom from the very air. A trace of a smile lifted her lips; then her eyes snapped open and she stared straight through the man before her.

"The lion of Macedon is invincible," the muleheaded priestess said, her voice smoother than the clearest honey. "As was Heracles before him. So Apollo has decreed and so it shall be."

I rubbed my forearms to ward away the chill that rolled down my skin, for everyone knew that Hydra poison had killed Heracles despite his supposed immortality, eating away his skin and exposing his bones. I'd rather fall on my sword than watch Alexander suffer such a gruesome death.

"There, now," Alexander crooned, oblivious to the prophecy's double meaning as he sheathed his sword. "Was that so difficult?"

He strode toward the entrance without a backward glance, but the priestess still looked down on us from her throne, her face mottled with rage.

"I shall ensure that Alexander leaves the god of light a sizable offering," I said, but received only a yellow gob of spittle heaved in my direction as thanks.

"Apollo shall not soon forget this," she growled. "No one in the history of this temple has dared treat the oracle in so foul a manner."

Apollo should have been glad his Pythia still possessed a beating heart, but I doubted whether the god or his priestess would view that as a boon after being insulted. Gods' memories are perilously short regarding all the sacrifices made in their name, yet long when it comes to slights, be they real or imagined.

It made me ache for an *amphora* of wine—or maybe an entire *krater*—just to think about it.

I grumbled a prayer to Ares and Zeus and any god that would listen that Alexander would vanquish Persia, although I doubted whether even all of King Darius' gold would placate Apollo.

And I wondered whether Alexander even cared.

CHAPTER 3

333 BCE

Issus, Persia

DRYPETIS

"Perhaps Ahura Mazda will send a plague that will turn Alexander's bowels to brown water and make his pretty face erupt with oozing boils," I said, standing on stiff knees as the red-robed priest extinguished Ahura Mazda's sacred flame and packed away the *barsom*, a twined bundle of myrtle and pomegranate twigs used to purify our prayers. I doubted whether the god of light and wisdom would hear my prayer, but at least it interrupted my mother's latest tirade against the famed Macedonian and his invasion, namely its inconveniencing us from our seasonal palace rotation. Right now we should have been in Nebuchadnezzar's famed palace in Babylon, but instead we were encamped on the stark plains of Issus. One might have thought we were in the deepest depths of hell instead of ensconced in a silken pavilion with eunuchs serving silver platters of sliced cucumbers and freshly curdled goat cheese while we were massaged, bathed, and doused in rose oil. I supposed the lack of saffron stems with which to paint my mother's cheeks *was* an affliction too terrible to be borne.

My father was Darius III, the mighty King of Kings of the entire Persian Empire. He would win this battle against Alexander and we'd soon return to our dozen palaces. My mother would be happy then, but I might die of boredom.

"I told your father he should offer a reward of gold bullion for the heads of Alexander's guards," my mother said, pursing her plump lips as the priest departed and a servant rubbed swan fat onto her hands. I refrained from pointing out that the grease would have been better suited to oiling the bowstrings of my father's archers. "Ptolemy and Hephaestion—how a barbarian and a catamite managed to save him at Granicus I'll never understand."

Alexander had driven his cavalry into our troops at Granicus and received an ax blow to the head; he'd been saved from feeding the vultures only by the stubborn metal of his helmet and his bodyguards who dispatched his attacker, Spithridates. My mother had proposed minting coins with Spithridates' profile, but my father had contented her with promising to kill Alexander himself.

"Alexander's bodyguards are sworn to protect him." My sister, Stateira the Younger, glanced up from her charcoal sketch, this one taking the form of our grandmother. Our father's mother, Sisygambis, was either 70 or 170 years old, and she sat in a corner with her wrinkled eyes closed, shrouded by winter's early darkness. Too refined to snore and unable to rest while her eldest son battled for his empire, she'd spent the morning in private prayer and now I guessed that she feigned sleep to avoid this conversation—and the beauty regime—altogether. I wished I'd thought of that tactic first.

"The *yona takabara*"—a Persian slur meaning "the Greeks who wear shields on their heads"—"should die a thousand deaths for daring to invade our shores." My mother lifted her head from her tasseled pillow and managed to sip lemon-infused water from the lacquered bowl held to her lips by another servant. As everyone from here to Babylon knew from all her grousing, her back had ached and her stomach had been sour these past days with her fresh pregnancy. A battlefield was no place for a mother and an unborn babe, but she had refused to tell my father of her condition after so many still-births and miscarriages.

Memories of another blue-lipped boy came unbidden. That terrible day still lived as fresh in my mind as if I were five again instead of seventeen.

"Persia is the most cultured civilization on earth," my mother said to me, "and your father shall remain its King of Kings until his hair has gone white and his back is bent like a crone's."

But war had already aged my father and there were streaks of gray at his temples when he'd kissed us and ridden out that morning, flush from a fortuitous dream that the Macedonian phalanx was spread before him in flames, a sure sign of the Persian victory soon to come. So certain of his triumph was he that he'd seen no reason to discontinue the practice of allowing his royal wives, children, and imperial concubines to accompany him despite the close proximity of the battlefield. It seemed to me that he had chosen poor ground on which to engage the enemy, for the sea, the mountains, and the river Pinarus would force him to divide his army. When I'd mentioned it this morning, he'd only tugged the end of my long braid underneath my favorite hat, a gift from him for my seventeenth naming day, hewn from the gray hide of an old war elephant.

"A battle isn't one of your machines to tinker with, Drypetis," he said. "It's made of men, not cogs and wheels, and men are capable of miraculous feats."

So too were swords and the fearsome Macedonian pikes, shield bearers, and mounted archers, at least if the corpses from Granicus were any indication. That defeat smarted, but my father hadn't led our troops at Granicus, so I held my tongue even as he winked and whispered in my ear. "Your mother wants Alexander's head, but I'll bring you back a Macedonian *sarissa*. You can examine it at your leisure, see how those wily Greeks reinforce the tips with silver."

Mithra's eyes, but I worshipped my father and wanted nothing more than to believe he was invincible. Yet I was no longer a child and recognized the very real possibility that today might end in disaster.

"They say Alexander claimed Midas' chariot after unraveling the riddle of the Gordian knot by cutting through the cords of the cornel tree," I said, searching for some topic to fill the encroaching silence.

"Only a brute would consider cutting the rope itself," my mother said. "I swear that upstart Macedonian will never rule more than the backwaters of Greece."

I resisted the urge to argue, biting my thumbnail, which was already ragged from the sleepless night I'd spent toying with a terracotta pot rigged with a copper cylinder and an iron rod. The contraption was rumored to conduct some strange current when the pot was filled with wine or lemon juice. I'd discovered nothing save that lemon juice stung the myriad cuts on all my fingers, while I worried about my father riding into battle this morning.

Fifteen thousand brave Persians had been slaughtered at Granicus and thousands more had been bound in fetters and sent as slaves to Macedon, and I feared many others might meet similar fates this day. Alexander's army *was* a sort of machine with no room for weakness, despite what my father said, for on our travels toward Issus, we'd encountered hundreds of Macedonian soldiers who'd been abandoned for being sick, wounded, or simply unable to march at their leader's commanded double pace. It was an appalling show of Alexander's barbarity and callousness toward his own men, but in celebration, my father had cut off their hands and burned them on a pyre in an offering to the fire god.

My grandmother cleared her throat. "You forget, Stateira, but that upstart Macedonian already rules the entire Greek peninsula," she said with her eyes closed. "I'd scarcely call that a backwater."

"Stop gnawing on your thumb like a starving rat, Drypetis," my mother said, ignoring my grandmother. "And take off that hideous hat."

My elephant hat was hardly hideous, but I knew this battle was one I'd never win, at least not without my father at my side.

My mother pulled herself to sitting and beckoned to my sister with one elegant hand. She wound a lock of Stateira's ebony hair around her finger and rubbed it with her thumb. "More almond oil," she ordered to a waiting servant. Our women were nobles chosen from Persia's illustrious Seven Families for the honor of serving the King of Kings' wife and daughters, yet for the way my mother treated them, they may as well have been slaves dragged in from slinging dung onto the empire's wheat fields. "And more whitening cream for Drypetis' fingers." She scowled at me. "I thought I told you to leave that water wheel alone."

That morning after the troops had moved out, she had forbidden my examination of the nearby irrigation *karez*, but hadn't said a word about the spare chariot that my father had left behind. Having abandoned the terra-cotta pot experiment and needing something to keep my hands busy and my mind off the nearby battle, I'd tackled changing the chariot's draft pole, which had given me a devil of a time, and then contented myself with polishing the white holly-wood axles. Then I'd uncovered an abandoned box of bronze scythes. The long bronze blades were an awkward length for one person to hoist and mount onto the axle ends, but the project had successfully distracted me, although by the time I was finished, my hair was disheveled and my hands were raw.

I extended my hands to the waiting servant with a wan smile and allowed my palms to be slathered with the whitening mixture of ground lentils, barley, and powdered deer antler. It smelled wretched, but afterward my hands would be as soft as a child's. No amount of rose oil or salt from the Dead Sea would ever make me as beautiful as Stateira, but my mother was determined to die trying, and I often enjoyed the results. Although my mother never said it aloud, there was no doubt that I was the greatest disappointment to her, the plain-faced second daughter of Persia's most renowned beauty. It was said that my father had swooned with love when he first saw my mother among the limestone towers of Cappadocia, that the very breezes themselves were heartsick from her perfumes. Yet I was plain and wiry as a field mouse during a seven-year drought, and my nose had acquired a decided ridge last year after I'd tinkered with an elevating winch and received a wad of lint shoved up my broken nose as a reminder to secure winch lines properly. Fortunately for the house of Darius, Stateira possessed all the grace and beauty that I lacked. My mother had even shared her name with my sister, while I was named after a mottled brown butterfly. Although a caterpillar might transform itself, a butterfly never would.

"Put away the perfumes and oils," my grandmother finally commanded, rising from her seat in one elegant motion. Her white hair was piled on her head in the same tight mass of stiff curls she'd likely worn when she'd married her brother, the former King of Kings, who now lay moldering in our royal mausoleum. "No one will care how soft our hands are if my son fails today, nor will they notice how we smell like roses if he returns flush with victory over the Macedonian hordes."

I mouthed my thanks to her and was wiping my hands on my oil-stained sleeves when the echo of hundreds of men's boots reached us and was joined by the snorting of horses outside. For better or worse, the battle must have ended and our army was now returning.

Stateira clutched my hand so tightly I thought my knuckles would shatter. I imagined my father riding triumphant in his golden chariot, Alexander's head in one fist and a Macedonian *sarissa* in the other.

Or perhaps Alexander was entering the king's huge pavilion, stealing its chests of gold and silver while his boots trod my father's blood over the intricately woven carpets.

We stepped outside to watch our men return. But it wasn't blue-robed and bearded Immortals with spears and long-shields approaching at a double march, but a whole host of beardless Macedonians armed with menacing swords and garish sun shields.

My mother screamed and dragged Stateira back into the tent, my grandmother following and issuing stern injunctions for them to remain calm.

I stood rooted where I was, watching as my father's camp was overrun with orderly lines of Macedonians, their metal helmets gleaming like a thousand moons fallen to earth. I trembled to see our Persian attendants being rounded up: my father's cooks, musicians, wine servers, and even his scent-makers. The camels that carted my father's concubines brayed and snorted, commanders barked orders, and leering soldiers carried towering stacks of golden bowls and ewers. A *yona takabara* stood across the way, almost a head taller than the rest and holding the reins of a black monster of a horse wearing a gold-horned helmet. He directed soldiers as they carried crates of coins and unminted silver from my father's tent, along with a royal purple carpet and a massive ibex-handled golden jar that contained purified oils to burn for Ahura Mazda. The authority the man wielded and his plumed helmet with its emblazoned lion told me whom I beheld. It could be only one man.

Alexander of Macedon.

I gasped and almost ducked back inside, but the warhorse shifted to reveal the terrible items behind him. My heart screamed with rage and pain, even as I stumbled forward.

It was the custom for an empty chariot drawn by white horses to accompany the King of Kings into battle, to invite Ahura Mazda to assist in leading the troops. Yet before me was both that chariot and another: my father's, its gold plate still gleaming with the image of Ahura Mazda as an eagle beneath the smears of mud and blood. The yoke glittered with the full panoply of rainbow-hued gemstones and I could just make out the hammered image of my father on the side, dressed in his king's cloak with his curled beard I'd loved to run my chubby fingers through as a child. Alongside the Chariot of the Sun lay my father's golden shield and his purple robe, now rent to tatters and stained with something almost black.

My knees turned to water, but somehow I managed to remain standing even as the world shattered about me.

"No, no, no," I moaned, stumbling toward all that remained of my father. Alexander swiveled and said something in heavily accented Greek, his eyebrow raised in question, but I only spat at his feet. "I curse you, Alexander of Macedon, for all you've done today!"

I expected a sword in my belly to end my trials, but instead I was greeted with a great boom of male laughter.

"Alexander?" the man repeated, touching a hand to his cuirass, smeared with another man's blood. "No. I am merely Hephaestion," he said in Aramaic, the language of my father's empire.

I knew not which surprised me more: that I understood the man or that he was not Alexander. I'd expected Alexander's catamite to be like my father's favorite eunuch, Bagoas, small and pretty with skin like rose petals, but this beast was certainly no eunuch, unless he'd been gelded after reaching manhood.

I drew ragged breaths to try to calm myself. "Well then, Hephaestion, you may inform Alexander of Macedon that the widow and daughters of King Darius request an audience." I barely managed to push the words around the stone in my throat. My eyes burned with unshed tears and I yearned to touch my father's chariot and breathe in the scent of him from his purple robe, yet I dared not.

Hephaestion glanced behind me to my mother's pavilion. "Darius' widow?" he asked. Confusion marred his coarse features, then cleared. "But Darius still lives."

"He lives?" I almost choked on the words. "But you've captured his chariot and shield. . . ."

"Yet not the wily king himself," Hephaestion said, as another commander with a smaller-plumed helm joined him. "His troops scattered in the four directions and the King of Kings bolted east toward Babylon."

My father had fled, meaning he'd left us behind to be captured by these *yona takabara*. My heart shriveled to something small and black at the thought, but surely my father had abandoned us only out of necessity, so he might fight another day.

And he *would* fight. Of that I had no doubt.

Hephaestion glanced back at my mother's tent. "Tell your mistress I will send Alexander to speak with her after his physician finishes with him."

Mistress? And then I almost laughed; this man thought me a slave to my own mother!

"His physician?" I asked. "Was he injured?"

"A sword thrust to the thigh, delivered by King Darius, in fact."

I felt a surge of pride. "And might he still die from the wound?"

"It's merely a scratch. He's suffered far worse."

"Pity," I muttered. "Someone will need to finish the job one of these days."

Hephaestion's eyes narrowed. "You may tell Queen Stateira that she shall be treated gently by Macedon, although Alexander has no use for slaves with whips for tongues."

I recoiled, then offered him my back and returned to my mother's pavilion. The women inside set upon me before the tent flap fell shut.

"You little idiot! Where have you been?" my mother began, but my grandmother cut her off.

"What did you discover?" she asked, her face a mask of calm even as her nails dug into my palm.

"Father is still alive," I said, my immense relief at his survival quashing the whisper of shame that he'd run from the battlefield.

"And Alexander will come once he finishes plundering my father's tent." I refrained from mentioning the pile of his treasures outside or my father's captured chariot.

Hephaestion was true to his word, and we didn't wait long for both him and Alexander to arrive, the latter's golden curls damp and smelling of fresh almond oil. He was shorter than I expected and more handsome, but I clenched my fists beneath the pleats of my robe to realize that this *yona takabara* had befouled my father's great marble bathing basin, carried west by a sledge and six matched horses from our palace in Babylon. My mother gave a sharp inhalation and cursed under her breath, likely troubled not by Alexander's bath but by the woman dressed in sapphire and gold on his arm, whom I recognized as Barsine, the widow of my father's Greek commander, Memnon. Until recently Barsine had spent almost her full thirty years exiled in Greece, so she was considered more Greek than Persian. Her face was shaped like a heart, framed by lovely black hair, but even her beauty paled in comparison with my sister's. I imagined Stateira on Alexander's arm and winced.

"Alexander, son of Philip of Macedon," my grandmother said. She too was drawn to the sheer size and power emanating from Alexander's guard, and bowed as she addressed Hephaestion. I cleared my throat in an attempt to redirect her misguided attentions, but she ignored me.

Hephaestion and Alexander exchanged grins, and it was Hephaestion who corrected my grandmother in fluent Aramaic. "This, Dowager Queen Sisygambis, is Alexander of Macedon."

"My apologies for so egregious an error," my grandmother said smoothly, but I thought I detected a rare flush of embarrassment on her cheeks.

"It is no mistake," Alexander said, his smile wide. "Hephaestion and I have been of one mind since we were boys, two sides of the same coin. Thus, he too is Alexander."

One mind and one flesh as well.

To my shock, he knelt on one knee, and I took satisfaction at his wince, although there was otherwise no sign of his leg wound. The rest of his retainers followed suit, but it was almost humorous to watch Hephaestion find his knees, akin to watching a poorly trained bear bow. "I am honored to be in the presence of King Darius' women."

"And we are honored by your attentions," my grandmother answered. "This is Queen Stateira and her daughters, the princesses Stateira and Drypetis."

Hephaestion stared at me as the men stood; then his lips curled into a grin. "Beware the younger one," he whispered to Alexander, his lips almost grazing the man's ear. "She hisses. And spits."

I did my best to look down my long, albeit broken, nose at him, but that was difficult considering the top of my head scarcely grazed his shoulder.

Alexander inclined his head to us, which I supposed was another honor. "I shall guarantee your safety and comfort while I make arrangements with King Darius for your return."

"You mean while you ransom us," my mother stated, ignoring my grandmother's pointed look.

Alexander shrugged. "So it is in the ways of war."

"As dowager queen, I believe I may speak on my son's behest," my grandmother said. "Perhaps instead of a ransom, you may be amenable to a more enjoyable arrangement?" She stepped past Barsine, sniffing as if she were rancid meat, then nudged my sister forward. To her credit, Stateira stared straight ahead, although she'd gone pale as milk. "My eldest granddaughter, Stateira, is of a marriageable age. Marry her, become my son's heir, and put all this foolish war business behind us."

My sneaky, slippery grandmother. Alexander would become my father's heir only if the babe in my mother's belly was another girl or, worse, another stillborn. But, of course, Alexander didn't yet know of my mother's pregnancy.

Alexander blinked at her boldness, then chuckled. "I like you, Sisygambis of Persia. However, there is one flaw in your otherwise cunning logic."

My grandmother smiled, and I realized with a start that she was enjoying this, the sly old she-cat. "And what might that be?"

"While I appreciate the women your empire has to offer"— Alexander tucked Barsine's perfectly manicured hand over his—"I've already taken your family as captives. I could marry all of you if I wished it, but as King Darius discovered when he fled today, wives and children are a costly burden to any campaign."

"You may be right," my grandmother said. "But in time you may come to see the beauty of my offer." The word *beauty* was pointed as her gaze flicked to my sister and prompted a genuine smile from Alexander.

"Perhaps," he answered. "But in the meantime, we break camp and you shall accompany me."

"We thank you for your generosity," my grandmother said, bowing over her hands and stopping just short of kissing her fingertips in a *proskynesis* as if she were addressing a god or a king.

Alexander turned to my mother, her face pale and her hands clasped over the still-flat belly that would soon burgeon with my father's secret heir. "I give you my word, Queen Stateira, that you and your daughters shall receive the same honors as my own mother and sisters."

"Says the man who murdered the husband of his sister," I muttered to myself. This man was our enemy and instead he was being feted like a powerful *satrap*.

Alexander ignored me to place his hands over my mother's, then turned away with a sweep of his purple cape. "May the gods keep you," he said to us, but I overheard him murmur in Hephaestion's ear, "Sisygambis I like, but the Stateiras both quake like terrified rabbits. As for the younger daughter, I've seen fairer-faced horses."

Hephaestion glanced back at us and for a moment I thought he might smile at me. Instead, his gaze fell on Stateira. "The elder daughter is lovelier than a nymph," he said under his breath. "And you never know—the younger one may one day prove useful. Perhaps for target practice."

Alexander's laugh boomed as they stepped into the encroaching dusk, ushering in a gust of chilled autumn air that bespoke ripening pomegranates and hearth fires at night. I resisted the urge to shout obscenities at them, mostly because their foul soldiers' mouths could probably outcurse me. Or their soldiers' swords could stake my tongue as Alexander had threatened.

I sagged with relief as the tent flap fell closed, shutting out the commotion of the camp and leaving us with some semblance of protection.

Today my father had been branded a coward, but we would be safe as Alexander's hostages.

At least for now.

CHAPTER 4

Balkh, Persia

ROXANA

I gave a squeal of disgust at the gaily painted wagon of *karakul* as it lurched across the rutted road, its cargo of prized fetal lambskins tipping dangerously while mud from the recent rains splashed onto the hem of my favorite orange robe. "Foul-faced peasant," I shouted at the driver, shaking my fist from the back of our rickety donkey cart. "Don't you know who I am?"

"A trussed-up little shrew," the man said, the black grime dug so deep into his lined face that he might have passed for a striped tiger. "With a mouth like a braying ass!"

"I hope you choke on a fish bone!"

"Roxana!" My father turned and snapped his whip overhead from his place at the front of our cart. "Well-bred daughters are silent as a corpse. Learn to keep your mouth shut, you little fool!"

Ha! I snorted silently. Well-bred I was not, certainly not with hunchbacked old Oxyartes of Balkh for a father. My mother had birthed my twin and me, then died and left us to fend for ourselves.

"This is the Mother of Cities?" I muttered under my breath, wrinkling my nose. I'd hoped for more from the birthplace of Zoroaster and its *satrap* Bessus, cousin to King Darius and the man next in line for the throne. I'd lived within a day's ride of Balkh for all of my thir-

teen years but hadn't left the crumbling walls of my father's rural estate
on the dusty outskirts of the city since I was six, both because we
lacked the coin to purchase anything the city might offer and because
my father feared that some accident might befall his lone daughter. It
wasn't tender feelings that made him worry for my safety, but instead
the fact that my dusky eyes and the long black hair that fell past my
hips were the most valuable pieces of property he possessed.

All my life my father had promised to make a return on his
investment in me. Today was that day; hence my short temper and
roiling stomach.

Now my ears rang with the braying of donkeys and my nose
twitched from Balkh's pungent stew of dung, sweat, and animals.
A storm cloud of gnats shifted in the air and the half-dead donkey
that pulled our cart shat with exuberance. "I didn't realize the Jewel
of the East smelled like our stables," I muttered.

"What did you expect?" My twin brother lay sprawled on the
cart's floor and lifted a hand to shield his face from the autumn sun,
peering at me through slitted eyes. Parizad was all elbows and knees,
with a giant fleshy apple at his throat. "That Balkh's rivers flowed
with honey and the walls were made of amber?"

The truth was, I *had* expected more from the Mother of Cities,
had dreamed of the comforts I would gain once I left my father's
crumbling walls. Bessus was second only to King Darius himself,
the powerful *satrap* of all of Bactria and my father's overlord. Where
were the jeweled towers and the marble palaces I'd been promised,
the slaves to weave ribbons into my hair and the scent-makers to
create exotic jasmine perfumes for me to swim in?

Instead, our father dismounted to lead our donkey and cart
through the sea of scab-kneed urchins and scowling merchants that
thronged the packed-dirt streets.

"Our hideous father is the most minor noble in all of Balkh,"
Parizad said, sitting up and twisting his perfect lips into a lazy smile.

"You should be honored that our great *satrap* would glance in our direction."

"I know that," I snapped. As if I could forget. For the past days, ever since our father had arranged my betrothal, he'd been scouting new horses for his perpetually empty stables and guzzling finer vintages of sweet raisin wine than had ever graced our table. Even the robe and the long-legged *shalvar* he wore today were new, a garish shade of yellow with blue embroidery that did little to hide his misshapen back or twisted foot, while my own robe was a piece of reworked silk from my mother's marriage chest. The only things of any value on my father's estates were his several metal foundries, as useful to me as pebbles in my slippers.

Parizad tapped his chin. A pathetic attempt at a first beard covered his jaw like the fuzz on a rotten peach. However, I was supposed to be silent and thus, I wouldn't point out the shortcomings of his few dark whiskers. "They say Bessus has a hundred concubines," Parizad mused, "but you'll be, what . . . his third wife?"

"Fourth." I practically spat the word at the reminder, then glanced at my brother and scowled. "And your beard looks ridiculous, by the way."

Ahriman take silence, and I hoped the black demon might turn my brother's tongue into a worm while he was at it.

But Parizad only stroked his chin. "I think it looks dignified. So did the pretty slave I tumbled in the garden shed this morning."

I snorted. "If you recall, I did ask Father why he couldn't find a nobleman to take me as his first wife," I muttered. The welts on my back were healed to bruises now, but I winced at the remembrance. My father had emerged from his mother's womb with a body twisted and bent like a fat harvestman spider—big-bellied with spindly arms and legs—and Parizad and I had once made the mistake of taunting him that his fists inflicted little damage on us. To our dismay, we quickly learned that his whip stung deeper than a swarm of hornets, and always avoided biting deep enough to scar or mark our precious faces. Fortunately, Parizad had discovered an interest in healing and kept his leather medicine satchel well stocked with rosemary and lavender salves, and chamomile and yarrow infusions, that eased the worst of the pain.

I yearned to one day be stronger than the hunchbacked spider, to take the whip from my father and flay the skin from his back. But the daughter of a spider could bide her time. . . .

We'd entered the heart of Balkh through its seventh gate, which led into its poorest and oldest section of town, and now we wound our way through a ramshackle market packed with carts of red slip pottery, frayed baskets overflowing with lentils and heads of garlic, and bloody hares strung by their back legs and bound for the city's dinner plates. I thought perhaps we'd reached the palace when my father clambered back into the cart, but the cobbled street opened up to villas of the affluent, the scent of water lilies and oranges wafting over their whitewashed walls. They might not be palatial, but they were certainly more lovely than my father's meager estate with its loose shutters, which had long ago given up pretending to block out the winter winds, and the stain of black mold that graced our hall's ceiling. The streets seemed to go on forever, beyond towering Zoroastrian fire temples and the sprawling granaries, each orderly street crammed with obstinate mules, packs of mangy dogs, and slaves hurrying to do their masters' bidding.

And then we came to a set of walls inlaid with turquoise and engraved with images of winged lions and bearded sphinxes. Guards with silver shields and lances stood at attention atop the immense wooden gates, their eyes hidden beneath beaten-metal eagle-wing helmets.

"Oxyartes of Balkh has answered the summons of Bessus, *satrap* of Bactria and cousin to the King of Kings," my father called up to the guards, craning his neck so deeply that his shoulders seemed dislocated. "I bring my daughter, Roxana, at his behest."

My father spoke like a polished courtier instead of a hawker selling trinkets with fake gilding and colored glass passed off as garnets. I could think of nothing save that beyond these walls lay Balkh's palace and my future husband, a man I'd never even met.

And my freedom.

Parizad leaned forward and squeezed my hand. We'd shared the same womb and wet nurse, so I knew all the squalls of my twin's temper, the smallest nuance of his laughter, just as he knew mine. Right now I wished he would press his lips to my forehead and talk of pearls the size of swallow's eggs and the famed Basra dates that Bessus would gift me with. Instead my brother leaned back in the cart, resting against the rough-hewn crate that contained my father's armor. Father would give me to Bessus, spend most of my bride-price, and then travel with the *satrap* to the west, to face the threat of Alexander of Macedon. If we were lucky, Alexander would crush my father beneath his boots. "I wonder if Bessus might allow me a position as a healer in his army," my brother mused, feigning nonchalance. "Then the bards might one day sing of my glory saving men on the battlefield."

"Perhaps I'll make Bessus fall so much in love with me that he'll make you one of his generals." I gave an impish grin, prompting a smile from my brother.

"I have faith in your powers, sister," he said, lacing his hands behind his black curls and winking. "For your beauty rivals only my own."

And it was true. Ahura Mazda, or perhaps the god's evil counterpart, Ahriman, had cursed us with a grasping, grotesque spider of a father, but somehow gifted us with enough dark beauty to make both men and women weep with envy, although Parizad had yet to grow into his new lankiness. Sometimes I wondered if that was why our father hated us so, because we'd been given everything he'd been denied.

For a moment I wondered why Bessus had deigned to negotiate with my father at all, but surely the *satrap* must be a great cultivator of all things beautiful.

"Shut your gullets, you two," my father commanded, rubbing his hands together as the palace gates groaned open on ancient hinges. "Bessus has just finished his council meeting following the recent . . . *unpleasantness* in Issus."

Parizad snorted under his breath. "More like a rout. And our King of Kings slunk from the field like a desert dog with his tail between his legs."

I jabbed my brother in the ribs, not wishing to listen to him drone on again about the Greek victory. I didn't care a whit for dead soldiers rotting on a battlefield; after all, the empty-headed imbeciles had volunteered to die in the first place. And despite what I had said to Parizad, I'd never send my beautiful brother to be slaughtered by some Greek pike, to let the carrion pluck out his sparkling eyes and tear apart his perfect skin. That would be akin to sending a piece of myself to die. No, he would stay here with me, right where he belonged.

If my father heard Parizad's comment, he ignored it and leveled his beetle black eyes at me. "You shall greet Bessus in the Hall of Columns. You'll scrape and bow, and make him think the sun rises and sets at the flutter of your eyelashes—"

"Thus sealing the alliance between our families," I recited, smiling prettily so my dimples cleaved my cheeks.

A smile spread across his face that had nothing to do with me. "Thirteen years I've fed and clothed you, endured your foul tempers and disobedience," he said. "But tonight it will be worth it."

Barely fed and barely clothed, but tonight I'd marry the *satrap* of Bactria. I would finally *be* somebody, with slaves of my own to gut newborn fawns for my dinner table, to oil my hair and polish the pearls and gems Bessus would surely give me as a bridal gift.

Only then could I begin to live.

B essus did have a magnificent palace, hidden from the prying view of lowborn eyes. We rode in silence along the manicured path that cut a swath through the orderly lemon trees, the fragrant air disturbed only by the flight of an errant white butterfly. Parizad helped me disembark and we continued toward the audience hall, my pale fingers held tight by his browned and calloused palm, my throat suddenly dry.

What if Bessus didn't want me? The *satrap* could have any woman as wife; why would he choose a girl clothed in moth-eaten silk with a spider for a father?

Outside the Hall of Columns, my father spoke to an egg-bald herald, who had the gall to arch an eyebrow darkened with *sormeh* powder in my direction. I pursed my lips, acutely aware of the fine weave of his robe and the gold disks sewn into the wide red *kamar-band* around his waist. I worried at my mother's gold bangles on my wrists—the cheaply gilded kind, which my father hadn't yet gotten around to losing on a horse bet—and brushed my black hair behind my shoulder, the better to show off her pearl earrings, although I wished they were larger than coriander seeds.

"I bid you welcome to the court of the *satrap*, Roxana of Balkh." The herald wrinkled his nose, sniffing as he touched the rumpled fabric of my sleeve. His voice was too high to be a proper man's—a eunuch, then. "Delicate bones and thick hair, blacker than a winter night," he said. "The *satrap* will enjoy this one, for a few days at least."

I resisted the urge to pinch the half man until he cried, a trick I'd often used on our idiot slaves when they didn't do what I wished. Instead, I brushed away his hand as if he were a pesky fly. "Don't presume to touch the *satrap*'s future wife," I said. "Lest he have you cut a second time."

The eunuch's eyes widened, but then he smiled and tucked his hands inside his loose sleeves. "Of course."

Ordering one's inferiors was a simple task, akin to training a dog.

"Do not look the *satrap* in the eyes when he greets you," the eunuch admonished me. "Sweep gracefully to the ground and press your forehead into the floor. Can you manage that?"

"Of course I can," I snapped. "I'm not a peasant you've plucked from the fields."

Although I wouldn't mind sending this mockery of a man to trudge through manure and mud.

At an impatient flick of the eunuch's hand the guards opened the ebony doors to the audience hall, the herald proclaiming my father's meager titles. I tilted my chin, but my cheeks still burned as the well-dressed nobles tittered behind their hands as my father limped and Parizad and I strode through the center of the hall under the watchful gazes of the gods of old and new: Ardokhsha, the goddess of good fortune; Bahram, the god of victory; and Ahura Mazda, the god of truth and light. But I cared as little for the gods in that moment as I did the unimpressive herd of nobles.

Seated on the far dais was a mountain of flesh with a craggy, receding hairline, his broad belly and chest gleaming with his silk and gold robes. He lumbered to his feet and every man and woman bowed before him like ripples in an insignificant pond.

"Is this her?" the man on the dais asked, rubbing his fat hands together as his eyes swept over me. "Roxana, daughter of Oxyartes?"

I stood rooted in place, short of breath as I watched my future husband stride toward me, feeling his every massive step reverberate through the floor tiles. Bessus' skin was pitted like an apricot kernel, his eyes close set, and his nose twitched like those of the rats I'd sometimes found in our pantry's sacks of grain.

And I was to wed this meaty rodent.

I never thought it possible, but my father had succeeded in betrothing me to someone as hideous as he was. My stomach curdled with revulsion and disgust, and I wanted nothing so much as to turn and bolt. Instead, I forced myself to stare at the magnificence of the Hall of Columns, to imagine the way my new silk robes would feel on my skin, and how sweet the glasses of honey wine would taste at the wedding celebration tonight.

Bessus halted, looking down as he circled me while his fingers tapped a nervous rhythm on one of his chins. "You didn't exaggerate about her beauty, Oxyartes," he said to my father, then reached out to clasp a lock of my black hair, twined it around his fat sausage finger, and gave a little tug, like on a mare's reins. I resisted the urge to jerk away as that pudgy finger traced my jawline. "I know we only discussed her maidenhead, but I might be interested in riding this filly of yours more than once."

I reared back, yanking my hair from his grasp. "I'm to be your wife, not your whore for a night."

"I already have three wives," Bessus said, his stomach rippling with his chortles of laughter. "And I'd sooner slit both my wrists than add to the collection."

My father joined the hall's laughter, then said, "Surely you won't begrudge Roxana her illusions, so fresh and naive is she in the ways of the world." He grasped my shoulders, his fingers digging into my flesh, but it was his new ring that caught my attention: a moonstone set in gold, the same ring the *satrap* gave to all his retainers. "I told you, Roxana, that the *satrap*'s attentions would bring great honor to yourself and your family."

My body went cold. My father had schemed and lied for his own benefit. And he had risen high because of it, while I was to be bedded by this heap of flesh, one of a hundred virgins he'd probably ruined, instead of becoming a pampered wife seated on a dais next to the man who might one day be the King of Kings.

I wanted only one thing in that moment: to crush my father and feel him break beneath the heels of my secondhand slippers.

I tilted my head and let my chin wobble, the very picture of youthful innocence. "My lord," I said to Bessus, ignoring my father entirely, "I would be honored to serve you in whatever manner you choose, but I thought only flowered women were given the honor of serving as bedmates."

A hush fell over the hall as every supplicant leaned closer to hear.

"Oxyartes . . . ," Bessus growled, his fat face turning the color of autumn beets.

"Roxana is thirteen and recently ripened into womanhood," my father said, scraping several hurried bows on his twisted foot before the fat *satrap*. "I swear it."

I shook my head. "That's not true. I told you that I'd not yet flowered."

"It is an affront to all the gods for a man to force a bud to blossom," Bessus said, leveling his frigid gaze at my father. "And it is also an affront to those same gods to lie, Oxyartes of Balkh."

Triumph surged over me, hot and golden, at the panic written clear on my father's face, that one of his schemes might unravel like a gossamer spiderweb attacked by a child's stick. He dared not call me a liar and spoil his precious goods before Bessus' eyes. For once, *I* would beat him.

"I swear I thought she was ripe for the plucking," my father said, mopping the perspiration from his forehead even as he speared me with a dagger-sharp gaze. "Perhaps if we return in a few weeks—"

"I have no use for children or liars." Bessus snapped his fingers at the eunuch. "Roxana of Balkh is to be returned to her father's house, but Oxyartes will accompany me as I leave to rendezvous with the King of Kings. I'm of a mind to have him pull my cart, but perhaps the Greeks will do us all the favor of shooting his miserable hide full of poison arrows."

"I thought you wished for the use of my weapon foundries," my father started, but Bessus cut him off.

"King Darius can make use of some other foundries for his fight against Alexander. Yours are tainted by Ahriman's shadow and no longer of interest to our king."

My father twitched, then whirled on me once Bessus' back was turned, his hand on my arm so tight it threatened to shatter the bone. "You stupid little idiot. Don't think I'll leave Balkh without making you wish you were dead."

A chill coiled down my spine, for I'd been so swept up in shredding my father's plans that I hadn't thought he might still find a way to make me suffer. I shuddered even as Bessus turned. "Oxyartes!" he barked. "I said you would accompany me. Must I teach you to heel as well?"

My hunchbacked father flushed an angry scarlet, but bowed and limped toward Bessus, leaving me to heave a shallow sigh of relief and wonder if perhaps I'd have been better off spreading my legs for the *satrap* like an obedient daughter.

I'd lied, but now I'd forgone one trap and stumbled into another of my own making.

Yet I was the daughter of a spider. And spiders are never caught in their own webs.

With nowhere to go, I dared to sit on the bottom step of Bessus' dais while the Hall of Columns emptied. Parizad sat beside me, rummaging through the leather satchel at his waist.

"Sometimes I think you're the smarter of the two of us," he said. "And then you go and pull a maggot-brained trick like that."

"You'd rather have a sister whored to that saggy elephant?" I plucked a loose string on my sleeve, watching with satisfaction as the entire edge came unraveled.

"I'd rather still have a sister, which isn't likely after Father finishes with you. There are worse things than spreading your legs for a man like Bessus."

Perhaps I *should* have accepted Bessus. My father might sell me to a leather tanner just to spite me now, leaving me smelling of urine and my hands wrinkled like prunes for the rest of my life. Still, his greed might prove my saving grace, for a tanner likely couldn't afford to outfit him with gold and moonstone rings.

"Piss and shit," I cursed under my breath. "I should run away."

"And where would you go, big sister?"

I breathed in the smell of dusty herbs and earth that always clung to him. "I was going to wear rubies in my hair and sleep on silk, and have an army of slaves to attend to my every whim. I might have been queen one day."

"I know," he said, stroking my head. "And you still might."

"What?" I lifted my head.

"I think you might be very ill, very soon. Violently ill, in fact," Parizad said, his voice soft.

"I feel fine, for now at least—" But I stopped when I saw in his open hand two misshapen glass vials filled with round yellow seeds and dried leaves the color of a twilight sky. "What are those?"

"Mustard and rue," he said. "I've gotten out of a few beatings myself by being so sick Father dared not touch me. Mustard and rue always do the trick. You'll feel terrible for half a day, but it's better than not being able to move for a week from the lashes."

I grinned and bumped his shoulder. "You sly demon."

"You really will call me a demon once these sour your stomach."

I opened my hand and let him empty the seeds and leaves into my palm. "You're sure this will work?"

"Take them quick enough and I might be forced to call Bessus' physician."

I caught his meaning. "I may have to stay overnight. . . ."

"And Father and the *satrap* will be gone by dawn."

I took a deep breath, then downed the herbs. My gorge rose at the overwhelming taste, but I swallowed. "I love you, little brother," I said. "Even if you did just poison me."

"And I love you, big sister, even if you are a lackwit with barley mush for brains."

It didn't take long for the herbs to make me feel as if I'd swallowed a host of poisonous, writhing asps. I moaned and curled into myself, vomiting into one of Bessus' alabaster urns as Parizad hollered for the physician. Through the haze of pain, I dimly recalled seeing my father's red face as I was carried to a set of empty palace chambers. Perhaps I'd get lucky and find a way to stay in the palace longer than one night—perhaps forever—if, of course, that didn't require bedding the mountain of flesh that was our *satrap*.

I felt a surge of triumph then, mingled with a hefty dose of agony as I begged Ahura Mazda to strike me dead where I lay.

I was free from the spider. But even I knew that couldn't last forever.

CHAPTER 5

Tyre, Phoenicia

DRYPETIS

My grandmother was a dowager with iron for bones, my mother a pampered queen who preferred that her feet never touch the ground, and I might have passed for a blacksmith with my scarred hands, permanently filthy from my fiddling with winches and jibs. Only Stateira was without fault, yet my father loved us all. Still the days passed into weeks and weeks into months, and no ransom came as we traveled south. We had only silence from my father, and from Alexander.

"To see Persepolis again," my mother moaned. "The throne room and the Damascus prunes . . . They're in season now and we're missing them. This dreadful sea air makes my nose twitch."

"At least Alexander has kept his word," Stateira said, trying to maintain the peace, as she had through these long months while the Greek army marched along the blue-waved coast toward Tyre.

My grandmother grunted, dismissing the chatter. "You'll have to let those robes out again," she said, eyeing the ever-growing swell of my mother's belly, and the flash of fear crossed all our eyes. We'd kept her secret so far, but for how much longer?

"I'll take to my bed," my mother said, massaging her belly. "If Alexander complains, we will tell him the constant traveling is wearing to my delicate constitution."

I snorted softly. If my mother was delicate, then I was a winged *simurgh* capable of carrying off a whale . . . but Alexander didn't know any better, and the secret held even as we came into Tyre, a home port for the Persian fleet.

Tyre was in the midst of its annual celebration to the god Melkarth, an ancestor of the Tyrian royal family whom the Greeks identified with Heracles. Hearing of our approach, the city's inhabitants had wisely fled the old quarters on the mainland in favor of New Tyre, the city-within-a-city situated on an island a mile from shore. Alexander deigned to ask permission to join the festivities and even made a great show of sacrificing two shaggy goats to their shared ancestor. But when Alexander sent messengers to sue New Tyre for peace, his heralds were killed and their decapitated heads flung over the walls into the sea.

Thus, Tyre sealed its fate.

The city's walls stretched like a mother's arms, standing as high as thirty men. Those stones had withstood a siege from King Nebuchadnezzar for thirteen years, yet that Babylonian king hadn't possessed Alexander's terrible war machines or his plan to build a mole, a colossal wooden causeway that would span the full mile to New Tyre so he might simply knock down their gates. I marveled with a grudging awe at Alexander's growing fleet of stone throwers and siege towers, cringing when the impressive inventions were turned to the buildings of Old Tyre for target practice.

Still, New Tyre defended itself, and its engineers were more creative than even Alexander imagined.

Alexander granted us permission to walk to the hill overlooking both Old Tyre and the island of New Tyre across the bay, under guard, of course, but I was glad for the freedom. Stateira and I went one afternoon and stayed out past sunset. It was a moonless night with a favorable wind.

Favorable for Tyre, but not for Alexander.

The wind whipped the hair about my face and the smell of the fresh-hewn oak and fir beams invigorated me. "The tallest of Alexander's siege towers have twenty different levels for archers and battering rams," I said to Stateira, prompting her indulgent smile.

"Twenty levels," she echoed, arching an eyebrow at my excitement, but I continued on undeterred. Stateira, a veritable font of patience, was the only person besides our father who indulged my love of machines.

"There's another marvel at the pinnacle: a stone thrower powered by twisted ox-sinew springs," I said. "They throw stones *and* metal-tipped bolts."

My sister cringed. "They sound dreadful."

Tucking my face deeper into my cloak, I touched a bolt I'd found left discarded on the earth, the cold iron that would soon find itself hurled into stone, destroying Tyre's illusions of safety.

"What is that?" I murmured, squinting at a dark shape drifting across the bay from New Tyre toward the Greek siege towers and the old city. Suddenly, orange flames streaked across a Persian transport ship on the water, its deck packed with iron cauldrons, as it approached the shore and Alexander's causeway. The explosions of the cauldrons were louder than any war drum, a cacophony orchestrated by the gods that shook the marrow of my bones.

Oil. The crafty Tyrians had filled the ship with cauldrons of oil, and a single ember had ignited utter destruction.

Macedonians screamed and scattered as the fireship collided with the mole and its wooden siege towers, lighting the night sky like a shattering crimson sun.

"We must go," Stateira yelled, covering her ears. "Mother will worry about us."

I ignored her, stomping my feet into the hillside, hollering and cheering for Tyre until I went hoarse and the last orange sparks fell to the sea. Only then did I consent to let Stateira drag me back to our tent, still craning my neck and grinning as the Tyrians trounced Alexander of Macedon once and for all.

"You'll never believe it," I whooped as I entered. "Alexander has lost—"

A wall of blazing heat hit me; a roaring fire had been lit in every brazier as if this were the dead of winter instead of spring. The tent smelled of sweat and something primal, and a terrible odor I'd smelled only once before, on the banks of a muddy river many years ago.

"What's happening?" I asked. Despite the late hour, the entire tent was a flurry of chaos like the battle I'd just seen, every oil lamp lit, and our servingwomen scurried about like retreating soldiers, laden with sloshing basins of water and piles of fresh linen.

"Your mother is about to deliver," my grandmother said. "I sent one of the eunuchs to fetch a midwife, but he hasn't returned."

"The camp is in an uproar," I said, casting a glance at my dumbstruck sister. "The Tyrians are using wildfire to destroy Alexander."

"I care little for Tyre right now," my grandmother snapped. "Not when your father's heir is about to be born."

An heir that Alexander would likely expose. We'd prayed to Ahura Mazda every day since our capture for another girl, after so many years of praying for a son.

"I'll fetch the midwife," Stateira said, surprising both of us as she darted back out of the pavilion, imbued with a sudden bravery, or cowardice.

"Go to your mother, Drypetis," my grandmother ordered. "She shall require all our strength in the fight to come."

I found my mother draped halfway over her bed, knees on the ground while she moaned into her swan-feather mattress. Her hips swayed back and forth, as if to entice the stubborn child to slide from her womb. I placed my hands over hers, knotted though they were in the soft sheets.

"This one may yet kill me," she groaned, clutching my hands so the bones threatened to splinter. "Promise me that you'll keep the child from the river. And from Alexander."

I recalled that terrible day, one of my earliest memories, as our family camped along the Euphrates while on progress from Babylon. It had been a fine day and my father had taken down several ducks and a magnificent white-plumed crane with his hunting stick. My elder brother, Cyrus, twice my five years and stronger than the hero Achaemenes to my young eyes, had snuck out in my father's skiff when no one was looking. My mother yelled for him to come back, but he stood on the prow in the middle of the river, hefting my father's bow and quiver of arrows onto his back. We watched in horror as he tottered and the skiff swayed drunkenly; then my dark-haired brother lost his balance and tumbled into the river with a violent splash. My mother screamed and my father dived into the water. Stateira and I clutched each other, waiting for him to resurface, but there was nothing. River debris matted Cyrus' hair and his lips had gone blue by the time my father pulled him back to shore. My mother collapsed and wailed into the earth even as my father pounded on my brother's chest and begged him to breathe.

The River of Copper had stolen his last breath. That same day we carried him to Babylon's Tower of Silence, exposing his pale body and allowing him to greet the gods and cross the Chinvat Bridge into paradise.

I'd refused to touch even my bathwater for weeks afterward and Stateira still mumbled pleas to Ahura Mazda's holy flame each time we traversed a river, the flickering light from the god's fire making her appear six years old again. Life had soured for my mother after that, then grown more bitter with each miscarriage and stillbirth that followed.

"I swear it, Mother," I said, kissing her brow. "No rivers. This child will be so overindulged that elephants shall carry her over every river in the empire."

But my mother didn't hear me, for an unexpected midwife had arrived with Stateira, swathed in her customary blue and gold. I wondered if Barsine would have preferred to plunge back into the turmoil of war once she took in the scene before her.

"The camp is in disarray," Stateira said, wringing her hands. My lovely sister detested having a single brush or charcoal nub out of place in her drawing box; the chaos of the fireship and our brother's birth might well send her sobbing into the tent corner before the sun rose again. "The midwife is nowhere to be found, but Barsine offered her assistance."

"You brought Alexander's whore to catch my child?" my mother nearly growled.

"Barsine's mother was a midwife before their exile," Stateira offered.

Barsine shrugged off her cumbersome head scarf, which fell past her waist and was covered with gold embroidery and a king's ransom in shining coins. "I've helped several of my handmaids deliver healthy children. The Greek midwives during our exile were averse to catching Persian babes. I swear I won't spit on the queen or her child as they did us."

My grandmother pursed her lips, but nodded. "We are grateful for your help, Barsine."

But there was another reason Barsine had offered to attend my mother.

"I have news from your father," she whispered to me as she submerged her smooth hands in a bowl of boiled vinegar. "Alexander received a messenger—a eunuch from your father—today."

"And?" I prompted. "What did the messenger say?"

She glanced at me, her eyes as blue as her necklace and almost as wide. "He spoke of your father's pain at your capture and begged for your release in return for ten thousand talents."

I gasped. It was a colossal sum that would overfill the largest treasury in the kingdom, but I was sure Alexander would demand no less. "When will the exchange occur?"

She shook her head and allowed a eunuch to dry her hands with a towel. "It won't. Alexander burned the letter."

"What?" My voice was so sharp it drew my grandmother's attention, but my mother's animal wail of pain saved me.

"He told his Companions that the Great King insulted him and demanded your freedom, claiming this war to be the fault of the Macedonians. You can imagine the Companions' reaction when Alexander asked their opinion on your release."

"They probably cursed my father and all of us to the furthest depths of *Duzakh*," I said, keeping my hands busy with refolding a stack of towels. "Right before they laughed the messenger all the way back to Babylon. Alexander toys with us for his entertainment." But I arched an eyebrow at Barsine. "Why would you risk telling me all this?"

She shrugged. "Alexander enjoys my company now, but his tastes may change in days to come. I hope that your family would remember my assistance and look upon me kindly should that happen."

"A practical plan."

Barsine was saved from answering by my grandmother's barked command. "I need your help examining her, Barsine," she said.

I didn't watch. The axles and suspension beams of chariots entranced me, but the workings of my mother's body held no allure. It was our duty as women to bring forth children, but I thought men had it better, for they could count on the strength of their sword arms when they risked their lives in battle. There was little a woman could do to guarantee her survival in childbed.

"The babe's feet are first," my grandmother muttered.

Despite the heat of the tent, a chill made me shiver as Barsine nodded. "We can try to turn the child, but it will cause the queen great discomfort. And she is no longer a young woman. . . ."

"We have no choice," my grandmother said.

Barsine, no doubt wishing she'd never answered the summons to attend to Darius' queen, helped my mother remove her sweat-stained robes and arranged her onto her back. No longer was my mother the regal consort of the King of Kings, but instead just a woman like any other, the skin of her stomach stretched thin and streaked with angry purple veins. My grandmother shoved pillows beneath my mother's hips, then placed the heels of her hands atop her swollen stomach and shoved hard. I winced at my mother's scream, a bloodcurdling shriek to rival any battle cry, and pushed back sweaty tendrils of hair from her forehead, feeling like the mother consoling her child.

Again, Barsine checked the babe, eliciting more exhausted moans from my mother. "The child still faces the wrong direction. I need sheep fat," she ordered. "Warm it over the brazier."

A servant scurried to attend to the fat while my mother cried softly to herself. "My girls," she whispered through her tears. "You must be brave. Whatever Alexander plans for you, remember who you are, daughters of the King of Kings."

I knew then she believed herself dying, but every laboring woman wishes for death just before bringing forth new life. My mother would survive this to outlive all of us and complain to our corpses about the quality of wine served at our funerals.

The sour tang of tallow filled the air and I watched in confusion as Barsine slathered her hand and forearm with the warmed sheep's fat. Confusion turned to horror as she waited for my mother's belly to slacken at the end of a pain. Barsine parted my mother's legs and worked first her fingers, then her entire hand and wrist into my mother's body. My mother screamed again, and hot tears slipped down my cheeks.

By the time Barsine finished, rivulets of sweat dripped down both her and my mother's temples. Alexander's pampered mistress sat back hard, her chest heaving. "The child is lodged firm," she said. "I cannot turn it."

My grandmother leaned over my mother to clasp her cheeks in age-spotted hands. "Stateira," she whispered. "You must push this child from your womb. Think of Darius, and of holding this child together when you see him next."

My mother seemed to rouse then, allowing my grandmother to help her squat next to the bed. I watched in horror as the skin across her belly tightened and she cried out in agony, her eyes bulging, as over and over the pains repeated and my mother, now on all fours and almost unrecognizable from the pain and struggle, pushed and screamed while her sweat soured the very air we breathed.

To no avail.

We took turns murmuring to her and whispering encouragement into her ears as each new pain sapped her remaining strength.

Still, she clung to life.

I tried to stay awake, but the sun rose and set, then rose again before the infant finally fell from her womb feetfirst, a son with a blue face like my brother Cyrus, strangled by the cord wrapped tight round his neck. My mother lay on the bed as her lifeblood flooded from her body, staining the mattress and floor with an oncoming tide of scarlet. My throat grew tight as my grandmother forced her to swallow a mouthful of consecrated Haoma water and barked for the slaves to fetch pomegranate seeds, both harbingers of immortality served to the dying. Barsine tried to stanch the flow of blood, but there was naught she could do. Even before the pomegranates arrived, my grandmother bent to press her cheek to my mother's nose, feeling for the breath that wouldn't come.

I choked as she removed a golden thread from her pocket—the sacred *kusti* always kept near a laboring woman—and girdled it about my mother's engorged waist, murmuring the *Padyab-Kusti* prayer to keep Ahriman's demons at bay. "Your mother awaits her entrance into paradise," she finally proclaimed. "Someone must inform Alexander."

Without waiting for a response, I burst into the garish sun's light for the first time in two days, gulping in the crisp air still tainted with the ash and smoke from the fireship.

My mother was dead. She had been alive when dawn tinted the sky today, but now she was dead.

I stumbled through the camp, ignoring the shocked stares, some of the soldiers making the sign against evil and death as I passed. I glanced down, only now realizing that the bottom of my stale robe was stained with my mother's blood. My heart was heavy with grief and guilt for all the moments I'd squandered these past months that I might have spent with her, for all the times my temper had grown short as she complained of her swollen ankles and aching back.

A Companion pointed me toward the waterfront when I asked where I might find Alexander, and I trudged in that direction, each step draining the last of my energy.

I found him standing at the start of the narrow causeway that was the ruined mole, the wreckage from the siege towers still floating in the turquoise waves like detritus after a storm. The Macedonians labored to lash two ships together with a massive battering ram atop their decks. Only two days ago, I might have marveled at the ingenuity of the Greeks in the face of such a terrible setback as the fireship, but now I only shoved past Alexander's assembled onlookers.

He looked surprised at my approach and some part of my mind noted Hephaestion sitting on a crate next to his friend, his eyes bloodshot and both of their faces covered in several days' worth of stubble. I felt as terrible as they looked and collapsed in a heap at Alexander's feet, too exhausted to remain upright any longer.

"Alexander of Macedon," I murmured, my throat raw. "I bear unfortunate news from the tent of Queen Stateira."

To my surprise, Alexander knelt beside me and his assembled Companions drew back like a wave, granting the illusion of privacy. "What has happened?" he asked.

"Queen Stateira is dead," I said, wiping away the sudden deluge of tears with the back of my hand, the same hand that still ached from being crushed during the labor pangs.

"How can that be?"

"She delivered a child this morning—a stillborn son." I forced myself to stop and draw a deep breath. "She didn't survive the ordeal."

Alexander stared at me with such distress that I might have told him of his own mother's death. He hadn't known of my mother's pregnancy or that he harbored Darius' potential heir in his own camp. Now he was spared from having to decide what to do with the child, although my sister and I had been served a double portion of grief. "You and your family have my deepest condolences," he said in a tone that sounded genuine.

My gratitude for his sincerity was quickly replaced by anger as I realized he was likely only relieved that he hadn't been forced to kill the child.

I struggled to my feet, ignoring his proffered hand. "Thank you," I said, remembering the other reason I'd sought him out. "My mother and brother must be exposed before the sun sets. You've taken Old Tyre; the city's tallest building is its Tower of Silence for the dead." And within the tower were the long-legged vultures that would purify their bodies, along with the deep dry well where their bones would be laid to rest. I only hoped a four-eyed dog could be found somewhere in Tyre's alleys to help guide them to the afterlife.

But Alexander recoiled and dropped my hand. "Exposure is a barbaric practice. Your mother shall have a funeral and burial befitting her rank as Persia's Queen of Queens. I myself shall make a sacrifice to the gods on her behalf. I will not let it be said that I allowed vultures to tear the flesh from her bones. For to do so would be a crime."

I stepped closer, my palms balled into savage fists. "All of Persia's kings going back to Cyrus the Great have been exposed in a Tower of Silence. Would you deny my mother the final rites that will see her soul to paradise?"

"I would indeed—," Alexander began, but Hephaestion cleared his throat.

"The Tower of Silence still stands in the northern district of Old Tyre, despite the heavy bombardment the city received in that area," he said, leaning forward to rest his thick forearms on his knees. He exchanged a silent conversation with Alexander, although I couldn't quite decipher its meaning. I felt a pang of jealousy, wishing there were someone with whom I might share a bond stronger than words. "Perhaps that is a sign that Queen Stateira was meant to be taken there."

A pulse ticked in Alexander's jaw and I expected him to lambaste Hephaestion, but instead he gave a slow nod, his face softening and the angry pulse calming. "Fine," he said to me. "Take your mother to the Tower of Silence and let the remaining vultures do as they will."

"Thank you," I said, not understanding his change of opinion but too weary to question it. "And will you arrange for a herald to carry the news to my father?"

"I shall inform Darius of the passing of his queen when I deliver the answer to his latest ransom demands."

"The ransom that you denied and then lied about to your advisers?" Now hardly seemed the time to discuss the release of my family, but I wanted nothing more than to leave this place, to escape to the mountains and valleys where our family had been together. Yet my family would never be together again.

"Drypetis has just lost her mother," Hephaestion interrupted, standing and clapping a hand on Alexander's shoulder. "Surely this discussion can wait."

"Of course," Alexander said. "We shall sort out the rest of this sordid business after Tyre has fallen."

"After Tyre has fallen?" I echoed. "When shall that be?"

"Weeks, perhaps months." He snapped his fingers and his Companions parted to allow a graceful young boy to pass in a cloud of myrrh perfume, bedecked in an immaculate white Persian robe and finely wrought golden bangles. My jaw fell at the realization that my father had dared part with Bagoas, his favorite eunuch, whom my mother had never decided whether to love or loathe, so often had he supplanted her in my father's bed. "In the meantime," Alexander said, "I hope you will welcome your father's messenger back into your family's service. Your mother was a noble queen," he said. "May Charon carry her easily over the river Styx."

Bagoas bowed to me, and I noted the way Alexander followed his every elegant movement and how Hephaestion frowned. My heart thudded as I realized the true gift Alexander had just placed in my hands.

My head spinning, I beckoned Bagoas to follow me and wound my way back toward my mother's tent, where my words would be drowned out by the servants' mournful wails.

"You must carry a message to my father," I whispered in Bagoas' ear. He was scarcely older than twelve summers, dark and lithe with skin like a lustrous pearl. "Tell him of my mother's passing and the games Alexander plays with the ransom demands. Tell him how many soldiers the *yona takabara* has and how the siege of Tyre is draining his food supplies."

Bagoas stepped back and pushed the dark curls from his face. It seemed unfair that even this boy was prettier than me with his dark eyes like polished river stones and lashes like a camel's. "But your father commanded me to stay until Alexander answered his offer of ransom."

"You heard Alexander," I said. "That could be months from now, if ever. You must go and tell him to ride against Alexander, to rout these Greeks and free us. Please," I said, clutching his delicate wrist. "Take one of the horses after dark and don't stop until you find him."

"I shall serve the house of Darius in this," he said. "I will not fail."

"Thank you." I pressed my forehead to his. "Travel well, and fast."

And thus, I put my last hope in the hands of a smooth-faced eunuch. I only prayed that Bagoas would reach my father before Alexander discovered my trickery.

We carried the bier of my mother and tiny brother through Old Tyre's deserted streets just before the sun fell that day, our footsteps echoing off the walls of abandoned homes and granaries, and accompanied by the steady thuds of Alexander's ballistae as the Macedonians hurled rocks at New Tyre's sturdy battlements. The Tyrians were fresh out of ships, but they had hung thick leather skins stuffed with fresh seaweed along their walls to cushion the blows and continued to drop stones upon Alexander's foundering battering ships, which swayed in the choppy seas. Alexander had ordered every spare man not at work repairing the causeway or manning the battering ships to attend the funeral procession, an honor my mother surely would have remarked upon if she'd been here.

Yet I thought only of the five days yet to come, calculating how far Bagoas would need to ride each day to reach my father in the east.

The fight for Tyre became more apparent as we approached the northern section of town, its buildings bearing gaping holes left from Alexander's ballista practice and exposing tables once set for evening meals that now fed swarms of flies and families of crows. We picked our way around piles of rubble from a collapsed building, the stench of something rotting coming from beneath the mud bricks and plaster.

The Tower of Silence cast a cold shadow over the wide avenue leading to it, which was broad enough for our funeral procession and all those that had come before us. Three interior concentric circles comprised every tower for the dead: the inner for children, the second for women, and the outer for men. My mother and brother would be laid in the proper circles, naked as they were when they entered this world, where first the vultures and then the sun might strip and bleach their bones. Only then would their travails on this earth be complete and the gods ready to welcome them into paradise.

The funeral procession halted before the tower, and the white-cloaked Companions carrying the bier disappeared within to carry the bodies up the flights of winding stairs to the topmost level, where the vultures and the afterlife awaited. As the only royal family members present, my grandmother, Stateira, and I would remain here for the next five days, keeping the sacred fire burning and ensuring that my mother's and brother's bones were stripped clean before they were deposited in the tower's communal well. Yet there was one thing missing, for although I'd glanced down each of Old Tyre's dark alleys for a sacred dog, it seemed even the strays had abandoned this beleaguered city.

A soldier approached Alexander's chariot. "My apologies," he murmured to the conqueror, "but the Tyrians have cut through the ropes anchoring the battering ships."

"By the gods," Alexander muttered. "Cannot the Tyrians wait until after this funeral to torment me? How in the name of Heracles did they cut the ropes?"

"Underwater divers," the man answered.

I snorted with mirth, marveling at Tyre's ingenuity, and mumbled, "If only you'd thought to use iron chains instead of rope."

Alexander swiveled to face me. "An apt observation," he said, then turned back to the soldier. "Ensure that the ships have all the iron chain they need."

My mother would have pinched me if she were here, or worse. Instead, I withered under the full wrath of my grandmother's glare, blazing fiercer than Tyre's fireship.

"They're running out of stones," the man said. "Soon they won't have anything left to throw at us, save their own walls."

Alexander gestured for Hephaestion. "Go with him and get the ships under control. Harpoon their divers if you have to, but I don't want to hear of my ships drifting again."

Hephaestion nodded, but didn't move away at once. Instead, he motioned to a waiting slave, who brought forth the most pitiful scrap of mangy fur with four legs I'd ever seen. The paltry excuse of a dog was missing patches of a coat that had once been mostly yellow, his pink skin surely riddled with fleas.

But he had two dark spots of fur above his eyes. A four-eyed dog.

"My apologies that he's uglier than Cerberus the hellhound," Hephaestion said, offering the dog's rope to my grandmother. "But I believe you have need of a four-eyed dog."

"The state of his fur doesn't concern Ahura Mazda," my grandmother said, standing straighter even as she took the rope, as if it were woven of gold. The sacred beast would be brought before the Queen of Persia five times during the next five days, his potent stare used to drive off the *druj Nasu*, the evil matter found in every corpse. "How did you know of our need?"

Hephaestion shrugged. "I've read the Avesta once or twice," he said.

I was shocked that the *yona takabara* knew how to read, much less that he'd studied our sacred text, but my grandmother only gave a terse nod and gathered her skirts, stepping over the threshold of the Tower of Silence. The dog and then Stateira followed, my sister's eyes downcast, but I hesitated as I passed Hephaestion and Alexander, knowing that gratitude was owed. "Thank you," I ground out, then hurried after my family.

My appreciation survived only until I reached the topmost floor of the tower, where Stateira and my grandmother stared at the span of blue sky gaping at us from an open hole shorn from the roof. Any long-legged vultures kept to service the dead had long since flown to feast on Tyre's corpses, although their white droppings still spackled the floor and stone walls. A breath of wind sent several gray feathers skittering across the flagstones like furtive mice.

I recalled the knowing glance Hephaestion had exchanged with Alexander when he'd appeared to accommodate my mother's funeral requirements.

Take your mother to the Tower of Silence and let the remaining vultures do as they will.

"That filthy, toad-faced liar," I said, kicking at the feathers and obliterating the tower's sacred rule of silence. The Companions laid my mother's white-clad body on the stone bier in the middle circle, while my brother's tiny, naked body already lay in the center of the chamber. The men exchanged worried glances, then bowed and strode from the room, their footsteps echoing down the stairwell.

"Perhaps Alexander didn't realize the state of the roof," Stateira offered.

But it wasn't Alexander I spoke of, though I knew Stateira was too generous. It was Hephaestion who had reminded Alexander of the location of the Tower of Silence. They had agreed to honor our mother, all the while knowing that her rites would be incomplete.

"Alexander dislikes the practice of exposure, so Hephaestion sought to pacify us and placate him—"

My grandmother cut me off. "It matters naught. We have the dog and fire, and tomorrow we shall have the sun. Your mother must be attended at all times; we will make do with what we have for the next five days. Then your mother and brother shall join the rest of the dead in the well, and we shall rejoin the living." She held her hands up to stop my argument. "From this moment forward we shall not speak, of this or anything else."

I bit my tongue and took my place at my mother's side, seething in silent anger. We might soon rejoin the living, but to repay the insult to my mother, I'd do everything in my power to make Alexander and Hephaestion wish they were dead.

Five days later I emerged from the Tower of Silence, faint with hunger and smelling of death after seeing my mother's and brother's bodies—still laden with flesh from this world—lowered into the deep well of bones in the barren courtyard. I expected to find Alexander waiting for us, but while my grandmother and Stateira gratefully accepted the litters waiting for them, I was instead greeted by a contingent of guards and the man I'd dreamed of strangling. Perhaps it was the lack of food or the company of the dead that I'd kept too long, but I gave little thought—or at least less than usual—to what I did next.

"You," I growled, lunging toward Hephaestion.

He moved faster than I expected for one so large, catching my wrists neatly in one of his massive hands. I kicked at him, but feasting only on hate and grief for five days had made me weak and the toe of my soft slipper on his shin might as well have been a playful nudge for all the harm it caused. The four-eyed dog had followed me and growled low in its throat.

"I hope you've not spent all your tears on your mother, Drypetis, daughter of Darius," Hephaestion snarled, "for you're going to have far more to weep about when I finish with you."

Alexander's lover could pulverize me with his fists if he chose, run me through with a deft attack of his sword, or bash my head against the wall of the Tower of Silence. My heart plummeted as I recognized a smaller figure with a mop of dark curls chained by iron shackles in a waiting cart, the fragrant smell of myrrh and the potent stench of fear in the air.

"Release him," I demanded, stomping on Hephaestion's foot and dancing from his grasp, gesturing angrily toward Bagoas. I gaped when the eunuch lifted his head, revealing a swollen eye with a bruise roughly the size of Hephaestion's fist.

"How dare you?" My voice at that moment rivaled that of any cat looking to rut as I whirled on Hephaestion. "Shall I find small children for you to beat next? Little girls with golden curls, perhaps puppies or a simpleton?"

Hephaestion stopped short, blinking as if taken aback before he shook the irons around Bagoas' wrists, the perfumed boy whose skin was accustomed to touching only the finest silks. "Five days ago, while on my way to deal with Tyre's ships, I discovered this eunuch of yours attempting to slip from camp, carrying a message *you* ordered him to deliver to your father. Explain to my poor, feeble mind how King Darius also deserves to know the strength of our numbers. And the exact movements of all our men?"

I cringed to realize that Bagoas had spilled all that information to Hephaestion. Better that I'd chosen a eunuch without a tongue than one without a backbone. I reminded myself that he was only a boy with no hope of ever becoming a man, but that didn't lessen my ire.

"Release him," I commanded, my gaze flicking to where Bagoas cowered behind Hephaestion. "He acted on my orders and has already suffered for it."

To my surprise, Hephaestion swallowed hard as if he might eat his rage before producing the key to the irons and freeing the boy.

"You may return to the tent of the dowager queen," he said. "Take the mongrel with you." It was only then that I noticed my grandmother standing behind me, her litter abandoned and her hands tucked into her sleeves with her chin tilted in a most imperious manner.

"It seems my granddaughter and I have much to discuss," she said to Hephaestion, allowing Bagoas to take his place behind her, although he held the dog's dirty rope collar between two dainty fingers. "I thank you for the return of my son's favored eunuch."

"You're most welcome, Queen Sisygambis," he said. He barked a command and the rest of the men parted to let us return to the litters. Hephaestion gestured me forward with a flourish, as if he had the power to command my very movements.

My hand itched to slap him, but I didn't relish the idea of a bruise to match Bagoas', especially as my wrists still ached. "I won't trouble you further," I said. "Thank you for not murdering Bagoas with those big fists of yours."

He inclined his head, then called after me, "But you still owe me something."

I stopped and turned slowly on my heel, gritting my teeth. "What might that be? A blood oath of obedience? My firstborn child?"

Hephaestion grimaced. "Obedience would be a start, but I doubt you could keep that oath past sundown. I leave to quell a revolt in Greece and I don't wish to hear from afar that you're causing Alexander problems. You'll swear now that you'll keep to your tent, or I promise I'll make Alexander clap you in irons before he marries you off to the first moldering Greek governor he can find, preferably a hideously fat one with a penchant for buggering pretty young girls."

"You wouldn't dare."

"Is that a challenge?"

I stared at him, then gave a neat bow. "I swear I shall not commit any further treason while you're gone."

Then I turned on my heel and stormed away, away from Hephaestion and my failure, away from my mother's bones, and toward whatever miserable future Alexander planned for me.

I'd promised I wouldn't commit treason while Hephaestion was in Athens.

But I'd said nothing about what I'd do upon his return.

CHAPTER 6

331 BCE
Pella, Macedon

THESSALONIKE

The brown whip snake twined its way up my arm, its scales as cool and smooth against my flesh as the night air. It didn't have a tooth in its mouth and its eyes were occluded with age, but still I stood motionless while Olympias poured a goblet of spiced wine from the painted *amphora*. The vessel's sides were emblazoned with stark images of Dionysus' initiates in various states of ecstasy, men's bare arms wrapped around the women's waists, their heads all thrown back in abandon.

And snakes. Slithering across its black and red borders were images of snakes to match the live serpents writhing beneath my feet and up my arm. Nonvenomous, they could still strike if provoked, yet they were the least of my worries on this evening of the harvest's full moon.

The very scene on the *amphora* would play out before me tonight, and I would wake not merely a fourteen-year-old woman, but a *maenad* initiate of the wine god, Dionysus.

Olympias had commanded that I partake of the Dionysian revels and I had no choice but to obey. My life had been empty in the four years since Alexander had left as I did my utmost not to attract Olympias' wrath. My childhood plumpness had hardened, so that

Olympias often muttered that I resembled my father, thick-boned and heavy-jawed, save my pelt of golden hair, which I kept braided tightly down my back. Wealthy suitors from all over the Peloponnese had begun asking for my hand in marriage, but Alexander had ordered his mother to refrain from making any alliances and I'd stewed in boredom until I almost wished some man would storm the walls and take me away from here.

Over the past weeks, I'd sacrificed and prayed to the god of grapes and pleasure that this ceremony would fill me with purpose, that my brother's frequent letters would cease taunting me with all I was missing in the wider world while I remained here to obey Olympias' every whim, saved from madness by only my brother Arrhidaeus and my menagerie of animals.

It seemed a trick of the gods that the very man who had conquered the world was my brother, yet I remained unable to breach Pella's walls until some man claimed me as his wife. I prayed that my future husband would be one of Alexander's generals, anyone except a future king.

I would *never* be a queen, not after I'd seen the monster Olympias had become once a diadem had graced her head.

"Drink," Olympias commanded me, curling my fingers around the goblet of wine. Arrhidaeus whimpered in the background, his fear growing palpable as slaves added more cedar and olive oil to the fire until the flames leapt taller than the barren apricot trees. Despite our move from Aigai to the palace at Pella, he'd been fearful of fire ever since the night Eurydice died; both the flames and the dark still provoked his terrible fits of crying. "Go, Arrhidaeus," Olympias said, not even looking at him. "The revels of Dionysus are not for you to enjoy."

"Go," I murmured to my brother, in a voice more controlled than I felt. "In the morning I'll take you fishing."

"You promise?" Arrhidaeus asked, twisting his meaty hands

together even as his eyes strayed toward the gate that led away from Olympias' garden and back to the safety of the palace.

"I promise," I said, although staring at the placid waters of a lake all day sounded as exciting as reading anything written by Homer. "Take my fat orange cat to bed with you to warm your feet."

I watched my brother tiptoe around the snakes (like watching an elephant sidestep mice) and lumber out of the garden. Just as he craved the solid safety of the palace walls, I thrilled at finally leaving them behind, at least for one night.

"Will Cynnane be at the revels?" I asked Olympias, smoothing the fawn skin that was draped over my shoulders and masking the hope in my tone. I desperately wanted to see my warrior half sister, to ask a thousand questions about where she'd learned to throw daggers and whether she thought I could ever learn.

Olympias sniffed. "Cynnane has no taste for the rituals, savage that she is."

She lifted the goblet to my lips and I drank deeply. The wine was potent, unwatered and full of foreign spices, and something else I couldn't quite name. It was cool to the tongue, kept in a clay *amphora* and chilled in the palace well all day, but it burned down the back of my throat and spread warmth like fingers through my belly. It would be a night of fire as we traveled from one bonfire to the next, drinking Dionysus' bounty of wine that would set our insides aflame.

Olympias only smiled. "More," she murmured. "You must drink it all to show the god of revels your willingness to accept him."

I hesitated but did as she asked, trembling as I stared unblinking at her over the rim. Olympias was made more beautiful by the power she wielded, but there was no denying how much she frightened me, especially tonight with the shifting shadows and snakes curling up her arms.

I drained the cup in a final gulp and wiped my mouth with the back of my hand. I'd dressed simply, barefoot and clad in only a white *chiton* made of the finest cotton. My pale hair fell loose past my shoulders and I shivered in the night air, gooseflesh rolling down my arms.

"You'll warm soon," Olympias said, her attire matching my own. "The god shall embrace you and wrap you in his heat." She turned, taking a torch from a waiting slave, then walked languidly to the gate that led away from the palace and toward the hills behind Pella. "You may dance and drink tonight, Thessalonike," she called over her shoulder. "But you shall not couple with any of the revelers. Do you understand?"

I blushed and nodded, but my feet grew heavier with every step toward her. Mist clouded my vision and I tripped, giggling as I stumbled. Olympias looped her arm through mine, setting me aright. "Dionysus favors you," she whispered in my ear. "To see the world through the haze of the god is a precious and powerful gift. Perhaps tonight he shall honor you with a vision as well."

I was entranced with the snakes twined around her neck and my wrist, their beady eyes glinting in the torchlight. A spotted leopard snake draped like a pendant at the base of her throat flicked its forked tongue at me. We continued on our way, drawn forward by the rhythm of far-flung drums and the golden glow of a crackling bonfire atop the hill, its embers tangling with the scattered stars.

We stopped, and I gaped at the pinnacle of a rugged hill encircled by a ring of torches held aloft by faceless shadows. The drumbeat reverberated into my bones, and this time when I stumbled, Olympias let me fall to the earth. Rocks scraped my hands, although I felt no pain.

"It is the earth that feeds our god," she proclaimed, and I watched an acolyte offer her a terra-cotta *rhyton* in the shape of a giant phallus. Olympias drank greedily before she handed the cup to me and I took a sip, luxuriating in the flavor this time before it was passed to the next initiate. "It is in his honor that we abandon ourselves this night," Olympias said, "to feel the power of the god flow through our veins. Rise and welcome the god of mysteries!"

Someone thrust a *thyrsus* into my hand, its wooden fennel stalk topped with a pinecone dripping with honey to symbolize a phallus and its erupting seed. I knew I should blush, but even that was beyond me with all the wine sloshing in my belly.

The female dancers burst into song then, a bawdy hymn to Dionysus, while they tossed another *thyrsus* between them in a mockery of the thrusting I'd seen bulls and dogs perform while mating.

To Dionysus do I pray,
A long man do I hope to catch,
But alas, only a thyrsus pole do I snatch,
With its pinecone I shall not lay!

I staggered to my feet as they dragged me stumbling up the hill, joyous at the heat that surged just beneath my skin. I looked at my arms, expecting to see flames there, but instead only the little brown snake was watching me.

"Dance with us and you dance with the god," someone whispered in my ear. I turned, expecting to see Olympias, but the world was slow in catching up. The hilltop had filled with other revelers, their eyes glazed and their heads thrown back in rapture. The heat flamed hotter, sounds grew sharper, and the rank smell of the torches and sweat filled my nose. Around me, men and women shed their clothes, and some clung to one another, their naked bodies writhing together in rhythm to the drums. The notes of Pan's pipes rose into the air and the sounds of a wood and cord bull-roarer circled like a giant wasp, crescendoing into the buzz of an entire hive.

Then someone shouted and women ran down the hill, chasing the unfortunate goat that had been brought to the revels. The *maenads* would catch the beast and tear it apart with their bare hands, offering the softest bits to Dionysus' fire before feasting on the bloody flesh.

The animal bleated in terror, the bell around his neck clanging with every step.

I ran, tripping several more times, and shoved half-naked women away from me, intent on catching the unfortunate goat and chasing it into the shadows. Several revelers in my path stumbled and one especially plump matron fell so hard that she rolled partway down the hill. Yet still I ran.

Until one of the *maenads* I elbowed whirled on me and an explosion of white lightning lit my vision.

I wheeled back, but recovered from the punch to lunge forward, grabbing fistfuls of hair and clawing at the blurred face I could scarcely see through the fog of wine. The goat forgotten, we fell to the earth with screeches like two cats in heat, rolling over and over in trampled grasses. I tasted dirt and my own blood, felt her fists, knees, and teeth as they attacked my soft flesh.

And I'd never felt so alive.

I crowed with laughter when the faceless *maenad* stumbled to her feet and lurched back up the hill. I knew now why Alexander and even my sister Cynnane craved the heat of battle, the euphoria of a good fight.

The faces and bodies that passed me became a blur of flesh lit by fire shine. I saw familiar faces long since gone: Alexander and Hephaestion, my mother and father. I laughed, but when I reached up, it was to find my cheeks were slick with tears.

Fear gripped my heart and I cried out, but the drums and the ecstatic cries of the revelers swallowed the sound. I crawled toward the exterior ring of torches, into the darkness that beckoned to me with its promise of quiet and calm. There was no euphoria this time, only a wave of panic, as my arms collapsed and I hit the earth.

I couldn't move.

I felt another surge of panic, wondering if I was dying, if my wine had been mixed with more than just spices, if I might be trampled by Dionysus' crowd. I prayed for the god's mercy then, to release me from his grip.

Instead, faithless Dionysus abandoned me to continue his revelry and I fell blissfully unconscious.

A brutal shaft of sunshine stabbed my skull as I blinked my way back to life the next morning, recognizing my light-filled chamber despite having no recollection of how I'd gotten there. A sound like boots hitting the floor sent more daggers grinding into my temples and I moaned in agony.

"She lives," a man's voice boomed, reverberating off the stone walls of my chamber. A familiar slow grin greeted me, one I'd not seen in four long years.

I groaned again, then wished that Zeus might strike me with one of his bolts.

"So, little Nike survived the Dionysian Mysteries," Hephaestion said, his voice louder than it needed to be. With his foot, he nudged away a jumbled tangle of wool yarn, an embroidered scene of Athena and her sacred owl that I'd started ages ago and had left neglected on the floor for the past year. "I expect you want to die about now."

Medusa's snakes, but he was right.

Hephaestion's eyes crinkled at the corners, his face leaner and the skin toughened from the time he'd spent riding with my brother beneath Persia's Eastern sun. I was no lovesick girl, but I'd have had to be as blind as Homer not to appreciate Hephaestion's brawny allure.

I'd expected to feel different after my initiation, more alive and worldly, but all I felt was a curdled stomach, a vise around my head and ribs where the *maenad* had kicked me, and utter mortification that Hephaestion was seeing the mess I was now. I'd count it a blessing from the four goddesses if I could keep from hurling the contents of my stomach into an urn while Hephaestion was here. His almost-black eyes sparkled now with mirth at my obvious discomfort.

"You shouldn't be in my chamber," I said, struggling to sit. "Olympias will have your hide."

"And miss this opportunity? Never." He sat beside me on the bed and lifted the lid of the wicker basket, then dropped it back on my snake with a grimace.

I wrinkled my nose and buried my face in my linen sheet. "You smell like you bathed in *garos*."

And from the way my stomach lurched, the fermented fish sauce was the last thing I should be smelling right now.

Hephaestion sniffed his tunic, then shrugged. "A drizzle of *garos* will go splendidly with the trout Arrhidaeus caught this morning."

"Arrhidaeus . . ." I groaned. "I told him I'd take him fishing today."

"He accepted me in your stead, although not without a fair bit of grumbling."

"You've already been and gone?"

"You slept the morning away, little Nike." Hephaestion chuckled. "And most of the afternoon too. I found Arrhidaeus waiting outside your door at dawn, his birch poles and a basket of worms ready to turn your stomach."

My gorge rose at the very idea, imagining the squirming worms and a morning spent gutting fish. "Thank you."

"You're quite welcome. Without you fidgeting and scaring away all of the fish, Arrhidaeus and I caught enough trout to feed a small army at the banquet tonight."

"What banquet?" I croaked.

"The one to celebrate the peace treaty I brokered with Athens." He leaned back in his chair, hands clasped loosely behind his head, a pose surely perfected to reveal his well-shaped arms with their glorious battle scars. "Alexander sent me to prevent the revolt of Agis from spreading to Athens. I negotiated a mean settlement with Demosthenes, not that I would ever boast."

I snorted at that, for Hephaestion possessed more than a healthy dose of confidence. Only days ago, Olympias had received a runner in her weaving room, a sweat-streaked messenger bearing news of Greek states allying against Macedon, led by Agis of Sparta. The Spartan *basileus* had died during a pitched battle, but the entire mainland had held its breath and waited to see whether Athens would join the cause and continue the revolt. Now it appeared we had our answer.

Hephaestion dropped a folded parchment into my lap. "I come on Alexander's orders. This just arrived from him."

I tore into the letter like a starving dog, knowing that the words within carried hazy visions of foreign lands I'd never see. I breathed deeply of the parchment and imagined its scent as that of blowing sand and aromatic spices, the boiling sun and musty tombs. Perhaps if I wished hard enough . . .

But when I opened my eyes, I was still sitting on my bed with Hephaestion opposite me, a bemused expression on his face. "It's only a piece of paper," he said. "There's no need to hold it like a lover."

I flushed at the very mention of a lover, for I'd never even been kissed, but stuck out my tongue as a cover for my embarrassment. I'd seen four winters and four summers come and go since Alexander had marched out of our city, and since then my brother had conquered the Peloponnese, Granicus, Issus, Tyre, and Gaza before moving on to Egypt, where he was welcomed with open arms. Each letter from him was exquisite torture, sketching for me pictures of places I could only imagine and never truly see with my own eyes.

"You wouldn't understand," I muttered.

"It's true that I'm just an insensitive dullard with a skull thicker than a marble pillar," Hephaestion said. "I'd certainly never understand why you'd want to leave Pella's little harbor to see the world." He moved to a nearby chair and kicked his heels up on my bed. I felt quite dignified as I ignored him, imagining Alexander's silken voice in my head.

Dearest Thessalonike,

This afternoon, as the sun-god Ra reached its pinnacle in the sky, I was crowned pharaoh of Upper and Lower Egypt. It is no boast, but only the truth to claim that my collection of crowns now rivals that of King Priam.

My men and I will winter here in Alexandria, thus far a veritable city of tents along the coast. The boundaries of my glorious new city were laid out with barley sprinkled by sacred priests draped in leopard skins, drawn in the shape of a proper Macedonian military cloak. This city shall be my monument to the world, the brightest jewel among my conquests.

I hope you continue to read your Homer—you shall marry one day and I shall require that your groom be well versed in all the poet's great works. Any man who cannot recite The Song of Ilium shall find himself unworthy of my sister's hand.

Your dutiful brother,
Alexander

And he'd scribbled an afterthought beneath his flourish of a signature. . . .

Eat an extra helping of beef at your next meal and think of me. I fear to repeat the acts of Artaxerxes, when he offended the Egyptians' sensibilities by roasting their sacred Apis bull for a feast. Thus, I've forbidden any of my Companions to eat beef while we travel along the Nile.

"What does it say?" Hephaestion's eyes were hooded, but I'd felt him watching me while I read.

"That he pines for beef," I answered, rolling my eyes. I'd have gladly sacrificed all the bulls in the world if it meant I could witness the fresh temples of Alexandria being built or see the leopard-bedecked priests performing their dedication rituals.

"Your brother suffers mightily for his ambitions," Hephaestion said, chuckling. "I told him to let the Egyptians eat donkey, but he claimed that would be an affront to his new father, Ammon."

"His new father?"

Hephaestion nodded, rising and going to the window that looked out over the hill where Dionysus' Mysteries had taken place. "He uses his adoptions to collect mothers and fathers like trinkets now, the better to solidify his hold on various territories. Widowed Queen Ada of Caria is his latest mother, and the god Ammon his newest sire."

"I doubt Olympias will approve," I said.

He shrugged. "Olympias is a practical woman. Ada honored Alexander by renaming her capital after him, and the hold of my ship contains a crate of gold crowns from her, a gift from Alexander to Olympias."

"The world shall grow weary of every city being named Alexandria."

"Perhaps." Hephaestion laughed. "Yet I fear Alexander never will." He leaned forward and dropped a kiss atop my head as if I were still a girl with scraped knees. I glanced down at my hands, wincing at the scabs from my falls last night. "I'll post a guard outside to let you sleep before the banquet tonight," he said. "Antipater is hosting and his son Cassander is freshly returned from Athens, so it promises to be a staid and very long affair."

I fell back on my pillow with a groan.

Whereas Alexander and Hephaestion had left Aristotle's Mieza school here in Macedon and marched off to conquer the world, Cassander was their junior by six years and had followed the famed scholar to Athens, where he'd continued to teach at the Lyceum. I cared little for an insufferable boor, who would likely spout his tutor's maxims while extolling the virtues of his father's cheese-stuffed cuttlefish, fried Egyptian goose eggs, and fine wines.

"I know," Hephaestion said. "I tried to beg off, but Olympias made me promise to stay so she might arrange for letters and gifts for Alexander."

I sat up again, too fast from the way my head clanged. "When will you leave?"

"Eager to get rid of me so soon, eh? We sail in two days, if the winds remain favorable. I only stopped here to deliver Alexander's gifts—"

I lurched forward to seize his hand, swallowing hard as the ground swayed beneath me as I clambered to my knees beside his chair. "Take me with you and train me."

For the first time I could recall, Hephaestion seemed speechless.

"Please," I babbled, sounding desperate even to my own ears. "I'll do anything you ask, shovel your horse's stall, fetch your wine, polish your greaves. Please, please, please. I can't breathe here, not under Olympias' shadow. I want to *see* things and to fight like I did in the revels last night." I winced at the fresh pain in my temples. "Only without the wine."

Hephaestion stared at me, my hand like a manacle around his thick wrist. "It isn't safe, Thessalonike, especially not for women."

"There are women with the army," I corrected him. "Alexander has Barsine."

"Your brother is worshipped as a god now. He can snap his fingers and have whatever he wants, but that's not how the world works for the rest of us mortals."

I crossed my arms, undaunted. "Darius brought his family with him on campaign, even his elderly mother."

Hephaestion threw his hands up. "And they were captured in battle!"

"I'd never be captured," I scoffed.

"Perhaps not. But you'd leave Arrhidaeus here? Alone?"

I sat back on my heels. I hadn't thought of Arrhidaeus. Olympias hadn't threatened him since the night of Eurydice's death, but I certainly couldn't leave him with her. "He could come to Persia as my bodyguard."

Yet even as I said it, I knew my half brother would never survive a campaign, leaving the home he knew to face iron and blood.

"Arrhidaeus is no soldier," Hephaestion said sadly. "His gifts lie elsewhere, in his loyalty to you."

"I'm Alexander's sister; that alone would protect me."

"I'd wager Darius' women thought the same, before the Battle of Issus. His youngest daughter, Drypetis, reminds me of you."

"Then she must be beautiful as Aphrodite, intelligent as Athena, and courageous as Artemis," I said, recalling Hephaestion's words to me when he'd first left to march off with Alexander.

"Actually," he said with no small dose of exasperation, "Drypetis is plainer than mud and more obstinate than a starving pig at a trough."

I glared at him. "Please, Hephaestion. I'm begging you."

His face softened and he touched my cheek as a knock came at the door. "I'm sorry, little Nike, but I can't. It's too dangerous, especially for a girl."

Meaning he might have taken me if I possessed a sword between my legs instead of a stupid flower.

"Get out!" I yelled. My pillow missed Hephaestion and hit the wall in an explosion of goose feathers.

"As you wish." Hephaestion stood and swiped a feather from the air, twirling it between his fingers. "Although I'd have thought you'd have better aim after trying to persuade me to take you into the thick of battle."

I grabbed the closest thing I could find and hurled it at the door just as Hephaestion closed it. Unfortunately, that resulted only in a dull thud and my half-blind snake slithering from its basket as I screamed in frustration, the walls of my chamber closing in around me.

Freedom was an impossible dream, yet one I couldn't quite shake. And if Hephaestion wouldn't help me—I cursed his name under my breath—then I'd find another way to escape Olympias and these palace walls.

On my own.

The banquet made me want to slit my wrists, or, better yet, Hephaestion's throat.

Being a guest of honor, he was seated alongside our family beneath the open oculus of the formal hall, next to Cassander and his father. Upon his arrival, I edged as far away from him as I could without falling off my chair. Olympias cocked an eyebrow as slaves served us platters of sow's udder stuffed with leeks and cumin, milk-fed snails drowned in a pepper sauce, and braised pigeon from the palace's domed dovecotes. "Is there a spider on your chair?" she asked.

"Not at all," I said. "Hephaestion doesn't care for the presence of *girls*."

There were several sniggers at that from eavesdroppers, but Hephaestion ignored them.

"He does like girls," Arrhidaeus said. "He was kissing one in the courtyard."

Hephaestion flashed a smile and shrugged. "I appreciate beauty in all its forms. Especially those forms that don't hurl things at my head."

And with that, he had the audacity to give me his shoulder to speak to Olympias. I listened with my ears buzzing as he delivered several letters from Alexander, and they discussed Alexander's adoption of the god Ammon as his father.

Yet I had a plan. I might still get to follow Alexander, to see Egypt and Persia and beyond. . . .

"They claim that Zeus visited me so I might conceive Alexander, that my womb was sealed with the mark of a lion that night," Olympias said, lifting her goblet, so the torchlight caught on the gold bracelet at her wrist, illuminating the serpent insignia there. She wore a sardonyx cameo at her throat, its raised relief depicting her regal profile behind Alexander in his plumed battle helmet. "Ammon is Egypt's name for Zeus, so of course he should claim him as his true father."

"Zeus should be worshipped in his true form," came the voice from my other side. "Ammon, Ahura Mazda, and the like are the false gods of *barbaroi* who speak with forked and twisted tongues."

Antipater's son Cassander was far from handsome, in fact downright ugly in this room of polished nobility, his face too harsh and his coloring darker even than Hephaestion's, but I showered my most golden smile upon him.

"And now that you've finished your studies with Aristotle," I said to him, "will you be joining my glorious brother in his campaigns in Persia? Perhaps see those barbarians for yourself?"

Cassander stared at me as if I'd started jabbering in Egyptian, his black eyebrows drawn together like a monstrous caterpillar. "Fortunately, no."

I waited for him to elaborate, but I may as well have ceased to exist.

"Pella must seem dull after the recent excitement in Athens," I prodded.

He sighed and grudgingly turned his attention back to me while the others discussed Alexander's progress in Egypt. "So says the sister of the world's conqueror. You possess the youthful ignorance of the young. Athens narrowly escaped her own destruction by signing Hephaestion's treaty. I prefer my studies to being slaughtered on the streets in the name of freedom."

Insulted for my gender and my age today. It was enough to make me want to throw snakes at him too.

"You're only a few years older than me," I said, strumming angry fingers along the base of my goblet, and calculating whether it would be worth hurling the contents into Cassander's pious, big-nosed face.

"I'm eighteen," he said. "And *I* wasn't careening about half-dressed in the moonlight last night. Were those really snakes crawling up your arms?"

"You were at the Mysteries last night?" I winced at his terse nod.

"Hephaestion's ship docked next to mine and he insisted that we witness the foul ritual." His eyes flicked to Olympias, but she was deep in discussion with Hephaestion and therefore wouldn't bite off his head for slandering her beloved celebration. "I hope you thanked him for carrying you to your chambers after you passed out from overindulgence. Otherwise you'd have found your virtue stolen by some drunken sot come morning. *If* you still possess any virtue, that is."

So *that* was how I'd gotten into bed. Still, I'd let scorpions devour my tongue before I thanked Hephaestion.

I rearranged the folds of my *peplos*, feeling my ears flare red even as I wished I could attack Cassander with my fists as I had the *maenad* last night. But it didn't matter, for I'd soon be sailing away from Pella. Cassander could rot here with his father for all I cared.

The rest of the banquet passed so slowly that I suspected Apollo might be delaying the sun's descent. I listened with feigned disinterest as Hephaestion spoke with Olympias of his plans to leave in two days' time, before turning to comment to Arrhidaeus on the quality of trout in Pella's streams.

I watched my brother lick the butter from his fingers, then blow his shaggy hair away from his eyes and give me a crooked smile. If only I could be more like him, so content within the security of these walls and the never-changing vista of Pella's hills and harbor.

I couldn't tell him what I planned without fear of him slipping the secret to Olympias, Hephaestion, or even a passing slave. And there was still much to do.

I rose, swaying on my feet. The conversation at our table stopped and Olympias lifted an elegant brow, giving me permission to speak.

"I'm overweary after last night's exertions—" I avoided looking at Cassander, feeling his derisive scowl at my back. "May I retire early?"

"You may," Olympias answered. "Rest well."

I left behind the chatter and warmth of the banquet hall, and padded softly down the silent corridors to my own chambers. An oil lamp staved off the darkness and illuminated the blue swirls of plaster waves and the motionless gray dolphins painted on my walls. A slave had arranged a vase of fragrant crocus blossoms on my table, and my bed waited for one of the last nights I would sleep there, its sheets freshly pressed despite my late rising.

In two days' time, I'd leave all this behind.

I opened a polished olive-wood chest that contained the majority of my *chitons* and removed the plainest one of sturdy cotton and a pair of unadorned leather sandals. I'd take little else, only Alexander's copy of *The Song of Ilium* and a cloak to hide my face.

And my snake.

I set aside the top of her woven basket and let her slither out, her unseeing old eyes still inquisitive as she stared at me. It pained me to think of leaving behind my orange cat and spotted nanny goat, but they weren't easily packed and hidden away. Especially not the cat, who howled if he'd gone without food for more than a quarter hour. "You need a name, and I think Aristomache fits you well," I murmured to my snake. *Aristo* meant "best" and *mache* was "battle."

"My father named me for a battle, and together you and I will see this war my brother fights."

She cocked her head and I replaced her in the basket, closing the lid. I didn't mean to sleep, but my excuse of weariness from Diony-sus' revelries must have been close to the mark, for soon I was lifting my head from the table and wiping the drool from my chin. I squinted through bleary eyes to see sunlight streaming through the shutters, setting the dust motes aflame. Tonight I'd sneak away with Arrhidaeus and board Hephaestion's ship. We'd hide below for at least three days—uncomfortable, but manageable—which meant I'd need to filch food from the kitchens today. Bread, hard cheese, and an *amphora* of wine . . .

"So, was Hephaestion as good at tangling as they say?" A girl slave with drab brown hair giggled and entered my room, flanked by two ebony-haired twins sent from Thebes after my brother had razed their city. The first carried a tray of apricots, goat cheese, and bread for my morning meal.

"Even better," one of the twins whispered back.

"We didn't sleep all night," the other twin said, pretending to hide a coy smile behind her hands. "It's no wonder Alexander keeps him close."

All three jumped nearly out of their skin as I stumbled to my feet.

"How long has the sun been up?" I demanded.

The closest girl, one of the dim-witted twins, ducked her head in obeisance. "It's the second hour past sunrise," she said.

"Where is Olympias?" I asked.

"I believe she's at the shrine of Dionysus."

Good. The last thing I needed was Olympias figuring out that I was up to something. "And Hephaestion? I need to speak with him."

To thank him for rescuing me from being trampled at the Mysteries, and to throw him off the scent of what I planned.

"Hephaestion's ship set sail before sunrise."

I whirled on her. "What?"

"He asked me to deliver this to you," one of the twins said, offering a rolled parchment bound with a leather thong.

I gestured for them to leave, then tore open Hephaestion's letter. I recognized the lazy slant of his handwriting, the inky whispers of the stylus where he couldn't be bothered to lift it fully from the paper from one letter to the next. The parchment quivered as I clenched its edges between my trembling hands.

Dearest Little Nike,

I expect that you're still cursing my name and inventing creative ways to ensure my death. (All I ask is that you make it quick, no lingering and painful ends where I humiliate myself by blubbering for Hades to claim me.)

Have no doubt, Little Victory, that you shall not be locked in Pella forever. My conscience is heavy with many things in this life— we both know I've a terrible fondness for drinking fine wine, indulging in mawkish poetry, and I am easily distracted by the curve of a beautiful woman's back or the breadth of a man's shoulders—but I shall sleep easy knowing you are far from the battlefield. I have no surviving siblings of my own blood, but you and Alexander are my sister and brother, and I could never forgive myself if anything happened to you. Instead of cursing me to Hades and back (which I know you will anyway), I suggest you seek out Cynnane to help you pass the time. Your half sister will likely bore you beyond tears with her claim of killing the Illyrian queen and will undoubtedly gloat that she once managed to disarm me. (She first got me drunk with a krater of wine, and thus, her claim is an idle boast.) Between sparring with a would-be Amazon and your communes with Dionysus, you'll find some small measure of entertainment, I expect.

I have no doubt that you will continue scheming, and in fact, I welcome word of your future exploits. Just know that I adore you too much to be the instrument of your death.

Your brother,
Hephaestion, son of Amyntor

I'm quite proud to say that I didn't scream then or dissolve into tears. Instead, I carried Hephaestion's letter and walked calmly to my balcony, rimmed by cypress trees that allowed me to glimpse slivers of tantalizing sea waves through their swaying branches. Zephyr's west wind tugged at the hem of my rumpled *peplos* and teased my tangled hair about my face.

Then I tore the paper into tiny pieces and sent Hephaestion's words flying on a gust of wind. A few scraps fell to the garden below, the same one where Olympias had begun my initiation only two nights ago, but others spun in the air, lifted up, and were carried toward the sea.

"You're right, Hephaestion," I whispered. "I will continue scheming. And I'll find a way to join Alexander, if it's the last thing I do."

CHAPTER 7

331 BCE
Gaugamela, Persia

ⅅRYPETIS

The ground outside our pavilion trembled as if it were being pummeled by Mithra's mace. I shielded my eyes in a vain attempt to make out my father's war elephants stomping their mighty feet across the plain choked with Greek and Persian soldiers, the beasts tossing their tusks and trumpeting louder than any herald's horn. The wooden siege towers balanced on their backs could hold three Persians armed with pikes, the perfect vantage point from which to strike down these invading Greeks. So great was Alexander's fear of the massive elephants that last night beneath a sweep of watchful stars he'd made a blood sacrifice to the gods, cutting the throat of a young bull and pouring its lifeblood into the ground. Alexander's distress lightened my heart as the sound of Persian hammer blows reverberated into the dark sky, the sweet sound of sharpened wooden stakes being beaten into the ground to reinforce my father's front lines.

The sound had almost been drowned out by Hephaestion's shouts. Freshly returned from the peace he'd brokered with Athens, the dark-haired beast was now the commander of Alexander's personal guard, who fought at his side. With the blessing of full sails, Hephaestion's oared trireme had reached the Euphrates well ahead of the plodding infantry and baggage train, giving him time to build a bridge across the entire river. I wished that Hephaestion's bridge might crack with a mighty roar and pour Greeks into the waters to drown in their heavy armor, sweeping away Alexander's army until the surface of the Euphrates was blighted with bloated bodies. Yet even Anahita, our fickle maiden goddess of the river, seemed smitten with Alexander's warrior-lover and allowed Hephaestion to stride from one bank to the other unmolested. I should have known better, for Anahita had forsaken my family since the day my brother drowned.

But there was still hope even without the goddess, for Alexander's contingent of Greeks was vastly outnumbered by the full might of the Persian army.

The site chosen for the battle was Gaugamela, a village situated at the base of a hill shaped like a camel's hump. The men on both sides stared at one another across the open plain, and the autumn sun glowered down at us from a sky marbled with clouds, yet Alexander remained abed.

My family and I stood outside our pavilion shaded by a silken awning, across from Alexander's campaign tent and flanked by guards as we awaited the Macedonian to show his face. So sure was my grandmother of Alexander's impending defeat that she'd ordered us dressed in our finest silks, embroidered with golden thread and studded with jewels. Inside our pavilion sat ready three cedar palanquins for our victorious procession out of Gaugamela. The great Dowager Queen Sisygambis had also commanded our serving-women to sew scented sachets of dried rose petals to hold to our noses after the battle, to keep the smell of the rotting Macedonian corpses at bay.

I knew from Barsine that Alexander's generals had urged him to make a surprise night attack to hide his inferior numbers, but he'd refused, claiming that he wouldn't steal his victories. Now the sun climbed higher and higher.

I shifted closer to Stateira. "Maybe he's plotting the best way to surrender in the face of his impending defeat," I whispered, but she ignored me.

"No amount of prayers to Zeus should take this long," Hephaestion finally said to the gathered generals, rubbing a hand over his freshly shaved jaw. "I'll see what's keeping him."

I smiled to myself, sure that the mighty Macedonian was trembling with fear in the dark of his tent while beseeching his many divine fathers for a painless death.

We waited in silence and I marveled at how straight my grandmother and sister could stand, gazing ahead with their hands clasped before them. It required all my willpower not to fidget, until I occupied myself with thinking of the scale model of Tyre I'd been working on in our tent, planning the wood pieces and plaster needed to construct Alexander's causeway and siege towers. With any luck, by the end of the day I might be showing it to my father.

It was another quarter hour before Alexander finally emerged, still buckling the shoulder guards on his cuirass, lines from his pillows plain on his cheeks as he rubbed his eyes. "You might have let me sleep until noon," Alexander grumbled to his generals, running a hand through his uncombed hair. "For the battle is already won in our favor."

My lip curled into a snarl like a feral dog's. Today would be a good day, for I would relish watching my father defeat this strutting peacock who could rival Narcissus with his conceit.

The Macedonians saluted Alexander as he passed with his lion helmet held in the crook of his arm, the gleam of its polished iron contrasting with the sunlight on his hair, while his neckpiece glittered with emeralds and rubies. The cloak that Hephaestion fastened around his neck was purple and embroidered in a dizzyingly intricate pattern of gold thread, as if stitched by a flock of haughty hummingbirds.

He offered us no words, only a terse nod as he nudged his new white stallion forward. Bucephalus came behind, led by a groom and dressed in a bronze equine frontlet depicting feline heads and frolicking nymphs. Alexander's favorite horse would wait until the battle's end to carry his conqueror to victory or ignominious defeat.

Alexander's men shouted their praises of him to the skies, begging him to lead them to triumph. And Alexander, the man who already claimed an Egyptian god as his rightful father, lifted his spear and shouted into the wind. "If Zeus truly sired me, then all the gods will strengthen us, and we will have our victory against the Persians!"

To add to the spectacle, one of Alexander's many seers was toted out, a crooked old man swathed in a white *himation* like a burial shroud, the hem of the fine cloth stained with red dust. I scoffed and resisted the urge to roll my eyes, for a trained monkey could have recited Alexander's convenient prophecies that all foretold his impending triumphs.

"There," the seer said, lifting an aged hand toward the cloud-strewn sky. All heads craned toward a black speck soaring above. "Zeus' mighty eagle gives his blessing to our cause, and this battle."

"An eagle, hawk, or more likely . . . a speckled pigeon," I muttered, earning Stateira's elbow in my ribs.

"You shouldn't mock the gods," she hissed.

"Zeus is god of the Greeks, but he is not ours," I reminded her. "Nor is he our father's god."

"Yet Zeus must be powerful to favor Alexander so."

I wrinkled my nose at that as the bent old prophet pointed to the sky again. "Zeus' messenger dives toward the enemy," he proclaimed. "Just as our spears and swords shall find their home in the hearts and ribs of the foul Persian invaders."

"We're not the invaders," I grumbled, not that anyone save

Stateira could hear me. "And the bird is soaring in circles, not swooping toward anyone."

But the generals marched to take their places before their troops, Alexander at their lead, riding into battle at the front wearing his foolhardy white-plumed helmet, which every Persian archer would surely aim at.

At least he was making it easy for my father to slay him.

As Alexander, Hephaestion, and all the other soldiers marched away in a choking cloud of dust, a woman clad in a sapphire *chiton* followed us inside our tent. Barsine was a frequent visitor to our pavilion and I found I enjoyed her honest company, despite her position as Alexander's bed warmer.

"I see you're prepared for a Persian victory," Barsine said, glancing at the palanquins laid out for our triumphal procession.

"Of course," my grandmother said. "Much as I admire Alexander, he cannot possibly defeat my son and his Immortals."

"Even though he's done so twice before?" Barsine picked up an alabaster jar shaped like a hippo and filled with perfumed resin, an Egyptian gift from Alexander to Stateira.

"My father has had time to prepare," I said, hearing the defensiveness in my voice as I sat before my model of Tyre, frowning as I righted the miniature fireship that had fallen over. I'd snipped tiny bells from the bottom of one of my hems and filled them with black pitch in imitation of the cauldrons of oil before they were lit. "He's entrenched and reinforced with elephants and scythed chariots."

"Which Alexander is ready for," Barsine said. "He was up half the night with his schematics."

"I suppose that excuses him for sleeping half the day away," I scoffed, turning away from the model.

But Barsine continued, unperturbed. "He plans to thrust the men onto the right, away from the Persian traps and elephants so he might encircle the Persian left. And there will be almost a thousand *sarissa* bearers guarding this very tent to keep his favorite Persian trophies safe and sound."

"All of which might be important factors," I said, "if the Greeks weren't outnumbered six to one."

My grandmother held up her hands for quiet. "There's no need to fill our ears with idle chatter while we wait. My son shall be victorious, but in the meantime we will pray to Ahura Mazda. Starting now."

We wore veils to cover our lips so as not to pollute the fire, and bent our knees before the ritual flames dedicated to the sacred triad of Ahura Mazda, Mithra, and Anahita, begging for their light and wisdom to shine down upon my father, to push back the Macedonian scourge and finally free us. Slaves brought meat from a freshly slaughtered sheep, although it was apparent the beast had been far from fresh itself, likely an old ewe past bearing age. We placed the meat atop dried myrtle leaves, allowing the smoke to envelop our offering to the gods while at the same time drawing the pure scent of fire deep into our lungs.

I'd performed the ritual at least a hundred times, but today it did little to still my mind.

"You of the thousand eyes and ten thousand ears," I murmured under my breath to Mithra. "To the friend of the just and honest man, and also the goddess of the waters, we sacrifice to you."

The air that stole through the floor cracks of the tent carried the cool of the month of *Bāgayādiš*, the season dedicated to the god Mithra, but my underarms grew damp. Bagoas and the other eunuchs fanned us with peacock-feather fans, which served only to rearrange the air with its stale scents of incense, smoke, and fear.

And then the ground rumbled beneath us and a harried servant burst into our tent. "The cavalry is here!"

I knew not which cavalry she meant, Macedonian or Persian, but fled from the tent to see with my own eyes. Too late, I reared back as a contingent of mounted soldiers surrounded us. A massive Persian barreled toward me on his armored warhorse, a flash of silver armor and yellow silk, just as my grandmother stepped from the tent.

"The Queen Mother," the man yelled in blessed Aramaic, snapping his fist to his chest and calming his horse. I recognized him then as Bessus, my father's cousin and *satrap* of Bactria. I was shocked that he'd found a horse able to carry his impressive girth, but his shield was dented and there was a wound at his temple weeping a scarlet trickle of blood. "Hello, cousins," he said, his eyes flicking over all of us and lingering on my sister. "I came to escort you out of this Macedonian pit."

For a single moment, there was a swirl of peace and hope. But only for a moment.

"Where is my son?" my grandmother asked.

"I rode into battle at the left of the King of Kings." Bessus' eyes scanned our camp and his horse pranced beneath him. "Just before he was engaged by Alexander."

"And you abandoned him?" My grandmother's eyes narrowed into a glare sharper than broken glass, regardless of the Persian soldiers and Indian mercenaries who streamed into our camp, their combined forces meant to halt Alexander's progress.

"The King of Kings never intended to allow you to remain in enemy hands after this battle," Bessus said. "I volunteered to lead the rescue while Alexander is engaged in the center."

And from the way he was surveying the carts and our persons, I could imagine he was already tabulating the reward he'd garner from seeing all of it safely returned to my father's camp.

He could have the entire treasury at Persepolis, so long as he got us out of here.

"And the *sarissas?*" I asked, cursing and choking on the growing cloud of dust. Barsine had said that the pike-wielding infantry would surround us, and I doubted that even a rout would cause Alexander to abandon his Persian prizes.

"Encircled by our right wing," Bessus said. "But Alexander's reinforcements will be on their way. We haven't much time."

So Alexander still lived. Dread unfurled from my belly, spreading its cold to the tips of my toes and fingers.

"Secure the baggage carts," Bessus yelled, his chins quivering beneath his helmet's too-tight chin strap. Hundreds of mounted Persians flooded around us, swooping about like dust-coated angels as they readied the carts filled with Alexander's precious spoils of war. "Ready the queen mother and the royal family for transport!"

Our attendants scurried to follow the barked commands, to secure the carts and harness the horses. I expected my grandmother to issue her own orders, but she only stood as if frozen, silent and pale.

"We'll ride together," I yelled to Bessus. "We'd walk on our hands from here if necessary!"

Bessus grinned, revealing teeth that gleamed a painful white against the grime of his face and helm. "I hope it won't come to that, daughter of Darius."

I scrambled into a scythed chariot commanded by a lithe Indian driver with a pointed beard, pulling my trembling sister and grandmother into the basket with me, choking on the hope of the tantalizing taste of freedom denied us these past two years. Barsine was nowhere to be seen, lost in the shining sea of silver helmets and wild-eyed horses trying to break loose.

And then came the cry that tore the air from my lungs.

"Darius has fled! The Greeks are coming!"

Bessus glanced at us, and I knew he was tabulating again: the price of his own skin over the reward he'd reap if he managed to free us.

The odds were against us. He knew it, and I knew it.

"Retreat!" he commanded, but his men weren't fast enough and a contingent of Greeks fell upon us like a swarm of armored locusts, their terrible battle cries ripping apart the very heavens. The last I saw of Bessus was the saffron flash of his robe as he galloped away.

And blood. Everywhere blood.

Following first my father and then Alexander from battle to battle meant that we'd seen blood and death before, but this was fresh blood from our attendants and soldiers alike, pouring in torrents from stab wounds wrought by *sarissas* and spears, spraying into the dust-choked air as swords slashed and clanged in hand-to-hand combat. There was a thud to my left and I turned in time to see our driver hit the floor of the chariot basket, impaled through his chest and out his back.

Stateira's scream clawed the air and I grabbed the dangling reins, wrapping them tight around my hand while searching for an escape. A corridor opened between the men and horses to our left, as if Ahura Mazda parted them with his own two hands.

"Hold on!" I screamed to Stateira and our grandmother. I whipped the horses as the chariot lurched over bodies of the dead and dying. Wind whistled in my ears, blocking out the sounds of battle, and we might have made it had it not been for the black-haired Macedonian rushing toward us on horseback, one arm bloodied from a gaping wound while the other raised his sword, ready to fell us where we stood.

Our wretched horses reared, jerking us forward so fast that I lost my grip. The platform lurched beneath my feet and the world slowed as I careened over the basket into the maelstrom. But I'd wrapped the reins too tightly around my hand, anchored to the chariot tighter than the thickest chains. A catastrophe of white light cracked from my shoulder, a streaking pain with more red-hot heat than a thousand forges, and my body snapped back with a shriek of agony. I dangled loose, my feet precariously near the churning wheels, whirling scythes, and pounding horse hooves.

The pain ebbed and my vision faded, but the din of battle followed me into the dark.

The Greek battle cry, the clang of kissing swords, and the screams of the dying. The darkness folded around me until I could no longer fight its smothering embrace.

Everything went silent.

CHAPTER 8

Gaugamela, Persia

HEPHAESTION

I loathed the bloody Persian Immortals more than the yellow dust that their thousands of feet churned up, clouding my eyes and choking me like an invisible hand around my throat. I cursed the bastards to Hades and back, yet still they came at us, a never-ending hive of wasps that bit and stung and buzzed until I roared in fury and slashed at them from atop my horse while around me Alexander's Companions took sword and spear wounds to their arms and legs. So close I could spit in his eye, some lucky Persian slashed at a Companion's neck and was rewarded with a spurt of Macedonian blood.

I cleaved off his sword arm, then dispatched him to his gods.

Before us, thousands of Persian javelin throwers clashed with our lines, some of them pulled from their chariots and hacked to pieces by Macedonian swords.

Beyond the wasps would be Darius, a prize greater even than Homer's Priam. But we couldn't get to the Persian coward as one wave of fresh Immortals after another replaced their fallen comrades.

"Die, you filthy bastards," I cried, feeling no small satisfaction as my sword found its home through a Persian soldier's ribs. They might be called Immortals, but they died the same as any other men.

"Pests, they are," Alexander yelled to me, his voice muffled by the metal of my helm and the crush of battle. I could just make out his demonic grin as he plunged his sword into another Persian from atop his warhorse. My sword arm grew weary as more Immortals met a similar fate, but I sensed the opening at precisely the same moment Alexander did.

Being in battle was akin to being lost in a sandstorm of writhing men, with opportunities opening and closing faster than the blink of an eye. It was Alexander's gift that he saw those openings before they even happened and was willing to pounce on them regardless of whether they swirled close, whether the gods damned his men's lives or his own.

This was a hole where the left wing met the center, like a gate swinging open to admit us to Darius himself. Even the dust parted for a breath to reveal the middle of the precious Persian defense, beckoning to us with more power than all the Sirens combined.

Alexander screamed the order. "Forward!"

And we charged, all of the Companions and the shield bearers, running double-time with swords and spears and *sarissas* toward victory and everlasting glory. Some were mired down by the enemy, but still we surged forward, swords flashing, and screaming our battle yell with one voice.

And there, beyond the Persian elephants—worthless beasts that had yet to join the fray—was Darius, the King of Kings, resplendent in his new golden chariot and his billowing red cloak. Alexander didn't hesitate; he slashed with his sword as if cutting away vines in a forest instead of mere men, even as I fought off a snarling Immortal with a beard tangled with dust and spittle, his teeth bared like a rabid wolf's.

And like a wolf, he lunged at my throat, but he attacked my left with his right, making it easy to parry his long knife as I slammed my shield into his other shoulder, then whirled around to finish him off with a blade in the back. The death wound was as neat as a sacrifice done by a priest's hand.

I glanced up as the cursed Immortals launched a volley of spears at us in retaliation and ducked my head beneath my shield on instinct, feeling one of the weapons clatter off the edge. Then, like an idiot without the good sense he was born with, I straightened too soon and bellowed as one of the Immortals' short throwing spears found a home in my right forearm. Dumbstruck, I stared at the wooden shaft embedded in my flesh.

I'd been wounded before, my legs and arms riddled with reminders of when I should have feinted instead of blocked, or withdrawn instead of lunging forward. But it's a rare day when a man has a spear buried in his bloody arm.

And blood there was, although no pain. At least not yet.

The weapon had missed the bone and only pinioned the flesh of my arm—thank Zeus I had thick arms and this one wouldn't be joining the other dismembered limbs strewn about the battlefield.

And there was no time to pull out the spear, not unless I wanted several more spears in my hide. Instead, I kicked my heels into my horse's ribs, muttering a prayer to Ares to guide Alexander through the haze of dust, far too easy a target in his shining helmet with its white feathers and dyed red horse's tail. And beyond that, within range and with only a handful of Immortals in between us, was Darius, the King of Kings.

Alexander saw the opportunity, lifted his spear, and launched it toward the target of Darius' red cloak. It was a flawless throw, but we weren't the only ones to realize that. In the basket next to the Persian king, the driver saw his chance for glory and shoved Darius to the side. Instead of marking its target, Alexander's spear skewered the charioteer, the weapon thrown with such force that it pierced the boiled leather breastplate of his armor. The unfortunate man stumbled, then pitched backward from the golden chariot, leaving Darius alone and unprotected.

But Darius had experience in this sort of maneuver, and I knew before he grabbed the reins what he would do.

"Stop him!" Alexander thundered, but it was too late. The cowardly King of Kings flogged his horse, his Immortals clearing a path to safety for their beloved leader.

The Royal Road lay to the southeast of Gaugamela, a haven stretching all the way to Babylon. A place for Darius to lick his wounds, raise another army, and plot to fight another day.

I knew Darius for what he was then: a dung beetle like those revered in Egypt, a shiny, indestructible insect that scurried from the earth after all manner of catastrophe.

Alexander's curse might have shaken the temples on Olympus, and I've no doubt he would have run even precious old Ox-Head into an early grave in pursuit had it not been for the cry raised to our left.

"Bessus has broken through Parmenion's line!" shouted a Companion, whose face was coated with dust and streaked with dark rivulets of sweat and grime. "Parmenion begs assistance to secure the baggage and avoid being flanked."

An attack on the baggage meant one thing: an attempt to steal back Darius' women. That was an insult Alexander would never let stand.

I felt his struggle as he turned and watched the dust swallow the golden gleam of Darius' chariot as the Immortals retreated to join their worthless king. We would pursue, but not today.

"Hephaestion!" Alexander roared, and I turned about and galloped toward the left, my warhorse vaulting blurred corpses mostly outfitted in Persian gold, with few crowned by the silver helms of Macedon.

The baggage line was chaos when I arrived, my sword ready to relieve Bessus, or perhaps incompetent Parmenion, of his head. Slain attendants watered the earth with their blood, and near Sisygambis' tent careened a chariot with three silk-clad women in its basket. The shortest of the women glanced to where an opening in the line temporarily yawned, her bent nose as sharp as a blade and her muscles corded all the way to her shoulders as she whipped the frantic horse.

I kicked my warhorse again, determined to reach the brilliant little idiot before she succeeded in stealing away to her father. It was in horror that I watched their horses rear and the chariot lurch over the bodies of the slain. Drypetis sailed from the chariot, then snapped back and was thrown against the exterior of the basket like a dying fish on a line, her shimmering silk robes shining like the rainbow-hued scales of a summer trout. She'd be dragged beneath the chariot, pulverized by the scythed wheels or her own horse's hooves.

On a battlefield full of heroes' corpses, one more death shouldn't have mattered. Especially not that of a reckless Persian princess with a mouth full of vinegar.

Still, I galloped forward, then grasped the back of Drypetis' silken robe even as her grandmother and sister clawed to pull the unconscious girl up. I threw her into the chariot basket with my bad arm and let out a mighty roar of blinding pain.

The bloodlust was broken with this act of mercy and, with it, my inability to feel the wound that now gushed torrents of blood.

"You two, into the tent!" I yelled. "Now!"

I waited only long enough to see Sisygambis acquiesce with a rigid nod, her lips set in a tight line. She was a good sort of woman, the same as my own mother, and knew when to cut her losses.

It was more than I could say for *some* women.

I drew a steadying breath—as steady as one could after the debacle this was turning out to be—and grasped the spear shaft embedded in my arm, yanking the weapon from my flesh and cursing the Persian who hadn't cared to fully straighten the shank of his spear as I felt the wood make an agonizing scrape against bone. Blood flowed from the gaping hole; it would leave a gem of a scar if it didn't supperate and kill me first.

I wished I could find the Persian who had launched the spear and skewer him through his neck with it, but barring that, at least I'd sent several of his brethren to greet Charon at the river Styx this day.

I tucked the bloody spear into my belt and marched toward the women's almost-empty chariot, the pain in my arm throbbing like a second heartbeat.

Drypetis regained consciousness as I disentangled her wrists from the reins, one arm hanging useless at her side and her face the shade of sour milk. She blinked hard, her pupils dilated as she struggled to focus on me.

"You're going to live to see another day," I assured her in a curt voice, recognizing her confusion as she came to. "Now that I've saved you from being trampled by horses and minced by your scythes."

I should have enjoyed the rare moment of silence, for it didn't last long.

She jerked away to hurl a stream of abuse at me. "You didn't save me! You're the one who made my horses rear in the first place, you spotty piece of dung! I wish your mother had drowned you at birth," Drypetis continued, cradling her arm and a hand that was quickly turning blue, "and fed your waterlogged corpse to the crows!"

Her curses were tame by any soldier's standards, albeit creative, but I had an arm that screamed as if someone had tried to saw, stab, and then gnaw it off, and wasn't in the mood to be entertained by a knob-nosed girl transformed into a fanged and hissing gorgon. I grabbed the neck of her robe with my good hand and hauled her from her chariot, ignoring her cry of pain as I pulled her into the decadent Persian tent. A miasma of incense choked me and several lamps still flickered, remnants of their prayers to the Persian god of fire. It was nothing short of a miracle that the whole damned tent hadn't burned to the ground.

An *amphora* of wine stood abandoned on a table and I helped myself to it, knocking away its wax seal with my knife and guzzling its liquid treasure like a dying man.

I'd seen death again today, and bested it on the battlefield. No small accomplishment, and simply being alive sweetened the wine as it hit my tongue.

"Cease your shrieking," I growled as Drypetis opened her mouth to continue her tirade, her gold-flecked eyes flashing.

"We might have escaped had it not been for you—" Drypetis started in again despite the fact that she swayed on her feet, but thankfully, Sisygambis stopped her this time.

"Hold your tongue, Drypetis," she said, once again the queen of her domain. "I forbid you from speaking to Hephaestion." She glanced at me. "Spare some wine for that arm of yours. The dust in it will make it fester and then you'll smell worse than a rancid chicken."

"Then, if we're lucky, he'll get blood poisoning and die," Drypetis said between gritted teeth. She held up her good hand. I could tell from here that the other was broken. "I hope he's in agony—"

"I'm fine," I growled, but it was a lie. Only the gods knew how much of my blood stained the plains of Gaugamela, but it was enough to make the edges of my vision blur.

"My physician lies skewered by one of your men outside," Sisygambis said, her lips disappearing again. "And you'll look a fool if you pass out from loss of blood before your men. Let them finish the rout and content yourself with the healing skills of a dowager queen."

"You'd tend the swine who captured us for a second time before helping your own granddaughter?" Drypetis muttered under her breath. "I hope you plan to poison him."

"I'll order your sister to gag you if I must," Sisygambis said. She waited a moment, but Drypetis didn't answer. "Hephaestion might well bleed to death here in our tent, which I doubt Alexander would forgive. You, however, will live to a ripe old age, despite your shoulder and hand."

She crouched next to me to inspect my arm, even that simple movement filled with elegance. "My son has fled again. Thus, we shall remain the guests of Alexander and his Macedonians for the foreseeable future."

"You're a pragmatic old bird," I said, not enjoying the way her voice came as if from far away.

She smiled and smoothed her silver hair with hands laden with golden rings.

"Bring a dinner knife," she ordered Stateira. "Boiled wine, a clean rag, and a pot of honey too."

Stateira was a welcome relief after the shrieking harpy that was her sister. Yet she took one look at the chunk of flesh missing from my arm, and her face drained of color. Thankfully, her grandmother was made of stiffer stuff. Unfortunately, that meant she was far from a gentle physician.

"Brace yourself," she ordered, twisting the iron blade over the remnants of her sacred fire while heating an *amphora* of wine with the other.

I did as she commanded, but roared like a stuck boar as the blade hissed against my flesh, cauterizing the wound before the white-haired queen upended the heated wine over my arm.

"Head between your legs," she said, and I might have protested had it not been for her insistent hand guiding my head where she instructed. "We don't want you passing out and marring that pretty face of yours."

"You should see to your granddaughter before she loses consciousness again," I said, light-headed from pain and not wishing for any witnesses as the dowager queen finished slathering my arm with honey. I glanced up briefly to see Darius' younger daughter sway in her seat, her elbow lifted so her forearm rested on her head, the same position as when she fell from the chariot.

"I've no experience setting shoulders or splinting hands," Sisygambis said, winding a length of white cotton around my forearm. "She'll have to wait until a field physician is available. A lesson in patience and suffering might do her good, considering the danger she put us in."

I thought of the men I'd seen holding their guts in with their hands, the countless javelin punctures and gruesome sword wounds. Across from me, Drypetis shifted on her couch, going almost green with the movement as Sisygambis tied the ends of my bandage in a neat knot. Darius' little gorgon had gotten what she deserved for trying to escape, but I had to admit that I was impressed with her lack of tears over her injuries. The dowager queen began to fashion a sling with a second swath of cotton, but I shook my head. "I'll manage without it," I said. I'd used one once for a sword wound on my other arm, but the thing was a damnable nuisance.

"You," I said to Drypetis, feeling the world start to right itself now that Sisygambis was done poking at me. "Lie down."

"Tell Alexander's plaything I'd sooner die than follow a single order of his," she growled, her knuckles white with pain as she clutched the pillow beneath her.

"Lie down so I can tell your grandmother how to set your shoulder," I said. "Or I'll knock you down myself."

"You're familiar with her injuries?" Sisygambis asked with a frown.

"The physician will have to splint her hand, but I fell out of a tree as a boy and landed on my shoulder. I thought I'd die from the pain, and my arm was stuck over my head too, at least until my mother's howling brought the physician running."

"It's unfortunate you didn't land on your neck," Drypetis muttered. I pretended not to hear, knowing what was to come.

I jutted my chin toward the silken couch where she sat. "On your back," I said.

"That might work with all the other women you've known—"

"Drypetis!" This time it was her sister who protested, while the dowager queen looked ready to strangle her youngest granddaughter. Yet Drypetis did as I commanded, the first and likely last time she'd obeyed any order in her life.

"Keep your arm up," I said. "Fingers pointed toward the ceiling."

"Tell the idiot it's not as if I can move it anyway," she said.

I felt no small satisfaction at her hiss of pain, yet Darius' troublesome daughter managed to get herself into position without any further curses, which was more than most soldiers might have managed. Then again, most soldiers didn't have their iron-haired grandmother standing over them with a glower that might have made Zeus soil himself.

"Push down on her upper arm and pull up on her elbow at the same time, then tuck her elbow into her ribs and pull her wrist away from her body," I said to Sisygambis. "Fast, sharp movements."

"This is going to hurt, isn't it?" Drypetis asked as she stared up at the striped silk ceiling, blinking hard. I almost wished she'd had some wine to soften what was to come, but a mouth like hers would benefit more from a dousing of lye.

"Unless I'm lucky," I said. "Then your grandmother will miss the socket and cause you excruciating pain."

Sisygambis took the position. "Your sister is going to count to three," she said.

"One," Stateira said, her eyes screwed shut. "Two . . ."

And the dowager queen shoved Drypetis' arm just as I'd instructed, eliciting a screech of pain from her granddaughter.

"Three," Sisygambis said.

Drypetis pushed the knuckles of her good fist into her mouth and two lone tears streamed down her cheeks. Then she rubbed her arm, moving it slowly. "It's better," she said, a slow smile spreading across her face as she wiped her cheeks, her broken hand still hanging at her side. "I amend what I said before," she said to her grandmother. "Hephaestion is only mostly an idiot."

Sisygambis turned her back on her granddaughter, her hands clasped so tight I was sure she imagined wringing Drypetis' lovely little neck. "You have my gratitude," she said. "How may we thank you?"

"So long as Drypetis refuses to speak to me, that shall be thanks enough." I gave her a succinct bow. "Try not to dislocate anything else, save your tongue."

With that, I turned and left, setting several soldiers to guard the pavilion and breathing a sigh of relief to leave behind the women's tent for the welcome carnage of the battlefield.

And carnage wasn't in short supply; the plains of Gaugamela were pockmarked with corpses already beginning to stink despite the cool fall air, abandoned and broken spears, and overturned chariots with some of their wheels still spinning in the breeze. Bards would later claim that the battlefield at Gaugamela was littered with arms, some with their shields still attached, and heads with their eyes still open.

The bards didn't lie.

But the horses . . .

I could gaze upon body after body and scarcely bat an eye; after all, these men had chosen to march after their king in search of glory and riches. But the horses that had ridden so bravely into battle now lay in twisted heaps on the earth and made the back of my throat grow suddenly tight. There were thousands of them, the gifts of Poseidon, the vision of their unseeing eyes clouded with a thick film of yellow dust.

And in the center of the battlefield, his hair gleaming like the sun fallen to earth, stood Alexander. The king of Macedon—*my* king of Macedon—was triumphant this day, for the vast majority of the corpses spread before him wore either the yellow tunics and white turbans of the Indian mercenaries or the blue of the Immortals, their helmets wrought with lion-headed serpents and sacred trees to ward off evil. Yet Alexander's face was darker than a storm cloud.

"Congratulations on your victory," I said as I approached, running my good hand through my sweat-streaked hair. I smelled almost as rank as the corpses that I picked my way over, and likely felt worse with my arm and all the blood I'd lost. Still, it wasn't anything a good vintage of Lesbos red and a tussle on a military cot wouldn't remedy.

"A sham of a victory," Alexander muttered. "Darius eludes me yet again."

"That's not the face to show your men." I gestured toward those very same soldiers who already swarmed over the corpses, searching for survivors and spoils. The movement sent fresh shards of pain streaking through my veins and I winced.

"You're wounded," he said, grasping my wrist so he could inspect Sisygambis' pristine bandages.

I pulled the spear shaft from my belt and handed it to him. "A souvenir. You should have seen it when it was still in me."

Alexander stared a moment at the weapon, then touched it reverently to his lips before pressing those same lips to my bandaged arm. "I'd hunt each and every Persian to the ends of the earth if this had injured worse than just your arm."

He kissed me then and I kissed him back, ravenous for him after the heat of battle, neither of us caring that the men would see. And I knew we'd share each other's bed tonight, for with all the distractions of Athens and the Persian campaign, it had been too long since Alexander and I had enjoyed each other.

After a battle, you bed a woman to forget what has happened. You bed a man because he knows exactly what you're trying to forget.

From the left came a mighty cheer, likely the discovery of one of Darius' abandoned wagons. I wondered how the King of Kings felt about financing the army that sought his defeat, for the spoils here would go a long way toward keeping the troops and the kingdoms at home happy. I'd no doubt Alexander would find a use for all the

Persian gold. "The enemy fled like frightened gazelles." I nodded
toward the mountain in the distance, the one shaped like a camel's
hump. "Or camels, if your hired poets prefer. The courageous Battle
of the Camel's Hump."

"That's a ridiculous name," Alexander said, but a glint of humor
kindled in his eyes in two shades of blue. Not for the first time, I
was grateful for the rare gift of being able to turn Alexander's moods.

"Something more poetic," I suggested. "And victorious."

Victory. *Nike.*

I thought of Thessalonike then, how she would have clapped and
cheered to witness this battle. Still, I was glad I'd left her in Pella,
for there was no way I could have kept watch over Alexander's mis-
chievous sister *and* Darius' women.

"Nikatorion," I suggested.

"The Mountain of Victory." Alexander stroked his chin, leaving
streaks in dust there. A horn sounded and we both turned to see
soldiers struggling to force one of Darius' elephants to move. There
were fifteen of the gigantic beasts, all standing as if awaiting a belated
order to charge, save one. The angry animal snorted and snapped its
trunk to and fro, throwing its long tusks from side to side as if intent
on goring a man.

"Run it through," one of the nearby commanders yelled. "Before
it kills us."

Alexander's men let their spears fly and one of the weapons
grazed the wild fiend's flank, drawing blood on the tough gray skin.
The beast trumpeted and reared back, snapping one of its halter
ropes. Fortunately, the rest of its anchors held fast and more men
stood ready, but a scream to rival the Furies stopped the fight.

"The gorgon flies again," I said, groaning. My fingers itched to lob
a spear at her feet, just close enough to put the fear of death in her.

Yet I doubted whether Drypetis, daughter of Darius, feared anything.

"Leave them alone," she commanded. Her arm was in a linen sling, likely the same one Sisygambis had tried to use on me, but otherwise she looked like she'd been dragged across the entire field of Gaugamela. Come to think of it, she might have been had I not interceded.

Not my finest decision, that.

"Impressive," Alexander murmured, watching the scene unfold.

"Far from it," I said. "Our little Medusa will screech at anyone who will listen."

Alexander glanced at me. "Not her," he said. "The elephants. I'd almost forgotten them in the wake of Darius' departure."

This, coming from the man who had sacrificed a bull to the gods last night when he'd learned of the ugly Persian beasts. Yet the elephants hadn't been loosed during the battle and several still stood with abandoned siege towers on their backs.

"Leave the beast alone," Alexander commanded, his voice carrying to the men. Drypetis glanced our way, her expression turning black as her gaze fell first on Alexander and then on me. "I have plenty of gold," Alexander continued, "but no animals such as these. They are a fine gift from Darius and shall join the ranks of Macedon for further use in our campaign against the King of Kings. I shall force the cowardly king to his knees to grind the bones of his ancestors in humiliation the next time we meet in battle."

I almost laughed as Drypetis' scowl deepened. She may have spared the elephant a grisly murder, but now that very beast might help bring about her father's defeat.

"You should confine Darius' daughters to their tent or, better yet, an iron cage," I said to Alexander, ignoring Drypetis as she shoved her way through the men to the nearest elephant, trailing meek Stateira behind her. "They became the target of a rescue attempt by Bessus today."

"I'm aware," Alexander said, his eyes continuing to scan the battlefield before finally settling on the east, the direction of the Royal Road and Darius. "I've sent Darius' little eunuch Bagoas ahead with a message demanding the king's surrender."

"Do you think he'll yield?"

"No. We depart in the morning for Babylon. After I receive the *satrap's* obeisance there, I shall deposit Darius' mother and daughters in Susa on our way to track the King of Kings."

"Susa? Why Susa?"

"Darius has a fortified palace there, but he'll retreat further into his kingdom, gathering reinforcements on his march to Babylon. The women will be secure in Susa."

"To hold as ransom."

Alexander shrugged. "They won't be informed of their new living arrangements until Babylon falls to us, to keep their spies from sending auxiliaries ahead to Susa. Darius' women are more precious even than these elephants. After all, one day I'll have to marry them."

I recoiled. "Perhaps Stateira, but surely not Drypetis too?"

Alexander's lip quirked with distaste. "Kingship is a heavy burden. I can trust no man to wed Darius' daughters, to lay claim to his royal bloodline." He looked at me askance. "Except perhaps you."

I looked at him in abject horror. "If you ever loved me, please, no."

He laughed. "You know I love you well." He lowered his voice, leaning in so close that I could smell the sweat of battle on him, but also the priceless cloves he liked to chew. "Come to my tent tonight and we shall celebrate as we did in the old days, just you and me, like Patroclus and Achilles."

Despite my being wounded and bone-weary, my blood raced and I grew hard for him as I always had. Aristotle had once described our friendship as one soul abiding in two bodies, and he was right, for Alexander's life was as vital to me as my own.

Some claimed that war was nothing more than horror and destruction, but they were fools. War *was* death, but it was also life, the constant reminder that, for now at least, we lived another day to drink and feast, to shit and screw.

Alexander's generals approached, ready to ply him with questions regarding the captives and spoils. "Will you come?" he asked, linking his fingers through mine.

"Gladly."

For I intended to enjoy all that this short life had to offer.

CHAPTER 9

Bactria, Persia

ROXANA

I lay on Parizad's moth-eaten rug with my eyes closed in a shaft of weak winter sunshine while my twin strummed his long-necked *tanbur*, singing along with a simple melody that reminded me of the call of a loon. One of the gut strings was dry, but my brother's masterful voice and fingers masked all but the worst of its sharpness. A deep lethargy settled into my limbs and made my eyelids heavy; life had been idyllic these past months while my father campaigned with Bessus. My brother and I lived like the lord and lady of a great estate: We ordered the cook and the handful of remaining slaves about by morning, slept away the afternoons, and spun midnight stories of golden futures that we pretended might one day belong to us.

Such a paradise couldn't last forever, but I hadn't expected it to shatter that morning.

Horses' hooves clattered into the courtyard below and Parizad's music stopped midnote. I scrambled to my feet, choking on my heart to see my father dismount, thinner from his time in the west, so he seemed more bent-backed than ever. I ducked away and Parizad took my place at the window.

"Parizad!" our father bellowed. "Roxana!"

My face surely blanched white and I gulped for air, taking a moment to appreciate my body, which was free from fresh, healing, or scabbed lash wounds.

"You should hide," Parizad whispered, but I shook him off with a strangled laugh. I'd spent these months of my father's absence contemplating what I would do upon his return, knowing that his humiliation would fester during his time away. I'd already imagined every scenario where I might run away or hide, but there was nowhere in Darius' kingdom where my father wouldn't find me.

And I had nowhere else to go.

"I'm coming!" I called down to my father. I'd face him with my head held high, for, after all, pride was the only thing I had left.

"Good," my father called up. His horsewhip dangled from his hand, twitching eagerly. "I still owe you for your flight of fancy with Bessus."

And thus, before my father could even change out of his dust-stained travel clothes, I confronted him alone in the courtyard, my skin tingling with the pain I knew was soon to come and as much hatred as I could muster in my expression.

"Kneel," he commanded.

And I did, enduring yet another whipping in a long line stretching back to my earliest memories. We both played our roles admirably: I refused to scream during the first strokes and he spared my face, snapping the whip until the cries were wrenched from my throat. I ticked off each lash on my fingers, but there were far more than I could count. And for the first time, I felt the lashes cut deep enough to draw blood, tearing into my flesh and leaving no doubt that the scars would forever remind me of my folly with Bessus.

Panting and with sweat dripping down his temples, my father finally left me tied to a hitching post in the courtyard, but Parizad undid the leather thongs at my wrists and carried me bleeding and shivering to my mattress, where he applied wet compresses of lavender and chamomile to ease my pain and prevent the worst of the scarring.

Fresh roots of pain dug deep into my back, wrapping tight around my bones. I turned my face to the cool air wafting in through the window, squeezing my eyes against the tears that threatened. My brother sang to me in his sweet voice as he always did after my father had beaten me, the song of a benevolent winged *yazata* that hinted of soft summer sunshine and air that smelled of newly blossomed roses.

"I'm a terrible son," he whispered after he'd finished his song, as if admitting to murder or treason. "Part of me hoped that Alexander's spears would dispatch Father to *Duzakh*."

"Only part of you?" I croaked. I'd prayed for the same every night, not that Ahura Mazda paid any attention to my meager pleadings.

"I'm so sorry, Roxana," my brother said. He pressed a damp cloth to my forehead. "I should have stopped him—"

"You couldn't," I said, grasping his hand. "And you must promise me that you never will. Do you understand me?"

For I would never survive this world without my brother at my side.

He hesitated, then nodded. "I promise."

I closed my eyes and must have dozed, but a fresh commotion in our courtyard roused me. Parizad hung halfway out the window as he tried to see what was happening.

"It's Bessus," he said. "The *satrap* is here. He must be meeting with Father."

My heart climbed into my throat. Freshly whipped, I could barely move. But I'd told myself what I had to do if I ever saw Bessus—or any man who might want me—again.

"Help me dress," I commanded my brother, turning to my side and hissing with pain as the wounds broke open anew, a warm wetness seeping across my back.

"Lie down. What do you think you're doing?"

"Saving us," I said, not bothering to cover my nakedness from my brother. I still wore my *shalvar*, but only bandages on my back. "Where are my clothes?"

"Here," he said, handing me my secondhand robe, a deep umber restitched several times to hide the worst of its wear. Hardly the gown I'd imagined putting on to see the *satrap* again, but I hadn't envisioned the bloody lashes on my back either.

"Help me?" I asked. I didn't want to say it aloud, but there was no way I could lift my arms or reach behind me, not for at least another day or two.

"Of course," Parizad said, relenting.

He held my robe and averted his eyes as I slipped my arms into its wide sleeves and let him fasten my jasper-studded girdle—the one missing several stones near the clasp—on its last loop so it draped around my hips instead of cinching my waist.

"Wait," he said, retrieving a bottle from a cedar box with a broken hinge. Spicy notes of spikenard filled the air as he removed the stopper and dabbed a few drops of oil beneath my ears and at my wrists. "So you'll smell like a queen."

I sniffed and wrinkled my nose. "Or a whore."

He didn't respond, but let me lean on him as we walked to my father's receiving room. The door's rusted lock had long ago ceased to latch, and we crouched before the thin door, our cheeks pressed together so we could squint through the crack. Riding and campaigning had whittled Bessus from a mountain of flesh into a mere hill, but he was still resplendent in a gold embroidered robe with a crimson *sarband* on his head. He sat across the table from my father in all his gold bracelets and jewels, ignoring a spread of day-old brown bread, freshly shelled peas, and a watery fish soup that the cook could barely coax the villa's feral cats to drink. But I worried about more than the threat of an empty stomach tonight while Bessus' eyes roved over the slave girl ladling steaming soup into his bowl.

"There is news that Alexander marches on Babylon," my father said, his hands twitching nervously as he tore off bites of bread. Crumbs fell from his mouth and tangled in his black beard. I wished a crow would fly through the open window and peck them free, and my father's eyes along with them.

"There's a good chance that the city will throw open its gates and allow the Greek hordes to pour into its streets," Bessus growled, removing his dagger from its scabbard and stabbing the tip of its blade into our table. "I desire your pledge, Oxyartes, and the use of your weapon foundries."

The same foundries that had sat cold and empty since Bessus had closed them down after my antics in his throne room.

"My foundries?" My father ceased stuffing his mouth and sat back in his chair, still chewing. "I shall always do as you command, *satrap*," my father murmured, bowing his head like a supplicant, but Bessus cut him off.

"I have no doubt that you will do as I command, provided there's a reward waiting for you. Unless there are *sarissa*-wielding chariots bearing down on you, and then you'll scuttle under a rock like a spider with a hawk flying overhead. The illustrious Seven Families already looked down their long noses at you before you hid with the lamed horses during the battle at Gaugamela."

"My foot—," my father started to protest, but Bessus gestured for his silence.

"You've given them more fodder for their scorn, but there may yet be a reward for you after I've assumed my place as the King of Kings."

I gaped, my fingers fluttering to my lips, but not at the revelation of my father's unsurprising cowardice. I might be only a fourteen-year-old girl, but even I recognized Bessus' words as treason. He was the *Mathišta*, the supreme *satrap* and chosen successor, as the king lacked a male heir.

My sound of surprise may have echoed in the receiving room, for my father's eyes flicked in my direction and I fell back into the shadows. "I believe the position of King of Kings is currently occupied by Darius," he said. "May Ahura Mazda bless his reign."

"May Ahura Mazda spit on his reign," Bessus said, leaning over the table. "Darius is a cowering weakling who has turned tail and run from the Macedonian whelp, not once, but twice. He does not deserve the throne he sits upon and the arms from your foundries will ensure that someone more suited to ruling assumes his place."

"You seek to relieve your illustrious cousin of so tiresome a burden?" My father's trembling thumb traced the gouge mark Bessus' dagger had left on the table. "And if you fail?"

Bessus shrugged. "You know the sentence for traitors."

My father swallowed hard and his eyes skittered about the room as if searching for an escape. He would scurry off to weigh his options, to find a way to prosper regardless of the outcome.

But Bessus was no fool.

"You will do as I say—remain here in Bactria to oversee the production of more equipment after we march," he said, dunking a piece of bread in the soup. He took a bite and grimaced, pushing the plate away as if the food was rancid. Perhaps it was.

My father bowed his head like a recalcitrant child. "As you wish, *satrap*. Of course, it would make my heart light if there was an alliance between our families. My daughter, Roxana—"

I almost gasped aloud, so startled was I to hear my name. Parizad's eyes widened too, his mouth a perfect O of surprise; then he pressed his cheek even closer to mine. Together we peered back inside as Bessus raised his hand. "Your daughter's name remains a bad taste in my mouth." He wiped his lips with a napkin. "Much like this soup," he muttered. "Prove yourself to me and I'll consider Roxana once again."

"Perhaps as your wife this time? After all, the King of Kings can take as many wives as he wishes. And if she gave you a son . . ."

I loathed my father, but sometimes I had to admire his audacity. Still, I knew he cared only that he might be the grandfather to the future King of Kings in that far-fetched scenario. My position was inconsequential, at least to him. I sat back on my heels, the lure of being the *satrap*'s—or perhaps one day the King of Kings'—wife dazzling me once again.

I'd refused the *satrap* once in order to best my father and had paid for it today in the courtyard. I wouldn't make that mistake again.

"Perhaps when I return," Bessus said, and I could hear the glare in his tone.

"As you wish," my father answered, bowing over his hands and kissing his fingertips in a *proskynesis*, giving the *satrap* the honor due only to the king, the temple's sacred fire, and the gods.

Parizad scrambled to his feet next to me. "Father's coming," he hissed.

I almost fell over in my haste to stand, the lashes on my back stabbing me anew, and together we ducked into an open storeroom packed with barrels of fermenting wine. My nose twitched from the dust, but I willed myself not to sneeze.

A choice lay before me, and it would be lost when Bessus left my father's house. And my father would be staying here, his whip constantly at hand. . . .

I waited for my father to pass, then nudged the door open. I'd scarcely peered into the dank corridor when Parizad yanked me back, jolting my back and making me hiss with pain. "What are you doing?" he asked.

"Go keep Father busy," I said. "Ask him how to hide extra grain from the collectors after the harvest, anything to buy me time with Bessus."

"Bessus?" A dark understanding dawned on his beautiful face. "Why?"

"Because I'm going to become his concubine and convince him to marry me after he becomes king." I bit my lip, for I knew not what might motivate Bessus to make me his wife once he'd already enjoyed me, but what choice did I have? Even a life as a concubine was better than this.

I gestured down at my shabby clothes and a crushing wave of doubt nearly stole my breath. "If he'll have me, that is."

"A beautiful woman can have a man eating from her hand," my brother said, pressing a warm kiss to my forehead. "You could have Bessus on his knees with the right words."

"And if I have my way, Father won't palm a single copper from the deal." Even as I said it, Parizad's eyes danced with glee and a grin spread across his face.

"Father can drown in the well of *Duzakh*," he said. "But he'll beat you within a breath of your life if he finds out you tried to circumvent him."

I'd strip naked in front of Bessus before I let that happen.

Parizad pressed another dry kiss to my forehead, then hurried down the corridor after our father. I drew a steadying breath and slipped into the receiving room.

But Bessus was gone.

"No," I moaned, almost falling to my knees. Yet the *satrap* couldn't have gone far in the time I'd been in the storeroom with Parizad. I couldn't blame him for not wishing to spend a single moment longer in my father's house than he had to.

I turned and ran as best I could, my breath shallow from the shards of agony in my back.

Pain overwhelmed pain.

I was dizzy from the torment of my lashes by the time I saw Bessus enter the courtyard. His chariot awaited and once it left our walls, my chance would be gone.

"Wait!" I cried out. "I request an audience."

An honorable man might have refused to see the unwed daughter of one of his underlings, but Bessus of Balkh only inclined his head at me, scattering his slaves with the flick of a beringed and swollen hand.

"Roxana," he said. "So we meet again."

I ignored the rush of sound in my ears as Bessus' eyes raked over me. He sniffed and his nostrils flared at the breeze. I sent my silent thanks to Parizad for the spikenard perfume.

"Out," Bessus commanded his driver, the axles groaning with relief as he alighted from his chariot. "Now."

My cheeks flushed with pleasure at this newfound power as his driver scurried after the slaves. I could command a man's attention with a drop of perfume and a conveniently draped robe.

Power emanated from Bessus, despite the pouches under his eyes and his fleshy nose webbed with red veins. He might have been handsome once, but those years were long since spent, lost to his banquet table and wine cellars. "I assume your father sent you?"

"My father doesn't know I'm here."

"No?" Bessus crossed his arms over his belly and twisted a gold band high on his arm, a lurid thing shaped into horned griffins inlaid with enamel and onyx. It glittered brighter than anything I'd ever owned. I longed to touch it.

"If your father didn't send you," Bessus asked, "why have you come?"

Was it because I was greedy and grasping, cast in the very image of the father I hated, or because I'd do anything to be free of him? Perhaps both?

My fingers twitched like dragonfly wings, but I clasped my sweaty palms behind my back, letting Bessus' eyes rove over my breasts.

A beautiful woman can have a man eating from her hand, Parizad had said. If only I knew the words to say.

"You desired me when I once came to your palace," I said, hoping he didn't hear the quaver in my voice. "I'm a woman flowered now, and hoped you might be willing to entertain my counteroffer."

"As fair-faced as any virgin, yet you speak like a lender ready to fleece me."

My tongue turned to rock and Bessus leered at me. "Pray continue," he said.

"I assume my father set a high price for my company the last time you negotiated with him. If you'll take me from here, I'll give you whatever you desire. No payment required."

His chins wobbled as if he was choking back laughter. "A girl like you only has one thing to offer a man like me. Do you know what that is?"

"I do." I tilted my chin. "And I'd give you my maidenhead of my own free will."

"Nothing in this life is free," Bessus said. "What do you want in return?"

I thought on that, although I'd already rehearsed my requests. "A position in your army for my brother."

"Is that all?" he asked.

I shrugged. "I wouldn't mind gold bangles and pearl necklaces, or silk robes and tooled leather slippers. And I'd require your promise that you'll keep me as one of your women. In your palace."

"Your father should beat you for this," Bessus said. "Women do not negotiate with men."

I didn't flinch at his accusation, only took his hands in mine and pressed them to my breasts, scarcely daring to breathe lest he feel the edges of the lumpy bandages that wrapped around my ribs beneath the worn orange wool. I tilted my chin so he could drink in the graceful curve of my neck. "This woman does."

"You're as slippery as a snake," he said, but his eyes lingered on the mounds of my breasts, pale as two full moons. "Bangles and necklaces I have aplenty. And there's always room for an extra woman in my palace."

Bessus reached out then and ran a coarse thumb over the soft flesh of my shoulder. I shuddered from a mixture of trepidation, fear, and the heat burning in his eyes. I thought of having my own slaves to massage almond oil into my hands and feet, and chests of silk robes and beaded headdresses to wear every day.

"You'll give me what I ask?" My voice came out breathy and I gasped as Bessus' lips dropped to my neck.

"No more negotiations," he said, his hand expertly unfastening my jasper girdle. It clattered to the flagstones, scattering several more shoddy gems.

"Not here," I said, glancing around the deserted courtyard before leading him to the stables, my heart thudding in my ears. Our father's horse was only just returned and penned next to our aging donkey, but the ramshackle building smelled of decades of accumulated hay and dung. The musty odor didn't faze Bessus, for he pushed me into a stall still scattered with the remnants of old straw. Before I knew what he was doing, my hair tumbled from its threads and he tugged at my robe until my breasts were exposed.

"You are glorious, Roxana of Balkh," he said. His own robe fell loose, revealing two sow's teats and a chest covered with thick black hair as he kicked off his *shalvar*. He wrestled with the tie that released his *zir-šalvar* and I forced myself to watch as the undergarments fell to the ground, for although I'd often gone swimming with Parizad as a child, never before had I seen a grown man in his full nakedness. His manhood stared at me huge and dark, standing erect from its nest of black hair.

I dared not let him see the hideous bandages around my waist or the ruined flesh of my back. Instead I tugged down my own *shalvar* to expose my pale thighs before he could undress me further, keeping my robe pinned at my waist. It occurred to me then that he might have me here in the stable muck and then rescind his bargain, but from the way he backed me into the stall, it was too late to change my mind even if I'd wanted to. Instead I arched my back to keep from touching the wooden wall as his fingers probed the cleft between my legs. Then with one adept movement he lifted me and hefted me against the wall, smashing my damaged back with a flash of scorching agony. The scream of pain built at the back of my throat, flying free as he parted my legs with his hairy knees and entered me with one hard thrust. I cried out in double agony as he began to move inside me, writhing and wrapping my legs around him to save my back, all the while staring down at the griffin's gleaming horns still perched high on his forearm.

I bit my fist while Bessus labored into me, grunting like a boar at a trough. My nails dug into the flesh of my palms, but the pain there wasn't enough to drown out the combined white fire of my back and the flesh between my legs.

I'd been wrong: Pain doesn't always overwhelm pain.

But I had to make pain look like pleasure, for otherwise Bessus would surely cast me aside like a bruised cabbage leaf. So I moaned my pain through clenched teeth as he thrust into me and used my nails to scratch his back, opening it the way my father had opened mine.

Bessus moaned and stiffened, then fell against me in a crush of flesh, sweat, and coarse hair. "You're a loud one," he finally said, standing and shrugging his legs into his silken *zir-šalvar*. I managed to cover my breasts, stiff-spined as I tried not to move the muscles of my back. I expected to feel something for the loss of my virtue, but I could scarcely think through the red fog. Bessus was retying his *kamarband* when his face changed and he pushed me aside.

"What is this?" he asked, running a finger along the stall, its wood marred by a dark stain on its smooth planks.

He held up a forefinger streaked with blood, and only then did I notice the dampness on my back and the cool air against my mangled skin. The bandages had come loose and I felt the gashes weeping warm blood, just like the tears that flowed freely down my cheeks.

"Turn," Bessus said. "And let me see."

I did as he commanded and endured a fresh wave of mortification as his hand twined in my hair so he might inspect my back. "Your father's handiwork, I presume?"

I nodded.

He sighed and some unnamed emotion flitted across his pock-marked face. "No wonder you threw yourself at me."

"We had an agreement," I said, my thoughts coming in a jangled rush. "I swear I'll heal and the scars will be small. My brother has poultices—"

"Have your slaves gather your things."

"What?"

"I gave you my word that I'd take you and so I will. After all, I can still use a bed warmer while on campaign," Bessus said, replacing his robe and the crimson *sarband* on his head. "It's within a father's right to beat his children, yet it's a crime against the gods to mar such beautiful flesh as yours."

"You'll take me on campaign?" I almost fell to my knees in gratitude that he still wanted me, even as I shuddered at the thought of traveling with an army. I'd hoped to be ensconced in a luxurious estate somewhere, not dragged along on dusty marches with only a cot of tanned hide to sleep on and dried ox flesh to gnaw on each day. But it would take me away from my father. . . .

"You're under my protection now, and I leave for this campaign against Alexander at dawn." Bessus looked at me askance. "There will be plenty of spoils to retake from the Macedonian baggage train, silks and baubles to make any woman's feeble heart flutter."

I heaved a sigh, gingerly rearranging my robe. It was a start.

"And my brother?" I asked. "Will you give him a position?"

"There's always room in the ranks for a young man eager to die for honor and glory. Now stop asking for things."

I wouldn't let my brother die on a battlefield anywhere. His talents with herbs and healing meant that he could serve as a healer for the half-wits who volunteered to fight. There was time enough to maneuver that from Bessus.

"Will you take me with you to meet Darius?" I dared ask.

"The King of Kings won't want you," Bessus sneered, the hardened *satrap* once again. "He prefers the company of his eunuch Bagoas even to his slew of concubines."

"But you plan to supplant Darius," I said, taking yet another chance. "I heard you with my father."

In that instant Bessus stood so close I almost gagged over the smell of fish soup he'd choked down with my father. "Not a word of that to anyone, do you understand?" he snarled. "Pretty face or no, I'll gore you myself if your tongue wags."

"Forgive me," I said, falling to my knees before him. "Take me away from here," I gasped, "and you'll have my unswerving devotion until my dying day."

He stared at me, then pulled me to my feet. "Nothing so dramatic as your death, I hope."

I followed him to his chariot as he yelled for his slaves and my brother, the hot glow of triumph making me grin as my father emerged, spluttering and demanding to know what was happening. Parizad followed in his wake, his questioning look transforming into one of pride as he saw my face.

"I've claimed your daughter as only a man can," Bessus said, removing the griffin armband and tossing it at my father like a bone to a dog. "Take this and be happy I don't flog you myself for the damage you've done her. Your son—" He glanced at me.

"Parizad," I provided.

"Parizad shall travel with me on campaign as well."

I allowed myself a malicious smile as my father dived for the gleaming armband. The next time we met, I'd be his anointed queen, and could command all manner of punishment to remind him of the years of torture I'd endured.

For now I turned my back on him, leaving behind the crumbling house of my girlhood. I was a woman now, and one day I might live in Babylon's grandest palace, sleep in the frescoed chambers of Queen Amytis, and walk in the Hanging Gardens.

The promise of jewels and silks meant that I could tolerate this bloated carp of a man, the pain in my back, and even the fire that still raged between my legs.

I'd endure the flames of *Duzakh* for a chance to be queen.

❧·❧ CHAPTER 10 ❧·❧

Pella, Macedon

THESSALONIKE

I raised my hand against the unassuming wooden gate and knocked, my heart clogging my throat. Cynnane's villa—formerly the home of her husband, Amyntas—sprawled far enough from Pella that someone like Olympias might pretend that the white smudge on the horizon didn't exist. I listened for grunts and the cries of swordplay to echo over the walls, but instead only the breeze and the occasional shriek of a cicada drifted our way.

Arrhidaeus and I had left Pella's walls after giving the palace guards the slip, and I'd followed my brother through town into the yellowing countryside, past barren orchards of apricot, quince, and olive trees, and farmers harvesting the late-season barley. Cynnane often invited Arrhidaeus to visit her, in compliments of their shared Illyrian blood and her affinity for our simpleminded half brother.

It stung more than I cared to admit that she'd never thought to invite *me*.

But today I'd invited myself, having stewed over Hephaestion's suggestion that I seek out her and her sword arm.

"Greetings, Arrhidaeus," the guard at the gate said, removing the wooden bar. "Come to visit with Cynnane today? I see you've brought a friend."

"My sister Nike," Arrhidaeus said. "She's taking me fishing after we eat pomegranates with Cynnane."

The guard allowed us inside with a smile, then relayed my stuttered request to see my half sister. We waited in the open courtyard and I helped Arrhidaeus cut into a pomegranate I'd pilfered while strolling up Cynnane's path. He dived into it, leaving smears of crimson across his cheeks, while I perused the household gods in the courtyard's center altar.

I shouldn't have been surprised to see bearded Hephaestus holding an anvil and tongs in the place of honor. The god of metalwork was a logical choice for any warrior to worship, to ask that the iron of a sword be true and the metal of one's armor be impenetrable. But there were two goddesses behind Hephaestus. The first was easily identifiable and I stroked the wings of my namesake: Nike. The second wore a helmet similar to Athena's but was otherwise unadorned, bearing no shield or identifying owl insignia.

A woman behind me cleared her throat and I turned to see Cynnane enter the courtyard. I'd half expected to greet an Amazon, a shield strapped to her back and one breast shorn off, the better to facilitate drawing arrows from the quiver at her back. But the woman approaching me could have been any proper matron, save that her measured paces might have been stolen from an infantry soldier.

And her hair. It really was a disaster, and I was scarcely one to notice as I still sometimes pulled brambles from my own unraveled braid after a day spent in the woods.

"Greetings, Thessalonike," she said. "To what do I owe this honor?"

As always, my words snarled together when I was around Cynnane. She was everything I dreamed of being as a woman: strong, independent, and worldly. Next to her, I was just a knob-kneed girl.

"Arrhidaeus and I were fishing.... Well, we haven't started yet, but we were almost to the creek and he had a sudden craving for pomegranates," I said, my heart beating a wild tattoo in my chest. "So I said we could stop at your villa."

"Arrhidaeus is always welcome here," Cynnane said, ruffling his hair and bending to wipe a crimson smear from his cheek with the corner of her *peplos*. "You are also welcome, Thessalonike, although I've not seen you since . . ."

"Father's death," I said. "I know."

When Cynnane had felled our father's assassin with a well-thrown dagger, and I'd managed only to throw rocks at his feet.

Silence fell, punctuated by Arrhidaeus' loud slurps and smacks.

"We share a patron goddess, I believe," I finally said, gesturing to winged Nike. "My namesake."

"The goddess of victory was our father's patron," she said.

"I've recently become an initiate of Dionysus," I said too quickly.

Cynnane clasped her hands before her. "Olympias' patron."

I wanted to tell her that the god of grapes was the only thing I shared with Olympias, but my protest withered under the full weight of Cynnane's stare.

"Who is the second goddess?" I asked. "Not one of the Olympians, I presume."

"No indeed," Cynnane said. "She is Metis, Athena's mother."

Metis was Zeus' first wife, swallowed by her husband while pregnant with Athena. Undeterred, Metis had worked inside Zeus' head to fashion a helmet for her daughter, causing such a racket that Zeus roared in pain, prompting the god Hephaestus to cleave open the thunder god's skull, thereby freeing Athena. "The original goddess of cunning and wisdom," I said.

"Naturally," Cynnane said. "A woman of any age must be cunning, but I fear she needs those skills even more nowadays."

With that, she turned and strode toward a room on one side of the courtyard. I worried for a moment that I'd been dismissed, or worse, that she was retreating to the *gynaeceum* to weave, as Olympias so often did, but instead she crooked a finger at me to follow.

"Do you mind if I borrow Thessalonike?" she asked Arrhidaeus. He shook his head, already reaching for another pomegranate in a bowl.

"I'll be right back," I whispered to Arrhidaeus, but he scarcely looked up from his feast.

I followed Cynnane not into placid rooms decorated with frescoes of gardens or frolicking porpoises, which so often denoted the women's chambers, but instead into the black and red chambers of what must have been Amyntas' *andron*. The stone floor was sloped toward the middle to allow for easier cleanup of the wine thrown during the men's *symposions* and its walls were lined with weapons fit for an armory: swords, shields, lances, and daggers. A girl needed to be careful in here; one wrong move and I might lose an eye.

"I spend most of my time here, at least while my daughter, Adea, is at her lessons," Cynnane said. I'd never met Cynnane's daughter, but she must be close to five by now, having been born just before her father's death. "She'll finish soon and go down to play with Arrhidaeus. They get along well." She mixed what I thought was spices into a *kylix* of wine, then poured and handed me a cup before arranging herself on one of the couches. "I suspect whatever you came here to discuss might best be done in private."

I'd expected the aroma of cloves and sweet raisin wine, but instead beheld a brackish beer with chunks of stale bread floating on top, its recipe likely stolen from Sparta's meanest barracks. At least it wasn't their famed black broth made from boiled pigs' legs, blood, and vinegar. I held my breath and took a sip, refusing to allow myself to choke.

I set the cup aside and folded my hands in my lap, but quickly took to turning the snake bracelets on my wrists. "I told you," I said, my courage failing. "We came for pomegranates."

"A meager lie, meagerly told. Let me guess." Cynnane sighed. "You've come to me because you fancy work with a sword. Why else would you seek me out?"

My head jerked up. It was possible that Olympias had sniffed out my motives and forewarned Cynnane; her spies were more plentiful than Medusa's snakes.

And Olympias kept me close, pulling me to follow in her footsteps with her serpents and love of Dionysus. She sought to mold me into her shadow so I might serve our family as she had. But I was *not* Olympias.

And I had no intention of ruling anything, not Macedon or Aigai or even the garbage midden outside Pella.

"Will you teach me to fight?" I asked.

Cynnane stared at me a long moment, then shook her head. "No," she said, and my heart fell. "I won't teach you."

"Why not?"

"A sword will only give you blisters, my pampered little sister. You ask for something to nibble on when a banquet is laid for you. You sneeze and a barrage of slaves arrives with rags to dab away your snot." She waved a dismissive hand at me. "Return to the palace and ask Olympias for a new puppy instead. I won't have you diminishing the honor and sanctity of my Illyrian steel with your playing at war."

A red rush of anger and embarrassment roared in my ears and I was on my feet in a heartbeat. "I'm not playing at war," I said. "I'll go mad if I stay in that palace with my only hope of escape tied to a husband and a far-flung marriage bed. I asked Hephaestion to take me with him to Persia, but he refused." I practically spat the next words at her. "I even snuck here without Olympias' permission, thinking you might understand, but I see I was wrong. I won't trouble you further."

With that, I turned and stormed away. I tried to open the door, but somehow I'd neglected to notice that Cynnane had locked it upon our entrance. It didn't budge, meaning either I would have to wait for her to produce the key or I could jump out the window and land in the juniper bush outside.

The bush wasn't too big. Perhaps I might escape with only bruises to my pride and scratches on my backside.

Cynnane cleared her throat behind me and I waited for her laughter to follow, curling my hands into fists.

"You truly asked Hephaestion to take you with him?" she asked. "And he refused?"

I turned slowly, trying to ascertain whether she would mock me next, but her expression was empty of malice. Instead, she bit her bottom lip, a mannerism she shared with Alexander when they were thinking deeply about something. "He did," I said. "He claimed a battlefield was no place for a woman."

She scoffed, then stood on tiptoe and removed a gleaming broadsword from its mount on the wall. "Hephaestion is an idiot."

I'd never heard him described as such, but I wasn't going to argue with her, at least not while she balanced the wicked blade in her palms.

"I wrote a curse tablet for him after that," I admitted. I'd taken my curse to a bent-backed old man in the market who made a living writing the tablets. The metal panel was a lovely little thing, what with its tiny letters that cursed Hephaestion's life, mind, memory, lungs, liver, and heart scratched into the lead. (I'd have cursed his eyes, nose, fingers, and even his big toe if it were up to me, but alas, the tablet had only so much room.)

Cynnane gave a snort of laughter that might have come from a swineherd. An ill-mannered one at that.

"You can add your tablet to my pile," she said. "Unfortunately, Hephaestion is protected by every god under the sun, and our brother as well. Curses roll off him like quicksilver."

I wondered then what had transpired between Hephaestion and

Cynnane. Hephaestion was as easy to love as summer, but that season's heat too often burned if one wasn't careful.

"Fine," Cynnane said, the single word as sharp as the sword she carried. "I'll train you."

"What?" I gaped for a moment, then clapped my mouth shut. "Really?"

"I'll surely regret it," she said. "But you'll go mad in Pella without something to occupy you and I'm already well on my way to madness. We can't have two of Philip's daughters turn into raving loons, now, can we?"

"Thank you!" I squealed the words and flung my arms open to hug her, but Cynnane hunched over and something metallic whizzed past my ear, followed by a wooden thud. A dagger protruded from the whitewashed beam behind me, and my ribs suddenly felt as thin as drum canvas being smashed by my heart.

"You wish me to teach you the ways of a sword and shield," she said. "Anything else?"

I remembered another dagger flying through the air and embedding itself in the flesh of our father's murderer.

"It appears you're handy with daggers as well," I managed to squeak out.

Cynnane gave a slow smile. "An Illyrian soldier is proficient in all weapons."

She tossed the sword to me, and I thanked Nike that I didn't drop it or, more likely, cut off my hand. "Let's see how strong you are," she said, digging through a chest and removing a wooden training sword, polished smooth but battered about its oak blade. She kicked a low table out of the way and opened her arms wide. "No sniveling and no whining, no matter how much it hurts."

And it hurt.

One wouldn't imagine that a woman with a battered wooden sword could inflict a lot of damage, but by the time Cynnane called the match, I was winded and bruised, and every muscle screamed in protest. Although I'd lunged and parried with a real blade, the closest I'd come to disarming or besting Cynnane was when I crashed into the ground, scraping my shoulder on the tiles and losing my sword. She'd pointed her blade at me, but I kicked it away and scrambled for my own weapon, rising and swinging wildly. Surprise had flared in her eyes, but she parried hard and backed me against the wall, this time aiming the point of her blade at the soft skin at the base of my neck while covering her yawn with her free hand. She'd released me and I thrust forward again and again, all while Cynnane's insults and instructions rained upon my head.

"Is that the fastest you can move? I've seen snail slime dry faster. Feint, don't block, donkey brain!"

My body was battered, but it was my pride that stung the most.

But pride led to hubris and hubris led to nothing good, as my father's grave could attest.

Finally, the torture ended. I dragged a sleeve across my face, ignoring the stink of perspiration that clung to me. My slaves would be hard-pressed to scrub the sweat stains from the underarms of my *chiton* and I'd have to invent a story explaining why the hem was ripped.

"I'm hopeless," I said, tears stinging my eyes.

If I'd yearned for sunny compliments and gentle words of wisdom, I'd come to the wrong place. For that matter, I'd been born into the wrong family.

"You are indeed," Cynnane agreed, removing her dagger from the wall and replacing it in an ingenious leather sheath strapped below her knee. "But you'll improve."

"When can I return?" I asked.

"Whenever it pleases you," she said. "I'm always here." I took some satisfaction in the fact that she was breathing harder than normal. She unlocked the door of the *andron*, leaving me to scurry after her.

Arrhidaeus had fallen asleep in the courtyard, curled up in a patch of sun like an oversized, snoring cat. Cynnane's little daughter, Adea, covered her giggle with chubby hands as we approached, surrounded by a veritable herd of multicolored kittens. She'd inherited her father's black hair instead of her mother's mass of copper tangles, and it captured the sunlight now. She said, "Uncle Arrhidaeus gurgles like a fountain between his snores."

As if on cue, Arrhidaeus did just that. It took the toe of my sandal on his backside to finally wake him with a snort worthy of a Cyclops. For a moment I thought I detected a hint of a smile on Cynnane's face as Adea wrapped her pale arms around my brother's leg.

"You're like a great cuddly dog, Uncle Arrhidaeus," she said. "I like you even more than my kittens."

To my surprise, Arrhidaeus gave a sheepish grin, then opened his arms and laughed as she launched herself into his embrace. "And I like you more than pomegranates," he said, setting her down.

"That's high praise coming from him," I whispered to her with a wink, earning another giggle.

I was still smiling as the gates closed behind us and Arrhidaeus chased after a yellow swallowtail butterfly, his big feet sending up puffs of dust. I paused to glance back at the villa's high walls and rubbed the growing pain in my shoulder. It would ache for days, but each twinge was a reminder of time not spent at a loom or wasting away in Pella's bathing pavilion, letting slaves rub me with rose-scented salves while streaking lemon juice into my hair.

Right now I wouldn't argue against a salve or two, although I still wasn't sure how I was going to explain my absence to Olympias if she asked. The sun hung closer to the horizon than I'd planned by the time we'd caught enough trout to cover our tracks, but we still might slip back into the palace undetected.

"Will we see Adea again soon?" Arrhidaeus asked, alternately swinging his pails of pomegranates and trout. "I miss her, and her kittens."

I gave him a stern look. "Remember what I said—that you can't tell anyone we went there together or Olympias will lock me away until I'm an old crone?"

Arrhidaeus nodded. "No one can know about you with Adea. Or Cynnane. But secrets are bad."

"This secret would mean you'd get to come back and eat pomegranates, to play with Adea and the kittens."

Arrhidaeus frowned, then gave a thoughtful nod. "Then, yes, I swallow our secret."

I smiled. "Then, brother, I think we'll see them often."

We'd barely closed the garden gate and paused to pet my shaggy goat, enjoying her dinner of grass, when a shadow darkened our path. Olympias waited with her arms crossed over her chest, and behind her stood Antipater, my father's former general and Alexander's regent here in Macedon. If the old boor wasn't bad enough, Cassander flanked his father, standing as rigid as any god's statue. He was as ugly as the god Hephaestus with a scowl that made his lips shrivel like the twisted god of the forge.

"Where have you been?" Olympias asked. Not even a snake's face ever looked so cold and calm.

"Fishing," I said, nodding to Arrhidaeus' pail and lifting my own basket. The smell made my goat *baa* and storm away to seek calmer pastures. "And filching pomegranates."

"So I see," Olympias said. "And did you have a fine day fishing, Arrhidaeus?"

My brother looked to me, then mirrored my slow nod. "I brought my best worms," he said, holding out the fish pail for inspection.

"The trout will make a fine meal for us tonight," Olympias said, her tone as smooth as if he'd offered her a pail of rubies. "Would you like to take them to the kitchen? I believe the cooks just finished a batch of sweet rolls as well."

Olympias knew the magic words to steal away my ally. Arrhidaeus didn't even wave to me as he bounded over the tiles, his pail swinging so wildly that several dead trout looked as if they were trying to escape. I was left alone to face Olympias, Antipater, and Cassander.

I'd rather have fought the nine-headed Hydra with only a spoon.

"You are not a simple peasant's daughter, Thessalonike," Olympias said. "And I am not a simpleton. Did you really think you could slink off to Cynnane's villa and no one would notice?"

"Cynnane is my sister—"

"And you asked her to train you to fight," Olympias said.

I didn't get a chance to answer, for Antipater crossed his spindly arms beneath his trailing beard. "It is unseemly for a woman to even think of engaging in swordplay."

"Thessalonike can learn to wrestle naked in the Olympic arena for all I care," Olympias said.

My eyes bulged, but nothing could have saved me from bursting out into laughter at the horror that warped Cassander's already ugly face.

"That's sacrilege," he stuttered. "Women are meant to wield a shuttle and loom, not a sword or shield."

"Thessalonike won't be fighting in the Olympic arena anytime soon," she said. "For as you've pointed out, she is a woman now and a sister to the *basileus* of Macedon, Egypt, and Persia. But she is a passionate young woman, and until she can funnel that energy into pleasing her husband and producing his children, she must have an outlet. You are valuable, Thessalonike," she said, turning to me while Cassander gawped, "yet you traipse across the countryside, begging all manner of men to take advantage of you."

"I'm learning to fight," I protested. "And surely no man would be tempted to risk Alexander's wrath."

"Your brother is far away," Antipater said. "And you invite all sorts of trouble with your degenerate ways."

"Do you expect Alexander to protect you *after* you are kidnapped, raped, and married against your will?" Olympias asked.

I had no answer for that.

Olympias only sighed. "Provided that you do not become negligent in your devotions to Dionysus, Cynnane will move into the palace to provide you with entertainment," she said. "Effective tomorrow."

My heart gave a gleeful somersault to know that I'd be able to train every day. Of course, I doubted how elated Cynnane would be to receive Olympias' royal command, which was likely already arriving at her gates. I suspected she'd take her wrath out on me; I'd be lucky if I could walk in the days and weeks to come.

I thought I'd won the day, escaped punishment, and received a double boon in Olympias' approval of my training and Cynnane's relocation, at least until Olympias' next words crashed over me like a basin of creek water.

"It seems that Thessalonike can still benefit from the guidance of a learned tutor," she said, already turning to leave the gardens. "Cassander, you will fulfill that role until I deem otherwise."

I expected him to sputter and protest, but I would soon learn that Cassander was far too stoic for such dramatics. His outburst about my training was out of character, and that was simply because I was the antithesis to the order he believed to be necessary and good in this world. Instead, we glared at each other while Antipater scurried after Olympias like a flea after a dog.

I wondered how long it would take before one of us killed the other.

CHAPTER 11

Korkura, Persia

DRYPETIS

The Eternal Fires of Baba Gurgan made a furious blaze in the falling darkness, the naphtha lake gleaming like a great golden round shield laid flat on its side. Scattered about the gray plain were molten slivers of intermittent blazes, the forgotten tailings of some giant's forge from days long since past. To the east, a hundred holes in the earth spewed smokeless fire and a daring soldier stabbed the ground, then yelped when a flame erupted to lick his helmet. There were rumbles of laughter from his companions, but the sound was tense, for the unnatural fire and stench of sulfur made these Greeks uneasy.

"It's said that King Nebuchadnezzar threw Jews into these fires for refusing to worship a golden statue of Ahura Mazda," my grandmother said to Alexander, but my sister and I exchanged a sly glance. Every Persian old enough to listen to a traveling singer knew that the flames from this lake were sacred and untainted by humans. The shepherds from Korkura huddled close to these fires in winter to keep their flocks warm, and women often came here to pray that their husbands' seed would flourish in their wombs and bring forth sons. The Father of Fires had smoldered to life with the old gods and would continue to burn long after our bones had turned to dust.

From here, the Royal Road branched east toward Babylon, but

dusk was falling and we would camp outside Korkura, the odor of Gaugamela's dead still fresh in our nostrils and the visions of the battlefield carnage seared into our eyes.

Not even the Father of Fires could cleanse us from the filth of that battle.

It wasn't dead men but the rearing elephants and fallen horses I saw each time I closed my eyes, their flanks ripped open by all manner of blades and glazed eyes covered with flies. Worse still was the memory of Hephaestion charging toward my family, the thundering hooves of his stallion grinding to dust our hopes of escape.

A bright shard of pain burst from my swollen hand as Alexander excused himself and our cart lurched to a stop. My shoulder had healed, but a physician had proclaimed my hand broken, which was obvious to any fool. He'd splinted it with wood and linen bandages, and admonished me to pray that it wouldn't set as a misshapen claw. I refused to dwell on his threat, but beseeched Ahura Mazda to spare my hand. I also suggested to the god of wisdom and light that if my hand was ruined, he might also turn Hephaestion's wound putrid. That seemed only just.

Exhausted from the day of travel, I stumbled from the chariot and collapsed onto a waiting crate next to my grandmother, watching with drooping eyelids while slaves worked to assemble our pavilion even as Alexander's tent rose like a newly formed mountain.

Our purple and white striped pavilion had become dull and battered in the two years we'd spent following Alexander's army, but it was home and despite everything, Alexander still insisted that we be treated as royalty. I sometimes wondered if that was because he feared his own treatment should he one day be defeated and captured.

A eunuch opened the wicker cage holding my four-eyed dog from Tyre—freshly washed and brushed now—and he barked happily, darting to take up his post at my feet. Despite the recent battle and the day's dusty journey, a herald bearing Alexander's lion insignia on his breastplate approached and bowed over his closed fist in the briefest acknowledgment as he addressed us.

"Alexander, *basileus* of Macedon, Greece, and Persia, requests the presence of the mother and daughters of Darius at his tent, to better enjoy the evening meal and entertainment."

I opened my mouth to protest that Alexander wasn't king of Persia while my father still lived, but Stateira's hand put gentle pressure on my shoulder.

"We would be honored to join the king," my sister said, standing as stiff and beautiful as an ancient statue of the goddess Anahita. "It is kind of him to remember us."

I didn't bother to suppress my groan as the herald ushered the three of us toward Alexander's tent, my mutt following at my heels, even as I longed for a bath and bed. The path glowed with sputtering flames, a showy gift from the residents of Korkura, who wished to impress the victor of Gaugamela and thereby escape his irascible and unpredictable temper. Inside, a richly spangled baldachin hung overhead and my armpits dampened with sweat from the naphtha fires burning in a hundred different oil lamps, while Alexander crowed about how he'd tamed the wild oil.

I ignored his boasts and joined Stateira and my grandmother to lean back on the silver-footed traveling couch farthest from Alexander, silently chanting the recipe of clay, egg whites, and goat hair to make *sārooj*, a special waterproof mortar, to keep from nodding off during the meal. Despite the Macedonians' best attempts to provide a sumptuous, movable court, there were grains of sand embedded in the leather. I picked at them idly, wishing I could find a more comfortable position but failing miserably due to my infernal hand.

"Where's tonight's singer?" asked Alexander, his voice carrying over the din of conversation. Barsine perched at the foot of Alexander's couch while Hephaestion and the other Companions lounged nearby, laughing heaps of muscle and sinew that had somehow survived Gaugamela while so many others had died. "I would have a song," Alexander commanded.

A boy with a face as plain as milled flour entered the tent then, and I recognized him as a singer with a girl's voice who often entertained Barsine, plucking the strings of his lyre with a curved talon stolen from a golden eagle. His elbows and knees jutted at odd angles, for he was just on the cusp of manhood, and he clutched his harp tightly, as if afraid he might drop it. He scurried to bow before Alexander, gazing up at the conqueror through his mop of hair with lovelorn eyes.

"Perhaps a recitation of *The Song of Ilium?*" Barsine suggested, pouring Alexander a cup of unwatered amber wine, one so fresh and young that several pieces of half-fermented grape also splashed into the cup.

I glanced about for a *sarissa* with which to gouge my ears, but sadly, there wasn't one at hand. The sun might stop rising if Alexander didn't get to compare himself to his idol, the shiftless, corpse-defiling demon Achilles.

"No," Alexander said. "I crave a new tale. One of Darius fleeing at Gaugamela."

I clenched my good fist, thinking to feign a headache. In the two years since our capture at Issus, I'd clung to the image of my father as a brave hero who would vanquish the Greeks from our lands, but that was harder to do now that my father had run from battle not once, but twice. We'd suffered listening to Alexander's men sing songs and boast of my father's cowardice, comparing him to a whipped dog and worse. I wasn't in the mood to suffer through more of their insulting ditties.

Yet before I could slump over the arm of my couch, Alexander beckoned in my direction. "And I would have our Persian guests come closer, so they may better hear our singer's sweet voice."

With leaden feet, I followed as Stateira glided toward Alexander with a serene smile, her bronze hair sewn into perfect whorls that gleamed through her transparent veil. We arranged ourselves as the singer began to pluck his lyre and then sang in a watery voice, gaining strength with each verse.

"He was King Darius, the King of Kings, the Lion of Lions, who turned tail and fled like a mewling house cat from the field of battle—"

I stopped listening.

Fortunately, Alexander wasn't listening either, a fact that caused the singer to wring the strings of his lyre as if strangling an obstinate chicken.

"We know that the naphtha will blaze," Alexander announced to no one in particular. He leaned over a golden urn at his feet, filled to the brim with the black oil that fed the Eternal Fires. "But will it consume that which it burns?"

Any half-wit knew that fire of any sort would eventually consume its fuel, be it wood, oil, or some other material. But I refused to give Alexander the satisfaction of an answer.

Hephaestion swirled his wine in a fluted silver griffin goblet, looking far too robust and entirely without a hint of the blood poisoning I'd wished on him. He avoided looking at the fire, his gaze searching everywhere save the flames. "I'm looking forward to inspecting the Hanging Gardens once we reach Babylon," he said as if he hadn't heard Alexander, his finger rapping an agitated tattoo against the goblet. "I wonder if something similar could be constructed when we return to Macedon?"

Alexander scowled briefly, then turned his attention to the rest of us. "Naphtha will be difficult to use as a weapon if one is unaware of its full properties." His voice rose in combat against the singer's wails. "What do you think, Drypetis?"

He'd caught me off guard, yet I tried not to let it show, ruffling my dog's ears instead. "I know little about the substance."

"You're interested in engineering and weapons. Would naphtha consume its fuel or would it burn itself out, leaving all it touched unscathed, as it does with water and earth?"

Alexander asked my opinion about a weapon he surely sought to use against my father and Persia, just as I'd once blurted out the suggestion of using iron chains in Tyre instead of rope. I'd thought it impossible to hate him any more than I already did, but my loathing of him expanded in that moment.

"Olive oil scorches, sputters, and smokes," I said, forcing myself not to snarl like a rabid wolf. "Why wouldn't naphtha?"

"But olive oil burns and sputters even on water," Alexander said, taking a swill of wine. "Naphtha doesn't. One is like a beautiful courtesan, the other a common bath slave."

Stateira flushed and became suddenly entranced with the weft of her sleeve. I gave Alexander a terse smile. "I defer to your vast knowledge of courtesans and bath slaves. But surely naphtha would burn anything weaker than water or earth, be it wood, fabric, or even flesh."

"What I really need," Alexander said, "is a test. Preferably on someone still living."

I recoiled as the music fell suddenly silent.

"Test your theory on your most humble follower," the musician said, collapsing to his knees before Alexander. His lyre clattered to the ground with a discordant twang. "I offer myself to you, Alexander of Macedon, that you may determine what sort of weapon you have."

"Don't be an idiot," my grandmother hissed, but I could see that was exactly what this empty-headed singer was.

"His face is plain enough, so nothing shall be lost if your theory fails," Hephaestion mused, finally glancing our way and raising his cup of wine to the singer. It was impossible to discern from his droll tone whether he spoke in jest.

"You can't be serious," I said to both him and Alexander. "Light yourselves on fire if you wish to test your theory on a living, breathing man."

"Or perhaps you'd make a fitting test subject," Alexander said. After traveling for so long with the Macedonian conqueror, I recognized the gleam in his eyes, a harbinger of his wildest mood.

A pinch on my back, so hard I cried out.

"My apologies for my granddaughter," my grandmother said. "I fear she may have hit her head as well as her shoulder in Gaugamela." She lowered her voice so only I could hear her. "And if not, I'll do the job myself once we return to our tent."

"Enough of this," Hephaestion said in a low tone to Alexander. "Fire is nothing to toy with, as you well know."

"This won't be like that, Hephaestion," Alexander muttered. "We're no longer children."

I wondered what he meant, but Alexander studied me through slitted eyes. I shivered as he patted the singer's shoulder. "Let it not be said that I lit Darius' daughter afire, especially not when we have a willing and pleasant subject."

The boy fairly preened with the feeble compliment.

Alexander gave a wild grin and tossed his cup of wine to the ground, spilling scarlet over the silken carpet as he grasped the golden urn of naphtha and poured it over the singer, then touched one of the hundred oil lamps to the boy's dripping flesh.

"Alexander, no!" Hephaestion lunged forward, but he was on the other side of the pavilion, too far to stop his madman lover.

I leapt from my couch with a wild cry of fury, but I was too late.

For a heartbeat I thought Alexander was right, that the Eternal Fire would do no harm. But in the span of a breath, the orange flame consumed the singer's chest, then snaked down his arms and legs. He lifted a hand and for a moment that plain face lit with wonder as he marveled at the flames dancing from his fingers.

Then he howled like a demon trapped forever in the flames of *Duzakh*.

The sound seared itself onto my memory, more terrible than my mother's death cries as she struggled to expel my brother from her womb. My dog howled and barked as the singer dropped to the ground, burning yellow and blue so only the dark silhouette of his writhing body could be seen through the flames.

"The rug," I cried, but everyone remained rooted with shock. I shoved the gaping Alexander from my path and tried to roll the burning boy into the precious silken carpet. The threads began to singe; he was flailing around too much to suffocate the fire. Strong arms shoved him down and held him immobile, and someone dumped a *krater* of wine atop the boy, finally quenching the flames.

Steam and the terrible stench of singed flesh filled the room, like some sort of altar sacrifice.

"Unroll him before his flesh adheres to the carpet," my grandmother said. She was holding an empty terra-cotta *krater*, the last few drops of wine dripping from its mouth.

The singer's skin peeled away in great sheets on his chest and limbs, the edges tinged charcoal black. The boundary of the flames remained a livid shade of crimson, raised and mottled like a slab of unpolished marble. His breathing came in lurches, as if the fire had seared his lungs. Only his face and left hand were blessedly untouched.

He still might pluck his lyre, then, but his right hand was ravaged and burned so deep that patches of red muscle showed through. Blisters were already beginning to form, pale pockets of shining skin filled with clear water. My stomach lurched and Stateira retched into the empty *krater* held by my grandmother. Barsine hurried her and my still-barking dog out of the tent and into the night air, but I fell to my knees alongside my grandmother, her clear gray eyes already ascertaining the damage.

"Can he be saved?" came a man's voice.

Alexander hovered above us. "Interesting," he continued. "See that he receives the proper medical attention."

"You dim-witted, arrogant monster," I said, gritting my teeth. I stumbled to my feet, but Hephaestion stepped between us. My grandmother grasped my bad hand to stop me, eliciting my yelp of fresh pain.

"You have your answer," Hephaestion said to Alexander. His fingers were singed and a fine sheen of perspiration covered his face. I realized then that it was he who had helped me with the rug. "Sisygambis is an accomplished healer and will need full access to your physician's chest of herbs."

"Of course," Alexander murmured, the mercurial gleam in his eyes finally banished as he snapped his fingers at a slave. "Fill a chest with the singer's weight in gold, a fitting reward for such a noble sacrifice." The slave nodded and scurried away, likely worried he'd be the next to be doused by naphtha.

"Noble sacrifice?" I choked. "You tortured your own singer! What songs will they sing of you now?"

I knew instantly that I had gone too far.

"You shall not speak," Alexander ordered in a frigid voice, the whites of his eyes bloodshot. "Lest I be required to send your father a letter detailing the death of his youngest daughter."

The singer moaned, but his pain-glazed eyes still stared up at Alexander. The foul Macedonian knelt and reached down as if to touch the boy, then recoiled. My rage burned hotter than the flames at the Father of Fires, for Alexander couldn't even bring himself to touch the ruined creature he had created.

"The *basileus* thanks you," Hephaestion said to the singer, and I was shocked to see his eyes shining, but then he blinked and I thought perhaps my mind was playing tricks on me. Alexander's slave returned then with the medicine chest and my grandmother poured a draft of poppy milk and dribbled it into the singer's mouth. It wasn't long before the boy's eyelids drooped, allowing him blessed peace.

"Does anyone know his name?" I asked, but no one answered. "What is his name?" I asked again, almost hysterical.

"He is Adurnarseh," Hephaestion said quietly. "He sang for me once or twice."

Adurnarseh. His name meant *the word of a fiery man*.

I closed my eyes against the irony. Adurnarseh had sought glory through fire, but it had lasted a single bittersweet moment. Now he would have to live with its aftermath for the remainder of his life, provided he survived his wounds.

"We ride for Babylon at dawn," Alexander said, looking everywhere except at the singer as the boy was levered onto a shield and carried from the tent. "There I shall expect the family of Darius to make public oaths of obedience and lend me their full support as I greet the Persian populace."

So Alexander required us to betray my father and persuade our people to accept him, after we'd just watched him immolate one of his own. Then again, perhaps this had been a warning to me, and to my family. The weight of everyone's stares fell upon my grandmother and me, as if daring us to defy Alexander. For once I held my tongue, even as I gritted my teeth until they threatened to crack.

I'd swear Alexander's petty oath if I had to. And then I'd destroy him and cackle with glee to witness his fiery destruction, just like Adurnarseh's.

Babylon was a decaying old queen, her gaily painted temples bent-backed and surrounded by moldering brick walls like a frayed robe trailed too long in the dust. The city of Hammurabi the Law-giver and Nebuchadnezzar the Builder was decrepit now, her glory squandered by heavy taxation and the incessant wars of the past decades. Yet even still, her seven-story ziggurat gleamed like a copper crown from its pinnacle in her skyline and she stood tall, waiting to greet this latest force assembled at her gates.

My father had brought Stateira and me here many times to marvel at the colossal Etemenanki ziggurat dedicated to Marduk, the blue and gold tiles of the Gate of Ishtar with its procession of aurochs and dragons, and Nebuchadnezzar's lush Hanging Gardens. Stateira had fidgeted as my father explained the process of baking and glazing the bricks of the Ishtar Gate, of arranging them into place like a giant puzzle, and building its cedar roof, but I had hung on his every word, enthralled by the vision he created.

It was the Ishtar Gate that swung open to receive Alexander exactly seven days after Gaugamela, the conqueror still smelling of the seawater and hyssop used to purify him after the singer's death. Even before the smudge of city had become visible on the horizon, the *satrap* Mazaeus rode out with his sons to pledge loyalty to the Macedonian marauder. The swarthy man with a beard of perfectly coiled ringlets had led my father's right wing at Gaugamela, but now he bowed and scraped to Alexander, hoping to save his derelict city and return it to its former glory.

Alexander drew up his army as if to advance, but the move was unnecessary. Officials poured out to greet their conqueror as priests lined the cobbled path with silver-plated altars burning so much frankincense that even Ahura Mazda must have cringed at the excess. The Processional Way was strewn with pink and white rose petals, and crowds cheered as Alexander rode forth in my father's golden chariot, pulled by Bucephalus and surrounded by his Companions. One word was chanted over and over, taken up by the crowd and echoed by grandparents and grandchildren, husbands and wives.

"Liberator!"

My eyes watered, but I blinked hard, praying that my father wouldn't receive word of this treachery. Alexander and his men passed beneath the watchful eyes of Ishtar and her stone lions, winged Marduk and his painted dragons, into the heart of the traitorous city. The streets that fanned out from the Processional Way were crammed with cages of pacing leopards and roaring lions, whirling acrobats and chanting priests. The music of stringed lyres, silver pipes, and skin drums drowned out the joyous shouts of freedom.

"People of Babylon!" Alexander yelled, and the crowd stilled. "I come here not as a conqueror but as your liberator, freeing you from the yoke of Darius' heavy taxation. Babylon shall once again assume her place among the grand cities of the world." Alexander flung one arm toward a pile of rubble and the other toward the copper-topped ziggurat. "The famed temple of Esagila shall be rebuilt with its gold and jewels to once again blind all who look upon it. And the gold statue of Bel-Marduk shall be recast and returned to its rightful place in the ziggurat of Etemenanki."

The crowd cheered wildly and Alexander waved and nodded, even daring to take off his helmet with its double egret plumes so all of Babylon might see him better. I prayed for a Persian arrow to find its mark in his eye or temple, but the herd of dumb sheep continued their incessant bleating, ecstatic in the presence of their conqueror.

Then Alexander turned toward us and the Babylonians calmed. "Darius, the supposed King of Kings, has fled from us twice on the battlefield, yet the gods have seen fit to trust me with the protection of his cities, his mother and daughters. It is my honor and privilege to enter Babylon on this historic day, to assume his place as your rightful *basileus*."

My grandmother and Stateira lowered their heads in unison, but I waited a moment longer, making sure that Alexander and those near enough could witness the hate burning in my eyes. Only then did I dare bend my head to the *yona takabara*, although I kept my back stiff and refused to kiss my hand to him in the sacred *proskynesis* as so many in the crowd now did.

Alexander of Macedon was not a god. He was only a man who had climbed too high and would soon discover how far he had to fall.

*   *   *

Alexander remained five sumptuous weeks in Babylon, minting new coins from my father's gold bullion—stamped with his own haughty profile—visiting Nebuchadnezzar's vast treasury, and gorging on pike liver, lamprey roe, and pig kidneys at countless banquets and poetry recitals. I wondered if Alexander ever thought of the poor singer left behind with a hill of gold in Korkura, if Adurnarseh still breathed or if his corpse now fed the worms. But if Alexander did wonder, he never asked. Instead, he charged blithely forward.

Forbidden from leaving the palace, I spent most of my days and even several nights in the famed Hanging Gardens. I climbed the open-air terraces that Nebuchadnezzar had built for his homesick Median queen, sitting beneath the canopies of almond and fig trees, spruce and cedars, cypresses and rosewood, juniper and tamarisk. A squirrel leapt from branch to branch over my head and a brown sparrow hawk soared into the clouds. If I closed my eyes, I could imagine that I was in the mountains of that queen's homeland, the whitewashed pillars of the terraces transforming to the snowy peaks above the forest. When Stateira had first visited the gardens, she'd feigned interest in the assorted trees, but I'd pressed a hundred questions to the eunuch who'd been commandeered as our guide, ceasing my queries only after I'd learned that the terraced roofs were made of reeds reinforced with bitumen and laid across cedar beams, then layered with baked brick and lead so the moisture from the top levels wouldn't compromise the stability of the whole. In addition, there were aqueducts to force water upward from the Euphrates via an ingenious screw mechanism, while rainwater could gather in cisterns on the roof.

Some were inspired to write poetry about the curve of their lover's cheek or the first burst of sunlight after the darkest day of the year. It was fortunate that I was no poet, for I'd have composed verses to the might of a lowly winch or the glory of an aqueduct.

It wasn't poetry I wrote today, but something much more vital.

There had been no word from my father since we'd reached Babylon, although whispers claimed that more *satraps* like Mazaeus were abandoning him, casting their lots with Alexander to avoid utter destruction.

I still prayed that my father would best Alexander on the battle-field, but that seemed less likely with each passing day. Fortunately, there was more than one way to win a war.

My hand had mostly healed—although a few of the fingers would likely always be stiff—and the Script of Nails flowed from my pen in a letter to Mazaeus, the turncoat *satrap* of Babylon.

Greeting to Mazaeus from Darius the Third,

The King of Kings wishes you to know that the combined treasuries of Persepolis and Babylon would throw open their doors for you if you should assist the chosen one of Ahura Mazda in fomenting a rebellion against Alexander of Macedon. Such a show of support for the one true king would be a demonstration of the utmost loyalty, for which the only fitting reward would be the eternal union of our families. The King of Kings would offer you the hand of his youngest daughter—

"She's a woman who must be constantly occupied," a familiar voice interrupted, "lest she wreak havoc on the affairs of men."

My pen scratched across the page, a black scar of ink across my carefully chosen words.

Words for which I could expect to be impaled, or worse, should they be discovered.

"What do you want?" I asked Hephaestion, crumpling up the

paper even as I fought the urge to flee with the evidence of my treachery. Today he was dressed in a long Persian-style robe, sumptuous and made of embroidered brown silk, mimicking Alexander's newly adopted style. I hadn't seen so much as the tip of Hephaestion's infuriating nose in the weeks we'd been sequestered in the palace, and had rather hoped that I'd be spared the honor for the remainder of my natural life, or at least until Alexander's pet was speared by a Persian charioteer. I was fairly certain I could rouse myself to attend his funeral.

Yet he came now, interrupting me while I was engaged in high treason. I willed my hands not to shake, but they refused to obey, so I crossed my arms before me, finding it suddenly impossible to breathe normally.

"I'm pleased the gardens are proving a pleasant distraction for you." He plucked a handful of figs from a tree and popped one of the fruits into his mouth. "Lest we find you fanning the flames of rebellion in the street."

"Are there flames?" I asked hopefully, even as I clutched my ruined letter tighter in my hand.

"None that I can tell," he said. "Babylon seems quite content with her new master."

"I asked you what you want," I said irritably, shoving the letter to Mazaeus into my sleeve. "Or does Alexander simply prefer to torture his captives? Perhaps you have a pail of naphtha you'd like to douse me with?"

Hephaestion sobered at that, and tossed the remainder of the figs into the bushes as if he'd lost his appetite. "I received word that Adurnarseh died from his wounds."

"May he pass easily into paradise," I said, and meant it. "Another example that no good can come from serving Alexander."

"Alexander is blessed by the gods," Hephaestion said, and I could see his hackles rising. "He's ruled by his passions and his ambitions."

"That's not a man you've described, but a demon flown from the very depths of *Duzakh*."

Hephaestion clenched his fists. "I bear a message for you from that very demon."

I waved a hand. "Then deliver it and begone. There must be a kitchen slave or a courtesan, or a perhaps even a goat, that you'd rather be buggering than wasting my precious time."

Hephaestion gazed at the cedar beams overhead, but a vein in his jaw throbbed in frustration. "Actually, there *was* a fine-looking ewe I saw on my way here. I think it's due in the kitchens for slaughter, but I'm sure no one would mind if I availed myself of it first."

I gaped for a moment, then flinched when his snide laughter mocked me. "You play that you're a woman of the world, Drypetis of Persia, but you're only a blustering girl."

"I wasn't aware that a Macedonian man-whore could insult the daughter of the King of Kings," I said, scrambling to my feet. "You have less than two breaths to deliver that message—*without* insulting me—or you'll find yourself facedown in the Euphrates."

It was an idle threat and we both knew it. Although I was sure Hephaestion had memorized the contents, still he made a great show of removing the scroll from his belt, sweeping an obsequious bow, and beginning to read.

"'Upon sunrise, the entourage of Alexander of Macedon shall travel to the end of the Royal Road to the Kara Su River, the source of the King of Kings' drinking water, and thereby rendezvous with the *satrap* of Susa, who offers a herd of camels and twelve warriors as proof of his friendship. The family of Darius, King of Kings, including his grandmother and daughters, Stateira and Drypetis, shall remain in Susa henceforth,'" he announced. "'So it is decreed and so it shall be.'"

The letter certainly sounded like Alexander—pompous and over-bearing. "Susa?" I stood, folding my arms before me. "At sunrise?"

No time to send my letter to Mazaeus, much less start a revolt. Hope withered in my chest, leaving my heart hollow. "How long shall we be in Susa?"

Hephaestion pretended to scan the missive again, then rolled it with a shrug. "Alexander doesn't say. Preferably until you die of old age."

I waved away his meager attempt at an insult as my hopelessness was swamped by a newly smoldering anger. "And what shall we do there?" I asked. "Weave and sew and compose songs of Alexander's glories in battle?"

"I've seen your sewing and heard your singing. You'd be better suited to scrubbing wine cups and polishing chariots."

I stomped my foot. "And you'd be better suited painted as a girl and serving in a brothel than on a battlefield."

"Be that as it may"—he dared to chuck me under the chin with the scroll—"it is you being caged at Susa, and not me." He saluted and marched off, his step downright jaunty.

I scarcely managed to hold in my rage until Hephaestion's footsteps faded, scattering sparrows and squirrels from Nebuchadnezzar's trees as I screamed and beat a gnarled tamarisk trunk with my palms, tearing open the flesh there until my throbbing hand forced me to stop. I collapsed to the ground, sobbing and breathing in the scent of rich earth.

Cradled in the roots of the tamarisk tree, I knew then how Nebuchadnezzar's wife had felt, pining for bygone days and family long since dead.

Yet there was no one to build me a magnificent garden of memories and ease my heartache. Despite my attempt of escape at Gaugamela and even inciting rebellions here in Babylon, there was only a long stretch of gray days that would lead to Susa and the inevitable word of my father's death.

I didn't mean to drift off, but my grief and rage were heavy burdens to bear, and the murmur of the water in the aqueducts and the chatter of sparrows lulled me toward sleep. I awoke sometime later beneath a darkening sky, a crick in my neck and my robe damp through from the earth. I sat and stretched, feeling for the letter in my sleeve, intent on tearing it into shreds and burying the evidence in at least five different holes scattered throughout the garden.

But the letter was gone.

CHAPTER 12

Susa, Persia

HEPHAESTION

In the height of summer Susa was reputedly a boiling scrap of sand where the air quavered with a choking heat and the city's streets scorched the bottom of a man's sandals like an earthen sun. If that weren't unpleasant enough, spending a winter in the ugly and ignored bastard of Persia's four capitals was even worse.

Susa was a bleak and vile smudge of gray, its people hunchbacked against the cold winds that sighed and howled and gnawed deep into their bones. It was a wonder that the city had been sacked so many times in its long history; had I lived here, I'd have begged any would-be conqueror to pull down its bricks to save myself the eyesore.

Yet it was in the open plain outside Susa that I stood bent over my knees with my chest heaving, having just run oiled, naked, and shivering beneath the city's sodden sky—admittedly not the best weather to show off a man's shaft and cods—with Alexander in farewell games dedicated to a whole bevy of Greek, Persian, and even a few Egyptian gods. Alexander had once boasted that he would run the *stadion* in the Olympic Games only if all of the other competitors were kings, but I could have beaten him by a good ten paces today. Still, the people of Susa were here to ogle their golden-haired conqueror, not me, before Alexander left them to their petty lives and we marched on Persepolis. So I'd slowed and let him pass, grinning as he embraced me at the finish, while slaves bedecked him in a laurel wreath and a thick purple *himation*.

He wrapped a thin red cloak around my shoulders. "I'll have to train more to beat you in a fair race, fleet-footed Patroclus that you are," he murmured in my ear, and I smiled at the old nickname from *The Song of Ilium*.

"If you think it would help," I said, chuckling. "But did swift-footed Achilles ever beat Patroclus?"

The crowd drowned out his response as they took up his name in a never-ending chant. There were only two responses for cities toward Alexander: to fawn over him in fake adulation in the hope that he would spare their lives, or to try to kill him. Much as I loathed Susa, I was glad they'd chosen the former and saved us the trouble of slaughtering their men in the streets.

I let Alexander bask in their cheers as I scraped the oil from my body with a bronze strigil and then shivered back into my discarded Persian robes, envying a group of old men draped in thick wool *himations* who were simultaneously throwing down knucklebones and cups of unwatered wine. They'd go home every night this winter to warm beds and even warmer wives, who'd swat their hands away before they decided to ward off the season's cold together. I, on the other hand, would don armor that weighed more than Atlas' globe and was so cold that it felt like a million knives to touch, thus to march in ever-frigid weather with only the heat of an impending battle to look forward to.

A woman dressed in brown sackcloth with a hairier upper lip than even these bearded Persian devils hawked roasted nuts over a portable clay oven in a voice that might have shattered glass, had there been any around. She screeched at the men playing knucklebones, making them all cringe in perfect unison. One shot her a withering look before muttering something to his companions and shuffling over, resuming his place beside her and behind the piles of steaming nuts.

"Nuts," he said in a monotone voice, warming his hands in front of the oven's open front, steam pouring from its smoldering black coals. He was as ugly as she, with a bulbous red nose and a tangled beard that might have housed a family of rats. "Pistachios, walnuts, and almonds."

I fished for a coin in my pocket and tossed the bit of gold to him. His face slackened with shock when he realized its value, but then twisted in annoyance as his wife grabbed it, biting the gleaming metal between brown teeth before shrieking and shoving it between her ample breasts.

"Women," I said to the man, shaking my head with a commiserating smile as she jabbered and filled the largest bag of steaming pistachios. "Can't live with them . . ."

"I could live without this one," the husband hissed, receiving a thunk on the head from his foulmouthed wife as she shoved the bag into my hands. She reminded me of another Persian woman, one whose slightly fairer face did little to make up for her fishmonger's mouth.

Yet the threat of banishment to Susa had silenced Darius' gorgon of a daughter, a feat on par with Heracles' slaying of the Hydra. I popped a warm nut in my mouth, wondering if perhaps I might persuade Alexander to commission a song or two in my honor for surviving another encounter with the ghastly she-cat.

Immediately upon entering Susa two weeks ago, Alexander had marched past the city's sissoo-wood temples to the inner palace and thrown open the doors to the throne room, its flame-scarlet and night-black walls studded with tasteful ebony and tiny flecks of glittering gemstones. One could fault the Persians for gelding their eunuchs and retreating like cowering dogs on the battlefield, but their palaces were luxurious and their gardens lush paradises, especially compared with the stark utility of our Macedonian architecture back home.

In the presence of Susa's *satrap* and priests, Darius' sour-faced womenfolk, and all his Companions, Alexander had mounted the short dais, hesitating only briefly before the solid gold throne beneath its gilded canopy, emblazoned with a purple and gold lion on the base and a bouquet of peacock feathers and gem-laden blossoms. He sheathed his sword, turned with a flourish, and hoisted himself upon the great throne.

His feet didn't reach the ground.

Among other things, the gods had endowed my friend, commander, and lover with a noble birth, a quick mind, and more courage than Achilles, but he was no taller than most men and apparently, he was far shorter than Darius.

A Persian king would never sully his feet with something as inane as the floor, and a low gilded stool waited patiently for Alexander's dusty boots. A eunuch scurried to place the stool, then glanced up at Alexander with an expression of sheer panic. Drypetis sniggered into her hand, silenced only by her grandmother's glare.

Alexander's feet still didn't touch.

His mouth tightened like a length of steel, but I jutted my chin to a short table at his elbow, its sides carved to resemble a winged sphinx with decorated clawed feet. The eunuch took the cue and moved the table to replace the footstool, thereby eliminating the dangle of Alexander's feet.

"There's dust and manure on his sandals," Drypetis groused under her breath. "Our father would cut off his feet for the insult." I turned to silence her—I'd stuff her veil in her mouth if I had to— but Alexander hesitated, moving his sandaled feet as if to admire the hammered gold filament of the sphinx's wings. "It is a fine table," he said, replacing his feet. "A fitting stool for the true *basileus* of Persia."

He continued as if nothing had happened, reappointing the Persian *satrap*, ordering sacrifices to our gods, and proclaiming a bout of athletic games fit for the twelve Olympians and possibly the Titans too.

Artemis' tits, but I was sick of running about naked for the honor of Zeus and his ilk. Let the lord of thunder gambol about in the cutting winter winds without his *chiton* and see how he enjoyed it.

"My troops depart for Persepolis before the solstice," Alexander informed Susa's *satrap*, a man with so much oil in his ringleted beard that walking by an oil lamp might set him afire.

I winced at the remembrance of the singer left behind to die at the Eternal Fires of Baba Gurgan. In the days since, I often wondered if I might have stopped Alexander from committing such a terrible crime against Adurnarseh, but my own fear had paralyzed me, recalling the fire Alexander had set in a cave while we camped in the Precinct of the Nymphs at Mieza as boys. We'd been sent into the foothills of Macedon's Bermius Mountains by Aristotle in order that we might observe the natural world via the lush orchards and waterfalls around us. We'd stayed up half the night as boys are wont to do, ignoring the bugs and bushes we were meant to be studying in favor of practicing our swordplay with wooden blades and telling haunting tales of vengeful gods, until I'd finally dozed off. We'd chosen a cave to sleep in and I'd dreamed of the forges of my namesake Hephaestus, the crippled god sweating inside his volcano while hammering armor and weapons for his family of gods. Instead, I'd woken to a cave filled with smoke and fire, the scalding flames that licked at my hair and limbs also obscuring the entrance. Disoriented, I might have died in that tiny rock tomb had it not been for Alexander's strong hand around my wrist pulling me into the clean, fresh air. I'd fallen to the ground, coughing until my smoke-scorched throat threatened to bleed while Alexander watched the flames in rapturous silence.

"What happened?" I had finally been able to ask, my voice rasping like an old hag's.

"I wanted to see how big the fire could get," Alexander said, a wild grin splitting his lips in two.

In that moment I wanted to split more than just his lip. If my wooden sword hadn't been left in the cave, I might have bashed in his head. Instead, I still crouched on the damp earth, my entire body shaking.

"Have you been breathing Apollo's vapors?" I'd gaped, incredulous. "You could have killed me!"

Only then did Alexander look abashed.

"I just kept feeding it with tree limbs and old brush . . . ," he muttered, staring at his feet as if I were Philip reprimanding him. "I'll give you my new copper sword to replace your training sword. And . . . I'm sorry."

It was Alexander's first encounter with the power of fire, and it wouldn't be the last.

I forgave him for the accident—my new copper sword was almost worth the terror and my singed curls—but since then, fire held the power to make the gorge rise in my throat. That fire at the Mieza cave was when I recognized that it would fall to me to rein in Alexander's passions, but my feeble actions at stopping him at the Eternal Fires had proved too little, too late. And while I'd scarcely known the singer, one day I'd greet Adurnarseh's shade in Hades and be forced to atone for my part in his death.

"I leave behind precious spoils," Alexander continued to the *satrap* with a graceful wave of his hand toward Darius' women, trussed like turtledoves in their full plumage. "I entrust to you my adopted mother, the Queen Mother Sisygambis, and her granddaughters Stateira and Drypetis. It is my command that they receive every comfort here in Susa, and that they enjoy the privilege of the finest Greek tutor that can be procured for their private use."

Drypetis balked. "We already speak Greek." The girl may have been raised in four palaces, but she possessed less polish than a kitchen slave wringing shit from the guts of a freshly slaughtered goat.

"It is my wish that you should learn to speak our tongue more fluently, and write it too," Alexander said. "As befits women of your station."

A station that should have guaranteed Alexander's marriage to one if not both of Darius' daughters by now. But he'd only shrugged when I'd asked him about the matter on our way to Susa.

"I'm scarcely twenty-six," he'd answered. "There's plenty of time for marriage *after* I've conquered Persia and wear her eagle diadem."

"We are honored at your thoughtfulness," Stateira said. "And we shall endeavor to please you by becoming adept at your language." She clasped Drypetis' wrist hard enough to break the bones anew. It was the first time I'd seen proof that Stateira possessed a mind of her own, and I suspected that she had one goal: pleasing Alexander.

"I shall be happy to receive letters written by your own hand, Stateira, daughter of Darius," Alexander said. He gifted her with a true smile, the one that shone with the sun's own warmth. "You shall bring great pride to your grandmother."

Drypetis snorted, but Stateira didn't answer, only bowed her lovely head so a lock of gleaming copper hair slipped from her veil as she backed slowly down the stairs. Alexander's gaze followed her the entire way. His weren't the only eyes on her; it seemed as if every man in the throne room had only just now taken notice of Darius' elder daughter. Stateira was everything her younger sister was not: elegant as the Graces, beautiful as Aphrodite, and demure as Hestia.

Drypetis tried to saunter past, but I caught her by the forearm. "A word, if you don't mind, Princess?"

She scowled. "I have more than one word for you, but I suspect the length and breadth of them would make your ears bleed."

"Interesting, because I have only one word for you." I leaned down to whisper to her, catching a whiff of her spicy cassia perfume, so different from the typical musk and myrrh perfumes most Persians favored. Strange, as I'd imagined that Drypetis smelled only of axle grease and rust. "And that word is *treason*."

Yes, I'm more evil than a venomous manticore and all manner of other monsters, for I reveled in her blanching face and wide eyes; she looked as though she might be sick all over my sandals. She recovered quickly, but the admission of guilt was there, although I already had plenty of proof.

"I don't know what you mean," she said, her pupils dilated like those of someone who'd overindulged in poppy milk.

"Don't insult either of us by lying. I have in my possession—not that you'll ever find it—a foul screed written in your hand, inciting the Babylonian *satrap*, Mazaeus, to rebellion and offering your hand in marriage. Granted, you claimed to be your father, but your skull must be full of gnats to think that anyone would believe that the King of Kings would beg one of his lowest-ranking *satraps* to save him and take his foulmouthed daughter off his hands."

"You stole that letter! You laid your hands on me while I was sleeping—"

"I did indeed," I snarled, "and when I read the letter's contents, I almost wrung your skinny little neck. Do you think Alexander will be so benevolent when I inform him of your plot?" I walked around her, hands clasped tight behind my back to keep from shaking her. I almost stumbled when she turned and stepped so close I thought she might shove me out of her path. I'd half expected her to cower with fear and beg forgiveness when I confronted her, but I must have temporarily lost my wits; Drypetis of Persia would make Medusa herself tremble in terror.

"Then why wait so long to confront me?" she demanded. "Why not proclaim my guilt to Alexander before we left Babylon?"

"Because the letter guarantees your good behavior while you're in Susa."

The little weasel dared to laugh in my face. "Why in the name of Ahura Mazda would it do that?"

"Because if I hear one whisper that you're rabble-rousing while we're in the east, I'll present it to Alexander." I stepped closer, ensuring that her next step backward pushed her against the throne room's magnificent frescoes. "But I won't tell him that you wrote it. No; instead, I'll tell him that it was written by your sister."

"You wouldn't dare. And he wouldn't believe you even if you did." Her words were bluster, her battle stance and bravado deflating before my very eyes as she realized she'd lost.

"You will stay in Susa as Alexander commanded," I said, stepping back and flicking imaginary dust from my robe. "You will learn Greek and be a perfect specimen of obedience, even though it may well kill you."

"Which I'm sure would please you to no end."

I shrugged. "It would save me the trouble of killing you later."

I'd thought we were alone, but someone cleared his throat behind me and I turned to see Alexander standing before the colossal ebony doors, his arms crossed before his chest and an annoyingly amused curl to his lips.

"Am I interrupting something?" he asked.

"Not at all," I said, even as Drypetis sounded her own emphatic *no*. I barely kept myself from quipping that I was hunting down traitors. "We were just finished," I answered instead.

"Seems like you were just getting started," Alexander said. Not even my stoniest glare could stop him from raising a bemused eyebrow in my direction.

My last glimpse of Darius' younger daughter was of her fists clenched tight, looking as if she might hurl daggers or any handy projectile at my back as I departed the throne room.

I'd silenced the gorgon, but I was under no illusion that I'd broken her.

It was enough, at least for now.

* * *

Days passed, and fortunately, I didn't cross paths again with Drypetis while we remained in Susa. Neither did I hear any rumblings about rebellion, so I was content that she'd behave herself in order to keep her beloved sister safe from harm.

We left behind thirty thousand Persian boys taken during our many campaigns, adolescents with breaking voices and brave attempts at beards who would remain behind and train to one day fill the ranks of Alexander's army. The boys lined the road leading toward Persepolis at least a hundred deep, and dutiful aristocrats that they were, Sisygambis and Stateira helped festoon the ground with dried rose petals when our regiments departed. Barsine too was there among the cheering crowds and crowing horns, dressed in her customary sapphire silk, for she had asked and received permission to remain behind with the royal Persian women. I watched her whisper something in Alexander's ear and he gave a mighty cheer, then kissed her with a rare ferocity even as I bade good-bye to a handsome young slave with the most stunning calf muscles—among other parts—that I'd ever had the pleasure to run my hands over.

I breathed a sigh of relief as Susa finally slipped into the gray smudge of the horizon. "I detest that city," I said to Alexander as I assumed my place at his side, giving Bucephalus my customary growl by way of greeting. Dependable old Ox-Head threw his head and snorted like a demon from Tartarus, but he lacked his golden horn helm today, making him seem like a normal, mortal horse. In fact, the noble steed's teeth were browning and going sharp like an old nag's, showing signs of his age despite his extra pails of alfalfa and constant brushings. Alexander didn't respond. "I wouldn't mind if Susa crumbled to the ground," I continued, "although I will say that spending the winter curled in bed with a pretty slave or two might trump chasing after Darius in this miserable weather. I swear I can barely feel my toes."

Alexander scarcely glanced at me, his brows drawn together over his mismatched blue eyes. "Barsine is pregnant."

I stared at him a moment, then grinned. That explained Alexander's display with her as we were leaving. "It was only a matter of time before the world was rife with little golden-haired terrors just like you."

But Alexander looked more like the corpse at a funeral than a proud father-to-be.

"The child will be illegitimate," he said, stone-faced. "I need an heir, Hephaestion, not a bastard."

"As you said before, there's plenty of time for you to make dozens of heirs."

"Perhaps," he said. "Perhaps I do need to take a wife, and soon."

"Then marry Barsine and be done with it."

Alexander's lips made a bitter twist. "I can't marry a Persian whore, and you well know it."

"One thing at a time." I clapped him on the back, earning an annoyed snort from Ox-Head. "Deal with Darius first and then you can find some pretty girl to make you all the heirs you want."

"Speaking of which," Alexander said, his expression turning suddenly sly, "I won't pretend to understand it, but I've seen the way you look at Darius' youngest daughter, homely though she is. That day in the throne room you looked ready to devour her. She's a far cry from the beauties you usually bed, but shall I make you a gift of her?"

I looked askance at him, grim-faced. "I'd never forgive you if you did."

He laughed and spurred Bucephalus with his heels. Moments later we were racing over Persia's drab winter plains like we had so many times as boys after escaping from Aristotle's droning lessons, no greater care in the world than the wind in our ears. Alexander leaned over Bucephalus' reins while the rest of the Companions hollered after us and struggled to catch up.

That was the last golden day before everything went to Hades.

Persepolis, the richest city under the sun, sent its letter of sur- render to Alexander before we even reached the city, and the Persians threw open the grand Gate of All Nations with its massive sculpted *lamassus*—winged bulls with the heads of bearded men— to allow Alexander entrance into its stunning palace. I'd dreamed of walking the halls of Darius' famed Apadana palace with its eagle- headed columns and porticoes embossed with exquisite carvings of the famed Immortals, whom I found I enjoyed seeing chiseled in stone far more than their screaming flesh-and-blood inspirations on the battlefield. I watched in awe as the entire court bowed to Alex- ander in a wave of perfumed silk, kissing their fingers as if they were greeting Ahura Mazda himself. The *satrap* in his flat-crowned blue hat surrendered 120,000 talents of gold bullion, priceless lapis lazuli plaques, and countless cedar chests of gemstones, so massive a trea- sure that it would take fifteen thousand beasts of burden to carry away the city's vast riches. Yet Alexander didn't even acknowledge the spoils, only marched farther into the palace with a face like one of the many exquisite marble statues being carted away.

I followed him into the Hall of Xerxes with its throngs of aristo- crats waiting to catch a glimpse of their new ruler, but I ignored all the overdressed peacocks, running an appreciative hand over the priceless frescoes showing the famed king stabbing lion-headed demons. A hammered golden plaque bore chiseled inscriptions prais- ing the first Darius' expeditions against Greece in the three tongues of Babylon, Persia, and Elam. Still, Alexander took no notice of the art or the aristocrats waiting to fawn over him, skirting the audience hall's hundred towering pillars and gesturing toward the treasury.

"There's more bullion inside," he told a regiment of Macedonian infantry, many of them slack-jawed at the opulence of Darius' ancient palace. "I want every single last coin melted down to send home to Aigai."

Alexander had an army to pay and feed, but that didn't mean that I was going to forgo the opportunity to stare at one of the great wonders of Darius' empire. I managed to shut my maw, but wandered into the throne room and whistled in reverence at the winged-lion statue rearing up over the dais, its mouth frozen midroar and massive golden paws ready to strike.

"You should build a palace like this in Alexandria," I mused aloud to Alexander. "Or perhaps even in Aigai."

But Alexander was gone, presumably knee-deep in gold bullion in the treasury.

Someone shouted and there came a series of thumps like bodies hitting the ground. On instinct, I drew my sword and the hairs on the back of my neck prickled as they did before battle.

I sniffed the air and panic seized my throat like a Titan's fist.

The acrid smell of smoke made my mouth go numb and every nerve in my body screamed in barely restrained panic.

Four Companions burst then from the Hall of Xerxes, leering in triumph and lugging one of Darius' many golden thrones between them, this one studded with lapis lazuli and emeralds arranged into a stunning *simurgh* raptor. Behind them, tendrils of gray smoke emerged from the hall, curling like claws to rasp at the walls and the ceiling.

Alexander emerged from the treasury, fists on his hips and watching with satisfaction as the smoke grew. The flames crackled with glee as they devoured the frescoes of Xerxes battling demons, their wall of heat searing my very lungs.

"Raze and plunder Persepolis, the most hated city in all of Asia!" Alexander cried, and lifted his hand in the signal to the waiting regiments armed with torches and swords. They streamed like starving locusts from every door of the throne room, headed toward the city's graceful columned terraces and splendid avenues. Statues of Persia's ancient history crashed to the ground—stone wings smashed from sphinxes and crowns obliterated from the heads of kings long since dead. Noblewomen screamed as they watched their husbands, brothers, and fathers being slaughtered, then screamed again as they were claimed by our soldiers as further spoils of war. All the while, more men streamed down the stairs, carrying bolts of shimmering silk and chests of gleaming silver, crates of bullion and armloads of golden bangles and necklaces.

"What in the name of the twelve gods are you doing?" I yelled, grabbing Alexander by the front of his leather cuirass, but he shook me off.

"This city harbored Darius. Let this be a lesson that I shall destroy his empire, city by city and brick by brick if I have to, until he surrenders." His eyes gleamed like one entranced and smoke seemed to roll from his skin. It scraped the back of my throat and dug into my eyes like grains of sand.

Fire. Zeus above, how I hated fire.

"Persepolis surrendered, Alexander," I yelled, hoping my words would shame him even as sweat gathered at my temples and ran down my back. This was the singer Adurnarseh again, only magnified a thousandfold. "This is the act of a tyrant."

Something flared deep in Alexander's blue eyes. "This is an act of vengeance," he said. "A repayment to Persia for their burning of Athens during the Great War and a clear message to Darius. I have finally done what my father set out to do: conquer Persia. Now it's time that Persia learned their lesson so they never rise against us again."

"The sacking of Athens occurred while your grandfathers were still shitting their swaddling clothes," I growled. "This temper tantrum doesn't befit a man who seeks immortality and claims to be a god."

He whirled about, deadly silent as he leaned so close that I could feel the heat of his breath despite the growing flames. "I *am* a god, Hephaestion," he finally said. "You cower there like a woman, ready to piss yourself in the face of a little fire and spilled blood, while I conquer the world."

My fist hit his cheek and he staggered back, looking up at me for a moment like a wounded child. Never before had we traded blows, not even as children. Yet he was no longer a boy, but the most powerful man on earth.

"You've been granted many gifts by the gods," I said, looking down on him from my superior height. "You are meant to build cities, not destroy them. Put out the flames, Alexander."

"It is only because I love you that I don't slay you where you stand," he growled. And then Alexander, my lover and friend, brother and commander, shoved past me so hard that I stumbled back. "Your fear shames you," he said, his voice echoing off the walls. "Run if you wish, away from the flames that so terrify you, but do not dare to speak to me again."

With that, I turned and walked away, forcing my steps into measured paces as the gilded cedar rafters of the Hall of Xerxes crashed to the ground behind me.

CHAPTER 13

Bactria, Persia

ROXANA

"And thus approaches our craven king," Bessus murmured in my ear, his breath hot against my skin. His voluminous green robe was edged with black silk and embroidered with gold thread, his earlobes and every finger bedecked with jasper and onyx rings. The bronze dagger I'd watched him sharpen that morning was now tucked into his vast black *kamarband*.

I gave a sly smile and trailed my fingers down his arm. "All shall be as you wish it."

And then all would be as *I* wished it.

Only days before, Bessus had used the promise of fresh troops to lure Darius to Bactria, for the King of Kings was in desperate need of men to march with him against Alexander. Cowardly Darius was a trusting fool and stumbled headlong into the trap, allowing himself to be imprisoned and taken hostage by Bessus' officers. Now I watched the tense rendezvous from beneath an awning of golden silk, dressed in a new yellow silk gown and matching veil embroidered with tiny stars, calfskin slippers dyed to match, and my beautiful brother at my side. Parizad was resplendent in his own robe the color of freshly churned butter, which denoted his improved position as one of Bessus' bodyguards, a position I'd procured after mastering several of Bessus' favorite positions both in and out of bed. Arms crossed tight against my ribs, I rapped an impatient rhythm along my forearms at Darius' approach, for I knew what was soon to come.

I'd expected Darius to be impressive, but the man who approached between the brandished spears of Bessus' soldiers was haggard as a beggar, his wrists bearing heavy golden manacles instead of sumptuous bangles and his eyes dark and hollow beneath their smudged lines of *sormeh* powder. Only the king's bedraggled purple-striped cloak and Persia's eagle diadem at his brow hinted that he had once been the ruler of the greatest empire on earth. Several soldiers whispered and averted their eyes, their pity for the beaten king apparent in their drawn faces.

I had no pity. Darius' sun had set and Bessus' was rising, with mine alongside it.

"Dear cousin Bessus," Darius said, his voice rasping. He was a tall man despite his bent back, but the chains at his wrists rattled as tremors shook his body. A king should be brave and courageous, but Darius' eyes rolled in their sockets like an animal awaiting slaughter. "What is the meaning of this?" he managed to ask.

"I would have thought that was obvious, cousin." Bessus bent to kiss his fingers in a *proskynesis* due to his king. "You have been tried and found wanting as king. Thus, I relieve you of your burden."

I'd been half the instrument of my mother's death, but I'd never seen a man killed until Bessus raised his dagger against the King of Kings. He hit home with practiced ease, the tip of the dagger neatly piercing the white silk of Darius' robe to plunge between his ribs. Shock slackened the king's face at the quick and underwhelming kill, but my stomach clenched as Bessus' men joined the fray, stabbing Darius again and again, the sounds from a butcher's block while the king brayed like a sacrificial ewe.

"By the gods," Parizad breathed, white-faced. He moved to stop them as Bessus' archers emerged with bolts drawn in case Darius somehow managed to escape. I grabbed my brother's wrist with a tight shake of my head.

"It's too late," I said, thin-lipped and suddenly light-headed. "Bessus is king now."

Parizad whirled on me, horror-struck. "You knew about this?"

"I share Bessus' bed," I said, watching still more soldiers fall upon Darius. "And soon I shall share his throne."

Parizad stared at me, but my fingers threaded through his as Bessus lifted the blood-spattered golden eagle diadem from Darius' brow and placed it on his own head. The old king's white robe was rent to tatters and his chest pockmarked with bloody gouges that seeped wet crimson.

"May you cross the Chinvat Bridge with ease, cousin," Bessus whispered, a grin cleaving his face in two. He leaned down and slit Darius' throat, allowing the feeble king's last breath to escape in a wet hiss.

"Darius is dead," Bessus proclaimed in a line I'd listened to him practice countless times over the past days. "We hereby proclaim ourselves the Great King, King of Kings, Artaxerxes the Fifth!"

For a moment no one dared breathe. I was the first to move, sinking to my knees in a graceful *proskynesis* I'd also rehearsed, my lips curving into a smile before kissing my fingertips. The men around me followed my example, hailing Bessus as their king.

But not all men . . .

"What have you done?" Parizad shrieked next to me. I tried to yank him to the ground, but he shook me off. "You've killed Ahura Mazda's chosen king in cold blood!"

Bessus glanced down at Darius' corpse. "Thank you for pointing that out, boy. Otherwise I might not have noticed."

A rumble of laughter started, but ceased when my brother stepped out from beneath my silken awning. "Do you really think men will follow you, the great murderer of kings? Or shall another *satrap* follow your example, slay you and claim the precious eagle diadem for his own?"

I was already scrambling toward them both. "Great King—," I began, but Bessus pointed his dagger at Parizad, then gave an easy nod to the archers. "Kill him."

"No!" I screamed, falling between Bessus and Parizad, my arms spread in an attempt to stop them both. "Don't hurt him!"

No one moved, but then Bessus flicked a hand.

"Stand down," he ordered, and the archers lowered their quarrels so they were no longer aimed straight for Parizad's stupid, noble heart.

But I was a fool to think Bessus so charitable as to forgive the brother I loved.

With a sharp gleam in his eyes, Bessus removed a helmet from one of the archers and tossed it toward Parizad, where it rolled haphazardly to a stop at his feet. "Since you bear such love for Darius, I charge you with protecting our former king from the marauding *daevas* who will seek out his rotting flesh." He yanked the embroidered bee scarf from my head, tearing away several pins and strands of my hair. "A final gift from your beloved twin," he said, throwing the gleaming scrap of fabric at my brother. "To tie over your nose when Darius' desiccated corpse becomes too rank to breathe!"

A snap of his fingers and a guard unlocked one of Darius' golden fetters and clamped the metal over Parizad's wrist.

I fought then, lunging toward my brother even as soldiers held me back. My love for my twin had spared him a quick execution and instead bought him a lingering death beneath the sun's screaming heat with only a dead king for company. My struggles against the guards made them clasp my arms tighter than Darius' golden manacles, and scalding tears blinded my view of my beautiful, doomed brother.

"Parizad, Parizad," I said, my brother's name tumbling from my lips like a fountain. "Parizad!"

But there was nothing I could say or do to save my stupid, gentle brother. I'd endured whippings, mustard seed poisonings, and even become Bessus' pliant harlot, but Parizad had thrown it all away with a few treasonous words.

And now I would lose him.

"Cease your sniveling," Bessus commanded, grabbing my chin between his thumb and forefinger so tightly that fresh tears sprang to my eyes. "Or I'll slay him where he stands and leave you to mourn his traitorous corpse."

"Go," Parizad whispered from his place in the dust, even as Bessus' men threw Darius' body into a derelict goat cart, dragging my stumbling brother with them.

"I'll stay with you," I said, wrenching my chin away from Bessus.

My beautiful brother shook with terror, but tried to steady his voice. "Go, Roxana, and be a queen."

But Parizad was my other half. Panic welled in my throat, for we had never been apart and now he was abandoning me for a dead man. He had torn out my heart with both his hands, leaving a gaping, bleeding wound in my chest that would never heal.

"But I love you," I whispered.

"And I you," he said, tears spilling down his soft cheeks as he lifted his irons in a gesture of helplessness. "And I swear we'll be together again, if only in paradise."

I wanted to throw my arms around him, but instead forced myself to turn my back on my brother, part of me dying with every step that took me farther from him even as Bessus lumbered to his waiting chariot.

I spared a last glance at Parizad, so tall and so handsome, his nose already beginning to redden under the sun's glare as it had when we were children.

Even if I did become queen, a crown would never fill the place where my heart had been.

Weeks of traveling to the capital of Bactria passed in a blur. I was sentenced to days spent in a lonely oxcart without Parizad at my side and resigned to nights spent bathing Bessus and using my long hair to dry his great folds of flesh before he took me on the ground, the bed, or anywhere he wanted. The people cheered for their newly crowned King of Kings as he approached them draped in an impeccable purple robe and golden cape he'd stolen from Darius' baggage cart. His thick waist was bound by an exquisite girdle woven of golden thread, like a colossal net crafted of the sun's rays. His gilded chariot was blinding, as were the two stunning white horses that pulled the vehicle while a eunuch rode beside him with a screen of goat hide and a bronze fly whisk.

I was carried in a holly-wood sedan several lengths back from Bessus, my wrists circled by golden bracelets topped by lynx head finials glowering with green jade eyes. Tiny golden doves perched on miniature altars dangled from my ears and I wore the finest silk robe I'd ever seen in my life, black as a winter night and embroidered with fearsome griffins. Bessus had promised me even more gold once Alexander was killed, claiming that he would drape my naked body with gold thread and weave gems and coins into my hair before he tumbled me on the floor of his treasury.

I'd wanted gold, pearls, and silk and now I had them in droves, and my own eunuch too, a lithe young man with a lilting voice named Bagoas. He had reputedly pleasured Darius but was taken as part of the spoils from Darius' baggage cart, then reassigned to serve my every whim. He did so with such silent dedication that I imagined myself with a collection of pretty eunuchs one day, far more impressive than a stable of matched horses. Even as Bagoas hooked the dangling doves through my ears, I knew that just weeks ago this largesse would have made me shriek with joy. Yet I would never be happy again, not while the sun bleached my brother's bones.

I would not cry. Not here, in front of the crowd.

Instead I forced myself to smile and nod at the mass of Bactrians until we passed beneath the gate to Bessus' palace. His waiting nobles bowed and thronged behind him in a perfumed current to carry him to his throne room. If I'd been Bessus' queen, I might have been permitted to follow and sit behind a filigreed screen, but as a mere concubine I was expected to wait on Bessus' pleasure in his chambers. Still, Bessus had sent his wives away for safety, two to Persepolis and one to the fortress at Sogdian Rock, so I had his undivided attention here in Bactria.

And I planned to make good use of the opportunity.

I took Bagoas' proffered hand, softer than silk and more lustrous than pearls, and stepped from the sedan with my head held high despite the many stares in my direction. One man in particular, Ariamazes of Sogdiana, had traveled alongside Bessus and leered at me every chance he had.

"I need a moment," I murmured to my guards, then hurried to the nearest alcove before tears of grief and frustration spilled down my cheeks. I'd scarcely leaned my forehead against the cool stone wall when a rough hand grabbed my elbow.

"You seem to have done well for yourself, spreading your legs for Bessus."

I clamped down on my cry of shock to see my father, his bottom teeth thrust forward while his eyes darted from me to the final carts and horses trickling through the palace gate. I could tell he was adding the figures for how much wealth Bessus had accumulated by seizing Darius' baggage train, his beady eyes bulging as he approached the total.

I smoothed the front of my robe, my palms suddenly sweaty. "I *have* done well."

"As well as could be expected," my father said. "For a whore."

That stung more than I cared to admit, but I squared my shoulders. "I have reason to believe that Bessus will soon marry me."

He snorted and waved Bagoas away, making the hump of his shoulder even more misshapen. "You're a fool to think that," he sneered. "Where is your brother?"

I looked past him, willing my eyes to stay dry.

"Dead."

A bolt of shock exploded on his face. "No," he said, shaking his head. And I could see then that, somehow and probably against his will, he'd felt some sort of affection for Parizad, a feeling that had never extended to me.

I almost reached out to comfort him, seeking a father's reassuring embrace—even if Oxyartes was a miserable excuse for a father—and wondering what it would feel like to feel his arms around me.

The fantasy didn't last long.

"Give me those bracelets." His gaze lingered on the golden lynx bracelets and I could well imagine him wiping the drool away with the back of his sleeve.

"No." I clutched them protectively. The courtyard had emptied as everyone followed Bessus, leaving me to fend for myself against my spider of a father.

"You still belong to me without Bessus' wedding girdle around your waist. And you will obey me when I tell you to hand over your pretty bangles."

"So you can melt them down?" I sneered. "Or sell them in the market? Have your foundries not proved as valuable as you'd hoped or have you already squandered all their earnings?"

My father stared at me. "You may spread your legs for the *satrap*—"

"King of Kings," I corrected him. "May you well remember it."

"But you're still just my mealymouthed daughter," he said, pointing a grubby finger in my face. "And you'll obey me or face Mithra's justice."

"I will *not*."

I flinched when his open palm hurled toward my face, then screamed at the unexpected agony in my ear. My hand came away bloodied when I touched the fire in my earlobe, but gold glinted in my father's hand.

My dove earring.

"You filthy, vile whoreson," I started, but recoiled when he lunged toward me again.

"You're a fast learner, Roxana," he said, grinning to reveal sharp teeth as he tucked the earring into the red *kamarband* at his waist. "I taught you well, perhaps too well. This little bauble only begins to cover the loss of my investment in you."

"I'm not an investment!" I screamed, still clutching my ear. "I'm your daughter!"

"You still believe that?" my father scoffed, then spat at my feet, the glob of yellow spittle landing on my hem and quivering atop one of my golden bees. "You're no seed of mine."

"What?"

He grinned, as if he reveled in uttering the words. "Your whore of a mother was born with a barrage of nursemaids to carry away her shit buckets and a pretty betrothal to some pampered noble's son, but she had fleas for brains and spread her luscious white thighs for some stableboy. No one wanted the soiled dove once her belly began to swell, that is, until her desperate father brokered an agreement that I take the empty-headed idiot off his hands along with her weight in gold. He got the better end of the deal, though, for she shat out you and your brother and then turned up her toes."

I sympathized with my mother, for any woman would have been tempted to die at the thought of Oxyartes of Balkh as her husband for the rest of her days.

I looked at him, really *looked* at the man I'd always thought to be my father. "There must have been any number of sewers you might have dropped us down, plenty of midden heaps you might have abandoned us on."

"I thought you might prove useful once you were grown." He leered again. "But even your mother's family knew you for the worthless bastard you are. Your brother might have been something, but you've repaid my generosity with treachery and deceit."

I stared at him, then burst into laughter, the first time I'd laughed since abandoning my brother. Parizad would have whooped with glee to know we hadn't been sired by the rotten seed of Oxyartes of Balkh.

"You beat and whipped us, treated us worse than rabid dogs. You might have been father to the Queen of Queens one day," I said. "But you're dead to me now. I hope you die alone, miserable and neglected."

He moved as if to rip the other earring from my ear, but I raised my voice. "Guards!" I called, sidestepping Oxyartes of Balkh. I tilted my chin like the Queen of Queens as my men snapped into place around me, forming a protective barrier and forcing the spider to let me pass unscathed.

The man who was no longer my father gave me one last festering smile. "Misery and neglect are dreams I share for you, Roxana."

I stormed from the courtyard with my ear still streaming blood. And I vowed in that moment that from this day forward, I needed no one except myself.

Bessus used me hard that night, bending me over a bed of silks and furs to pound into me until tears squeezed from my eyes and I feared he would tear me in two. Afterward, I wrapped a priceless leopard fur around me with trembling hands, breathing in the scent of animal musk.

Pain overwhelmed pain. . . .

"I'm going to miss these little interludes of ours," Bessus said, scratching the mat of hair on his belly as he sat in a chair near the fire, his shaft shrunken and glistening with the clear scrum of his seed.

"Miss them?" I asked, doing my best to sweeten my voice as I knelt before him and laid my head in his lap. He often liked to play with my hair and he did so now, threading his fingers through the dark strands. "But I'm not going anywhere."

"You're going to the fortress at Sogdian Rock," he said. I jerked away, yanking my hair from his hand.

"What?"

"My third wife has family nearby and is already there for safe-keeping until I've dealt with Alexander." Bessus spread his naked legs and slouched farther in the chair. "Your father suggested that I send you as well."

I opened my mouth to inform him that Oxyartes of Balkh was *not* my father, but promptly snapped it shut. Oxyartes was the poorest of nobles and a worthless man to claim as a sire, but the other option was to admit that my true father had been a callus-handed and manure-footed stableboy. Bessus' wives were all his cousins with illustrious pedigrees stretching back to at least King Xerxes. A stableboy's misbegotten bastard could never be Queen of Queens.

I would remain the daughter of Oxyartes of Balkh, even if it threatened to kill me.

And yet, I wondered what he stood to gain from sending me to the ends of the empire.

I crossed my arms beneath my breasts. "I refuse to go."

One corner of Bessus' lips tilted in a half smile and he placed a finger on my lips. "I've always admired your tenacity, Roxana, but you have no say in the matter. Truth be told, I've become attached to you and would be quite inconvenienced if anything were to happen to you."

I held perfectly still, stunned by his announcement. I harbored no tender feelings for Bessus, but it occurred to me then that there were two sides to the king before me, that beneath the conniving power-monger who had left my brother to die was also the man who had seen fit to relieve me from my father's house after he'd discovered my whipping and now claimed to care for me. "You leave in the morning," Bessus continued, "but the eunuch Bagoas shall accompany you. No man shall touch you until I return to claim you."

"And you *will* reclaim me?"

"Of course." He stood and pulled me toward him, one fat finger tracing the top of the leopard fur along my breast, his finger darting beneath to jab my nipple. "Now let's see that beautiful body of yours one last time before you leave."

I let him push the fur away, his member stiffening once again from within its tangled nest of dark hair, but my mind had already flown to Sogdian Rock.

The fortress was a veritable city reputedly balanced on sheer rock three miles in the air, impenetrable to all who tried to scale its walls. The marauding Greeks would never take the mountain citadel, and I'd have to fight Bessus' third wife for the queen's diadem.

Oxyartes had made his move. He might have won this battle, but somehow, I would win the war.

I'd have rather stayed in a cavern filled with snarling cave bears than in Sogdian Rock.

We were removed on our desolate mountaintop in the sky, iso-lated from all things save the ever-howling wind that threatened to drive us all mad. Few dared make the ascent up the narrow trail to the citadel's single set of iron gates, so high that the clouds obscured the world below. I'd have been richer than a queen if I had a copper coin for every perfumed refugee who whimpered that she would never leave this place alive. The only contact with the outside world was the occasional far-off groan of a wagon at the base of the cliffs, bearing another *satrap*'s wife or the rare letter from some noble to his wife or children, its news of the campaign against Alexander shared aloud by a eunuch, as none of us women or even the soldiers knew how to read.

Bessus never wrote. As the days turned to weeks and the weeks to months, I no longer knew what I was. I was fifteen, no maiden but no wife, neither daughter nor mother, only the discarded and neglected mistress of the King of Kings.

"The daughter of Oxyartes," Bessus' fat wife had announced when I'd arrived. Her hair was the stark black that came from countless rinsings of *amla* and black walnut hulls and her cheeks were jowly as that of a gray-snouted bitch. I'd prepared for the meeting at least a hundred times in my head, how I'd look down my nose at her and throw my hair over my shoulder, letting her jealousy take full root as she saw for herself my pert breasts and trim waist, the sheen of my glorious hair and my plump lips. Instead, the rain had lashed my face so I squinted from the rivulets of water running from my bedraggled hair, and I could hardly straighten from the stitch in my side from the climb up the cliff, leaning on Bagoas like a cane as I finally hobbled inside the torchlit citadel. "I'd expected my husband to have better taste," she had said, "but it appears he'll rut with anything that moves these days. This one still has the stench of a brothel about her."

Before I could answer, she turned and walked away, leaving her attendants to follow like a gaggle of dumb goslings after a waddling goose while I sputtered with rage.

"Ignore her," Bagoas murmured. My pretty eunuch removed a musty-smelling shawl from my lone chest and wrapped it around my shivering shoulders. "The gift of your beauty sets you apart. Men may love you for it, but other women never will."

I glared after them but said nothing, for Bagoas was right. Let them hate me, for I'd ensure that they rotted away here on this godforsaken rock when I was the Queen of Queens.

Still, had Bessus' wife not been such a hateful bitch, we might have lived in a silent truce, ignoring each other's existence. Instead, she exerted her influence to ensure that none of the other women would speak to me save to call me jade or whore, Astarte's daughter, or a she-wolf. The soldiers were simple creatures deprived of physical relief for too long and at first, believing I was for sale, they pulled me into darkened doorways for a quick grope and asked how much I charged for a tumble. They sang a different song when Bagoas presented them with an imperial seal from Bessus, claiming me as his own and ordering that I be housed with all the comforts the fortress had to offer.

Meager comforts they were, what with the frigid drafts that blew between the door cracks and meals of gray sludge that had once been barley and dried meat, probably horse.

If Bessus lost on the battlefield . . .

He couldn't lose.

We had news that Alexander was on the move. I prayed for someone to stab, spear, or behead him so Bessus would reclaim me and I could once again travel in my holly-wood palanquin and drape myself in rippling silks and shimmering gold. Here I had only Bagoas for companionship and I spent the endless days allowing him to brush my long hair and massage almond oil into my hands.

"Your beauty is wasted on this godforsaken rock," he said with a sigh one afternoon as he coiled a plait around my head. The length and the thickness of my hair were too much for me to manage alone, so Bagoas sewed my hair into place each morning. All the love and adoration I'd showered on Parizad I now gave to my secondhand eunuch, recognizing in him the loneliness I felt every time I thought of my twin. I'd even allowed Bagoas to sleep next to me on my mattress stuffed with musty old hay, the warmth of his back pressed against mine reminding me of Parizad when we were children.

Bessus had claimed that no man could touch me while I was at

Sogdian Rock, but Bagoas was no man, castrated in his youth so his voice trilled as high as a girl's, while his face remained as smooth as an infant's. And while Bagoas could never truly be my lover, one night his warm hands caressed first the small of my back and then my breasts, my thighs and then the damp cleft between my legs, making me feel an exquisite, trembling pleasure I'd never known existed.

And I wanted that pleasure. I *ached* for it.

I could well understand why Darius had kept Bagoas as a pillow slave, as he'd teased me until my back arched and I wrapped my legs around him, yearning for him to fill me as he never truly could and gasping when his fingers slipped inside me instead. It was he who taught me how to caress the insides of a man's thighs and make him moan with pleasure, how to trail my tongue along his earlobe in a way that sent him shuddering.

My beauty was like ambrosia, so sweet a nectar that not even a eunuch could avoid its heady allure.

"If Bessus doesn't hurry and win this fight, I might well die of boredom," I said to Bagoas as he finished sewing the last of my braids into place with his nimble fingers. "The soldiers are growing bolder; the ones who think Bessus will lose ogle me like a naked slave on the auction block."

"The men here are common soldiers who spit and defecate like animals," Bagoas said with a sniff. "We aren't meant for such beasts."

I knew that one soldier in particular—a man set to guarding Bessus' queen—had treated Bagoas worse than a beast, bending him over and using him as a woman while his friends cheered him on. I'd bullied the story from Bagoas after he limped to my dark room with his normally pristine robe askew. If it had been any other soldier, I might have stormed out and threatened retribution when Bessus came to reclaim me, but my threats would be worthless against Bessus' wife. Instead, I'd lain with Bagoas in the dark that night and sang to him as Parizad had sometimes done to comfort me, but after that, Bagoas had lost what little of his smile he still possessed.

"Save your beauty for Bessus," he said. "At least for now."

"And if Bessus loses?"

Bagoas tilted my chin so he could kiss my forehead. "Pray that he doesn't. It won't be long either way." He pinned my veil so that the ebony of my hairline showed in perfect contrast to the orange silk. "There's word that Alexander has swung north into Bactria, ostensibly chasing Bessus. He set fire to his wagons of spoils in order to travel faster and ordered his men to cast off all their loot, although he was benevolent enough to allow them to keep their Persian concubines. Satibarzanes of Aria rebelled, but Alexander used naphtha to set aflame the wooded hill where the Persians camped, burning the soldiers alive before marching onto Satibarzanes' capital of Artacoana, slaughtering and enslaving the town. Of course, the new town built on its remains will be called Alexandria Ariana."

I listened with only half an ear, for Bagoas often chattered and gossiped about the war like a girl twittering about a well-muscled stableboy. I knew nothing of Alexander's movements, nor did I care. Instead, I plaited three scarlet ribbons together to add as a trim along the neckline of my robe.

And then a wail of grieving rent the air like an eagle's talons.

The hair on my arms stood on end and a tremor of foreboding trailed down my spine, but I shook off my unease. Messengers often delivered unwelcome news of some noble's death in combat.

But this time countless mouths picked up the mourning wail so that it grew and echoed throughout the stone citadel until I could scarcely hear my own thoughts. I dropped the ribbons, but Bagoas was already at the door. "I'll see what happened," he said, slamming it before I could argue.

If Alexander was dead, it would mean that Bessus would soon

reclaim me. But no one here at Sogdian Rock would caterwaul in such a manner for the Macedonian lion. If Bessus was dead—

I'd have better luck hurtling myself from the ramparts than facing the soldiers outside.

Bagoas returned before I imagined too many versions of half-starved Persians pushing me into corners. He slammed the door behind him and my heart plummeted when he slid the feeble lock into place.

"Which brave Persian has fallen in battle this time?" I asked him, feigning cheerfulness as I picked up the scarlet ribbons with trembling hands. "He must have been well loved to cause such a racket."

"Bessus has been captured," Bagoas said evenly. "He is being put on trial for his crimes against Darius."

"What? How can the King of Kings be put on trial?"

"His own men abandoned him as Alexander approached. They left him naked and bound to a wooden collar on the side of the road for the Macedonians to find."

"Alexander will kill him," I said with grim awareness.

Bagoas nodded slowly, as if he was afraid that admitting the truth might somehow cause me to shatter. "He may have already done so."

The scream built at the back of my throat and exploded like an eagle's shriek. My hairpins went flying and I ripped my perfectly coiled braids loose from Bagoas' careful stitches, falling to my knees and beating the cold flagstones with my ineffectual fists. I raged and sobbed for all I had lost, for with Bessus would die my dream of being queen, of being anyone other than the bastard daughter of no one knew whom, abandoned by my dead brother and unwanted even by hunchbacked Oxyartes of Balkh.

Only once I was spent did Bagoas lift me from the floor and spread me on my poor excuse of a bed. I let him undress me and soothe me with his caresses, tears still seeping from the corners of my eyes until his lips kissed them away. "Your life isn't over, Roxana," he murmured, his voice like the purr of a dove as he lay down beside me. "We are survivors. No matter what happens, we keep our head above water."

"Like rats on a sinking ship," I said, feeling his chuckle reverberate up my spine.

"Like rats on a sinking ship," he agreed.

CHAPTER 14

330 BCE
Pella, Macedon

THESSALONIKE

Sweat dripped down the backs of my legs, pooled inside the wool *strophion* that bound my breasts, and threatened to blind me (as if my helmet didn't do that enough already) as Cynnane came at me like a she-demon freshly released from the depths of Tartarus.

"Again," she cried, hefting her sword overhead. "Faster—guard up—angle your shield—*again!*"

I was so intent on not taking a sword to my ribs that I didn't notice we were being watched until a woman clapped her hands, breaking us apart.

"Your games are finished for today," Olympias announced. "We must discuss Antipater."

Olympias' rare and unexpected visit should have soured my stomach, but the fact that my arms were about to fall off made me almost grateful. I tossed my blade to the ground and glanced beyond the gurgling fountain where Arrhidaeus and Adea played with her latest litter of kittens and my aging orange tomcat. Cassander waited at the courtyard's entrance, ostensibly to begin my lessons on Plato's endorsement of philosopher kings or something equally dreadful. Antipater's son was scarcely out of earshot and he stood rigid as always, as if bracing himself against the unpleasant chore that was his life.

Perhaps there was one benefit to Olympias' presence, for if she stayed long enough, I might weasel my way out of whatever lecture he had planned for today.

"Cassander!" I relished his flinch, which I knew by now was no gesture of surprise but instead a reaction to a woman raising her voice louder than the coo of a dove. "Fetch us wine. And glasses too."

I settled back in my leather-slung chair, watching the apple of his throat work hard as he swallowed his lecture about the impropriety of sending a nobleman's son several years my senior to do the work of a kitchen slave. Instead he gave a tight bow under Olympias' watchful eye and left the courtyard. If he were anyone else, I'd know to look for spit in the wine I'd ordered, but I doubted whether such a crass insult would ever occur to Cassander.

"What has Antipater done this time to displease you?" Cynnane scarcely looked up as she kicked the heels of her Macedonian silver-studded boots onto the wooden table. She unbuckled the clasps on her greaves and let them fall to the ground with a clatter, ignoring a look from Olympias that might have chilled the fires of Mount Etna.

"Antipater has grown too powerful since he quelled the Agis revolt in Sparta," Olympias said, her lips drawn tight as a rope as she crossed her arms over her chest, the sardonyx cameo of herself and her son winking at her throat. "Alexander agrees that Antipater's power must be checked."

I recalled my brother's most recent letter, his pen stroke so heavy that it had indented the parchment when he claimed that while he had been conquering King Darius, a battle among mice had broken out on the Peloponnese. My brother was accustomed to being obeyed and adored, both at home and abroad, and the tone of his letter had swung between anger and sulking.

"And how do you propose to check Antipater?" Cynnane asked with a brusque chuff of laughter. "Raise an army?"

I chuckled along with her, but fell silent as Olympias leveled her cold glare at me.

"I will welcome that day when it comes," she said to Cynnane. "Unfortunately, the time isn't yet ripe for us to meet on the battlefield."

Because try as she might, the Macedonian army was loyal first to Alexander and next to Antipater, its aged general and regent.

"But Antipater defers to Alexander in everything," Cynnane said. "Even when Alexander proclaimed the Spartans could keep their freedom after their revolt, despite the Macedonian blood they'd spilled."

"Still, the soldiers love Antipater," I said. I knew this because I'd lost count of the times Cassander had bemoaned the injustice of being relegated to instructing me when he might have been learning diplomacy and military leadership at his father's elbow.

"All the more reason that Antipater is a threat," Olympias maintained. "He pretends contentment as Alexander's subordinate, but that is the facade of a patient man biding his time. Alexander still has no heir and it falls to me to protect his interests at home in his absence. I'd prefer to see Antipater slain, his body burned and his ashes poured into a funerary chest, but the army would decry the execution of its leader."

"So," Cynnane repeated, "what shall you do?"

"I go at once to Epirus, to my brother's palace."

"Alexander of Molossia?" I asked.

"An excellent deduction, Thessalonike," she said, closing her eyes and pressing her middle finger to her forehead as if pushing away an ache there. "Considering that I have only one brother."

Cynnane clasped her hands behind her head. "But you haven't been on speaking terms with your brother since he abandoned you in your exile in Epirus."

Just before the wedding that had set my father on the path to be murdered in his arena.

"I haven't spoken with my dear brother since then, nor shall I ever," Olympias said, examining the heavy emerald rings on her hand. "For he's dead."

Cynnane set her feet on the ground and brushed back her frizz of hair. "You have my condolences."

Olympias waved away her words. "My brother was never going to amount to anything. He trundled off to Pandosia to become a hero against the Lucanians and found himself instead skewered by one of their spears in the heat of the battle. So now I must travel to Epirus to honor what little is left of him."

Cynnane and I exchanged a frown. "What do you mean," she asked Olympias, "what's left of him?"

Olympias snorted. "The Lucanians wished to make an example of him and cut him in half. They pelted one side with stones and javelins until almost nothing remained."

She spoke as if describing the menu for tonight, but my gorge rose at the very thought. I'd hardly known Alexander of Molossia, but no man's body deserved such desecration. "But there will be no rituals for your brother," I said, swallowing hard. "No *prothesis* to ready his body or procession to honor him. Surely a man fallen in battle deserves more. . . ."

I let the thought hang, for if my brother Alexander fell in battle, I knew that Olympias would demand his body be returned to Macedon preserved in a coffin of the clearest honey so she might prepare his body and consign him to the flames herself.

"A woman stumbled upon the execution and asked for the rest of my brother so that she might ransom her husband and children, who had been sent back to Epirus." Olympias yawned. "I've no need for my brother's worthless bones—and only half of them at that— but my infantile brother left our cousin Aeacidas as his heir. The boy is still a child."

"So you shall leave for Epirus," I said slowly, fitting all the pieces together. "And rule in your cousin's place?"

Leaving me in Pella without Olympias' constant surveillance. The very thought made me feel as if Atlas' burden had been lifted from my shoulders.

Olympias patted my hand like I was a doddering old crone, then rose regally to her feet. "Antipater will believe we are going to mourn my brother, but in fact, I shall rule as Aeacidas' regent while we consolidate our power, waiting for the right time to strike."

"*We?*" Cynnane asked, sitting up straighter.

"You would both prove valuable assets for Antipater's ambitions," Olympias said, her eyes narrowing dangerously. "Surely you're not proposing you remain here, vulnerable to his many plots and schemes?"

I waited for Cynnane to protest, for she was less vulnerable than the hunter goddess Artemis with her gleaming bow and immaculate aim, but my half sister's eyes only flicked to where Adea fed daisies to my shaggy goat, having abandoned the cats. Both Adea and Arrhidaeus squealed as Pan munched the early blossoms, her hairy lips tickling Adea's fingers. Cynnane had filled my ears with colorful curses about the trouble of having to leave her own estate when she'd first relocated to Pella's palace, but I'd caught her amused smile on more than one occasion as she watched Adea play with Arrhidaeus during our training sessions. Cynnane's own husband had fallen on his sword for Alexander's and Olympias' ambitions; I knew she'd protect Adea with her very life.

"Of course not," Cynnane said, answering Olympias' barbed smile with one of her own.

"Be ready to travel within the week." Olympias lifted the hem of her flawless *peplos* and stepped over Cynnane's discarded greaves, then swept away from the courtyard, leaving us aghast.

Cynnane sighed and thrust her long legs out in front of her, her *chiton* barely reaching the tops of her knees. "Your wish is my command, Olympias," she muttered.

"I'm still not sure why she wants to take us with her," I said, frowning at my blurred reflection as I polished my sword with the hem of my *chiton*.

"Because she can't have Philip's warrior daughters throw their support behind Antipater's army," Cynnane answered. "She might intend to marry us off for convenient alliances, or at least keep Antipater from doing the same. Olympias can scheme all she likes, but not even a sword at my throat will induce me to marry again. Being widowed once was more than enough."

It was difficult to imagine anyone, even Olympias, holding a sword at Cynnane's throat. I, on the other hand, was fifteen, a ripe age for marriage, an idea toward which I was still ambivalent. Cynnane had been a wife, a mother, *and* a warrior, proving that a woman could combine the seemingly irreconcilable domains of Hera, Demeter, and Athena. Marriage would free me from Olympias, but might saddle me to a man who was even more domineering.

Perhaps a man whose presence I suffered through each day . . .

"I can think of one good that shall come of this trip," I said, damping down the smile that threatened to spread across my face.

"That's one more than I can think of," Cynnane said. "What might that be?"

I jutted my chin toward Cassander as he returned with the wine and a tray of clay cups. He stopped directly in front of me, so close that I could smell the mint on his breath. After all, Cassander could never upset the natural order of the world with something as heinous as less than perfect breath.

"You took so long that we're not thirsty anymore," I said. He looked ready to dump the *amphora* of wine on my head, but I had good news for the both of us. Olympias had turned on Antipater and thus, surely she wouldn't wish his son lurking about where he might spy on us.

"I'm pleased to inform you that we're finally free from the torture of each other's company," I said. "I travel with Olympias to Epirus this week and therefore shall no longer require your services as my tutor."

Nor would I require his commentary on my unconventional behavior, the way I styled my hair, or how I shouldn't count my scars and bruises the way most women did their pearls and bangles.

Cynnane arched an eyebrow at me. I glanced up to find Cassander still standing there, as if baffled by the fact that no one wanted him.

"You're free," I said, waving an impatient hand. "You can return to your father's house, roam the streets, or take up residence in a whorehouse for all I care. May the gods keep you."

"May they keep you as well," he answered by rote, his eyes widening in an expression akin to Heracles' relief after cleansing the Augean stables of the dung accumulated from one thousand immortal cattle.

Not that I cared to equate myself to thirty years of animal dung, but I felt the same about him.

Cassander turned on his heel and left the courtyard with what might have been described as a jaunty step, ostensibly to return to his boor of a father and while away his days memorizing his even duller collection of books.

Whereas I would finally leave Macedon to journey to the mountains of Epirus, something I'd only ever dreamed about. Yet visiting Epirus under Olympias' shadow was worse than waking in the golden Fields of Elysium with a fanged viper wrapped around one's throat.

I'd have to tread carefully, lest the viper strike at my first misstep.

We might have traveled overland to Epirus, but Olympias decreed instead that she wished to skirt the coast aboard a string of red-oared biremes carrying everything our entourage would require for a lengthy stay to bury and mourn Alexander of Molossia.

Yet I'd peered into one of the many crates on the dock and found neither silks nor jewels nor even her collection of slithering snakes, but instead hundreds of neatly stacked and gleaming swords.

"A queen must always guard her resources," Olympias said as she pressed the box closed, nearly shutting it on my fingers. "Our foundries shall not make weapons for Antipater to use against us."

And so we would sail down Pella's narrow inlet into the Thermaic Gulf and around the Peloponnese, docking along the way to view the glories of Athens, Corinth, and Sparta. I suspected that Olympias' true motive for our travel by sea was to allow the opportunity for her to reinforce support for Alexander while drawing it away from Antipater, but she might have schemed to dance naked on the Parthenon's roof and I wouldn't have cared. And although we weren't marching directly into battle, for the first time, I was going to peer beyond Macedon's hills, to smell the briny ocean air and see myriad wonders that I'd only ever visited in my daydreams.

It was enough, at least for now.

"Can we fish?" Arrhidaeus asked me, leaning over the railing of the largest ship. "I brought my hooks and worm pail."

I patted him on the shoulder, then leaned my head there. "Just be careful you don't hook a *tonno* so big that it pulls down the ship."

I felt a gentle tug on my hand and glanced down to see Adea gazing up at me with big brown eyes. "Will you play with me, Nike?" she asked, jostling a leather bag I knew to be full of carved wooden animals. Her other crate contained smaller versions of Cynnane's Illyrian swords and shields, for her mother had already started training her in swordplay, just as Adea would one day train her daughter.

"I'd be happy to, little one," I said, dropping a kiss on her forehead. "Can Aristomache play too if she promises not to eat the mice?"

"Yes," she chirped, opening the bag and riffling through it before offering Arrhidaeus an oaken fish, slightly irregular around the tail where she'd chewed on it while teething as a baby. "Here's your favorite," she said to him. I felt a pang as she withdrew a painted goat figurine, for I'd left Pan behind to eat her fill of juniper and gorse bushes in our absence. My cat and the kittens too had been left behind, for it seemed a cruel torture to confine them to a wooden ship for several weeks.

I released Aristomache from her basket and let her slither about on the deck of the ship, the sunshine gleaming off her brown scales. "We may not get to see Egypt and Persia," I murmured to my pet snake, picking her up, "but this is a start." Her dull black eyes seemed to gleam with happiness even as heavy footsteps walked up the gangplank. "Cynnane," I said, straightening. "You're just in time—"

But it wasn't Cynnane.

"Medusa's snakes!" I cursed at Cassander. "What are you doing here?"

And then I saw the blanket roll and the pack he carried. He was outfitted like a common soldier embarking on an extended campaign.

"No," I said, shaking my head while Adea and Arrhidaeus gaped. "Not you too . . ."

Cassander wore the scowl of an executioner as he strode aboard and set down his pack. "Olympias informed my father that my services were still required and requested that I accompany your family. You lied about my dismissal, Thessalonike."

"I didn't lie," I said. "I only *hoped* that you were dismissed."

It was rude, but I didn't care. Now I'd have grim-faced Cassander lurking in my shadow while I climbed to the Parthenon to visit Athena's famed statue and explored Corinth's wondrous Temple of Apollo. Cassander would likely lecture me on both, droning on like an obnoxious wasp in my ear.

Why had Olympias commanded that Cassander accompany us, especially as she sought to draw support away from Antipater and raise her own army?

And then I knew.

Cassander was a hostage, although I guessed he didn't realize it, at least not yet. I almost felt sorry for him then, for he was merely another powerless pawn in Olympias' game. But then, weren't we all?

"There aren't enough cabins for you to have your own room," I said. "You can share with Arrhidaeus or sleep on deck with the rowers."

Arrhidaeus grinned at that. Despite my best attempts to persuade my brother that Cassander was as enjoyable as a brick wall, Arrhidaeus fawned over Cassander. I told myself that was only because he missed Alexander and Hephaestion.

"Shall we fish tonight, Arrhidaeus?" Cassander asked him, and I knew then that I'd lost. I turned my back on them and settled in to play animals with Adea, letting Aristomache slither back onto the deck, where she wrapped herself loosely around a tiny cedar elephant.

"I wish I could strangle someone too," I murmured to my snake.

I stalked off from Cassander in high dudgeon, but I soon forgot my pique as the bireme found its first heavy swells.

"I want to die," I moaned in my dark cabin, eliciting a chuckle and a perfunctory pat on my head from Cynnane.

"No one ever died from a sour stomach," she said. "We'll be on deck if you decide to join us for grilled fish and shrimp."

"I'd rather swallow rusty nails," I said, throwing an arm over my head and willing the world to stop swaying. I'd taken ill almost as soon as Pella had slipped from view amid the blue sky and cavorting porpoises. Thus far I'd offered Poseidon several impromptu sacrifices from my stomach until it was wrung dry, yet it somehow still churned like sea waves in a storm.

"Chewing mint settles Adea's stomach when she's ill or I've trained her too hard," Cynnane mused. "Perhaps we can fetch some when we next go ashore."

The door closed, leaving me to die in darkness on my hard little pallet.

Mint.

Cassander chewed mint.

"Cynnane," I moaned as loud as I could, hoping she'd fetch the herb, but she was already gone.

Even in my present agony, I wouldn't ask Cassander for anything. Still, I wasn't above stealing a few leaves from his pack.

I dragged myself from my pallet, wrinkling my nose at the fetid smell that followed me. Arrhidaeus' tiny cabin was across the empty corridor, and so cramped I had no idea how both he and Cassander would stretch out to sleep.

The door creaked as I opened it, but Cassander was sitting on his pallet. He hastily folded the letter he'd been writing and shoved it into his pack.

"What are you doing here?" he demanded.

"I was looking for Arrhidaeus," I lied, but the ground beneath my bare feet rolled and I clutched the doorframe. "Do you have mint?" I asked. "It's for my stomach."

I expected him to refuse or at least taunt me, but Cassander took one look at my disheveled state and retrieved a paper bundle from his pack.

"Thank you," I said, grabbing the precious leaves and leveling him with as haughty a glare as I could muster when he pulled them back.

"I'll give it to you," he said, "in exchange for information."

"I'm in no condition—," I started, but stopped when he opened his mouth as if to eat the leaves himself. "What information?"

"What is Olympias up to?" he asked, gesturing above deck with the mint. "Everyone knows she doesn't care two drachmas for her brother, yet now she's relocating her entire court to the other side of Greece to mourn him? It doesn't make any sense."

"She is a dutiful sister," I said, pushing the words between my gritted teeth.

"She *is* dutiful," Cassander agreed. "But only when it comes to protecting her son."

"Are you writing to your father?" I asked, to change the subject, jerking my chin toward his half-finished letter. "Did he tell you to make good use of your time and spy on us?"

"My father is no fool," Cassander said. "And neither am I."

"Then I'm confident you can figure out all of Olympias' plans on your own," I said. "And be sure when you do to share that information with me."

I turned to leave, but Cassander cleared his throat.

"You forgot your mint," he said, tossing me the packet and popping the other leaves into his mouth. I caught the precious bundle and turned again to stumble back to my cabin, making it to the copper basin Cynnane had left for me just before I made Poseidon yet another offering.

With any luck, it wasn't mint that Cassander had just given me, but an expeditious poison to put me out of my misery.

I survived that night and the next, but barely. When we docked in Piraeus' harbor, I went ashore and clutched fistfuls of loamy earth, nearly weeping at the solid ground beneath me. Crowds of curious onlookers had assembled to gawk at our purple sails and cheer for the royal family of Alexander. Olympias had already disembarked, forgoing the trip to the Acropolis so she might meet with the city's archon. Cynnane planned to visit a nearby temple to Metis with Adea and Arrhidaeus, but Cassander had insisted that he accompany me to Athena's famed temple. I planned to ride from the port to Athens, but found myself so weakened from lack of food and illness that I struggled to mount the modest mare that waited for me. I colored to the roots of my hair when Cassander knelt, allowing me to use his knee as a step.

"Thank you," I muttered, but he didn't answer as I arranged myself in the saddle, save to incline his head before mounting his own horse. I patted my pocket to ensure that the tiny vial of olive oil was still there, my offering to Athena today as we visited her famous statue. Apollo had driven his sun chariot halfway across the sky by the time we reached the base of the Acropolis and dismounted. My guards cut through the swath of grumbling politicians, yawning slaves, and bare-headed pilgrims by bellowing out my titles, but only halfway up the gravel path, I cursed my shortness of breath even as I marveled at the new sights around me.

A patchwork cat meandered among the olive trees on the rocky white slopes and I paused to rub her chin, relishing her purr as I caught my breath while my guards hung back. "It's a pleasant day to visit the Acropolis," Cassander said, directing his gaze at the rocky precipice as I rubbed a painful stitch from my side. "Aristotle often had us meet here to sit and discuss political theory in the shade of Pericles' achievements."

"You do realize how pretentious that sounds, don't you?" I said, taking my steps more slowly with the excuse of peering down at the columned Odeon, roofed with timbers taken from captured Persian ships and home of the world's finest musical competitions. The stray cat followed until I finally picked her up to stop her rubbing against my legs as if I carried dead birds in my pockets.

"It's not pretentious if it's a fact," Cassander said. "Any more than you draping yourself in your brother's gold is pretentious."

"I don't drape myself in Alexander's gold," I said, even as the cat batted at the pearl necklace around my throat. "I prefer cats and pearls instead."

I caught what might have been a smirk or a smile flit across his face as I set the cat back on solid ground. We walked in silence the remainder of the way until the hill leveled and opened to the rocky platform dedicated to Athena. The olive tree that the goddess had given the city spread its branches as if to clutch the rags of blue sky overhead. The white marble temple gleamed like a building stolen from Mount Olympus and I was too slack-jawed to protest as my guards ushered out worshippers laden with offerings of fruit and flowers.

"It's beautiful," I whispered.

I moved forward as if in a trance, drawn beyond the smoking altars alight with incense and into the empty sanctuary to gaze in wonder at Athena's ivory statue. The goddess of wisdom was clad in a *peplos* of flowing gold and wore a sphinx- and griffin-headed helm instead of a crown. She brandished her customary long-spear in one hand, while her owl-emblazoned shield waited discarded at her feet.

She reminded me of Cynnane, except that the goddess' hair curled in perfect ringlets around her face instead of a mass of kinks and tangles to rival Medusa's snakes.

"Just the chance to behold her is a treasure far greater than any gold," Cassander murmured next to me. There was no one else in the temple, so even his low voice seemed to echo off the ceiling. "It's something you've longed for, isn't it?"

I could only nod.

"And," he said, pointing toward Athena's outstretched hand, "she's holding your namesake."

I smiled against my will, for Athena held the winged goddess Nike in her palm.

"Your brother seems blessed by the goddess of victory," Cassander said, "yet he bypasses wonders such as these or, worse, destroys them as he did in Persepolis. I wonder how much time will pass before Nike withholds her gifts from Alexander?"

I should have known that Cassander would find a way to mar even this moment with his moral platitudes.

"Go away," I commanded, the earlier levity we'd shared suddenly dashed to pieces. I wished Athena would smite him where he stood. "Your dour tidings aren't welcome."

He looked about to speak, but instead bowed his head and backed toward the entrance, leaving me to scowl after him.

I didn't care to admit that Cassander's words troubled me, that I'd wondered the same morose thoughts sometimes as I drifted off to sleep. However, instead of leaving the olive oil for Athena, I laid it at the altar of Nike's nearby temple when no one was looking.

"Spread your wings over Alexander and keep him safe," I beseeched my namesake. "If only to spite Cassander."

For although I hadn't seen Alexander in more than five years, I couldn't imagine a world without him.

I loved Epirus' town of Cassope the moment I laid eyes upon it. The stark white city clung to the edge of the southeast cliff of the Zalongo Mountain as if daring the very winds to shake the entire city loose from its moorings. The picturesque city was famed for its Molussus hounds, the massive, long-nosed, shaggy dogs that fiercely guarded their flocks from wolves and thieves. We'd been in Cassope only a week before I had a pack of the beauties to claim as my own.

Olympias made short work of assuming the position of regent for her young cousin after her brother's desecrated body was finally laid to rest in the family tomb. Less than one week after our arrival, she sent word that I would skip my afternoon sparring exercises with Cynnane and accompany her to the city's coin forges instead.

Not a request, but a command.

"Cassander will think I've been kidnapped if I'm gone too long," I said, my hounds running along the path as I walked with her to the mint, one of the columned buildings that branched off the town's *agora*. My loss wouldn't trouble him, but losing me to brigands or rebels would mean that he'd be unable to finish yesterday's lecture on the great war against Persia, a tragedy from which he might never recover.

"I sent word to Antipater's son that you would be with me," Olympias said, stopping to straighten the pomegranate-topped pin that secured my *himation* around my shoulders. "Has he offered to marry you yet?"

I gaped, then sputtered. "Marry me?"

She arched an eyebrow, then gave a dainty sniff. "I assume not."

She turned and left me to scuttle after her into the coin forge, the smell of molten metal making me wrinkle my nose. "Why would you think Cassander would propose?" I asked, motioning for all the dogs to wait outside. They sat on their haunches without protest, better behaved than I'd likely ever be.

"Because Antipater hopes for a union between our families to guarantee his continued power," she said, ignoring the coin smiths as they scrambled to bow before her. "He believes himself to be Alexander's regent and his successor too, should my son fail to produce an heir."

"So I should rebuff Cassander," I said. That would be the first simple task Olympias had set me to.

But Olympias shook her head. "Far from it," she said. "You will encourage him in every way possible."

"What?"

But now it was I whom Olympias ignored. She nodded indulgently at the eldest of the coin smiths as he rose, white-haired and with hands more scarred than not. "You honor us with your presence," the man said. "It isn't often that the ruling house deigns to visit us."

"An error I seek to rectify," Olympias said, gifting him with a rare smile. "I wish to see how the coins I've ordered are progressing."

The smith snapped his mottled fingers and an apprentice hurried forward bearing a small wooden chest. Copper coins gleamed when he opened the box, freshly minted and slightly irregular from their stamping. Olympias plucked one from the trove and turned it over in her palm, her smile widening with unadulterated pleasure as she handed it to me.

"A thunderbolt and a wreath," I said, placating her as I inspected the other side. "And a thunderbolt on a shield."

"The three symbols of the Molossians, Chaonians, and Thesprotians," Olympias said. "This one coin shall unite all three Epirean city-states."

"Making Epirus a power to rival even that of Macedon," I said. "A threat at Antipater's back door."

Not for the first time I yearned for the simple life I'd built for myself back in Pella, sparring with Cynnane and fishing with Arrhidaeus. Against my will, Olympias had dragged me back into a royal's world of backstabbing politics.

She nodded. "It's a threat which shall either goad Antipater into action or terrorize him into inaction."

"But I still don't understand why you wish me to encourage Cassander," I said. "He's spying on us for his father."

"Of course he is. He sees nothing I don't wish him to see." She replaced the coins and commended the smith before answering the rest of my query. "And his father will think twice about attacking Epirus if he believes Cassander has a chance of securing your hand in marriage," Olympias said. "By then I'll have the entire region eating from my hand."

It shouldn't have surprised me that we were all bit players in Olympias' game, an amusement that might plunge us into a bloody civil war.

"Does Alexander know of all this?"

"He has given me free rein at home while he pursues his campaigns in the east," she said, her eyes narrowing as she glanced up from her inspection of the remainder of the coins. "Everything I do is for Alexander, to protect his interests in Greece while he pacifies our enemies and earns eternal glory. Heroes in centuries to come shall beg on their knees for the opportunity to kiss my son's feet in the Fields of Elysium."

I shivered then despite the heat of the forges, wondering what sort of simpleton Olympias took me for that she expected me to believe all her plots and schemes were a sacrifice to be laid at the altar of Alexander's greatness.

And I wondered what other sacrifices she was willing to make in the name of her son.

CHAPTER 15

Persepolis, Persia

HEPHAESTION

Persepolis burned like dry kindling in summer.

Whether Alexander planned for the fire to spread and consume the whole city, I knew not, but spread it did.

In later years bards would sing the tale of an Athenian courtesan named Thais, Ptolemy's favorite in his gaggle of mistresses, and boast that she challenged Alexander to punish Persia for sacking her native city and putting its remaining men to the sword. The song claimed that a garlanded Alexander swayed on his feet and followed the trail of dancers and flautists in Thais' wake, stopping to watch as she flung a sputtering torch onto the floor of Xerxes' throne room and danced beneath the cedar rafters as the wood caught the blaze.

That was a lie, for Alexander commissioned a singer after the ashes of Persepolis had settled in order to save his image from being forged into that of the ravaging conqueror he'd so sought to avoid.

He had become a demon, a man I no longer knew.

In a great irony, the Tower of Silence and the tombs of Persia's dead kings had survived unscathed, but the rest of the city may as well never have existed. The ashes in Xerxes' throne room stood tall as my knees and I keened like a grieving man when a messenger informed us that the ancient archives had burned, including the famed copies of the Zoroastrian Avesta and Zend, written on cow skins with ink of molten gold. My first thought was of Darius' women, how Sisygambis, Stateira, and even Drypetis would mourn the loss of their sacred texts, their words now ashes scattered by the very flames that their god held so dear.

But soon Darius' women would have more to grieve than words on paper.

Alexander and I hadn't spoken since the night of the fire and I'd spent many sleepless nights wondering if I should remain behind as he pushed into Bactria. I had hardly a memory without Alexander's smiling face and golden hair; to leave him would have been akin to cutting off my sword hand. So instead, I swore that I'd make him atone for what he'd done to Persepolis by designing a greater palace, constructing a larger library, and rebuilding the city to rival even his Egyptian Alexandria.

To save him from himself.

We left the ruins of Persepolis as the wild red tulips blossomed, drawn east by the lure of Darius' crown. Reinforcements had joined us and rumors of the King of Kings' ever-changing course reached us daily, first that he had retreated to Balkh and then to the Caspian Gates. We followed at a pace so blistering that good men fainted in their armor on the side of the Royal Road and horses collapsed, left to rot beneath a blanket of their own lather.

Then came news of Darius' arrest by Bessus, his own cousin and the *satrap* of Balkh. We abandoned the infantry and rode at a brutal gallop across the desert by nightfall, not bothering to stop for food or to refill our water flasks. Finally the sun rose in shades of vivid purple and orange, illuminating a line of abandoned baggage carts on the horizon.

Alexander and the other men prepared to ride ahead at the

promise of riches and abandoned weapons, but all I craved was a flagon of water to wash away the grit that filled my mouth, reminding me of the ashes of Persepolis.

The soldiers pulled away dusty blankets on the line of carts, revealing baskets of grain and chests of iron shields, but nothing of substantial value, nor any *kraters* of water. A lone cart remained untouched and abandoned off to the side. With any luck, it would be a water cart or, even better, one filled with *amphorae* of sweet date wine.

Another soldier beat me there, a Macedonian named Polystratus who had been cursed with the most terrible jutting chin the gods had ever sculpted. The wagon was high off the ground, but not covered by any blanket. Polystratus tested a wheel spoke with his weight and hauled himself up.

"You should see this," he said, burying his nose into his shoulder even as the morning breeze carried to me the inexplicable stench of death and decay.

I clambered up the other wheel, my metal breastplate clanking as I peered into the rude cart and promptly swallowed the sour bile that rose in my throat.

Two corpses, one an attendant dressed in a plain yellow robe. But the other . . .

Flies crawled upon its eyes and inside its gaping maw, bloody tears in its exposed flesh proof that the vultures had already been here. A dark stain of old blood on its robe, striped white and purple as only the King of Kings could wear. Gold manacles on its wrists as befitted a Persian king and yoked to the other corpse.

"Alexander," I called, my voice rasping with the first words I'd spoken to him since Persepolis. "I believe we've found what you're looking for."

Darius, the King of Kings, had been stabbed by his own people and left to rot in the sun. The man had been a coward on the battlefield, but even so, this was an ignominious death for a king who had ruled half the world. Further proof that even the greatest men sometimes died inane deaths of blood fevers and old age and petty vengeance.

Such was the humor of the gods.

I should have been joyous that the long-sought prize had been won, but instead, I removed my helmet and bowed my head to the decomposing man in the mud-daubed wagon. I gritted my teeth as Alexander strode past Polystratus, and waited for his whoop of triumph.

"It is Darius," he said quietly, and I nodded, for we both recognized the man who had fled the battlefield twice before.

Then Alexander—*my* Alexander, my Achilles, and not the demon who had burned Persepolis—removed his cloak and spread it over the dead Persian king, sighing as he relieved Darius of a ruby signet ring and slipped the treasure onto his own finger. "May his gods keep him," he said. There was a moment of quiet, surrounded only by the meager desert breeze in our ears and the overwhelming stench of death. "He shall be returned to Persepolis, his body to be interred in the royal tombs with all honors."

In that moment I was glad that the underground mausoleum of Persia's kings had survived the fire, protected by the earth.

"And Darius' family?" I asked. "Shall they be allowed to leave Susa to attend the funeral?"

"Yes, yes," Alexander said. "I shall send them my condolences."

Somehow I doubted that would be enough.

But then the yellow-clad corpse alongside Darius stirred.

I almost fell from the cart in shock as Alexander cried out in alarm, but I managed to recover enough to grab Alexander's water-skin from his belt. The half-dead attendant sputtered as I dribbled the lukewarm liquid into his mouth, but then he clutched at the skin and sucked at it more greedily than a dying carp.

"Easy," I cautioned in Aramaic, pulling it away from him before he threw it all back up. "It would be a shame to drown yourself so soon after escaping from Hades' clutches."

The boy's face was so badly burned that skin peeled away on his nose, and his hands were scratched as if he'd fought off a flock of vultures. It was suddenly clear why the carrion hadn't stripped Darius down to bones by now.

"What is your name?" Alexander demanded when I'd allowed the boy enough sips to drain half the skin. He tried to sit, a shock of dark and dusty curls obscuring his eyes.

"Parizad," the youth said, his voice trembling as he dared look up. Despite the damage the sun had done to his face, he was delicate about the shoulders, with a face that might have graced the finest courtesan, the promise of supple lips, and almond eyes fringed with camel's lashes. The manacle at his wrist clanged as he reached up to brush his dark hair from his forehead, even that simple movement languorous like a cat's despite the days of filth that streaked his skin and the golden shackle that bound him to a dead man.

"Our last reports claimed that Bessus had taken Darius hostage," I said, gesturing to Darius' cart. "Was this done by his hand?"

The boy nodded. "I saw it with my own eyes. Bessus stabbed Darius, then lifted the golden diadem from the king's head and placed it on his own. He proclaimed himself the new King of Kings."

Alexander's eyes narrowed, and I had no doubt that he would not be so magnanimous toward Bessus as he had been to Darius' corpse. More self-proclaimed kings would crop up like weeds if Bessus wasn't quickly rooted out.

"And you remained behind?" I asked the young man, sniffing out any possible subterfuge before I ordered his shackles broken. "What sort of soldier refuses to follow the newly proclaimed king?"

A loyal one, or a stupid one.

"I'm no soldier, although I wished to be," he said. "Bessus didn't take kindly to my questioning whether the remaining *satraps* would follow Bessus after his murder of a chained king."

"And he left you here to rot in the sun," I said.

Alexander clasped my forearm, his thumb brushing my wrist in a way I'd missed, as Polystratus used his sword to break the manacles' chain. "We'll take this boy with us and hunt down Bessus," he murmured, his lips warm against my ear. "Together, we shall kill the traitor in such a way that no other Persian shall dare challenge me."

So Bessus would be the next Persepolis, a warning to the world of all that Alexander was capable of. But Bessus was a vile turncoat, one man, not a city already ancient when the Olympians were still being born.

"If you wish," I said, but Alexander was already walking away, the new ruby ring on his finger glinting under the climbing desert sun.

Parizad had overheard and tagged behind me, rubbing his wrists and stumbling so I had to steady him. "My sister, Roxana, travels with the *satrap*," he said.

"As his wife?"

"His concubine. You won't harm her, will you?"

I swung my leg over my gelding and gestured for a soldier to help Parizad mount behind me. "Is she as pretty as you?"

Parizad didn't stutter or look abashed, only stared up at me with hazel eyes flecked with green that would have been charming on any woman but were stunning on a man, especially with his long lashes. "She's my twin."

I grunted as he settled into the saddle behind me. "Then she'll be safe from harm. I only kill ugly people."

But as I flicked our reins and headed toward the rising sun, I realized that it might do me good to take a new mistress, perhaps this Roxana or another passably pretty Persian. Perhaps even Parizad.

I was weary of death and destruction, of chasing dead men into the desert.

Yet I could begin to see that so long as I followed Alexander, that was to be my lot in life.

Weeks later, I woke drenched in enough sweat to drown a man. My heart thudded like the pounding fist of some furious god, while next to me, Parizad snored softly, his bare chest rising and falling in the feeble lamplight. I focused on the scattering of dark hair on his otherwise smooth chest while willing the nightmare to fade from my mind.

But when I closed my eyes, the bloated, ghoulish face still gaped like a gray fish freshly dredged from the Oxus River, bloody gashes where his nose and ears should have been. And the eyes stared at me: glassy and accusing.

Yesterday, I'd listened as a court of Macedonian soldiers condemned Bessus to death, then watched at Alexander's side as Companions held down the impostor king and another came forward with a pair of heated iron tongs. To his credit, Bessus stared straight ahead, at least until the instrument touched his pockmarked face with a hiss of searing heat. Not even Zeus could have withstood such pain without screaming into the horse rag tied against his mouth.

One quick motion of the tongs and Bessus' nose fell to the earth, a knobby lump of blood and pink flesh. The ears followed in quick succession.

Alexander grinned like a feral cat at the first bit of justice done to the Persian usurper, then turned on his heel and marched down the wooden platform, the golden eagle tiara that Bessus had stolen from Darius now gleaming at his brow. "See that the remainder of his sentence is carried out," he ordered me. "Make an example of him in the Persian manner we discussed."

"Are you still intent on leaving?" I asked, low enough so only he could hear me.

"I am needed in the east to subjugate the mountain rebels."

"Send someone else," I said, but he only narrowed his eyes at me.

"Finish this task and travel to Persepolis to oversee Darius' funeral," he commanded, flint in his voice. "All shall be as we discussed."

And thus, Alexander the Great turned his back on this grisly execution, unwilling to linger lest it be said he enjoyed it as he had lighting poor, bumbling Adurnarseh on fire.

Bessus deserved to die, and painfully too, but listening to his defenseless screams and the smell of his shit as he lost control of his bowels was less enjoyable than razing a town of rebellious Persians.

"Bessus of Bactria," I proclaimed, his pig eyes bulging as a Companion removed his gag. "A Macedonian court found you guilty of regicide and a shouting vote proclaimed that your nose and ears be removed in accordance with Persian law for your treason. To complete your sentence, you shall be executed. Do you have any final words?"

He licked his flaking lips with a pale tongue, the gaping red holes where his nose should have been making wet rasping noises with each bloody inhalation.

"I am not a marauding Macedonian," he breathed, eyes rolling from the pain. "I am a Persian king and thus, I am not subject to your backward laws."

I sighed. "I've read your code of law; a Macedonian execution seems far kinder than what Darius would have given you for your treason."

"You know nothing of Persian law," Bessus said, blood from his lost nostrils oozing into his mouth.

And just like that, he stumbled into Alexander's waiting trap.

"Fine," I said. "Who am I to refuse a dying king's command?" I turned to the Companions. "Bessus of Bactria finds himself in need of the boats."

Bessus' eyes bulged in terror. "You wouldn't," he said, this time with less bravado.

"Alexander is a just and benevolent ruler." Even if he didn't care to witness the full measure of his justice. "He is happy to observe your request of a Persian punishment."

Bessus began to blubber, so I ordered him gagged again. A parade of slaves brought two boats—not watercraft at all but a massive tree trunk hollowed out and hewn in long halves at Alexander's command for this very occasion—and hefted them onto the dais. Holes had been carved into the trunk for Bessus' head, arms, and legs, in order to lock the impostor king inside. But the cramped and awkward space was only the beginning of the agony to come.

"Ready a paste of milk and honey," I ordered, then turned to Bessus. "That is the prescribed recipe, is it not? And you'll sit and partake of the regimen, lest the singers and poets remember you as Bessus the Spineless." I lowered my voice. "Demonstrate the bravery you lacked when you stabbed Darius through the stomach and I might find a way to speed this farce to its natural conclusion."

He looked scarcely human without his nose or ears, but there was a flash of very human terror in his eyes followed by resignation as almost a dozen guards ripped away his clothes, then smeared the paste of milk and honey on his hairy gut and what remained of his ruined face. The Companions watched spellbound, but my stomach crawled into my throat as moments passed and the first fat flies landed on Bessus' face, drawn to the sweet scent of milk and honey even more than they were to that of rotting flesh. Before long the air seemed to hum with their beating wings and the black devils landed on the gashes left from his nose and ears. They filled his eye sockets, their iridescent wings and bodies creating a new pair of eyes already glazed like death. Bessus flinched at first, then writhed in silence. Several times he gave such a sudden lurch that the flies disassembled in a shimmering black cloud, then resettled again, their buzzing the music of Hades.

Alexander had ordered a Persian punishment and I'd carried out as much of it as I planned to. I raised my hands to quell the men's muttering, although a few banged their swords against their shields as Bessus continued to writhe. "Bessus, the impostor King of Kings, requested a Persian punishment, a gift which he has now enjoyed." This was followed by a few more cheers and several thumps on shields. My men hadn't read the Persian annals of kings long since dead to know how this scenario was meant to conclude: with Bessus trapped between the boats for countless days, filling the basin with his own excrement until his face erupted with maggots and he finally expired. One Persian chronicler had even outlined the necessity of continuing to feed the victim in order to prolong the torture.

I had seen more than my fill.

My dagger flashed silver, and had it not been for the flies, I like to think that Bessus would have looked at me with gratitude as the blade sliced across his neck. As it was, the insects scarcely shifted as Bessus' blood poured from the artery in his throat.

I turned my back and marched down the dais with my cape flapping. "Remove the head," I commanded to no one in particular. "Pack it in salt and I shall present it to Sisygambis."

The mother of Darius would appreciate the sentiment, knowing that her son's murderer had been duly punished.

I paused a moment once I was out of sight, scratching like a madman against the swarm of imaginary flies crawling on my arms, beneath my greaves, and down my back. I closed my eyes and drew great heaving breaths of dry mountain air.

I'd killed plenty of men before Bessus, but this was the first time

I'd tortured a man. Alexander had lit the fire that killed Adurnarseh, but this time I had *let* him use me.

There are a few things in this life that make a man a man: his ability to drink and screw, his honor, and his loyalty.

I'd given my honor and loyalty to Alexander, but now they were tarnished and slipping away along with my ability to temper the worst of his excesses. I wanted to blame Alexander, but I knew I had no one to blame save myself.

I'd scarcely blinked to discover Parizad waiting in my tent, clay cups of the sour swill that passed for wine in these mountains in each hand as if he'd known precisely what tonic I needed.

I would do as Alexander commanded, travel to Persepolis and bury Darius' bones. But in that moment I wanted only to forget what I'd done.

And so I didn't turn Parizad away, but instead kissed him with a ferocity that made him drop the cups, spilling wine over our feet. He was no Alexander, but he was eager and willing, which was all I needed. Together we grappled naked flesh against naked flesh, as if I might devour him.

But not even that was enough to purge my mind of Alexander's feral smile, the stench of Bessus' fear, and the drone of the flies.

I forged on to the stark fortresses of Sogdiana without even bidding Alexander farewell as I departed for my mission of diplomacy to Persepolis. Parizad accompanied me, proving his worth as a dependable bed warmer and silent companion. He answered my new spells of brooding and flares of temper with patience and forbearance; and I had to remind myself afresh each day that it wasn't fair to compare him with Alexander.

Nor was it lost on me that Parizad absorbed the worst of my

moods as I had always done for Alexander. The realization only made me snarl and snap like an ill-tempered dog.

After several long weeks of travel, we finally entered Persepolis. The once stunning capital still reeled from the fire that had ravaged her ancient treasures, her streets empty save those poor souls who were unwilling or unable to leave. The city's future was made bleaker by her grief for her lost King of Kings.

As I entered Persepolis' temple to Ahura Mazda, which remained blessedly unscathed, I realized that the men I'd left behind with Alexander had the easier task, for facing a tortuous mountain pass naked in a blizzard with ferocious tribesmen bearing down on me would have been more pleasant than greeting Darius' dowager mother and daughters. Transported here from Susa, the three royal women were veiled and swathed in ebony mourning garb that accentuated their paleness, their expressions reminding me of men preparing for a battle in which they were hopelessly outnumbered. Behind them, guarded by a regiment of priests wrapped in white raiment, was a massive copper fire altar ringed by griffin and siren-men protomes, its basin cold and empty. This temple had housed the flame of the King of Kings, lit on the day that Darius had assumed the Eagle Throne and to be extinguished only when he had breathed his last in this life. Now, like so much of Persepolis, it too was barren and abandoned, save for the impassive bird-men and striding sphinxes meant to ward off evil that had been carved into the walls.

I carried before me a ceramic ossuary box depicting the lush gardens of paradise and behind me Parizad held a second unmarked porcelain chest I'd done my best to ignore during our journey here.

"May Mithra be benevolent and may the maiden lead your son to paradise," I said, offering the box of Darius' disarticulated bones to Sisygambis. She hugged it to her frail chest for a moment with liver-spotted hands, rare tears filling her haggard eyes.

"I have only one son now," she said, "Alexander, and he is king of all Persia. I pray that Bessus will be dragged into the depths of hell," she said, blinking away the tears as if they'd never existed. I wondered whether she would have said the same had it been Alexander who had killed Darius.

"Bessus' spirit shall never know the pleasure of roaming Ahura Mazda's gardens," Parizad said, bowing to the dowager queen before offering her the second ossuary. Distaste flickered over her expression even before Parizad lifted the lid and released a smell of rot so strong that I had to force myself not to breathe.

The former queen pulled the corner of her black veil over her sharp nose and glanced inside. "Throw that to the carrion at once."

"All shall be as you command." Parizad's head bobbed up and down like a dark-plumed crane searching for insects as he backed from her presence.

"The three-day rituals for your son were observed at the oasis," I said. "Darius was honored as the greatest of kings."

"Even still, the rituals shall be repeated after the flame ceremony to ensure that all were done correctly," Sisygambis proclaimed.

Stateira sniffed at that and blinked several times, but Drypetis' gaze remained fixated on the porcelain box her grandmother held. The cruelty of it all struck me then, for although Darius had been more cowardly than a whipped dog, it had been two years since his womenfolk had seen him and now they greeted only his bones.

Yet our reason for meeting here today was twofold. I'd delivered what remained of Darius, but now a new flame had to be lit. White-robed priests moved in like pale vultures, the most decrepit and bent of them each carrying a silver oil lamp.

"You have known Alexander longer than any of us," Sisygambis said, her thick-knuckled grasp on the ossuary tightening. "Will you light his flame?"

I almost retorted that Alexander *was* fire, but bit back the words as I recognized the glaring message from the gods.

The fire in the cave.

The singer Adurnarseh.

The city of Persepolis.

The flame I was to light now was only one more of Alexander's fires. I prayed it was not a blaze intent on death and destruction, but instead a blaze to light his way in darkening times. I prayed to Ahura Mazda and all the other gods as the fire sputtered to life amid the fresh black pitch.

Sisygambis studied me with iron eyes. "It is the duty of the king to honor his predecessor and as Alexander's representative, that responsibility falls to you. You must join us in the Tower of Silence for the customary three days and nights to see my son's soul safe into paradise."

Drypetis' head jerked up as if she'd been whipped, a glimmer of the gorgon that I knew lurking beneath the shell of the grief-stricken daughter. "No," she started to protest, but I cut her off.

"I shall join you, if it pleases you," I said, to which Sisygambis answered, "It does." She swept past, carrying the bones of her dead son in her arms, while her granddaughters followed in her wake. I willed Drypetis to turn and impale me with one of her witticisms or comical attempts at cursing, but she only glanced behind to skewer me with a glare, trailing a cloud of familiar cassia perfume. My eyes lingered too long on the drape of her robe, the way the material moved over the curve of her backside.

I knew I had lost my mind then that I would be thinking of sour-mouthed Drypetis in my bed. Or more accurately, pushed up against a wall with her head thrown back in abandon and her lips parted in a moan.

So it was that I found myself dressed in black Persian robes and immersed in a haze of incense and prayers within Persepolis' great round Tower of Silence. The barrage of white-masked Zoroastrian priests shook their sanctifying *barsom* twig bundles to purify our prayers and floated like faceless shades in the underworld. Yet Darius' silent women moved with purpose, lighting sacred lamps and burning the special *sedra* shroud to clothe their son and father in paradise, all the while ignoring Drypetis' drooling four-eyed mutt of a dog now that he'd played his ceremonial role in confirming the king's death. This tower was larger than the one in Tyre, with four covered offshoot wells surrounding a great circular courtyard. My eyes burned as I snatched at scraps of sleep beneath the stars from dusk to dawn, the daylight hours passing slowly under a sun as cold as a whore's heart.

All I had was time to think, and that was the last thing I wanted.

That final, fateful night I sat with my back to the cold stone walls of one of the well corridors, a mostly full *amphora* of wine tucked into my side. The winter air had wormed its way into my bones and my empty stomach gnawed hard after three days of fasting. We were allowed wine, but I'd rationed myself only a cup, which was as useful at driving off the cold and hunger as the fruit and water perpetually denied to Tantalus in the dungeons of Tartarus. I nodded off in fits and starts, shivering and hungry, only to wake to the sound of stifled sobs echoing off the walls.

I pulled my *himation* closer around myself and waited for the sound to subside, but it continued while the priests kept their vigil around the sacred fire. Stateira and Sisygambis lay swathed in warm bearskins across the way, Stateira's face relaxed in a peaceful sleep despite the occasional snore from the dowager queen. Drypetis' dog curled at the foot of their makeshift bed, but his vinegar-mouthed owner was nowhere to be seen.

Come to think of it, neither was my *amphora* of wine.

And still, the sobs echoed.

I heaved a sigh and stood, stomping my feet to get the blood circulating again as I followed the sound down the nearest well corridor.

I knew whom I would find at the end of the passage, but it was still a shock to see Drypetis—proud, loudmouthed princess though she was—huddled inside a black silk cloak and shaking with sobs. An oil lamp sputtered next to her, illuminating my missing *amphora* tucked in her arm and the massive copper cover to the well below, a pit that held the bones and dust of countless souls who had come before us. Drypetis' veil fell away as she lifted a tear-streaked face, revealing dark hair shorn just below her ears, presumably in a show of mourning for her father. Her gold-flecked eyes widened as she saw me, but I took solace in the fact that she was sworn to silence until the sun rose.

Still, she reminded me of a caged beast, wild-eyed and savage, akin to one of Pindar's most famous closing lines.

Here danger lies.

The poet was surely right and it would have been easier to take back my wine and leave Drypetis to her storm of tears, but taking the easy path meant that I'd watched a singer immolated, a city torched, and a man tortured. This time I forced myself to take the hard road and sit next to Drypetis, my movements slow and measured. To my shock, she didn't bolt and run, only shuffled farther from me and tucked her knees tighter beneath her chin.

Our vows of silence meant I wasn't allowed to offer her trite words of solace. Instead, my hand hovered near her shorn hair for a moment before I finally dared touch her. She flinched, then relaxed as I stroked the curved line above her ear where hair fused with pale skin, untouched by the sun.

And then I kissed her.

She stiffened and I expected her to lunge at me with bared claws and teeth, but instead she clambered closer, pressing her lithe body to mine and knocking over the oil lamp in the process, plunging us into blackness. Her lips were desperate under mine even as she tugged me to my knees, both of us fumbling in the dark.

Wine. She tasted of sweet, sweet wine and salt from her tears.

Her persuasive hands tugged at the *kamarband* of my robe. I recognized her grief—and perhaps the wine too—making her grasp at this most basic act of the living, but even more shocking was the discovery that I wanted *her*, wanted to bury myself deep within her and forever smell that heady cassia perfume that made me feel like I'd drunk several *amphorae* of wine.

Drypetis tumbled like she did everything else, fast and fierce, our robes hastily discarded and her long legs wrapped around me while her nails dug into my backside. I was far from noble, teasing her until she whimpered and taunting her with my lips and fingers. Finally, neither of us could take any more and I felt a moment's guilt when I pushed into her wetness and past her maidenhead, but she only gasped and clutched my shoulders tighter, her lips devouring mine until she cried out. Afterward, I pulled my discarded cloak over the both of us.

By Zeus, I enjoyed the feel of her naked body pressed against mine.

I dozed, a heavier sleep than any I'd experienced in the tower, but woke to the wrinkled face of an old woman, the lines etched around her eyes and mouth chiseled deeper by a flickering oil lamp. The orange haze of dawn lit the corridor behind her, breaking our three days' vow of silence.

"Fuck me," I muttered.

"It appears my granddaughter already took care of that," Sisygambis said. "Although I'm surprised it took you both so long." The dowager's lips pursed tight even as her eyes laughed at me. Drypetis' shaggy yellow mongrel sat patiently at her feet, cocking his head before shuffling forward to lick his owner's sleeping face. Drypetis groaned and Sisygambis nudged her granddaughter with a slippered toe. "Rise and dress before the priests find you."

"Mithra's mace," Drypetis murmured as she sat up, petting the slobbering dog absentmindedly. Her eyes, which seemed to absorb whatever color she wore—black today although still flecked with gold—slanted at me in question. Then her hands flew to her lips as she looked first at her grandmother's retreating back and then to me again.

Ah yes, the shock and shame that came after a night of debauchery. It was a feeling I knew well, although I couldn't remember ever being the subject of such mortification.

I scowled and knocked the remainder of the broken seal from the *amphora* of wine she'd filched from me. The container was almost completely full, meaning that my little gorgon had, in fact, come to me without a fog of alcohol blurring her mind.

Bugger shame, then.

I arched an eyebrow at her and took a long draft of the old, sweet-tasting Lesbos vintage instead of grinning as I wished to.

"Nice hair," I said, gesturing with the *amphora* toward her shorn locks. It wasn't what I'd meant to say, but it seemed a safer topic than anything else that came to mind. I actually liked it short, framing her face in a tumbled mess so she really did look like a gorgon.

"Shut up," Drypetis snapped. "I got it caught in a pulley."

I barely kept from laughing as she stumbled to her feet and shoved her arms back into her robe so fast that the dog took a step back before settling onto its mangy haunches. Everything Drypetis did was forceful and full of purpose, never delicate or graceful.

And while I wouldn't have minded a repeat of last night's forceful performance, the way she looked ready to spit knives told me she felt otherwise.

"I'll be gone soon enough and then you can forget this ever happened." I sighed, wiping my mouth with the back of my hand.

Her startled pause gave me hope. "What?" she asked.

"I leave today. I'm to rendezvous with Alexander in Sogdiana."

"Of course you are," she snapped. "Will you always come when Alexander crooks his finger at you?"

I rubbed a knuckle against my ear with an exaggerated wince. "Perhaps. Will your tongue always lash me like a whip?"

"It's no less than you deserve," she said, looking down her nose at me, "from the daughter of the Persian eagle and the one true king. After all, you're nothing save Alexander's man-whore."

My gorgon had returned, despite the allure of her tumbled hair and the faintest trace of cassia perfume that clung to my skin. Some things were truly too good to last.

"You're the one who wrapped her legs around that man-whore last night," I said. "So what does that make you?" I thrust my arms into the sleeves of my robe and gave it a slight shake before tying the *kamarband*.

I'd never had a woman slap me before, but I assumed Drypetis' assault was as thorough as I could expect, a veritable bolt of lightning across my cheek. Her chest heaved and for a moment I wished I could push her against the wall and kiss her once more.

And why the hell not?

So I did, pinning her wrists behind her and exulting in the way her lips softened against mine even as she struggled, her breasts pushing against my chest.

I released her then and leaned back against the cold wall, my arms crossed and a smug smile on my face as her expression contorted in rage. Her hands curled into fists as the fire from her slap flared fast across my face. "I hope a Bactrian arrow finds its way into your miserable heart," she threw over her shoulder before whistling for her dog and storming off.

And as I watched her stalk down the corridor like an angry cloud, there was only one thing I could do, even though I knew it would fan the flames of her fury even more.

I laughed, a great, hearty laugh, feeling fully alive for the first time in months.

❋ CHAPTER 16 ❋

327 BCE
Sogdiana, Persia

ROXANA

The sharp winds yanked my hair from my veil and I mused anew how my body might shatter on the rocks below the citadel's precipice. Some months ago I had almost fulfilled the daydream, freshly broken as I'd been by the lonely soldiers who knew Bessus no longer protected me. I'd even invoked my father's name, but Ariamazes, our new commander, who had ogled my breasts when meeting with Bessus, had only laughed at my suggestion that Oxyartes would avenge my honor.

"Oxyartes of Balkh?" he sputtered. "A few coins would have him singing a different song. After all, he allowed you to whore for Bessus, didn't he?"

Ariamazes had been the first, but he was a fair and popular general who allowed his men their turns as well. I'd tried to fight in the beginning; I'd slapped one soldier, spat at another, and kneed a third in his stones. I screamed that I wasn't a common camp follower looking to hike her skirts up for any man with a hard shaft between his legs, but it didn't matter.

I'd had two choices after that night: to fling myself from the rock walls or to use my one gift—my beauty—to shape my life into something I wanted.

Now I no longer fought Ariamazes and his men, but instead wheedled from them bags of dried dates, wine, and the rings and silk scarves they'd been given by wives and lovers back home, in return for my pleasuring them as Bagoas had taught me. I'd become the Whore of Sogdian Rock, but I'd been a whore since I first spread my legs for Bessus, so what did it matter?

I took solace in the knowledge that Bessus' first two wives had been killed in Alexander's burning of Persepolis. The last remained here, still fat and jowly but more often ignored now that she'd never wear the queen's diadem.

I knew this wretched wasteland in every season, its scalding summer heat and screaming winter blizzards, the way the stark cliffs below us changed from wheat gold in the spring to mud brown as the shadows of the tamarisk shrubs stretched longer until finally snow blanketed the mountain peaks. I knew that the long-nosed niece of Ariamazes tumbled a flat-faced soldier behind the henhouses each night. I also knew that we received only sporadic provisions now that the stream of traveling merchants had decided the promise of bored, rich widows wasn't worth confronting the might of Alexander's army. Sogdian Rock had grain stockpiles to last two years, but the earth of the citadel's root gardens had grown barren with winter's snows, the clumps of dirt frozen harder than any paving stone.

The sheep and goats grew thinner, as did the rest of us, but a tentative spring had finally arrived, bringing with it the promise of easier living and warmer weather. And an army bent on our destruction.

Alexander had finally come to Sogdian Rock.

Greek mercenaries and Macedonians filled the plain below the fortress in a black sea of death. The path upward had been destroyed after we'd received word of Bessus' execution, news that had decimated my dreams of being queen even as it freed me from having to fake smiles and moans of false pleasure for the fat bastard who had sentenced my brother to die. To keep our stronghold impenetrable, soldiers had bludgeoned the bottom with hammers and hacksaws, prying loose the rocks of the narrow ledge that led into the clouds. It was a dangerous, backbreaking job and several of the men plummeted to their deaths when they lost their footing.

I bade them good riddance, especially the one who had liked to wrap my hair into a rope as he rode me from behind. I hoped the maggots below enjoyed feasting on his miserable carcass.

Now the fortress was truly impregnable, a prison that guaranteed survival to those of us inside.

I stood on the ramparts surrounded by jeering soldiers and curious women, the mothers and young children having retreated to the center of the fortress at the approach of the cunning Macedonian and his troops. The tops of our walls were just out of reach of their archers and too tall for any ramparts to be built, so Alexander and his Companions stood at the base of what had once been the ledge leading to the top, wearing their elaborate helmets and red woolen winter capes that fluttered in the wind. My fists tightened as I realized that one of them was likely Hephaestion, the same demon who had tortured Bessus with flies and honey.

I recalled Bessus' boast that he'd dress me in a net of gold and gems and have me on the floor of Persepolis' treasury, that we'd make love in each of Darius' beds in every one of his palaces.

He was a foolish, boastful, worthless man, just as Darius had been before him. Whoever had thought to give men swords and put crowns on their heads must have had raw eggs for brains.

But now the crowd fell silent as another would-be king shouted up at us.

"People of Sogdian Rock," Alexander yelled. Even from this vantage, I could see that he was shorter than most of the Companions who flanked him, but his voice boomed like a god's. "It is my wish to see you saved from the slaughter that has met so many of your countrymen."

"Slaughter at your hands," Ariamazes shouted down. Before his men had rendered our rock path impassable, our bold commander had plagued Alexander by leading revolts throughout Sogdiana. "Take your men and march back from where you came. Then there shall be no further Persian blood spilled, Alexander of Macedon."

"I am your King of Kings now," Alexander said. "Crowned in Babylon and anointed by your priests and gods."

"And yet you put Persepolis to the torch, even after you were crowned," Ariamazes said. "Proof indeed that you are no true king."

"You may return unmolested to your homes if you surrender this citadel," Alexander answered. His voice had taken on a hard edge; apparently he didn't care for being accused of false kingship. "You have until dusk to give me your answer."

"We can give you our answer now, you addled nanny goat," Ariamazes said. "You'd need men with wings to capture this fort. Seeing as you have none, we leave you to either fashion some or continue on your way."

With that, Ariamazes turned his back on Alexander and stalked away from the wall, but the deafening cheers mixed with laughter tumbled like boulders down to Alexander and his men.

Yet while our Persian soldiers clapped one another on their backs and women bent their heads to twitter like dumb sparrows over Ariamazes' daring, I stared down at Alexander.

And he stared back, his hands clasped behind him as he studied our ramparts that touched the clouds.

His was not the stance of a man who had given up. I should know; I saw it daily in my own mirror.

Winter's teeth dug deep that night despite the approaching spring, and the plains to the west were dotted with thousands of Macedonian campfires like tiny orange stars. Ariamazes had held a celebration for the soldiers of Sogdian Rock to honor their bloodless victory over Alexander and my services had been required for three separate soldiers, each of whom had drunk at least his weight in wine and taken an eternity to squirt his seed into me. I peered into the darkness on my way to my room, wondering whether wily Alexander had ordered his men to light several fires each to trick us into believing that their numbers were larger than they were.

"Drink this," Bagoas said as I entered, setting a steaming cup of boiled herbs before me. Having spent time among Darius' concubines, he knew how to prevent unwanted pregnancies, and he'd managed to procure a tincture of dried wild carrot, rue, and pennyroyal before the trickle of traveling merchants had shriveled up. It was something my brother, Parizad, would have done for me, although I'd never used such herbs with Bessus. Growing fat and birthing some unknown man's child here on this godforsaken rock was the last thing I wanted.

"That's the end of the almond oil," Bagoas scolded me as I massaged a bit into my hands and brushed it through the ends of my hair. He organized the black and white pawns on an enameled board of Twenty Squares, the same game I'd played with Parizad when we were children; the game was a recent payment from a soldier with the first fuzz of manhood on his upper lip.

"This siege might yet kill me," I said, choosing one of the scorpion pieces and moving it from the center of the board. "I dreamed last night of bathing in a vat of almond oil while slaves fed me lamb stew with limes and fresh cherries. And then I woke and choked down a bowl of barley gruel."

"There won't be any of that once Alexander departs," Bagoas said in his girlish voice, countering my move. "Unless you can persuade one of these soldiers to claim you as his own. Preferably Ariamazes himself."

I shuddered at the thought.

The throwing sticks were against me that night, but we played until Bagoas captured the last of my scorpions with his carved bird-of-prey pawns. We abandoned the board and Bagoas lifted the ragged blanket on our mattress and I settled in next to him. We rarely pleasured each other now that we both whored for the soldiers, those parts of our bodies too abused by others to be used for our own enjoyment, but we often curled together like two nestling cats.

The sound of his steady breathing lured me to sleep. I awoke to a brazier long grown cold and the haze of spring sunshine creeping under the door.

And a storm of hundreds, perhaps thousands, of marching boots. It was the sound of an entire army.

I stumbled in the semidarkness, knocking the game of Twenty Squares to the floor with a clatter of pieces.

"Don't, Roxana," Bagoas warned me, but I cracked open the door and gasped to see hundreds of Macedonian soldiers standing and marching alongside many of our own captured men in the small square.

Alexander had breached the walls.

But there was no slaughter, no screams, no blood running in the streets.

There were even a few women about and one in particular caught my eye with her dyed black hair beneath an askew veil and her pale pink silk robe that strained around the bodice and hips.

I grabbed Bessus' widow by the arm and yanked her into my room, slamming the weathered door behind us.

"What's happening?" I demanded even as she tried to pull away.

"By Mithra, unhand me!" she shrieked, prompting me to squeeze her arm harder. "Let me out of here, before I end up with nits or Astarte's whore-pox!"

"Piss on Mithra," I growled. "Tell me what is going on or I'll slit your throat. No one will notice the body of a dead hag on a day like today."

Her eyes darted from me to Bagoas, but he only shrugged. "Best do as she commands."

I worried that I'd have to make good on my threat, but she wrenched her arm away and relented. "Alexander armed three hundred of his men with iron tent pegs and lines of flax. They climbed all through the night after he offered twelve gold talents to the first man to scale the walls."

Men with wings.

Ariamazes had taunted Alexander, but the wily king of Macedon had outmaneuvered him with iron picks and thread. I would later learn that thirty men had perished during the long climb when they lost their footing, but for now I marveled at his daring, and also at his men's willingness to follow him in such a dangerous escapade. They must love him well, or be touched by the gods.

"And Ariamazes and his men won't kill them?"

"Ariamazes fled," she said, her lip curled in revulsion. "Lowered himself down in a basket used for supplies. That bag of bile he called a wife ran with him while our worthless men laid down their swords."

"May he rot forever and vultures pluck out his miserable eyes. And may his prick shrivel and fall off," I added for good measure, although Ariamazes' prick had been laughably short to begin with.

I'd heard all I needed to and hustled her to the door, surprised when she hesitated. "Where shall you go now, Roxana?" she asked, her voice thorny with spite. "Back to your father?"

I'd sooner go to *Duzakh*.

But I offered her a smile just as honeyed and just as treacherous. "I'm not sure yet," I said. "I'll think of something."

I pressed my forehead to the door after I closed it behind her, my mind reeling as I felt Bagoas drape a moth-eaten blanket around my shoulders. "I hope your fingers are deft this morning," I finally said to him.

"What are you planning?"

"We can't scurry like rats in a sinking ship this time," I said. "For there's nowhere to scurry to, unless you care to climb down the cliffs using tent poles abandoned by the Macedonians."

"I can't face all of those soldiers," Bagoas murmured, and I was shocked to see his hands trembling. "I'd rather you slit my throat."

I closed my eyes against the possible fate that awaited us, used among countless Macedonian soldiers that would make the Persian regiment pale in comparison. Why was it that women bore the brunt of war's aftermath, while men escaped via an easy death?

And poor Bagoas, caught between two worlds, was neither man nor woman.

"You shall not have to face them." I wove my fingers through his hair and kissed his eyelids. "Alexander loves beauty and I am beautiful," I said. "His men won't dare molest me, the daughter of Oxyartes of Balkh, if I'm dressed like the Queen of Queens."

"Oxyartes of Balkh isn't your father and even if he were, he's the most minor of nobles," Bagoas said, for I'd spilled that particular detail after a night of too much wine. "How can you be so sure you'll catch Alexander's attention?"

"I swear to you that I'll catch at least the eye of one of his generals," I said. "Or I'll slit both of our throats."

Bagoas looked about to argue, but finally gave a rueful shake of his head. "I hope you know what you're doing."

"Help me dress," I said, my heart racing and my palms suddenly damp. "We haven't much time." I wondered if this was how soldiers felt before charging into battle, suddenly alive at the very real possibility of victory or destruction.

I would emerge triumphant, or die trying.

B agoas sewed my hair into an elaborate set of curls and coils worthy of a queen's tiara, dressed me in my black silk embroidered with griffins, and belted my waist with a simple silk girdle before clasping my lynx bracelets high on my arms. I peered outside for the second time that morning and slipped into the crowd.

Every child's wail and mother's snivel set my teeth on edge. Still, I supposed mingling with the sweaty masses was preferable to being molested or murdered.

A hush fell over the dozens of soldiers and captives, but the air hummed with tension. Alexander was easy to recognize from the day before, shorter than almost all his men despite the egret plume and horsetail helmet he wore. A soldier with shoulders like a galley rower and crowned with a fish-spine helmet stood at his side, but it was Alexander who stepped forward and spoke, his voice booming over the huddled crowd.

"People of Sogdian Rock," he said, opening his arms. "I have proved that your fortress is not impenetrable, and thus, your soldiers have agreed to join my army. The rest of you may travel in my retinue as my honored guests, until the time when your own families shall swear their allegiance and claim you, or you may remain here under your newly appointed governor." He turned his palms up to the sky in a gesture of benevolence. "You may rest well in the knowledge that you shall not be harmed."

Mothers and wives around me sagged and sobbed in relief, but I fought down a wave of panic as Alexander turned to depart. The fish-spine soldier murmured something to him and Alexander gave a tight nod. I thought I detected a grimace of pain there, perhaps the stiffness of an old wound, but then he turned back to address us once again. "Hephaestion here has reminded me of my manners, for I shall host a banquet in the former house of Ariamazes each night for the duration of our stay here. Sadly, the quarters are cramped and will not accommodate so large a crowd at once, but each of you shall join me one night until I've had the pleasure of meeting all the wives and daughters of Persia's ancient nobility."

With that, he turned again, but a red rage threatened to overwhelm my vision even as the bearish soldier he'd spoken to jogged down the citadel's stairs.

Hephaestion.

The man with the fish-spine helmet was no common soldier, but the man who had tortured and executed Bessus.

My fingernails bit my palms and a wave of pure hatred surged through me. He'd made Bessus suffer, and for my brother's sake I wasn't sorry for that, but in killing my protector, Hephaestion had cost me a crown and turned me into the Whore of Sogdian Rock. The order may have come from Alexander, but I'd have to charm the conqueror if I ever hoped to leave this place. It was easier to blame Hephaestion for every soldier that I'd swallowed down, and for that, I'd loathe him until the end of my days.

Better yet, until the end of his days.

Yet I rearranged my features and pushed my way forward through the crowd, adopting a smile so sweet that a hive of honey-bees might have flocked to it.

"I shall dine with Alexander tonight," I said, daring to touch Hephaestion's wrist as he paused to speak to a portly matron. A flutter of annoyance passed over his face, but he offered both the matron and me the same lazy smile. "Is that so?" he asked. I could see that he appreciated what he saw as his eyes swept over me, but his gaze didn't linger as I'd expected. "You Persians prefer to try to kill Alexander or run in the opposite direction. You're the first to demand his presence, but you'll see him when he decrees it, and not a moment before."

With that, Hephaestion turned and ambled back into the crowd, the flock of idiots parting to let him pass as if he were some sort of king.

I'd deal with him later. First, I had to get to Alexander.

Ariamazes' quarters were identical to all the rest in Sogdian Rock, cramped, windowless, and built of the same straw-colored stone as the cliffs that held the fortress. Yet the door was flung open, a singer's voice warbled from inside, and a healthy fire burned on the brazier to ward off the evening's chill.

From Ariamazes' distraught daughter I'd managed to borrow a delicate red head scarf sewn with tiny seed pearls, their knobby surfaces gleaming like tiny misshapen moons. I'd dabbed the last remaining drops of my spikenard perfume behind my ears while the poor girl blubbered about how she might never see her father or mother again now that they'd fled the fortress, leaving her behind to be claimed as Alexander's captive rather than lose her to violence on a battlefield.

"There, there," I said over her caterwauling, dropping a perfunctory pat on her shoulder. "I'm sure Alexander is much too busy to hunt down cowards like your father."

Bagoas walked with me to Ariamazes' former home, where the noisy gathering had already begun. Just days ago these women had been cursing Alexander's name and now they flocked to him like a gaggle of empty-headed ducks. If I were Alexander, I'd have tossed them all from the top of the citadel just to end their squawking.

"Alexander's mistress Barsine carries his child, but he left her behind in Susa and has yet to replace her. The Macedonian conqueror is a lover of all beautiful things," Bagoas said as he adjusted my veil. "He won't be able to resist you."

I kissed the tip of his nose and ducked inside, glad for the firelight that danced on the sheen of my silk and brought a flush to my cheeks. A table had been set and rugs had been thrown hastily onto the stone floor, but it was still a garrison room filled with the birds of Persia's finest families, dressed in feathers long past their prime. There was a dance under way dedicated to Mithra, the ancient god of light, a chaste performance by Sogdian Rock's eligible maidens. I spotted Alexander immediately, seated alone at the longest table and looking as if he might fall asleep despite the drum and lyre music. I knew the steps to the dance, but I wasn't here to copy the bland movements of these dry virgins. Instead, I clapped my hands overhead as I joined in, twirling so my veil and robe spun around me as I moved to the center of the line. The girls chirped angrily among themselves, but I didn't care.

In Persia there are dances for women, but even more dances for men, infused with ritual and the lore of bull sacrifice in Mithra's honor. But there are other dances that Parizad had taught me, performances meant to demonstrate the virility of the dancer, with moves to simulate riding a horse. These dances were reserved for warriors, but it was those steps that I danced now.

Alexander sat straighter as I bent forward and rose like a wave, as if I were galloping into battle, my legs spread as if astride a great warhorse. The conqueror's eyes never left my body as he lifted his wine cup to his lips and took a long draft. I swayed in ways that left little to the imagination, while around me the rest of the girls continued their uninspired movements, out of tempo as the musicians followed my lead.

When it finally ended, I fell to my knees, my skin damp with perspiration and my chest heaving as I dared glance up. The gaze of every man in the room was fixed on me.

And Alexander looked ready to devour me.

I raised my eyes to his and gave a small smile, parting my lips as I maneuvered my way to stand before him.

"Alexander of Macedon," I said before he could speak. "I am Roxana of Balkh, daughter of Oxyartes."

"It is a pleasure to have you here tonight, Roxana of Balkh," Alexander said. He was daunting in full Persian dress with a gape-mouthed lion pendant gleaming at his shoulder, but his clean-shaven face in the Greek style jarred against his purple silks and the golden girdle at his waist. His curls were bound with a leather thong across his forehead, embellished with filigreed golden juniper leaves, as if he were a boy playing at being king.

But the man who stared at me was no boy.

"You must be weary from your exertions just now," he said. "I've never seen a woman dance like that."

"It's an uncommon dance," I said, "meant to strengthen the muscles and stimulate the blood flow as if one were riding . . ."

I let my voice trail off with a sly smile, letting him imagine what sort of riding I meant.

He flicked a finger to beckon me closer, desire making his blue eyes burn like the hottest flames.

I ignored barbed glares from the assembled girls and their mothers that might have made tremble even the *simurgh*, the ancient dog-headed bird that had witnessed the destruction of the world three times over. The women hissed like asps, flicking their forked tongues in my direction with whispers of *whore*, *harlot*, and worse.

Yet I had Alexander's attention, and they did not.

"Will you do me the pleasure of dining with me?" he asked.

"Of course," I answered. "You do me great honor," I said breathlessly, marveling at the fact that the King of Kings was standing to move a chair for me so I could assume my place beside him at the banquet table.

"I would do a woman like you many honors," Alexander said, setting my head whirling.

"Is that so?" I settled into my seat and pushed his chair back with my slippered foot, letting my toe brush across his muscled calf.

"It is indeed," he said, his smile slow and enigmatic. I felt a heat start deep in my belly and spread still lower. Alexander possessed the power of a small sun in this dark, cramped chamber, a heat from which not even I was immune.

I tasted none of the simple garrison fare the servants spread before us: bread and dried apricots, dates and roasted pecans; several goats had been butchered and cooked in a gravy with fresh butter and onions and garlic from someone's winter stores. My thoughts were an eddy of wind as Alexander watched my every movement.

"Is it true that you climbed to the fortress using only tent pegs and canvas?" I asked, letting my fingertips brush his arm. It's a well-known truth that every man enjoys having his pride cosseted, and Alexander's pride was surely larger than most. I almost mentioned that the Persian soldiers must have pissed themselves to see him standing at the precipice come dawn, but bit my tongue so he didn't think me crass. "The soldiers here were fools to believe themselves invincible against a son of Zeus," I added.

"A mistake other men have made before them."

I smiled slowly, tilting my head so his eyes could follow the length of my long neck. "And so you took the fortress without spilling a single drop of Persian blood. An impressive feat."

I neglected mentioning the thirty Greeks who had plunged to their deaths. Surely that was a small price to pay for a man like Alexander.

"And now I plan to enjoy the fruits of my cunning," he said.

"I'm sure you do," I purred, but I didn't get a chance to ask what that entailed, as the soldier I now knew to be Hephaestion arrived with a wicker basket in his arms. I glowered at him as he stopped before Alexander, bowing with his fist over his heart.

"My apologies for the interruption," he said, braving Alexander's black glare. "But this arrived from the wife of Ariamazes. We rigged a pulley and winched it up the cliff so you might have it tonight." He leaned forward, his dark brows drawn together. "You may lose your appetite after you view its contents."

Alexander's hand hesitated on the basket, yet I could see the curiosity deep in his eyes as he glanced around the room, ending with me.

"Open it," I urged him.

"You're a curious one," he said.

"Always," I taunted him with a dangerous smile, then wished I hadn't when the soldier revealed the basket's contents.

Nestled in a bed of hay was a man's head, freshly severed from its body, its eyes open and jaw gone slack to reveal two lines of perfect white teeth.

Teeth that had grazed my ear and nipped at my breasts as I was bent over the bed in this very room.

Ariamazes' teeth.

"A rather foul thing to serve at a banquet," I murmured as I fanned myself with my hand, trying to control the urge to vomit as Alexander withdrew a note from inside the basket. I'd never learned to read, so the scribbled characters meant nothing to my eyes, but Hephaestion stood and read over Alexander's shoulder.

"A gift from Ariamazes' wife," he said. "And an offer of peace."

I drank a hasty gulp of wine, then laughed into the back of my hand, masking the chortle as if I'd choked on my drink. The old lech had ogled my breasts and thought nothing of whoring me out to his men, but now he'd met this grisly end despite his cowardly escape. And at the hands of his wife!

"Ariamazes' wife is a wise woman," Alexander said, beckoning for a servant to take the befouled basket away. "For her husband's head is more valuable than gold."

"The rest of these godforsaken rocks will fall without Ariamazes to lead them, for they're all held by incompetent fools," Hephaestion said.

Alexander nodded and grinned like a child with a honey roll. "Thus clearing our way to India so I might rule from one end of the earth to the other," he said as if dazed, then turned to the messenger. "Send Ariamazes' wife a message of my deep appreciation." He removed the golden lion brooch from his shoulder and tossed it to the messenger. "This should more than cover her disquiet at her sudden widowhood."

I scarcely stopped myself from gaping as he swept from the dais with a flourish of his purple cloak, taking with him the spicy aroma of incense stolen from some Persian altar to Ahura Mazda.

And leaving me like a child's forgotten plaything.

I must have stared too long, for it was Hephaestion's low chuckle that shook me from my shock at Alexander's abrupt departure. "Don't be disappointed. Alexander has a penchant for all things shiny and bright. The allure of India's riches just happens to sparkle brighter than you at this moment."

"Leave me," I commanded, for I doubted whether I could mask my disappointment, or my hatred for this man.

But he didn't obey, and had the audacity to assume Alexander's chair and drain the remainder of his wine. "Rather demanding for a captive of Sogdian Rock, aren't you?" he asked.

"I'm no captive," I said, nearly knocking over my chair in my haste to stand and depart. Ariamazes' rotting head had squandered tonight's opportunity with Alexander, and now I had to remaneuver to arrange another encounter with the powerful Macedonian. "I am Roxana of Balkh."

"Roxana of Balkh?" Hephaestion's brow furrowed. "Daughter of Oxyartes of Balkh?"

I swept past him, unwilling to waste one further breath on this man, but his hand clamped down on my wrist.

"I have in my possession something you'll want to see." He smiled, more snarl than grin. "Follow me."

And there was nothing I could do, save act as he commanded.

"I thought you were dead," I sobbed into my brother's chest, breathing in the scent of life and herbs that had always clung to him. I'd hurled myself into his arms the moment my eyes had adjusted to the dimness of Hephaestion's lamplit chambers, screeching with wild joy once I'd realized it was truly my brother I beheld and not some trickster spirit.

Parizad hugged me tight, but not tight enough, for I wanted to cling to him as if a thunderstorm roiled overhead and never let go. "But I'm not dead," he murmured.

"I should kill you for all you did," I said around my hiccups, "spewing treason after I'd weaseled a position for you from Bessus."

His hand in my hair pressed me closer to him and I could taste the salt of his tears mingled with mine. "Everything happened as the gods willed it, Roxana."

At that, I shoved him away and grabbed the first thing I could find. The silver urn missed him and collided with the stone wall, then crashed to the floor like a lone clap of thunder. I searched for something that might shatter, but unfortunately, Hephaestion didn't have any alabaster vases or glazed pottery available, only books.

Cedar chests and wooden boxes full of books.

I grabbed one in each hand and hurled them at my brother. One broke and its yellowing pages littered the ground, the scrawled figures on their pages indecipherable to my eyes. Suddenly two strong arms salted with black hairs picked me off my feet and held me so my toes dangled off the ground.

"I'd forgive your denting the urn or even your own head, Roxana of Balkh," Hephaestion growled in my ear as I tried to squirm from his grasp, "but I didn't have my favorite volumes of Pindar winched up to this godforsaken fortress only to have you destroy them. Make peace with your brother and leave my copies of Ovid and Homer out of your quarrel."

I gave a tight nod, breathing a sigh of relief as my feet touched stone again.

"I'll leave you two to get reacquainted." Hephaestion spoke over my shoulder to my scowling brother. "Bind her wrists if she so much as breathes on my books again."

"I shall protect them with my life," Parizad said, the slow grin I'd once loved tugging on his lips. Then he lifted up on tiptoes and

kissed Hephaestion, his fingers splayed over the cheeks of Bessus'
murderer in a display of passion.

Stunned, I could do nothing save stare, struck dumb and blind.

My brother was alive. And he was a catamite. Hephaestion's
catamite.

"Thank you," he whispered to Hephaestion, who gave only a tight
smile in answer.

The door closed behind my brother's lover, making the oil lamps
flicker and the shadows on Parizad's face dance. Neither of us spoke
for a moment.

"You died," I said in a small voice, "and then I was chained to this
foul rock and Bessus was executed."

I wanted to tell him about Bagoas and all the soldiers, and our
father, or lack thereof, but didn't trust myself to speak further without turning into a sniveling mess.

Parizad cupped my face with his hand. "Have you been mistreated?"

I thought of Ariamazes and the other soldiers and my chin
wobbled. "I needed you *here*," I whispered.

My brother gathered me in his arms again. "You need no one,
Roxana; you only imagine that you do. The rest of us . . ." His voice
trailed off and he glanced at the door, toward Hephaestion.

I pulled away. "It seems I need play the whore no longer, for you
do it instead."

Parizad didn't bother to deny it, only grinned. "Are you jealous?"

"Of your bedding that dark oaf?" I scoffed, trailing my finger over
a crate of books. They seemed worthless objects to haul over mountains and deserts. "When he killed Bessus and sentenced me to—"

Parizad shrugged, interrupting me. "Bessus committed regicide
and Hephaestion only acted on Alexander's orders. I've often spoken
of you to him."

"And what did you tell him?"

"That my sister is the most beautiful woman in all of Persia."

"You must help me, brother," I said. "I won't return to Balkh and I can't stay here."

"I'll do what I can." He chucked me under the chin. "You should rest now and we can catch up more in the morning."

"Can't I stay with you?"

But I knew the answer even before he gestured to Hephaestion's crates of books, his bed. "My place is here." He bent and removed a copper dagger from one of Hephaestion's chests. "But take this. In case you and your lovely eyes have captured the attention of Alexander's soldiers."

My fingers closed around the cold metal. I'd never held a blade before, not one made with the intent of ending a man's life. This simple weapon meant that I'd no longer be the Whore of Sogdian Rock.

"All will be well," Parizad said. "It always is, in the end."

"I love you, brother," I whispered.

"And I love you."

I tucked the dagger into my girdle and pulled my cloak closer as I ducked into the night air and retraced my steps toward to the squat little room that Bagoas and I shared. I hadn't gone far when I heard male voices raised in argument.

"The men dislike these Persians and even your new affectations. Now you want to further upset your army by taking a Persian wife. You want to disappoint the same loyal soldiers who have followed you for almost ten years all the way from Macedon?"

Of course I stopped to listen, clinging to the shadows as I recognized Hephaestion's voice. *Persian wife?*

"You're wrong. The men will go where I lead."

Alexander.

"This is unnecessary," Hephaestion continued, the frustration tightening his voice. "I've quashed plenty of angry grumbles regarding your thirty thousand captives sent to train in Susa, green boys to fill your future ranks, and you've already ordered the older and infirm soldiers back at the Oxus to sire children with their Persian mistresses to fill the future army."

My skin prickled. I'd heard the stories of survivors of Alexander's sieges being rounded up, the women given as slave-mistresses to the soldiers. Was that what Alexander was planning here at Sogdian Rock? Were we women the treasure he sought to distribute to his slavering men?

I'd cut off their shafts with Parizad's knife before I let them have me like a common whore again.

"The gods smile upon me and all my ventures," Alexander answered. "I must marry and have an heir. A Persian queen at my side will garner the support of the Bactrians and the rest of these far-flung Persians. There remain only a scattering of rock fortresses to defeat until Sogdiana is secure. From there, the path to India shall be wide-open."

Marry.

Alexander planned to wed a Persian and make her queen, but I was no queen, only the Whore of Sogdian Rock. And Alexander wasn't likely to take me as his mistress if he'd just taken a wife.

Piss and shit.

Just like that, all my hopes had been dashed. Again.

I swallowed a cry of outrage as Hephaestion cleared his throat in the dark. "Surely you could choose a different woman, Alexander. You don't have to marry a whore to sink your shaft into her."

"She's noble," Alexander said, his voice taut. "And she's the woman I've chosen. The men will accept her because I tell them to."

"I hope you're right," Hephaestion said, his voice stretched just as thin. "For your sake, and theirs."

Footsteps came my way and on instinct I ducked into a dark doorway, holding my breath until they passed.

I recalled the way Alexander's eyes had burned for me at the banquet, for I knew of only one woman here who fit the description of a noble Persian whore.

Surely I was somehow wrong, for never in my wildest fantasies had I imagined that Alexander would ever marry someone like me: the grasping bastard daughter of Oxyartes of Balkh, discarded mistress of a traitor king, and foulmouthed whore to half the Persian forces of Sogdian Rock.

Still, a desperate hope blossomed in my chest and I nearly laughed into the night, hurrying on my way with my heart thudding in my ears.

I'd tucked Parizad's knife under my mattress and had barely lain down next to a sleeping Bagoas, my mind churning as I stared into the dark, when someone pounded at our weathered wooden door. It wasn't the first time a drunken soldier had come carousing, but it was the first time I had a weapon to stop him.

"Go away," I yelled, clutching my blanket to my breasts as my fingers curled around Parizad's knife.

"No chance of that," Hephaestion bellowed from the other side. "Open the door or I swear I'll break it down."

And he would. Probably with his head.

I nodded to Bagoas and wrapped the blanket tighter around me. The door opened to reveal a scowling Hephaestion, with Parizad behind him looking like he'd just been given a king's palace.

"Get up," Hephaestion grunted. He opened my wooden chest, grimaced, and let the lid drop as he glanced at Bagoas, who was cowering in the shadows. "You're going to the shrine of Ahura Mazda, so have your eunuch drape you in your finest fripperies."

"Why?"

I suspected I knew the answer, but I wanted to hear him say the words.

Hephaestion whirled on me, impatience rank in his expression. "Because, Roxana of Balkh, you're getting married."

"To who?" I asked, as sweetly as I could manage even as I shivered with excitement.

"To Alexander," he roared. "Now get dressed before I truss you like a pig and drag you there myself!"

He turned and stormed from the room, but my brother's exuberant grin matched my own as the door slammed shut.

And I cackled with glee then, great chortles of laughter that threatened never to end, knowing that my most wild dream was about to come true.

CHAPTER 17

326 BCE
Punjab, India

HEPHAESTION

Alexander had informed me upon discovering Barsine's pregnancy that he couldn't marry his Persian whore, but that was only a convenient shadow of the truth. What he really meant was that he didn't wish to wed a Persian harlot that he'd already bedded and whose pretty face he'd grown accustomed to. However, now the real truth was revealed: Alexander was willing, if not eager, to bind himself to a different Persian whore who simpered with practiced ease.

He'd lost his head over this one, for Roxana had him twisted tightly around her perfectly manicured little finger. Oblivious to his men's blatant stares, Alexander leaned down from his horse to kiss her in her ebony traveling sedan, a passionate embrace with wandering hands and devouring lips better suited to their wedding bed— which they hadn't left for days, until I'd finally dared to barge into Ariamazes' former chambers and remind Alexander that he had a kingdom to run and another to conquer, if he could rouse himself from Roxana's sweet thighs and luscious lips.

He had, but only barely.

And yet I knew Alexander, and knew that this infatuation would soon burn itself out, leaving behind the sorry truth that he'd chosen his bride with his prick instead of his head, saddling himself with a harlot instead of a better-born and better-bred Persian princess, a woman like Darius' daughter Stateira.

Alexander claimed his marriage to Roxana was a political alliance to sway the remainder of the Persian commanders to his side and to give him an heir, but there was no denying Roxana's sloe-eyed beauty, her high cheekbones and pelt of glossy black hair. The swell of her breasts, the lush curve of her lips, and the sweet spikenard perfume that heralded her every movement would have stirred any man's blood, be he eight or eighty.

And Alexander was no child or old mossback, but a hot-blooded man.

There were the rumors too that Roxana was well trained in the art of pleasuring a man after her time spent as Bessus' unofficial mistress. Only Alexander could confirm that bit of gossip—although I could guess the truth at the way he could scarcely keep his hands off her—and for that I felt a twinge of envy, quickly quashed as I had Parizad and any number of camp women to entertain me this night and all the others to come.

Since Persepolis and the fires, I'd been like a starving man grasping at crumbs. All save one encounter in a darkened tomb . . .

I smiled at the remembrance, but I'd have been half-dead not to feel jealous that crass Roxana of Balkh had managed to ensnare *my* golden Alexander.

"All hail the wife of Alexander, our new Queen of Queens," I mused to Roxana from atop my warhorse. She lounged back in her litter beneath purple silk curtains that protected her fair skin from the devious heat, a ridiculous extravagance as we traveled from the subdued fortresses of Sogdiana toward Alexander's next targets in India. A diadem twisted into a Heracles knot and studded with emeralds twinkled at her brow, a thinly filigreed cap of gold I'd caught her fingering as if she couldn't believe it was there, even as she watched Alexander canter away. "That's a fine accomplishment for the daughter of Oxyartes of Balkh."

Roxana's gaze flicked in my direction. "Is your remark an insult against my birth, Hephaestion of Macedon? I won't tolerate such insolence, not even from my husband's *chiliarch*."

Chiliarch. I'd served as the torchbearer for Alexander's wedding, watched him cut the ceremonial loaf of brown bread with his sword and feed a piece into Roxana's parted and well-rouged lips, and then received this new title as a gift, handed down to the second-in-command of all Persian kings. I had yet to see its benefits, save the lack of sleep all the extra work wrought.

"Of course not, my queen," I said, offering her a smile that would need polishing in the days to come. "I think you mistook my remark. After all, your father has proved quite an asset to Alexander."

An asset insomuch as Oxyartes had appeared out of thin air after Roxana's marriage and convinced Sisimithres, the commander of the Rock of Chorienes, to surrender without a fight, claiming that no fortress could stand if Alexander decided to take it. Sisimithres had opened his gates and his larder, filling our men's stomachs with fresh flatbread, dried ox flesh, and decent vintages of wine. Of course, Sisimithres was a man who had married his own mother, so there was no guarantee that he wouldn't have capitulated without Oxyartes' prodding. Alexander had rewarded Oxyartes handsomely, but strangely, Roxana rarely acknowledged her father. I'd hoped that Alexander would deposit both Roxana and her father in some far-flung citadel, but it was quite likely that our new Queen of Queens would remain with us far longer. She was a symbol to all of Persia of Alexander's goodwill, a cease-fire of flesh and blood with the promise of a permanent treaty that might one day drop from her fertile womb.

"How long shall it take for us to reach the court of King Taxiles?"

Roxana asked. She fiddled with the silver stitching on the sleeve of her cloth-of-gold traveling robe. I'd made up my mind that she was a grasping siren when she'd complained that surely Darius' wife had owned more than one crown, prompting Alexander to commission several more to outdo his predecessor, including the new diadem Roxana now wore. It would be a kindness to supply her attendants with tufts of wool with which to stuff their ears.

"Alexander plans to reach the court of King Taxiles by the end of summer," I said.

"The end of summer?" Her pupils widened beneath the black *sormeh* powder she'd used to line her eyes. I thought I even detected a faint dusting of pale white powder to lighten her skin, a trick most practiced whores used. "Piss and shit," she whispered under her breath.

Ah yes, our vulgar guttersnipe of a queen.

"Surely you jest," she said to me.

"I wish I did," I replied, although truthfully I wouldn't have minded if the journey took three years instead of three months. "In fact, today I ride ahead to oversee the building of a bridge across the Indus River, the better to ease our travel. I'm sure Alexander will keep you in great comfort in the long months to come."

"My husband is indeed a generous man," she said. "Yet it pains me to see you ride a stallion more magnificent than his. Is it seemly for you to outshine your King of Kings?"

I forced myself to smile. "Alexander prefers to ride Bucephalus, and whichever other beasts please his fancy. In fact, I hear he's taken a liking to that eunuch of yours."

"Bagoas would never dare such a thing," she said, but I reveled in the unsettled glance she cast in the eunuch's direction. If she thought to play at being queen, she'd have to learn to temper her emotions, or at least disguise them. "How dare you insinuate such a thing?"

"My apologies," I said, baiting her. "I assumed you knew of Alexander's varied tastes."

It was clear from Roxana's expression that she'd had no idea. Surely she hadn't believed that Alexander would be faithful to her, not after he'd bedded her and done her the unthinkable honor of making her a queen.

Yet as her mouth worked to form words and her face darkened, I could see that impossible dream was precisely what she'd expected. I almost pitied her then. She'd thought Alexander would be an easy conquest, further proof that she didn't understand or deserve him.

"Parizad," I barked, turning about. "Guard your sister. Enjoy the long journey to India, Queen Roxana."

I kicked my horse's ribs and galloped forward, thankful that I had a bridge to build to ferry Alexander's troops into the heart of India.

After all, attacking a regiment of Indians armed with tusked elephants would be preferable to speaking to Alexander's new wife again.

I crossed the Hindu Kush Mountains with a contingent of men and oversaw the construction, reveling in the sound of hammers and smiling to myself as I heard in my mind a woman's familiar voice questioning the spacing and the thickness of planks as we sank piers into the riverbed and lashed the beams atop. I wondered what Drypetis was doing then, whether she had somehow found contentment in Susa.

I chuckled to myself at the thought, for I had yet to witness Drypetis' contentment with anything this world had to offer.

I enjoyed the quiet freedom of the work, but too soon, the rest of the army rejoined us. Alexander commended the bridge and together we continued to cut a swath of destruction through India, beckoned by the lure of lands reputed to be lusher than Egypt, where the air was filled with the scents of saffron and cinnamon. The red earth was parched, its pine trees lifting their branches like hands beseeching the sky for rain. This was a land rumored by the historian Herodotus to be populated not by humans but by giant ants, and while we encountered plenty of foul, oversized insects, so too did we meet dark-skinned people on our way to what Alexander claimed was the sea at the end of the world. I'd encountered Indians as mercenaries only on the battlefield at Gaugamela, but these Indians were slim and foreign creatures who carried parasols against the sun and dyed their beards white, red, purple, or green. We passed their bald-headed holy men along the road, sitting or lying naked in various postures. I considered stopping to discuss philosophy with them, knowing Aristotle would berate me for missing such an opportunity, but Alexander continued doggedly on.

And I followed, as I always did, Aristotle be damned.

Some of the Indian inhabitants begged us via gestures and gifts of precious spices to leave their cities in peace, while others attacked and forced us to litter their streets with corpses rancid with the stink of death. Our men grew wearier with each step of the march that took them farther into this foreign land, but now there was the promise of new riches as we faced off across the Hydaspes River against the general Porus, who was famed for being as tall and as wide as one of his many cavalry elephants. There were so many of the gray beasts on the other side of the swollen river that we could hear them stamping and trumpeting while the rains lashed down upon us, pouring from the rims of our helmets and threatening to rust our swords where we stood. I spared a wry smile to think of pampered Roxana attempting to weather this belligerent storm, even as our men let fly the Macedonian war cry and beat their shields in an attempt to strike fear into the hearts of the Indians.

Lightning strikes flashed from the clouds and shattered the curtains of rain that obscured my vision. Zeus' favored weapon felled some unlucky bastard—one of our Persian recruits—not far from where I stood, burning his flesh and rendering him mute.

An ill omen, by any man's standard, and one that reminded me of Adurnarseh.

Yet Alexander ordered his generals to provide distractions while the main force of our army traveled upriver to cross. Under the cover of night and lashing rains, Alexander waded into the raging brown river dressed in full battle armor before hauling himself into one of the newly constructed straw and oxhide floats. Muttering and cursing all the while, I bellowed over the clamor for the Companions and cavalry to follow in the rest of the skiffs.

The blood-warm river and incessant rains overturned several of the rafts, and we emerged on the other side stinking of wet leather and panting like dogs.

Artemis' tits, but I was sick of being cold and wet and exhausted.

Unable to fully see us in the storm and falling for the distractions we'd arranged downriver, Porus had split into two his army of javelin throwers and archers armed with strange Indian bows as tall as a man. His fatal error allowed us to flank both his regiments. Alexander had prepared three thousand shield bearers with axes to slash at the elephants' legs and tusks. The beasts screamed their retreat even as their blood joined that of their riders, turning the muddy river to a sluice of red as if the veins of the earth had been slit open as the waters churned in violent death throes.

The rest of the battle passed in fits and starts, hours reduced to fragmented images of an Indian soldier being brained by the broadside of a Macedonian sword, horses screaming in terror, and Alexander roaring orders, his men moving like a living extension of his arm.

"We've got him," Alexander said to me as the fight neared its end, his face alight. "The great Porus himself shall bow and scrape before me."

"Like so many other kings and generals," I said.

"And I shall never grow tired of it." Alexander grinned and clapped me on the back. "Come with me to receive him."

For once, the rumors were true, for Porus was so large that when he was brought to us upon his largest elephant, he seemed a normal man astride his horse. His hair was gathered into a topknot in the Indian style and he wore a light cotton cloak over a massive leather cuirass that might have covered half a newborn elephant. He rewarded Alexander with a rare hunting bitch rumored to share the blood of tigers, thousands of four-horse chariots, lizard skins and tortoiseshells studded with beryl and onyx, and crates of fragrant cardamom, balsam, and sweet rush. Yet Alexander was so impressed with Porus' daring and the tenacity of his men that he named him *satrap* over the tribes of his remaining Indians.

It was a victory, followed by a tragedy.

A horse handler found me just as Alexander finished negotiating with Porus, the servant's eyes darting to our king while he wrung his hands.

"What is it, man?" I asked. "You look as if Porus' elephants have stampeded all of our geldings into the Hydaspes."

"Almost as bad," the handler stuttered. "Worse, perhaps."

I wiped the sweat and grime from the back of my neck. My sword arm throbbed and my shoulders ached as the thrill of the battle slowly leaked from my bones. I was fast approaching my thirtieth summer, certainly not yet old, but no longer the brash, invincible idiot I'd been when we first left Aigai almost ten years ago. We used to drink hard and carouse even harder to celebrate our victories, but tonight I craved nothing more than a cup of spiced wine and my copy of Aeschylus' *Seven Against Thebes*.

I snorted. Perhaps I *was* getting old.

I motioned again to the tongue-tied handler. "The skies could rain blood and Alexander wouldn't notice after a victory such as this. Spit out your news."

"It's Bucephalus."

"Ox-Head?"

He nodded, then bit the tip of his thumb. There was a welt of blood there already, as if he'd gnawed the unfortunate digit all the way here. "The king's horse, well, he was almost thirty summers old. . . ."

The same age as me.

The handler looked up, pulling a sliver of thumbnail from between his teeth, and flicked it to the ground. "I kept Bucephalus penned with a trough of sweetgrass, just as Alexander ordered, but the horse lay down and died just after the rains began. It was fatigue and old age—I swear it—not negligence on my part."

Artemis' tits. I'd hated Ox-Head with his ridiculous horned helmet, but it was no wonder that the poor handler looked ready to jump out of his bones every time his gaze skittered to Alexander.

"Go and prepare the beast: Brush the black demon and weave flowers into his mane." The man's panic twisted into confusion. "No flowers," I amended. "Just make him look like the hell-horse he was, carrying Alexander to eternal glory. I'll break the news to him myself."

The handler scurried away before I could change my mind. I waited until Porus lumbered off to his new illustrious posting; there was no need for the new *satrap* to see his conqueror rage, or more likely weep, over a dead horse.

"A glorious victory, is it not, Hephaestion?" Alexander asked, rising and gesturing to the plain choked with mounds of corpses like freshly turned earth. A mist of rain still fell as he paused to squeeze the shoulder of a dazed and shivering shield bearer. The man stuttered his thanks, yet another soldier who would tell his children and grandchildren of Alexander's largesse and the way the sun seemed to follow him.

"It is indeed," I said, counting to ten to give him a few more moments to enjoy his triumph. His bronze cuirass was stained with blood and he stank of hard-earned sweat, but he grinned like the boy I'd known in Aristotle's Mieza. "Yet I fear the day is not done."

"What do you mean?" His brows knit together as if he were finally seeing me, and not some battle map in his mind.

"Bucephalus is dead," I said. "He breathed his last before you crossed the river."

Alexander didn't speak for a moment, then let out a thunderclap of a curse, drew his sword, and flung it like a discus away from him. I thanked the gods there was no unfortunate soul standing in his path to be gored by the blade. From his shattered expression I might have been delivering news of the death of Olympias or Thessalonike, rather than a mere horse.

"I loved that horse," Alexander said to me, his blue eyes shining brighter than usual, his visage that of a gutted man. "He was the best horse a man could have."

Ox-Head was a hell-horse fit for Hades and had been since before Alexander had broken him as a boy, but I realized I'd actually miss the cantankerous old beast. Whatever his faults, Bucephalus had been fiercely loyal to Alexander, which was something I could appreciate.

"I know," I said, wrapping my arm around Alexander's shoulders and fitting him into my side. Sometimes I forgot how much smaller he was than me, so much space did his energy seem to eat up. "We shall burn him tonight so the crows cannot have him."

"And let the stars keep us company while we regale ourselves with stories of his victories," Alexander said, wiping a hand over his face.

So much for Aeschylus' *Seven Against Thebes*.

But I nodded to this man who was a brother and so much more than a brother to me.

"We shall greet the dawn," I said. "And still have stories left to tell."

In fact, we might have put our younger selves to shame that night, drinking enough wine to fill the Hydaspes River in honor of that black demon horse. Ptolemy and Craterus and the other generals joined us to sing dirges of dead gods and ditties extolling the ripeness of a maiden's breasts, so that together we spilled enough wine to make offerings to all twelve Olympians and their countless offspring. We played *kottabos* until our sword arms threatened to fall off, the inane drinking game that involved flinging wine dregs at a copper disk target floating in a basin of water. Finally, the others drifted away and took their songs with them, Ptolemy to seek out one mistress or another, while Craterus passed out with an empty *amphora* tucked under each arm.

It was just Alexander and me.

And as we lit the pyre, Alexander drew me close and kissed me, his lips hard, demanding, and warmer than a smothered fire. I answered by pushing him against a tree, intoxicated by the smell and feel of him, so familiar and yet so exotic. "I need you," he whispered to me, with a groan of desire close to pain.

And I needed him. I suspected I always would.

"What is all this?"
Roxana stood overhead, her arms akimbo and a glare that I might have mocked had the clouds over her not swayed alarmingly as I struggled to sit. The air was still salted with the smell of smoke from Bucephalus' funeral *pyra* and a light dusting of gray ash clung to my arm, the result of the meager wind changing direction in the night.

There might have been a poem in the ashes of a great warhorse armoring a living soldier, but my head clanged too loudly to pluck the words from the air.

I groaned and shielded my eyes. "To the left a little, if you please, Queen Roxana. The sun is blinding today."

And so was the humid heat, so thick Alexander and I had slept outside like common soldiers, wrapped together in our cloaks under the stars. Now we disentangled ourselves, the flesh of my chest and arms damp from where they had been pressed against his in our sleep. I stretched my legs out in front of me, in no hurry to move despite the harridan who glowered down at us.

"I'm not accustomed to repeating myself," Roxana said to us through gritted teeth. "What is all this?"

"It's quite simple, really," I answered for Alexander as he crouched by the banks of the river, returned to its original muddy hue, and splashed his face. "After such a resounding victory, Alexander treated us to his finest wines and asked our opinions on the name of his newest city. We agreed it should be named after his most favored, most beautiful companion. . . ."

Of course, the simpering wench took the bait, preening with every word.

"And so," I continued, "we agreed that Alexander should rename his next conquered city after his horse."

Roxana whirled on Alexander. "Your horse? Basileios—"

"Bucephalus," I corrected her before Alexander could order her tongue cut out.

"—was a beast of burden. Nothing would warrant renaming a city after an animal."

"I would never rename a fallen city after my horse," Alexander said, rubbing a hand over the golden stubble on his cheeks. For the first time I noticed wisps of lines at his eyes, as if the three fair-haired Horae of time had waved their hands before his face and left their imprint there.

"You wouldn't?" Roxana said. "But Hephaestion said—"

"I am building an entirely new city here, on the banks of the Hydaspes, and naming *it* after my horse," he finished.

"Bucephalia shall indeed be a lovely city," I said. I needed an infusion of willow bark to calm the pounding in my skull; each blow was like the thundering of Roxana's shrill voice. And Bucephalia *did* have a nicer ring to it than Ox-Headia.

Alexander swept past his wife, the conversation at an end. I stood and picked up my helmet, sniffing it and wincing at the stench of wine fumes. I shook the wine dregs from its interior, remembering that it had worked passably as a cup after I lost my golden *kylix* last night. I'd have to check Ptolemy's tent; the man was notorious for making off with things that didn't belong to him.

Roxana stared openmouthed as Alexander poured an offering from the last *krater* onto the remnants of Bucephalus' *pyra*, the horse's white skull and long bones covered in ashes and a few flies, which Alexander kicked with his boot. To her credit, Roxana waited until he'd stumbled out of earshot before she spun on me.

"This is *your* fault," she said, her lovely eyes narrowed into unattractive slits. "You entice him to drink and carouse when he should be spending his nights in my pavilion."

"My deepest apologies," I said, feigning a yawn. "Although perhaps I might offer you some advice regarding Alexander?"

"And what is that?"

"You've a pretty face, Roxana—more than pretty, actually—but you shriek like a crow and fill our ears with your complaints. Perhaps you should cease your squawking until your belly swells with Alexander's heir."

Her hands balled into fists and she stepped so close that I almost choked on her spikenard perfume. "Perhaps I'd have more of a chance to conceive if Alexander wasn't always sinking his sword into you and Bagoas!" She actually stomped her foot like an angry child. "I'm the Queen of Queens, yet I'm treated with less respect than a horse!"

I shrugged. "Perhaps if you proved yourself more useful than a horse, Alexander might name a city after you as well. Last night he claimed he plans to name his next after his favorite female."

"Really? When?"

It was far too easy to goad Roxana. But then, I'd met only one woman whose tongue and wit matched my own, and she was probably harping at some unfortunate soul in Susa's grand palace.

"After we cross the Ganges," I said, throwing the words over my shoulder as I tossed my helmet in the air, my head suddenly clearer after exchanging insults with Roxana. "He plans to name it Peritas, after his favorite hunting bitch."

The gods had never denied Alexander anything: the whole of Persia delivered to him on a golden platter, Darius conveniently killed by his own cousin, and the wealth of the world counted and stacked in tidy piles awaiting his approval. The tapestry of his life had been woven with thread of gold, but the Fates began tugging at it after Bucephalus died, and not even Alexander could avert the touch of Hades. And then things truly began to unravel.

The Ganges was a long, sluggish snake of a river, the sun glinting off its green waters like scales, and our men muttered among themselves that the river was more than a hundred fathoms deep. Our scouts returned with reports that more than eighty thousand Indian soldiers and six thousand war elephants waited on the other side to slaughter us. It was there that the generals suggested we turn back, retreat to Persia and then to Greece, leaving the remainder of India untouched.

I expected Alexander to give a rousing speech or ford the river himself as he'd done at the Hydaspes, but instead his face merely turned black with rage and he stormed into his tent.

We waited for him to emerge laden with books or maps or battle plans to persuade them of their folly, but heard instead the crash of something heavy and surely expensive. The generals cast shocked looks in the direction of Alexander's gold-columned tent. The flap flicked open, but it was pretty Bagoas who emerged, his wide eyes darting behind him as his feet kicked up puffs of dust. A fresh laceration on his shoulder marred his smooth skin and his elegant hands shook.

"The King of Kings is not to be disturbed," he said to me. I almost pitied the eunuch then—more than I already did for his lost shaft and cods—for he was unaccustomed to the squalls of Alexander's temper and apparently unwilling to fight back.

"Return to your men," I commanded the generals. "Tell them that Alexander is taking their comments under advisement, but that they must prepare to ford the river come dawn."

The generals hesitated as if they might protest, but then filed past, still casting furtive glances at Alexander's tent. "Alexander has won us many battles," the captain of the shield bearers said to me, his tone bordering on reverence at odds with his tattered Macedonian *chiton*. "Yet he is a man, not a god. And Tyche is a fickle goddess; a man can only do so much before the blind Mistress of Fortune deserts him."

"Tyche is indeed a fickle bitch." I thumped the captain firmly on the back. "I'll speak to Alexander."

I sent Bagoas for wine and found Alexander cross-legged on the ground of his tent, his chest heaving as he clenched and unclenched his fists. He didn't even look up at me before roaring like a wronged lion. "Get out!"

"Is this the Alexander whom the entire world looks to?" I asked. "Throwing a tantrum on the floor like a child?"

"You forget yourself," he growled. "I haven't given you leave to speak so freely."

"And you've forgotten whom you're speaking to," I said. I was

grateful that the night we'd spent together after Bucephalus' death
had worn away the thorns between us so I could say my mind to
Alexander again. "I'm Hephaestion. I've earned the right to speak
to you however I wish, and you well know it."

I tossed myself into a leather-slung chair, knocking the wax seal
off a nearby *amphora* of wine and drinking my fill before passing the
container to him, breathing a sigh of relief when he took it instead
of flinging it across the room.

He wiped his mouth with the back of his hand. "Those men
outside and the worthless maggots that follow them have betrayed
me with their refusal to march further into India. I'll have them all
killed if they won't obey me."

"Those men have won you many crowns and still more titles." I
leaned down and swiped the *amphora* from him. "And I suggest you
don't call them maggots in their hearing."

"I don't care if they hear," he said, jumping to his feet and beginning to pace. "They ask me to retreat, but doing so would mean
admitting defeat at the mere threat of being outnumbered."

"Severely outnumbered," I reminded him, but he didn't hear.
"And if I recall, you recently received a letter from Thessalonike.
This could be the perfect opportunity to return home in glory,
unvanquished, and settle the squabble between Antipater and your
mother."

"Their feud is a petty grievance, scarcely worth my notice. I will
never be vanquished," he muttered. "Not here. Not ever. Like Achilles, I shall not leave this ground."

I groaned inwardly. I'd survived many of Alexander's recitations
of *The Song of Ilium* and still more of his boasts that he would outdo
even Achilles in this life.

"I will not leave," he said. "Not until they stand outside my tent
and beg me to ford the Ganges, to march with them into the heart
of India. Let them rot on their way back to Macedon."

"Fine," I said, for there was no use arguing with him now. Not for the first time and especially after seeing so many crowns placed upon his head, I wondered if Alexander carried too much now, if he had in fact become as capricious as the gods he sought to emulate. "Remain in your tent to pout, and then see if they spin epic tales about your leadership and acts of bravery."

"They cannot doubt me," Alexander said so softly that I had to turn to hear. "They must go where I command, Hephaestion."

I threw my hands up. "They do. But they've grown weary after ten years of fighting in your name. They aren't gods like you, merely men who miss their homes and families."

He walked to me, then laid his hands on my shoulders and pressed his forehead to mine. "Then they must remember that I am their family, just as you are mine. I will go forward into India, or I will stay here and perish on the banks of the Ganges. The choice is theirs."

In the end, the generals agreed to cross the Ganges, but I'd known even before then what their decision would be. For what man would dare claim that he turned his back on Alexander?

"Over the top!" Alexander screamed, and we rushed forward in a sea of metal armor and round shields. Despite their renown as the fiercest fighters in the whole of India, the Mallian archers had fallen back and our scaling ladders clattered against their walls like the long legs of some carnivorous insect. Alexander sheathed his sword, his blazing sun shield still strapped to his forearm, and leapt onto the first ladder before practically running up the rungs. I followed, a dagger clamped tight in my mouth as I scrambled to keep up with him.

"They'll sing about this for ages!" Alexander called down to me, a maniacal grin splitting his sun-beaten face. The madman was enjoying this.

The walls were the height of perhaps seven or eight men, and I'd have commanded the main gate broken down before I'd ordered scaling ladders. More men clambered behind us, each adding his own weight to the mango-wood ladder—hastily constructed after we'd pillaged the Mallian orchards—and making it tremble and groan. Arrows rained down at us as more Indian archers from above took aim. A soldier behind me screamed and the ladder wobbled as if released of a man-sized weight, but I dared not look down unless I wanted to join him.

Above me, Alexander leapt over the ramparts and I followed just as there came a terrible cracking sound below. Angry brown faces shouted down at us and arrows whizzed past so close I could feel them, but I turned to see the ladder bow and then splinter at its midline, shedding screaming men as its middle smashed and then scraped down the stone walls like some giant's claw struggling for purchase. Armor and swords flashed in the melee before yellow dust enveloped them all. The soldier directly behind me, an old Macedonian veteran named Peucestes, had just made it to the top rung, but now he grasped at stones, his torso and legs dangling over the edge of the wall.

I hauled him over, then turned, dreading the scene I knew would be worse than what I'd just witnessed.

We three were alone.

Well, alone save for the hundreds of armed Mallians facing us.

And Alexander, fool that he was, lunged into their midst with a bloodcurdling yell.

I'll never know what the Mallians thought—whether they glimpsed a god fallen to earth in a blinding flash of silver or whether they realized that their walls would soon be overrun with snarling Greeks wielding swords against their wooden arrows. Whatever it was, the Mallians hesitated.

But only for a moment.

Then they fell upon us, screaming like a flock of a thousand eagles. And we fought.

This was no battle, only a feint from death as we tried to hide from their arrows behind our shields. Deep within their mass of swords, a swarthy Mallian a head taller than the others drew his bowstring.

And aimed his arrow at Alexander.

The world slowed even as I slashed with my sword and smashed the skull of a shrieking Mallian with my shield. But that lone Mallian arrow flew forward just as Alexander opened his shield arm to strike another man with his blade.

The arrow pierced cleanly through his unprotected cuirass, just as Pausanius' dagger had done to Philip more than a decade ago. Alexander's eyes bulged, one knee bending so he came to the ground as if bowing before the shrine of some foreign god.

Or the altar of Hades.

Then the Mallian archer ran forward, his scimitar drawn over his head to steal Alexander's life.

I'd be damned to the farthest depths of Tartarus if I'd let him succeed.

Peucestes too had seen and together we pushed forward, striking the Mallian so hard that the blow into bone and flesh reverberated up my sword arm.

But from the melee and dust to our left lunged another snarling Mallian, this one wielding a wooden club. And this time, there was nothing we could do to stop him.

That club came down on the back of Alexander's neck with a sickening thud and I reached out in vain to clutch his *chlamys* and keep him from careening over the wall's edge into Hades' waiting arms. The stones caught him just as our men streamed over the rampart from a new ladder.

"Surround him!" I screamed, and the blessed Macedonians moved to form a protective barrier around their wounded king. "Lift him and cover us!" I commanded, for now that the ladders were in place, we would quickly outnumber the Mallians. Shield bearers and Companions spread their gleaming round shields around us as we carried Alexander from the fray.

If Alexander died, I'd see every last Mallian put to the sword, their town torched and their fields salted.

Alexander would not die. He *could not* die.

The wooden shaft of the Mallian arrow had to be sawed off, so embedded was it in the boiled leather of Alexander's cuirass and his pale flesh that no amount of cajoling by the surgeons could loosen it. All the while, Alexander lay insensate on the cot, his face the shade of a long-dead corpse. Bagoas had entered once, but I'd sent him away, unwilling to share what might be Alexander's last moments with anyone else.

It wasn't until the surgeons in their bloodstained *chitons* un-strapped Alexander's leather breastplate and sought to remove the arrowhead from his ribs that he roused with an animal groan of pain that made his eyes flutter. His pupils were dilated in agony, obscur-ing the blue irises so that both of his eyes matched for the first time I'd ever seen.

I willed him to speak, to rage against the Mallians, but he only gurgled and gasped in pain as the butchers dug into his wound with their iron tools, his hands like fetters around my wrists. The arrow-head was three fingers thick and nearly four long, and it took all my willpower not to bash the physicians' heads together as they debated how best to remove the cursed thing.

Worthless men masquerading as Asclepius' disciples. I threatened to have them all impaled on sharpened stakes if they didn't remove the rest of the arrow. That seemed to get them moving instead of bickering.

Midway through a procedure that involved opening the wound with scalpels and prying the shaft loose with a long-necked spoon, Roxana arrived. She was dressed in orange silk, her dark hair piled high on her head and a wasp pendant secured between the mounds of her breasts, creating a pull between the silk there that I might have found alluring had I not been drenched in Alexander's blood. She took one look at Alexander stretched out on the table and swayed on her feet. "By the holy flame of Ahura Mazda," she said. "Will he live?"

The physicians ignored her as they poked and prodded at the hole in Alexander's barely rising chest. "He will if I have any say in the matter," I said.

"You," she said, as if she hadn't noticed my presence before. "You were with him when he was injured?"

"I helped kill the bastard who thought his ribs could make good use of this adornment, yes," I said. "And my sword took a liking to the man who clubbed him over the head."

If I'd expected any gratitude, it was only because I'd forgotten to whom I spoke.

"You imbecile," she screeched. "It's your responsibility to *protect* Alexander! Instead, you may as well have gored him and offered him to Ahriman yourself!"

I had her arm twisted behind her back before she could blink, smearing her pristine silks with Alexander's blood. "You will return to your tent until Alexander summons you," I growled.

"And if he doesn't recover to summon me?"

"Then you'll stay there and rot."

She didn't flinch as I shoved her away. I waited only until she'd retreated in a swirl of orange to clasp Alexander's hand, even as the surgeons gently eased the head of the arrow and the remainder of its shaft from his torso.

"Give it to me," I said, reaching out my free hand for the ruined weapon.

They looked at me as if my mind was garbled, which perhaps it was, but turned over the arrow. I watched in silence as they sewed Alexander's wound with tight stitches of white silk, like spiders weaving a macabre web in human flesh.

"You may wish to avert your eyes," one said, and I saw then that he held a knife over the dancing flame of an oil lamp.

But I forced myself to watch as he pressed the heated blade to the wound, cauterizing it with a hiss of steam so painful that Alexander roused himself to consciousness long enough to scream before falling into blessed oblivion once again.

Then the surgeons' deft hands packed the injury with a honey poultice even as they applied a bloody chunk of meat onto his swollen neck.

"From a freshly butchered ox," one of the surgeons assured me. "To draw out the ill humors."

"Will he survive?" I asked, echoing Roxana's earlier question.

The surgeon finished wrapping the meat around Alexander's neck. "We should all pray to the twelve gods that the wound in his ribs doesn't turn rancid." He gave me a neat bow. "Is there anything else you require, *chiliarch*?"

I was Alexander's second-in-command. If he died, I would become the lone commander of his massive armies. Yet I had no taste left for conquering and would trade every soldier beyond the infirmary's goatskin walls to keep Alexander alive. I shook my head and the surgeons departed, leaving the King of Kings, the conqueror of the world, on a stained military cot, balanced precariously between life and death.

I know not how much time passed, only that the stench of sweat and blood hadn't dissipated when I heard a sound sweeter than the clearest honey.

"I've bested them again, haven't I?"

His voice was a mere croak, better suited to a crone's mouth than to a golden lion, but it might have been mistaken for the trill of Apollo's lyre to my ears.

"You're an utter fool," I said, trying to snarl even as my voice cracked with relief. "Scaling the wall first and giving the Mallians the whole of you for target practice. The next time you want to die, I'll save everyone the trouble and kill you myself."

"A god cannot be killed by mere men," Alexander said.

I recalled Alexander's head wound at Granicus, his thigh wound at Issus, and a stone strike to his head just before Sogdian Rock. It was a wonder the man was still alive at all.

Still, he needed to learn a lesson, right here and right now.

I wormed my thumb beneath the bandages at Alexander's chest so hard that he cried out, then shoved my thumb under his nose.

"This is the blood of men," I said. "Not golden *ichor*. And this," I added, revealing the spear shank stained with his blood, "is the arrow that almost killed you."

He stared at it a moment, then grimaced. "We should add it to my collection," he whispered, closing his eyes and brushing the scar on my arm. "For I still have the arrow that gave you this."

"You almost died," I whispered.

He grimaced. "That explains why I feel less than godly. Where is Bagoas? And Roxana?"

"I sent them away," I said. "You'll have to make do with me."

His eyes fluttered and his lips curled up in the hint of a smile. "Good," he whispered. "It shall be just like old times."

And just like old times, I kissed him, although his lips were pale and dry instead of wine-spiced and demanding, then maneuvered myself around him until we fit together on the cot, provided neither of us moved too suddenly and toppled the other onto the ground. And I sang to him then, songs of our boyhood that would usher him to sleep and away from the dark allure of Hades and the Fields of Elysium.

There would be time for death later. For now, Alexander would live.

And that was all that mattered.

CHAPTER 18

325 BCE
Cassope, Greece

THESSALONIKE

The myths all claimed that the gods came down to earth, but I'd never seen one. Unless you counted Olympias in her sapphire *peplos* with its golden snake shoulder clasps and her hair studded with tiny seed pearls—and she possessed an incinerating glare worse than any goddess' as she stalked into the potter's yard. I eyed the kiln, but it was too cramped for me to crawl inside and escape Olympias' inevitable rage.

Her eyes flicked disdainfully over me, at my hair in a straw-colored braid, at the dog hair that covered my dark *chiton*, and at my hands streaked with the rose madder dye I'd used to paint a clay soldier for Adea. "You look like a shepherd's daughter," she said.

My skin tingled at the insult even as the heat of Olympias' temper receded into her typical icy demeanor. I'd brought eleven-year-old Adea to the local potter this morning, and been bored to tears until I'd watched her gasp with pleasure as the ruddy-faced potter released clay figurines from the terra-cotta molds. The dolls held no allure for me, but the visit was a reward for having sparred with Adea at Cynnane's behest. I'd felt no small rush of pride at the suggestion, as if *I* possessed skills worthy of teaching Cynnane's daughter. Now Adea clutched a finished soldier figurine. A quick nod from me sent her scuttling inside.

Olympias snapped her fingers and a waiting slave came forward with a letter. "This just arrived from Alexander," she said, jutting her chin toward the rumpled scroll. "You should read it, for it concerns your future."

I hesitated, for we'd received so much bad news of late, first word of Alexander's Mallian injury and then the loss of many of his soldiers to disease and famine on the terrible retreat back to Persia. We'd had rumors of Alexander's growing Persian affectations and how he had kissed his eunuch Bagoas after a dancing contest in view of the entire army, then how my brother had demanded his Persian and Greek friends perform the *proskynesis*, bowing and kissing the tips of their fingers as if in reverence to a god.

I scanned past the salutations written in Alexander's pristine hand to the bottom of the missive. My brother described feasting for seven days on a platform drawn by eight horses through Gedrosia, the parade of purple-canopied chariots that followed behind to carry the harpists and singers, and the dancing girls celebrating the rites of Dionysus. His men wore no helmets and held no weapons during that week, he claimed, and were instead crowned with flowered garlands while they raised golden goblets to their own glory.

My throat grew tight as I read about his lack of precautions. Alexander believed no harm could come to him, but that was pure hubris, the same that had slain our father.

"He commends you for your swift action against Antipater," I said, shaking my head as I came to the end. "And asks that you do whatever necessary to ensure Antipater's power remains in check." I folded up the letter and placed it in her open palm.

"Alexander is in need of fresh men after his disastrous journey from India," she said, gazing toward the east, where, somewhere, her son sought still more lands to conquer. "Antipater and his son will rendezvous with him in Persia with extra Macedonian forces. With any luck, Antipater will die on the way and save us all the trouble of killing him."

"It seems a thorough plan," I said drily, bending over and pushing kindling into the kiln's fire chamber. If Antipater weren't such a bore, I might have felt pity for him for earning Olympias' ire.

"It is indeed a thorough plan," Olympias said. "Most especially the bit where I send you to accompany him."

I slammed the kiln door shut so fast I almost caught my thumb in it. "What? You'd send *me* to Persia?"

To Persepolis with its famed Gate of Nations, the Hundred Columns Palace, and the Tomb of Kings. To Babylon with its Ishtar Gate and Hanging Gardens.

To a war to be fought, and battles to be won.

"If that must be my punishment," I said calmly, although it was difficult to speak as my thudding heart had leapt to my throat in excitement.

Olympias' lips thinned to a tight line. "You shall accompany Antipater and prove your renewed loyalty by reporting on his movements and those of his son."

"When do I leave?"

"The ship is already waiting in the harbor."

And just like that, Olympias would excise me from her life, like a surgeon slicing out gangrenous flesh. Would that I could do the same to her.

"I'd take Cynnane with me. And Arrhidaeus."

Cynnane for protection, although I could handle a sword almost as well as she now that I'd seen twenty summers, and Arrhidaeus so he wasn't left unprotected from Olympias. After all, save for Barsine's illegitimate son, Arrhidaeus was our family's only male heir should anything happen to Alexander. I couldn't leave my brother in Olympias' clutches.

"Take them," she said. "I have no need of them here."

"Thank you," I said, forcing a smile. "I shall do my best to ensure Alexander's continued success."

She kissed my forehead and I had to force myself not to cringe. "See that you do."

"An army is no place for a menagerie," Antipater said, scowling, as I approached the entourage of soldiers and baggage waiting to escort us the remainder of the way to Babylon. Once again, I'd almost died from a sour stomach on the ship from Cassope to Pella and was thankful that the rest of the journey would take place overland by horse and cart.

I'd give at least a year of my life to never see the ocean again, five years to never step foot on the heaving deck of a cursed ship.

Olympias had commanded that I attend her Dionysian sacrifices for Alexander, and I could still smell the copper-coin reek of blood on my hands and feel writhing snakes on my skin. Now the road to Babylon and beyond stretched before us and my fingers itched to crack my whip overhead and race the whole way there. Antipater, on the other hand, looked ill as he gestured toward my baggage cart, stuffed with every sort of basket and cage imaginable. "Is all this really necessary?"

"I couldn't leave my darlings behind," I said as a slave lifted Aristomache's basket onto the top of the load. It might be well worth the punishment to hide my lovely little snake in Antipater's cot one night, just to hear him squeal like a child.

"Thessalonike is the protector of all creatures lost and broken," Cassander said to his father, in a tone that might have been mocking or serious.

"And apparently half the animals on earth as well," Antipater muttered as Cynnane mounted her stallion beside me. Pan, my shaggy goat, let out a loud *baa* as her lead rope was tied to the wagon. She'd given birth to a pair of kids while left behind in Pella and would provide fresh milk during our overland trek.

I'd never thought of myself as a protector of broken creatures, but Arrhidaeus sat in the cart with my newest companion nestled in a cage on his lap: an owl named Athena whose broken wing I'd healed. An excellent hunter, she was a sort of replacement for my orange cat, who had died of old age while we were in Cassope. Adea clambered into the cart next to Arrhidaeus and giggled as she fed the owl a strip of dried oxhide. Cynnane had insisted that her daughter accompany us in order to continue her military training, but that was a ruse to keep Adea away from Olympias.

And hidden in a secret compartment at the bottom of the owl cage was a letter Olympias had given me that morning, along with the command that it was for Alexander's eyes only.

We'd see about that.

We left behind Pella's fields of barley and grapes, passing men harvesting olives and sun-browned women braiding together green garlic stalks to dry. We rode until twilight spread across the sky like a black tide. The pace we kept was comfortable to accommodate the baggage train, but despite my training with Cynnane, my legs trembled as I dismounted late that night, ignoring Cassander's proffered hand.

"You're still with us, I see," Antipater sniffed, as if he hoped that I might beg him to let us return to Pella instead of continuing on to Persia. Or that perhaps I'd expired in my saddle.

I gave him a honeyed smile, sweeping past both men with a flounce of road dust that made Antipater sneeze. "Dearest Antipater," I said, "I'd ride halfway to Hades before I returned home to Pella."

Little did I know but that threat would one day come true, in ways I could scarcely fathom in that moment.

I stroked the top of Athena's feathered head through the bars of her cage and huddled into my *himation* before a roaring fire, shivering in the night cold and finally daring to pull loose Olympias' letter while everyone else collected their portions of teeth-snapping barley groats, chewy dried dates, and hard white cheese. Several of the common soldiers ate a gray gruel straight out of their helmets, even dunking black strips of dried tunny into the mess.

My ears perked up at the rumble of men's arguing voices, and I thought I detected Cassander's low tone and his father's barked commands, but I cared little for their family squabbles. Let them suffocate each other in their sleep and save us all the trouble.

With the fire shielding me from the rest of the royal entourage, I made as if warming my hands, holding Olympias' parchment close enough to the flames that the seal grew soft. The warmed paper gave off the scent of Olympias' musk perfume, as if she were scowling over my shoulder. I eased the wax away and read quickly, swallowing my disappointment.

Dearest Alexander,

It is with no small measure of relief that I deliver your siblings to you so that I might better attend to your interests in Macedon and Epirus during your prolonged absence. Antipater has answered your convenient summons to Babylon, in order to serve in whatever capacity you see fit. In the meantime you may rest assured that I shall govern the lands of your birth as you would rule them.

Your dutiful and loving mother,
Olympias of Epirus and Macedon

I resisted the urge to crumple the paper and throw it into the fire. There was nothing damning or inflammatory in Olympias' words, nothing I hadn't already heard from her lips countless times.

So annoyed was I that I didn't hear the heavy footsteps approaching until a shadow fell over me.

"I have one of those too," Arrhidaeus said. His paws were full of gray barley crackers with precarious towers of dried dates balanced atop them.

I rolled up the paper and hid it within the folds of my *himation*. "Have what?" I asked.

"A letter," he said. He jumped as the wood popped and hissed, then dropped all his dates and crackers as he clamped both hands over his mouth. "Olympias made me promise not to tell," he said, his gesture likely in response to both the spilled secret and the upset food. "She told me bad things would happen if I told."

"Nothing bad will happen," I assured him as I knelt to pick up his treats, but my curiosity was piqued. Olympias could scarcely stand to be in the same room as my simpleminded brother, yet now she recruited him to deliver messages to Alexander?

"We could read it," I said slowly. "Together."

Arrhidaeus made a face as he bit into a hardened barley groat, then snapped the cracker in half as he shook his head, his shaggy brown curls swinging over his forehead. "Silly Nike. I can't read."

I shrugged. "I can read it to you. I won't tell if you won't."

He shook his head gravely. "I won't tell."

The tickle of guilt I felt for making Arrhidaeus into my accomplice dissipated as soon as I began reading.

Arrhidaeus' letter was much more profitable than the one I carried.

Dearest Alexander,

As your mother, I shall speak plainly. It is dangerous for a man whose rule spans both edges of the world to remain without an heir. It is time for you to set aside your childhood toy, your eunuchs, and your mistresses. You must take more wives and set about the business of creating many sons to secure our family's legacy.

In addition, there is the matter of your siblings. As Philip's only other surviving son, the simpleton Arrhidaeus must remain unmarried and childless. You should have no qualms with Cynnane's refusal to remarry as that deprives the would-be Amazon of the opportunity to rally some new husband's forces against you.

Thus far, Antipater thinks to match together his son Cassander and your troublesome sister Thessalonike, but that hope shall die when you make Antipater heel like the dog he is. I send Thessalonike to you and bid you to use her marriage as an alliance, perhaps with one of your generals: Hephaestion, Ptolemy, or the like. Regardless, you must use the pieces at hand to your best benefit.

> *Your loving and dutiful mother,*
> *Olympias*

I stared at the parchment and then flung it into the fire.

"Nike, no!" Arrhidaeus yelled, then gaped as I burst out with empty laughter.

"It was a silly letter, Arrhidaeus," I said to him, watching it twist and burn as I threaded my fingers through his and gave them a squeeze. "One that would have upset Alexander."

Olympias thought I should marry Ptolemy or Hephaestion? I wasn't averse to the idea of a husband, but I was averse to Olympias dictating who that husband should be. I sobered at the thought of marrying Ptolemy with his hair that stank of goose fat and his even oilier personality. But then I wondered what it would be like to have Hephaestion feed me olives at our wedding ceremony and take me to our marriage bed. . . . I colored then, thankful that no one could hear my thoughts.

Arrhidaeus was still looking at me anxiously, so I smiled and laid my head on his shoulder. He might be simple, Cynnane a misfit, and me . . . I didn't even know what I was, like an extra shell in a child's game of *ostrakinda* that no one quite knew what to do with. Despite our different mothers, we were Alexander's family, come what might. I hugged Arrhidaeus' arm, but my hand clasped the dagger at my waist when a man cleared his throat behind us.

"Put your knife away. It's only me," Cassander said. The man was almost Arrhidaeus' size, but he made less noise than a snake on sand even as my owl hooted at him. "I only wish to speak to you, if you have a moment and Arrhidaeus doesn't mind, that is."

"I don't mind," Arrhidaeus said, scrambling to his feet before I could stop him. "I'll play animals with Adea before bed."

And just like that, my brother was gone, leaving me without the shield his presence would have provided.

Antipater's son tapped on Athena's cage and sat next to her on the trampled grass. "I fed your overgrown sparrow some jerky earlier," he said. "But I'd wager she'd prefer fresh mice to military rations."

"Don't," I said.

"Don't what?"

"Try to get on my good side."

"I wasn't aware that you had one," he said, tossing blades of grass into the fire as if trying to divine some message from their smoke.

"I'm overweary from the journey," I said, feigning a yawn and lifting Athena's cage so fast that it jostled her from her perch. She hooted in indignation and rustled her tail feathers. "I think I'll retire for the night."

"You're a miserable liar," Cassander said, glancing up as I stood. "Even a man as blind as Homer could see that traveling agrees with you. Or perhaps you're simply happy to be free from Olympias with the promise of the campaigns still to come."

"Perhaps," I said. I wouldn't acknowledge that he was right, at least not out loud. But the air smelled sharper under the dome of stars, and I actually looked forward to tomorrow, a brand-new day with no one to answer to save myself.

"What will you do when we arrive in Babylon?" Cassander asked, tossing another innocent blade of grass into the fire. "I don't suppose you plan to wait obediently for Alexander to marry you off as Olympias commands."

I swiveled to face him. "How do you know about that?"

He made a sound that might have been a laugh. "Olympias' desires are as transparent as water, Thessalonike, as are my father's."

There was no arguing that.

I set down Athena's cage, glancing east. "I don't know what I'll do in Babylon. At least not yet."

"I know what you should do."

"And what might that be?"

"Marry me."

I choked, an indelicate sound no maiden should make upon receiving her first marriage proposal, and prayed to the four goddesses that Cassander couldn't discern the laughter through my coughing.

He scowled and stood, half blocking the firelight with the heft of his shoulders. "I'll take your mirth as a rejection."

There was the Cassander I knew: morose, dour, and dull.

"You assume rightly," I said, looking at the stars overhead to avoid having to blink back my tears of laughter. "But now you can tell your father that you made a valiant effort to ally yourself with my brother."

"You must marry, Thessalonike, as must I," he said slowly. "I'm not a golden lion like your brother, nor do women flock to me as they do Alexander and Hephaestion. But perhaps one day you'll crave a husband who will do his duty by you."

I snorted. "I'd sooner wed a goat than marry a man who considered me his *duty*."

Cassander's smile this time almost reached his eyes. "Then I wish you and your goat many years of happiness."

I swallowed a smile, unwilling to allow this rare glimpse of Cassander's lighter side to disarm me. "I'm to marry Hephaestion upon our arrival in Babylon," I said with an uneasy sniff, made suddenly self-conscious by Cassander's humor. "It was Olympias' idea."

It was still odd to think of Hephaestion as my husband, but the idea was something I could probably reconcile myself to. After all, Hephaestion wasn't so old as to be half-dead, nor was he likely to beat me with his fists. In fact, I could probably challenge him to a match or two and win.

"I see," Cassander said. "I knew you fawned over him, but I wasn't aware the feeling was reciprocated."

"That just shows how little you notice," I retorted, but it occurred to me that my announcement had pricked him, something not even my sharpest words had managed before.

"Then I wish you both many years of happiness." He bowed and stalked off into the darkness, likely to seek out his father and inform him of his abysmal failure at wooing me.

Cynnane passed Cassander as he retreated, and she arched an eyebrow in his direction as she nibbled a plate of half-eaten barley cakes and cheese, her mess of hair like a tangle of ill-kept brambles. "Did I miss something?" she asked as she sat next to me, handing over the food.

"Nothing at all," I replied, taking the dented plate and stuffing several barley cakes into my mouth as I watched Cassander disappear into the darkness, feeling almost sorry for him.

Almost.

※ · CHAPTER 19 · ※

324 BCE
Susa, Persia

DRYPETIS

The horn blast was so deafening that the rock crystal slipped from my fingers, sending both the precious stone and its polishing paste of sand and water scattering across the floor.

"Mithra's eyes!" I cursed aloud. Curled at my feet, my motley dog barked and flicked a yellow ear as if shaking a tiny fist at whoever dared disturb our peace. It had taken me much of the morning, not to mention the sacrifice of several of my fingernails, to grind the crystal to the specifications given by an astronomer from Nimrud. He claimed that, with patience, the stone would turn to magic and enlarge anything seen through the opposite side.

If I could get the cursed thing polished without breaking it.

"Probably another wandering merchant or scraping ambassador coming to pick at the carcasses of worthless royals," I grumbled to my dog as I stepped over the wet sluice of sand and brushed the stone clean. Seated primly on the bed, Stateira scarcely looked up from her copy of Plato's *Symposium* in Greek, her lips moving silently over each word and meaning; no doubt later, I'd be subjected to a philosophical discussion on the finer points of love. Convenient, then, that I felt a headache coming on.

Alexander had deposited us in Susa with orders that we learn

Greek, and learn it we had, until we might have debated the Olympians themselves. After all, there was little else for us to do here. Stateira read until it was so dark that lamps had to be lit, while I constructed countless models of ramparts and scaling walls, rebuilt wheelbarrows for the slaves who emptied the night-soil buckets, and did everything in my power to keep from going mad.

We were afforded every luxury, yet forbidden even to visit the palace's pistachio grove without a full contingent of Macedonian guards. The nearby foothills of the Zagros Mountains with their paths amid the white milk vetch and yellow Jerusalem sage were beyond our reach, as Alexander had decreed that our feet should never pass through the city gates. I ached to explore the nearby domed *yakhchal*, an ancient subterranean structure that stored and kept mountain winter ice frozen even during the hottest summer, yet even that excursion was strictly forbidden. The one exception to our imprisonment had been when we traveled to Persepolis to lay my father's ruined body to rest in the Tower of Silence. I'd spent many a dreary day and even more long nights thinking back to the evening I'd spent there with Hephaestion, alternating between heated remembrances of his touch and self-recriminations for such utter foolishness. But then, I'd been a fool in everything where Hephaestion was concerned.

And so we lingered here, pampered and forgotten pets.

I rubbed the rock crystal between my thumb and forefinger, peering through its occluded surface just as our door was flung open with the force of an attacking assassin. My harried grandmother stood there breathing hard, and paused a moment to smooth her white hair as she stepped over the threshold.

For my grandmother to have hurried anywhere meant that the world must be burning. Or worse.

"Dress their hair," she ordered between breaths to the army of slaves coming into view behind her. Stateira closed her book, her thumb holding her place in Plato's long-winded rants. "Fetch their jewels and perfumes."

I knew not what was happening but took one glance at my sandy fingers, ruined fingernails, and stained robe. "Best fetch the vinegar and almond oil too," I said.

"You mad girl," my grandmother said, lifting the hem of her robe to step over the mess of sand on the floor. "Your dear mother should have ordered you whipped more often."

"I fear she found my tongue too similar to yours to chance it," I said, making my grandmother pinch my chin between her knob-knuckled fingers.

"You're hopeless, Drypetis," she said, patting my cheek as our attendants trooped in with more chests of unguents and perfumes. One immediately opened a giant white clamshell incised with a scene of musicians in a palm-filled garden and began slathering some sort of cream onto Stateira's face. A eunuch set himself to the unfortunate task of plucking the space between my eyebrows with copper tongs that looked better suited to torturing traitors and murderers. "Luckily, your sister has always been more biddable, which is fortunate considering that Alexander has been sighted just beyond the hills."

Thus solving the mystery of the horns and my grandmother's frantic state. Alexander and Hephaestion were the only two people I'd never managed to bend to my will, Alexander because he was as cold as the icy breath of the winged *daevas* and Hephaestion . . .

Well, because he was Hephaestion.

My grandmother looked to Stateira then, to my lovely sister with her skin that glowed like a ripe peach and her hair that shone like moonlight on a black river. My own hair had grown to my shoulders after the pulley accident just before my father's death, but I was tempted to chop it all off again just for the freedom it afforded me. She said, "There can be only one reason Alexander returns to Susa now."

"He's coming for his pets," I muttered.

My grandmother ignored me. "Alexander has commanded a massive wedding ceremony to marry his Macedonian soldiers to Persian women."

I saw immediately the genius of Alexander's plan, for the children born of these marriages would be loyal to both Greece and Persia, ensuring peace for years to come.

Including any children my sister or I bore him.

After all, it would be foolish to think the unions of his men to Persian brides wouldn't be crowned by his own wedding to Persia's two princesses.

Stateira set down her book with a delicate gasp and allowed the slaves to pin back her thick hair for the impending barrage of beauty treatments, but my grandmother's words rattled in my mind. "Surely Alexander has no need to marry *me*," I said. "After all, he already has another Persian wife in Roxana of Balkh."

A spasm of distaste ruffled my grandmother's visage as it always did when Roxana's name was mentioned, despite the fact that we'd never laid eyes on Alexander's wife. "We shall not speak of *that* woman," my grandmother said, the thin wattle of pale skin under her chin quivering with emotion. "Persia is secure, but Alexander cannot leave either of you unwed. He must strengthen his bond with the royal house of Persia, especially after allying himself with the tramp of Balkh."

"Roxana's father *is* noble," Stateira said, calmly enduring a thick painting of snail mucus and ground fish scales on her face, a foul concoction that left our skin as soft and unlined as newborn babes'. Still, it seemed a pointless sacrifice on the part of the fish considering the fairness of my sister's skin; one could see the faint web of veins along her hips and breasts when our attendants undressed her each evening. "And Alexander was within his rights to choose whomever he wished to be his bride."

"Oxyartes is a grasping spider with pretensions at nobility, and Roxana spread her legs for a traitor." My thin-lipped grandmother spat on the floor at the mention of Bessus, whose name she hadn't spoken since the day Hephaestion brought us my father's bones. "Alexander should not have lowered himself to marry into so base a family."

"They say Roxana is very beautiful," Stateira said, but she bit her lip. Only I knew of the bitter tears she'd shed into her pillow the night we'd learned of Alexander's marriage to Roxana. And while once I might have railed against her yearning to become Alexander's wife, there was no denying after all these years that our stars were yoked firmly to Alexander's.

"As are you, sister." I smiled at the pleasure that lit her eyes. Stateira was indeed lovely, and I knew she worried that her twenty-seven years meant she was too old to secure any man's heart and bear his children. "And Alexander will treasure you."

"We'll be together, sisters forever, Drypetis," she said, waving away the mucus-wielding attendant to clasp my hands. "Alexander will treasure us both."

I swallowed a chuff of laughter at that. Alexander was a lover of beauty, which I would never have, even if I swam in a vat of snail slime every day. If he did marry me, it was only because he wasn't brave enough to leave a daughter of Darius unwed as a possible lure for some other man seeking to seize power in Persia. I took solace in the fact that he'd certainly never bed me, not when he had both Stateira and Roxana to slake his desires, not to mention his clutch of other bedmates.

Thus, when I wed Alexander, it would be only because neither of us had any choice.

Susa's main square was a haze of gold that I glimpsed through my wedding veil, my every movement accompanied by the jangle of gold coins sewn below my chin. Yet even through the blur of gold, it was plain that Alexander was no longer the mighty lion that had besieged Tyre and delivered us to Susa, but was instead a weather-beaten pelt that had lost its former glory. He moved stiffly, bearded and dressed in an extravagant Persian robe with embroidered flower roundels reminiscent of the first Darius' famed Robe of Honor. Hard lines from the sun and wind had etched themselves around his eyes, making him look at least a decade older than his thirty-one years. On the lower dais and to his left stood his general Ptolemy, his hair gleaming from what appeared to be a full bottle of olive oil upturned onto his head. My traitorous heart tripped at the sight of the man to Alexander's right, of Hephaestion in his gray silk robe, slightly thinner after the miserable journey from India but easily the largest commander present. I tipped my nose in the air just as he winked at me so fast that I might have imagined it.

Why did the man have the ability to fluster me even on this, my wedding day?

My proud grandmother stood at the bottom of the dais and across from her was a woman swathed in garish orange and black with so much gold at her wrists and throat that it was a wonder she could still move.

Roxana, Alexander's first wife and the Queen of Queens.

Her eyes glittered like flecks of obsidian beneath all their *sormeh* paint, but Stateira and I swept past her to bow before Alexander in a rustle of rainbow-hued silk. Stateira wore the same deep shade of royal purple as a ripe pomegranate, golden bands at her wrists, moon-disks dripping to her shoulders, and a lion pendant draped between her breasts. Her hair had been knotted into plaits to rival the famed knot of Gordius, and our mother's diadem, a cacophony of golden disks, crowned her like a living goddess.

I fidgeted, for my golden belt and sphinx pendant were so heavy that I feared I'd collapse before Alexander could marry me. I wished for nothing more than to be wearing my favorite brown robe with the tear under the arm, my fingers coated in oil while I tinkered with the magic crystal from Nimrud.

Our cousin Parysatis took her place behind me, a silent girl wearing a king's ransom of gold and a startling crimson veil that covered her gaping cleft lip. Sadly, the royal blood of the former king Artaxerxes in her veins had done nothing to avert the terrible disfigurement she'd carried since her birth, one that marred not only her face but also her speech. She'd arrived this morning with Alexander's entourage after he'd gathered her from Persepolis. It seemed that the Macedonian conqueror was determined to wed all the remaining royal daughters of Persia.

Macedonian soldiers in full armor and Persian women dressed in their finest robes packed the square. In years to come, some claimed that nine thousand people attended the weddings, but I know only that I wished I could run into the hills as I faced Alexander.

"Soldiers and wives of Macedon and Persia," Alexander said from atop the dais. "Today is but the first of five days of weddings and celebrations during which we shall mark the unions of our two peoples. In addition to the bread, wine, and entertainment, I decree that every man who takes a wife here at Susa shall find his debts paid and a dowry provided for his wife from the spoils of our campaigns. Thus his future happiness shall be forever secure."

The resulting cheers likely deafened faraway Macedon, and died down only as Alexander raised his arms for silence.

In a traditional wedding, the bridegroom sits with his bride beside him before they cut a loaf of brown bread dotted with sesame seeds, a symbol of fertility. Chairs had been placed along the lower dais stretching to the far ends of the square, their size and order meant to dictate the grooms' prestige. The largest, a throne with gilded lion armrests and an inlaid mother-of-pearl back, waited behind Alexander, flanked by two smaller chairs.

But there should be three, for there were three royal brides to wed the Macedonian King of Kings today.

Alexander lowered himself onto his throne like an old man with swollen joints, then motioned to the chairs reserved for his brides.

"Stateira, daughter of Darius," he said, gesturing to the first, "and Parysatis, daughter of Artaxerxes. I take you both as my wives. From this day forth, Stateira shall be my Queen of Queens."

Stateira's eyes mirrored my shock and confusion before she and Parysatis lifted their hems to assume their thrones in a cloud of rose and myrrh perfumes.

However, my sister and I weren't the only ones stunned by Alexander's declaration.

Roxana's fists clenched and a foul storm of fury, hurt, and outrage swirled in her eyes at her sudden demotion to Alexander's least royal, and therefore least important, wife. I doubted if he'd even had the decency to inform her until this very moment that he planned to give the title of Queen of Queens to my sister. I'd been reared on stories of dangerous harem intrigue and feared for my sister then. We'd need to keep an eye on Alexander's vulgar little tart from Balkh.

Without even a glance in our direction, Alexander lifted my sister's veil and kissed her full on the lips to a hailstorm of cheers. He deftly avoided revealing Parysatis' cleft lip by kissing her through the veil even as my father's former eunuch Bagoas brought forth a single great goblet filled with sweet wine. Alexander drank first, followed by my sister, but Stateira dared look over the rim of the cup at me, the question apparent in her eyes. Every soldier in the square cheered and raised a smaller goblet filled with golden wine, then drank to the health of the new royal unions.

I remained standing, alone and forgotten. I wasn't sure whether to be insulted or relieved.

Hephaestion sat in the second groom's chair to Alexander's right. I suddenly didn't like the way he was looking at me, as if he was about to make me the target of some joke. "Drypetis, daughter of Darius," he said, his voice booming to reach the farthest fringes of the crowd. "I take you as my wife."

I gaped at him, stricken dumb and rooted to the cobblestones even as he returned my stare.

"Move, girl," my grandmother hissed as she prodded me in the back. Across from her, Roxana had recovered enough to manage some semblance of a smile, but it was far from pleasant.

Yet I couldn't very well refuse the command, nor could I stand here slack-jawed like a dead sea bass all day. There was no denying my relief that I wouldn't wed Alexander with his mercurial moods and fiery temper. Still, to marry Hephaestion . . .

I crumpled the pleats of my delicate wedding robe in two fists and forced myself up the dais. I'd have traded my rock crystal to hear Hephaestion's thoughts then, but his face was a mask, with no hint of the wink from earlier or his usual obnoxious smile.

I lowered myself stiff-backed onto the carved wooden chair, leaning as far away from Hephaestion as I could manage without falling on my rump.

"I swear on Zeus' bolts that I don't bite," he whispered, the brush of his arm against mine making me suddenly light-headed. "At least not in public."

And yet my cheeks burned as I remembered the marks his teeth had made on my neck in the Tower of Silence, and how difficult it had been to hide them from my prim sister.

Alexander reached over Stateira to embrace Hephaestion like a brother. "Enjoy picking her lock," he said, loud enough for even Stateira and Parysatis to hear. My ears flared, for Hephaestion had already picked my lock, as Alexander so eloquently put it. "She'll be fulsome and bidding as any wife after this night."

Hephaestion snorted. "You mistake my bride if you believe that to be true."

Alexander raised his cup to us, nodding to me reverently. "I've given you the greatest of wedding gifts," he said to me. "For Hephaestion is the best man I know."

"Then you must know few men," I muttered, prompting a sigh from Hephaestion.

He moved to lift my veil to kiss me and claim me as his own, but I batted his hand away, removing on my own the haze of gold with a tinkle of coins, the sound of all the gods and goddesses of the world laughing at me.

I closed my eyes so he couldn't read my thoughts, but Hephaestion scarcely pressed his lips to mine, a pale shadow of the passion we'd shared just once. He raised his goblet to the crowd, took a deep pull, and passed the cup to me amid further cheers.

I was a wife now, married to the man I'd already bedded in a fit of grief and lust. So why did my hands tremble like leaves and my heart thud in my ears? And why was I disappointed by Hephaestion's lackluster kiss?

I startled as his warm hand closed over mine.

"I believe these vows are binding until Hades parts us," he murmured in my ear. "There's no getting rid of me now."

"Then I'll offer a newborn calf to your god of death tonight," I snapped, prompting his further laughter.

Apama, daughter of Ariamazes, was married off next, followed by Barsine's younger sister to Alexander's general Ptolemy. Alexander drank from his goblet with each marriage and the common soldiers wed their Persian prizes in quick succession, but the swirling maelstrom of my thoughts drowned out all the words exchanged between the women and their new husbands.

"What did Alexander offer you to go through with this?" I finally asked Hephaestion as the last of the couples assumed their places. My hands closed around our goblet, a masterpiece hammered with images of cavorting winged lions. "A great ship filled with gold? A troupe of nubile dancing boys?"

"Actually," my husband said, without looking at me, "a golden ship filled with naked dancing boys coated in gold dust."

If I could have hurled daggers with my eyes, Hephaestion would have been a dead man a hundred times over.

He sighed. "Alexander wished me to marry and join his family to mine. In fact, he commanded that we set to work making his nieces and nephews this very night."

"Nieces and nephews," I repeated dumbly. The most important happening these past years at Susa had been the arrival of fresh peaches; the events of this day were coming too fast even for me.

Hephaestion nodded, expressionless. "At least a dozen of each, I should think."

I had nothing to say to that, only flushed and shrank back in my chair. I sat in silence, remembering every kiss and caress from the Tower of Silence, while Hephaestion jested with Alexander and loaves of crusty brown bread were distributed. The bridegrooms withdrew the swords from their belts and cut the loaves cleanly down the middle. Hephaestion handed me my half with a flourish and tore off a hearty chunk with his teeth.

I forced myself to swallow, but the bread may have been milled with spiders and flies, or ground pearls and precious cinnamon, for all I tasted.

Alexander's own loaf was split in three, for among all these men, only he had taken more than one wife today. He stood and spread his arms in a grand gesture of munificence, his purple cloak spreading behind him like imperial eagle wings. "May the gods bless today's many unions. Those of you eager for your marriage beds are free to go, and with my blessing. We shall need hundreds, perhaps thousands, of midwives to catch all the babes that shall be born nine months hence!"

This was met with hearty laughter and jeers, although crimson flushes stained the high cheekbones of many of the aristocratic Persian ladies. Some were pulled from their chairs and picked up by their husbands to be carted off to Susa's bedchambers and tents. My grandmother mounted the dais, whispered something to Alexander, and then ushered my sister and Parysatis from their chairs.

Stateira shot me a commiserating glance over her shoulder as she followed our grandmother, but soon she was gone and I was alone, watching the couples empty from the square.

I waited for Hephaestion to move, but instead, a woman in an exquisite sapphire blue robe and veil bowed before Alexander and then came to stand before us. Barsine's face was rounder after she'd given birth to baby Heracles, but she was as regal as any queen. I hadn't noticed her before the ceremony, and was relieved to see her now.

"Many blessings on your union," she said, kissing my cheeks first and then Hephaestion's, lingering there for an extra breath. For a moment I wondered if she too had succumbed to my husband's broad shoulders and lazy smile, but then she pressed her forehead to mine. "Your grandmother must ready your sister for Alexander," she whispered. "So I volunteered to attend you."

I squeezed her hand in appreciation, thankful for her calming presence.

"You may meet us at your tent, Hephaestion," she said. "Return before the sun kisses the horizon."

"Banned from my own tent on my wedding night," he grumbled, running a finger along the rim of the wedding goblet. "I knew I shouldn't have traded Aphrodite for Hestia."

"That was your choice," I said, my voice sharp. "Not mine."

I tried to replicate my grandmother's dignity as I stood, but failed miserably as the chair scraped loudly over the stones. Part of me thrilled at the thought of what was to come, for I'd experienced Hephaestion's prowess with bed-sport firsthand. The other part was consumed with such anxiety that it seemed as if a demon had lodged itself in my stomach.

Barsine tutted under her breath once we'd left the square. "Do you know what I think?" she asked.

"What?"

"I think the lovemaking between you two is going to be earth-shattering."

"Barsine!" I exclaimed, but she only laughed and pulled me through an alleyway to Susa's main gate, where many enterprising vendors had set up carts of dried fruits and roasted nuts. Beyond that, a handful of royal pavilions had been erected since this morning.

"I can tell just by watching the two of you," she said, her voice lilting with merriment. "You'd as soon tear each other's clothes off as strangle each other."

Our lovemaking *had* been earth-shattering and my knees grew weak at the thought of Hephaestion's solid chest beneath his robe, though I'd never admit as much aloud.

Hephaestion's tent was situated to the right of Alexander's massive campaign pavilion with three smaller tents surrounding it like moons, one for each of his wives. Hephaestion's canvas was larger than my chambers in Susa, its white panels striped with orange like the rays of the rising sun. My brow furrowed to see that my yellow dog was already tied outside and he barked in greeting at our approach, his tongue lolling from his graying muzzle and his tail wagging happily. Barsine must have read the question in my eyes, for she only smiled. "Alexander's wives have their own tents, but you're to share with Hephaestion, at least for now. Your grandmother ordered your things sent over during the ceremony."

Not for the first time, I cursed my grandmother's efficiency.

My dog jumped up on me, decorating my silks with dusty paw prints, but I ruffled his ears and kissed his muzzle before stepping inside. The tent's interior walls continued the white and orange pattern and there were shelves and crates of books everywhere. I recognized my cedar toolbox near the door and my chests of robes. An ornate copper lamp hung from the center, illuminating the golden braziers, the low table, and the eating couches. I ignored the wide bed beneath the lamp with its plush mattress and elegantly woven bedcovers.

Behind me, Barsine cleared her throat. "Sit," she said.

"What shall you do now?" I asked as she removed the golden veil from my hair. I wondered whether it had pained her to watch Alexander take two wives today, an honor he'd never offered to her.

Barsine answered, "My father and I shall retire to Pergamum now that Alexander no longer requires our services. My son is well cared for, but Alexander has made it plain that he wishes him to be raised away from his court, so as not to muddy the succession." She coaxed several strands from my intricate knot of hair and twined them around her fingers before arranging them loosely down my back.

"You'll garner respect wherever you go," I said, "the woman of a king and mother of his son."

"I prefer it this way," she said. "A quiet country life away from the intrigues of court shall suit me. After all, no one cares about an aging mistress and her bastard son."

"Take me with you?" I asked feebly, but Barsine only smiled.

"You'll be happy with Hephaestion," she said, dimples cleaving her cheeks as she smiled. "If you let yourself, that is."

She nodded toward a package wrapped in pale silk the color of clotted cream and tied with a bit of string. There was a tag attached with my name written in both the flowing Persian script and blocked Greek letters. "I believe that's for you."

"From Hephaestion?" She nodded, and I poked the package. "It's probably a viper or scorpion."

Barsine laughed. "Open it!"

I removed the silk wrapping and revealed a carved box, a work of art in its own right with its flock of hook-beaked *Homa* birds along the edges. But the contents of the box were the true treasures.

Barsine peered inside as I lifted the lid. "Is that an ax?" she asked in the same tone she might have used if it were a pile of dung. "And a chisel?"

I nodded and removed the tools with more reverence than if I were holding baby Heracles. Hephaestion's gifts were plain and utilitarian, lacking embellishments of gemstones or gold. Yet their blades were different from the iron I was accustomed to, likely some strange sort of metal he'd encountered while on campaign. "Hephaestion knows my penchant for tinkering," I said.

"Either that or he wished to provide you with the weapons for his own murder," she quipped, motioning for me to stand before her. "He's a brave man."

I replaced the tools in their box and spread my arms so she could unclasp my golden girdle and remove my outer robe with its dusty paw prints. I let her finish preparing me, then squeezed her hands as she kissed my forehead one last time. "Be kind to him," she admonished me. "You might surprise yourself with how happy you can be with Hephaestion, if only you'd stop sniping at him long enough to find out."

I sat alone on the bed once she'd gone, staring at the olive and laurel branches hung over the doorway—a traditional Greek wedding decoration—but within moments Hephaestion ducked inside as if he'd been waiting for Barsine's exit, his sheer size suddenly making the tent feel cramped.

"I see you found your gift," he said, his eyes flicking to me in my diaphanous robe before darting away as if he felt scalded or repulsed. My heart fell. He gestured to the ax and chisel, saying, "They're Damascus steel, harder than any iron."

"They're lovely," I said, wishing I could duck into an old robe and stuff my elephant hide hat over the perfect curls Barsine had rendered.

I felt like a half-dressed fool for all the notice Hephaestion seemed to take of me. "I don't have a gift for you," I nearly growled.

Of course I didn't have a gift for him, considering I hadn't known I was going to marry him when I woke that morning.

"I'll take the fact that you didn't demand to marry someone else on the dais this afternoon as my gift."

"Was that a choice?"

He ignored me to rake his hands through his thick hair. The beginnings of black stubble darkened his jaw, although I noted a few gray bits had crept in. "If you're not careful, Drypetis, I swear you're going to make me regret asking for you."

"What?" My eyes widened. "Why would you ask for *me*?"

"Because against my better judgment I wanted you!" he answered in a rush of frustration. "Is that so hard to believe?"

"Coming from the man who insults me at every turn?" I stood now, flustered and angry. "The same man who has made my life a living hell since we first met outside my father's tent at Issus?"

Hephaestion's face darkened like an oncoming storm. "Would you prefer that Alexander asked which woman I wanted from Persia's stables and I offered to take you to spare him the trouble of breaking you? Do you prefer that version?"

My heart juddered hard against my breastbone. "Would you like to measure my teeth to make sure you made the right choice?"

"What I'd like to do is gag you," he said. "But I have a better idea."

Before I had time to react, his lips were on mine, hard and demanding. My hands came up to push him away, but a burst of heat exploded below my belly at his touch, spreading to my fingers and toes like bolts of flame so that it was impossible to care about anything save the scent of his skin, the magic of his hands, and the intoxicating taste of his lips.

I wanted him. By Mithra's eyes, I wanted him more than I had in the Tower of Silence when I'd felt so lonely and empty that I'd wanted to die. And I could have him.

"It's time for bed, wife," he murmured, his warm lips tracing the delicate skin up the base of my throat and making me shudder with pleasure. "Don't you dare argue or I'll drag you there myself."

"Shut up, husband," I said, pulling him down onto the bed with me, my lips managing to find his even as I loosened the *kamarband* of his robe with impatient hands. "You talk far too much."

And Barsine was right.

It was earth-shattering.

CHAPTER 20

Susa, Persia

HEPHAESTION

I'd anticipated my bride gouging my eyes out on our wedding night, or at least threatening to embed her new ax in my skull. Instead, Drypetis surprised me, so much so that I planned on repeating several of those surprises when she woke.

I had no water clock with which to mark the time, yet I lay on the plush bed listening to my wife's even breathing in the flickering lamplight. Zeus help me, but I grinned like a besotted idiot then, recalling the gasps of pleasure I'd teased from her full lips and the way she'd pulled me deeper inside her. Her fearless approach to lovemaking had been the same as if I were one of her machines, experimenting until she found just the right place and correct use for her fingers, her mouth, or the slick cleft between her long legs. The simple remembrance made me grow stiff with wanting again, and I almost roused her awake so I could push us both beyond the heights of pleasure once again.

Instead, I stood and poured a goblet of wine, swirling the crimson liquid before taking a deep draft. Drypetis lay on her side with her hands folded beneath her sharp chin and her knees tucked up under her. The bronze lamp above cast enough light to accentuate the sweep of her lashes against her cheek, her barely open—and slightly bruised—lips, and the curves and valleys of her breasts and hips beneath the silk coverlet.

Drypetis had changed since those first days after Issus. She was still temperamental but no longer the knob-kneed, reckless girl responsible for the wild chariot escape at Gaugamela and attempts to foment revolts in the streets of Babylon. The years of captivity in Susa had filled her out, softened her body if not her temper. I pushed a stray tendril of hair from her forehead and smiled as she swatted my hand away in her sleep.

And it struck me then that in all my thirty-two years, I'd felt this overwhelming pull for only one other person.

Alexander.

It was damnably inconvenient that no matter how many singers Alexander murdered or how many cities he burned down, I would always love him. And he would love me.

Yet there was more to life than just Alexander. . . .

I stood silently, drinking in the sight of Drypetis until I could stand it no more. I crouched naked beside the bed, letting my hands wander while teasing her nipple with my mouth through the thin silk coverlet, feeling it turn hard and taut even as she groaned with pleasure.

"It's cold," she whispered, her eyelids fluttering as she opened the blanket for me, revealing the glorious length of her naked body. "Come warm me."

I knew not what the future would hold for us, but I knew one thing for certain.

Life with Drypetis would never be dull.

I'd hoped to be woken by my wife's deft hands rousing me to ravage her again, but instead we were wakened by a never-ending wail that threatened to make my ears bleed.

"What fresh hell is this?" Drypetis moaned, burrowing her face into my shoulder. "Did you order a herd of angry goats to be slaughtered?"

I'd already reached for my sword in case of attack, but the racket outside was no war cry. It was mournful, as if someone had died.

And it was coming from the direction of Alexander's tent.

A surge of energy coursed through my veins and my mouth filled with the metallic taste of fear as I shoved my arms through my discarded wedding robe and burst into the thin spring sunshine. I stopped short at the crowd of veteran Macedonians gathered outside Alexander's massive red and white striped tent, the majority of whom had taken new wives yesterday.

These were no happy bridegrooms, but the start of an angry mob. Their heads were freshly shaved in a gesture of mourning, so freshly shorn that I could see where a few had nicked themselves with the blade. Alexander was nowhere to be seen, yet a contingent of bearded and unblinking Persians stood guard outside the entrance to his tent.

Guards wouldn't protect a dead man, unless perhaps that dead man was Alexander of Macedon.

"What's the meaning of this?" I demanded. "Where's Alexander?"

One of the soldiers ceased his warbling. "Alexander has replaced us," the grizzled old warrior said, his voice seething with anger. He and his men were stubborn Macedonians, dressed in the Greek style and with the weather-beaten skin of their jaws shaved clean. "Instead, he plans to conquer the world with thirty thousand oriental dancing boys. We're soldiers, not old nags ready to be put out to pasture."

It took a moment for me to realize what he meant, that the thousands of Persian boys left behind in Susa six years ago were now old enough to join our ranks and replace the veterans who'd marched from Macedon more than ten years ago. Veterans like me.

"Alexander is inside?" I asked.

The soldier nodded. "He refused to speak to us after we demanded that he keep us on."

My panicked surge of energy dissipated, leaving me light-headed. These men were mourning their lost honor, not Alexander.

"Therein lies your first problem," I said, rubbing a tired hand over my face. "Beseech, beg, or bargain, but never *demand* anything from Alexander."

The soldier colored at that. "You're Alexander's closest companion," he said, his flush deepening, for we both knew I was more than that. "Can't you speak to him on our behalf?"

I stared hard at the striped canvas walls of Alexander's kingly pavilion. "I won't disturb any man after he's taken not one but two brides to his bed." That was an empty boast, for I knew full well that Alexander would never take Parysatis and her harelip to his bed. "I'll seek out Alexander before the twelfth hour, *if*—and only if— your men cease their caterwauling."

"But we require an answer—"

I held up my hands. "I have a comely and surprisingly flexible young wife waiting in my bed who requires my immediate attention. Go back to your new wives—or a different woman, or a boy, if you prefer—and keep yourselves occupied until I can speak to Alexander."

To their credit, these men were not so old that the suggestion of a tumble no longer held any allure. Their wails ceased and a few offered crude jokes before most wandered off.

"You swear you'll see to this?" the leader asked.

"I swear it on Ares' sword," I said. "So long as you give me peace and quiet in which to enjoy my wife."

The man nodded. "You shall have your peace, until the twelfth hour."

I watched him leave, then turned toward Susa's main gate, where several dozen vendors had set up bustling businesses to take full advantage of the army's arrival, realizing that I should probably bring back something for Drypetis and me to eat. I laughed aloud when

I spotted an old merchant with a tangle of beard like rotten seaweed hawking paper bags of roasted nuts.

"I hope your almonds are as good as the last time I was in Susa," I called to him, my stomach growling at the salty aroma. I fished for a coin—I had several of the freshly minted gold staters that bore Bucephalus' horned head, an honor to old Ox-Head that had made Roxana rant and rave—but the hawker's eyes sparked with recognition and he handed me a bag.

"You paid for half a harvest last time," he said, but his smile didn't reach his eyes. "And that coin of yours meant my wife got to prance about in silken slippers and buy herself a pure white goat kid. Slept curled up to that goat more than me, as a matter of truth."

"And where is your lovely wife on this fine day?" I asked, popping several nuts into my mouth. They were rich and buttery, the perfect accompaniment to the *amphora* of red wine I had tucked beneath my bed. I wondered then if Drypetis liked nuts, imagining her soft lips parting as I fed them to her.

The almond hawker cleared his throat and I frowned to see tears gleaming in his eyes. "My wife is dead," he said. "Died of a fever some months back."

"You have my sympathies," I said, daring to reach across and squeeze his shoulder. One would have thought being released from such a woman might have been a relief, but the man snuffled and dragged a sleeve under his bulbous nose.

"You're one of them soldiers who took a wife yesterday, aren't you?" he asked.

"I am," I said. Another soldier beckoned to the nut seller, already digging in his belt for a copper obol or two. "A woman who can never sit still for more than a moment's time and who possesses a tongue sharp enough to have competed with your late wife's."

"Enjoy every moment with your old girl," the man said, bowing his head to me as he took the soldier's money, biting it to check its purity. "You never know when it will end, or how much you'll miss her when it does."

I nodded my farewell and absentmindedly chewed a few more almonds as I walked back to my tent. I didn't get far, for a perfumed boy sat like a sentinel outside my tent.

"Greetings, Parizad," I said, wrinkling my nose against the haze of frankincense that clung to him like a god's altar, so costly a fragrance that only his sister could have given it to him. "What can I do for you?"

"I just thought . . ." Parizad gestured with a graceful hand toward my tent. "I hoped that you might be interested in a different sort of entertainment now that you've done your duty to Darius' homely daughter." He spoke quickly, his eyes flicking from my face to the ground and back. "I've been retelling the stories of your gods to Roxana, but I've run out of new tales. Perhaps you could read more to me, and after that . . ."

I smiled, for I recognized the symptoms of his cow-love and had once been flattered by it. However, it had been months since we'd been together in or out of my bed, for I'd volunteered Parizad for a special duty, guarding Roxana during our miserable retreat from India. I'd scarcely spared a thought for Alexander's first wife since the morning after Bucephalus' death, save to hope that she might perish in the snows of the Hindu Kush Mountains. Unfortunately, she was half-spider and had emerged from the ordeal with scarcely a hair out of place.

"My duty to Drypetis extends longer than a single night," I rebuked Parizad gently. "But I appreciate your offer."

His face fell even as I squeezed his shoulder. He was young—twenty-two, if I remembered correctly—and would recover from this infatuation as soon as a well-built soldier with dark curls crossed his path.

I ruffled the ears of Drypetis' yellow dog tied outside my tent and ducked within, a grin spreading across my face to find my wife seated on a dining couch. A tumbled fleece was tucked about her legs and shoulders, her hair loose, as she used the Damascus steel chisel to whittle a bit of wood that might have once been a drill bore. Mount Olympus would likely crumble to dust before I ever came upon her in a moment of female domesticity, spinning wool or gossiping with her attendants. "The wailing has ceased," she observed without looking up, biting her lower lip as she concentrated on her carving.

I nodded and offered her the nuts, smiling as she set down her tools and devoured a handful. "So it has. And we have until the twelfth hour before it starts again."

"Is that so?" She stopped chewing and swallowed hard, as if self-conscious now in the light of day. "And what do you propose we do until then?"

"So many things," I said, kneeling before her and setting aside the chisel and bore. I kissed her fingers. "Like this." I trailed my lips up the sensitive flesh of her arm. "And this."

I took my time, grinning as I pinned her arms above her head and used my tongue to drive her to madness before she mounted me, taking me inside her so we both cried out at the brink of ecstasy, her fingers pressed into my hair and her back arched against me, urging me still deeper. Afterward, she fell atop me on the narrow couch, our bodies slick with sweat and her hair fanned out over my chest. I fingered a few dark strands until she touched her lips to the scar on my forearm.

"You know," she said, tracing the puckered skin with her fingertips, "I was glad that you didn't go unscathed at Gaugamela."

"And I wasn't too upset that you almost pulled off your own arm. Served you right for trying to escape."

"You mean my trying to use the battle to my advantage?" she asked.

"You could have gotten yourself killed," I said, my voice suddenly gruff.

"All these scars of yours tell a similar story," she said, touching each nick and scratch I'd won by following Alexander. I knew her mind wasn't still from the impatient thrumming of her fingers against my shoulder. "Will there be much more fighting, do you think?"

"No one can know Alexander's mind. He may return to India, Macedon, or strike out somewhere entirely new. Only the ends of the earth can contain that man." I touched her chin so I could see her eyes, a deceptively easy smile on my lips. "Don't tell me that you're worried for me now."

I saw the flash of vulnerability in her gaze just before she rolled from my chest. "I don't care to be widowed, at least not just yet."

"We could travel together," I said, watching her as she sat up and slipped into her robe, tugging the silk tight so it pulled across her breasts in the most tantalizing way. I forced myself to retrieve my Persian *shalvar* from the floor and shove my legs into them, even though putting clothes *on* was the last thing I wanted to do.

"Travel?"

"Many of the veterans want to continue fighting," I said. "But some may choose to return home to Macedon, regardless of where Alexander goes next."

She cocked her head, eyes widening in disbelief. "You'd leave Alexander?"

I shrugged, unsure of that answer myself. "We march first to Ecbatana and then Babylon. That leaves plenty of time to decide which road to follow after that."

"You astonish me, Hephaestion of Macedon," she said. She sat opposite me and bent her legs so her chin rested on her knees. "Tell me something else that will surprise me."

I clasped my hands behind my head. "There's not much to tell outside of my deep intellect, dashing good looks, and Herculean strength."

She nudged my ribs with her toe. "Surely even your deep intellect can manage to think of something no one knows about you."

"I hate apples."

She made a face. "And I hate raisins. Better than that."

I thought for a moment. "I've always liked the way your eyes flash when I've angered you, like Medusa getting ready to turn me into stone."

Drypetis rolled those same eyes. "Flattery doesn't count."

She uncurled herself and shifted, laying her head in my lap. It was such a simple, trusting gesture that I hesitated, then plunged ahead, uttering a truth known only to Alexander. "I'm afraid of fire."

She tilted her chin and made a face akin to one I'd seen when she was tangling with a difficult angle for a winch or an obstinate chariot axle. "You, the great Hephaestion, afraid of fire?"

"My Achilles' heel," I said, trying to sound nonchalant. "Ever since Alexander tried to kill me."

It seemed almost a betrayal of Alexander's trust, but I recounted the story of the cave at the Precinct of the Nymphs, how I'd scarcely escaped with my life and how to this day the sight of flames made my stomach roil.

"That explains your reaction after Adurnarseh was burned," Drypetis said. "I thought it odd that a man who has seen such atrocities on the battlefield would be softhearted toward a mere singer."

"He didn't deserve such torture," I said quietly, threading my fingers through her hair to massage her scalp. "And that might have easily been my fate as a boy."

Drypetis nodded, struck silent for once. "My brother died before he reached manhood," she said after a long moment, her voice soft and vulnerable. "Drowned in the waters of the Euphrates."

Fire and water, disease and old age. Such simple things had the power to steal our very souls.

"I'm sorry," I said, and meant it. "Our lives are ruled by the whims of the three Fates. All we can do is enjoy the time we have before they decide it's time to cut our lifestrings."

And with that, I lifted Drypetis from my lap and guided her lips to mine, drinking deeply of the scent of her skin, her cassia perfume, the vibrant life of her.

Little did I know, but the three hunchbacked crones with their single eye and foul breath hovered over us even then, snipping their rusty shears and cackling with glee at a dark future that only they could see.

CHAPTER 21

Susa, Persia

ROXANA

I dressed with care the day after the mockery of the Susa weddings, outlining my eyes in thick lines of kohl in the Egyptian style Alexander admired and draping myself in my wedding finery. Timid Stateira might be the daughter of the former King of Kings, but her father was only a pile of dusty bones and *I* was Alexander's first wife, despite my empty womb.

Parizad suggested that perhaps Alexander was incapable of siring a child, that Barsine's sprat, Heracles, might have been sown by another soldier. I was beginning to believe him, for I'd used every trick Bagoas had ever taught me to please Alexander and drunk down countless foul-smelling concoctions to urge his seed to take root. Yet the nights since India had found him most often with Hephaestion and even that treacherous weasel Bagoas, and I had a sneaking suspicion that my husband had bedded his whore Barsine after she'd ridden out from Susa to meet him the afternoon before the weddings.

I knew then that I'd been right to protect my heart from Alexander, to give him my body but never my love.

I refused to be cast aside. No coy princess with the golden blood of kings running in her veins would stop me from conceiving Alexander's heir and becoming the mother of the future King of Kings.

And when I did, I'd force the rest of them to swallow their sly smiles and eat their insults against me.

Parysatis had gobbled up my advice when I'd visited her this morning as the sun rose. The hideous little fool knew nothing about how to please a man, and she'd seen neither hide nor hair of Alexander since yesterday's ceremony. Of course, no man could be expected to sleep with a woman who constantly slobbered into that veil of hers and could barely make herself understood. It would take more wine than Alexander could ever drink for him to do his duty to his disfigured wife, not that toad-faced Parysatis realized it yet.

Stateira, on the other hand, possessed enough beauty to lure our husband to her bed. She would require a different tack.

Yet I stopped short to see Bagoas outside her pavilion, its canvas walls fluttering in the meager spring breeze. "What are *you* doing here?" I sneered at the half man who had supplanted me in Alexander's bed.

And despite all the heartache and the nights in Sogdian Rock that we'd shared, Bagoas only tucked his arms deeper inside his sleeves and looked down his nose at me. "As her family's former servant, Queen Stateira requested that I attend her."

"I didn't realize that Stateira preferred the company of rats."

Bagoas dared shake his head at me, a mixture of pity and reprimand. "Alexander prefers his women soft and pliable," he said. "A lesson it would have served you well to learn."

I swore that I'd hardened my heart against Bagoas when he'd first betrayed me by letting Alexander into his bed, but his words still stung.

I sniffed. "And you'd have done well to learn that I don't take kindly to traitors."

"I did what I had to," Bagoas said softly, but I ignored him.

He lifted the tent flap and announced me, raising his lilting voice to be heard over the second round of wailing from the Macedonian soldiers outside. The racket grated on my nerves and made me wish someone would slit their throats to save all our ears.

"Roxana of Balkh." Unruffled, Stateira rose and approached, offering her smooth cheek for the *proskynesis* kiss that would have marked me as her inferior. Her eyes widened as I clasped her wrists instead and kissed her lips in the gesture between equals.

Her purple blood might have stolen my title, but I'd never bow and scrape like a commoner before her.

I dared motion to her couch. "Please, let us sit and get to know each other."

"It would be my pleasure," she said. Her proper breeding was more impenetrable than a Macedonian sun shield, but I caught the spark in her eyes before she quelled it. I gave her my most winsome smile even as I clenched my teeth at the sight behind her: Alexander's wedding robes, folded into a perfect square at the foot of her bed.

And she moved stiffly, as if she'd been well used last night.

"Stateira," I said, my nails biting into my palms. "I came to offer my apologies."

Her flawless mask of calm slipped a fraction. "Your apologies?"

"It pained me to no end yesterday to watch a woman of your stature herded among the cattle to be married. Surely you deserved a wedding of your own, such as Alexander afforded me."

Stateira smiled, although the gesture didn't reach her eyes. "Please don't worry yourself on account of me."

"My dear," I said, patting her hand. "As Alexander's first wife, it's my responsibility to worry."

She didn't answer as Bagoas served us cups of watered wine in strange silver vessels, carved to resemble the heads of hunting dogs.

"I presume that you are an animal lover," I said, taking a sip from the top of the beast's head. Drab little cups in terrible taste; I'd have expected more from the daughter of Persia's king.

"My father kept many dogs to assist with his lion hunts," she said. "The cups belonged to him."

"And now he is dead as well," I said, relishing the flash of shock in her eyes. Now I knew that her sun shield could be cracked if struck at the right angle.

I might have taught her a trick or two about hardening her heart, but I would be otherwise engaged in the coming days, ensuring that her usefulness to Alexander reached its speedy conclusion. He had his marriages that bound him to Persia's royalty, but they were the past.

I would be his future.

I flicked my hair behind my shoulder, silently celebrating the fact that the copper highlights of my long tresses far outshone hers. "One of the first things I learned when I married Alexander is that a camp of men is a lonely place for a woman. It is my most ardent wish that we be friends."

She swallowed, hard, and offered me a terse smile. "I'd like that very much."

We sat in silence for a moment, sipping our wine and glancing at the stark white walls of her pavilion. Voices approached from outside and I stood. "This has been a lovely visit," I said, setting down the distasteful dog cup. "And I look forward to many more pleasant interludes in the days to come."

The darling's nose actually wrinkled, but she caught herself as she rose carefully to her feet. "As do I," she said, although her tone claimed quite the opposite.

The tent flap opened and, unannounced, in barged Darius' second daughter. I took a step back in disgust, for the addled half-wit was dressed like a farmer's wife in a plain silk robe with her dark hair loose around her face. It was no wonder that King Darius had fled the battlefield not once but twice, and then allowed himself to be stabbed to death. This family of his was ill prepared for anything save the basest of manual labor.

I paused, waiting for Drypetis to sweep to her knees and kiss her fingers in the *proskynesis* of an utter inferior, but she hesitated only long enough to press a kiss to my cheek. I recoiled before she could touch the other side.

"Dearest Roxana," she said. "You're looking well this afternoon. Will you stay and visit with my sister and me?"

"Sadly, no," I said, dabbing my cheek with the hem of my sleeve. "I have much to do to prepare myself for this evening. Alexander will surely visit me as he does almost every night."

It was a bit of a lie, but they needn't know that.

"Marvelous," Drypetis said, and then the little beast dared to pat my arm. "We all pray that you'll soon conceive." She dropped her voice to a whisper. "Of course you know that the empire worries that your womb is too parched to quicken."

"Drypetis!" her sister exclaimed, but neither of us paid her any attention.

I hadn't expected the worthless second daughter of Darius to challenge me, but my hackles rose at the provocation, like those of the snarling dogs I'd sometimes watched Oxyartes bet our bread money upon.

"You just can't stand it, can you?" I snarled. "It galls your illustrious family to no end that Alexander chose *me*. That he discarded you here in Susa and married *me*."

"A situation he rectified with his weddings yesterday."

I'd have slapped her then, or worse, but Bagoas suddenly stepped between us. "It's time for you to go," he said to me.

I ignored him. "The gods shall bless my womb when the time is right," I growled over his shoulder at Drypetis. "And while Hephaestion surely did his duty and plowed your dreary field last night, your snatch will shrivel and fill with cobwebs soon enough."

"And thus, the Bitch of Balkh's true colors are revealed," Drypetis said, folding her arms and looking down her bent nose at me so I felt suddenly small and inconsequential. I hated these two haughty Persian bitches then, for making me feel every bit like the filth under their feet. I was the one who had to secure my place at Alexander's side lest I be cast out again, whereas they'd been born and would die pampered princesses. "In case you came here breathing lies and professing friendship for my sister, now we all know where we stand." She tsked under her breath. "I spoke to Parysatis already. She may be disfigured, Roxana, but she's not an idiot. Did you really think she'd follow through with all the depravities you suggested, just to capture Alexander's attention? You'll leave our cousin alone, just as you'll leave us alone."

"I don't know what you mean." My voice rose slightly, for perhaps I had suggested Parysatis act out a few of the tricks I'd picked up as the Whore of Sogdian Rock, perversions I knew would repulse even Alexander. How was I to know the little twit would see through my ruse? "My visits today were done with goodwill," I said, gaining control of myself, "which I see is not reciprocated. I shall not trouble myself in that manner again."

And with that, I swept from Stateira's pavilion, thankful to see Parizad skulking outside Hephaestion's tent. A yellow mongrel dog was tied outside and growled a threat, but I grabbed my brother by the forearm and dragged him to my tent.

"Begin tonight," I commanded as we entered its dark interior, the comforting scent of spikenard perfume soothing my ragged breathing. I dabbed more on my neck from an alabaster elephant bottle with shaking hands. "One at a time—Stateira first. Then we shall deal with the rest of them."

"You sound like our father."

There was a crack like a whip as my palm slapped the side of his face. He reared back. "What's wrong with you?" he howled, clutching his face like an injured child.

"Don't ever compare me to Oxyartes of Balkh. I do this for us. *We* do this for each other."

He rubbed his cheek and lifted gleaming eyes to mine. "Hephaestion rebuffed me, Roxana," he said, his lower lip trembling. "I need him."

Piss and shit, but I wanted to slap him again.

"Don't snivel," I said, instead caressing his smooth cheek, which was already flushing with the outline of my hand. My beautiful brother, like a mirror into my own soul. "It doesn't become you. Your lust for Alexander's plaything has made you weak."

"But I love him."

I scoffed at that, for how could my brother love that catamite? Of all the people on earth, Parizad and I had only ever loved each other and I refused to share him with Hephaestion of Macedon any longer.

Everyone I might have ever loved—my mother and father, Bagoas, and now Alexander—had betrayed me. I'd forgiven Parizad for abandoning me in the desert with Darius, but I'd never let him leave me again.

He was all I had left.

I embraced him, and kissed the angry handprint on his cheek. "You shall soon have Hephaestion on his knees, weak with gratitude for your love."

"You swear it?"

"On my very breath."

He pulled back. "And if we're caught?"

"We won't be," I said. "Everything shall be as we will it."

In the end, only one of Alexander's queens would remain at his side. Me.

CHAPTER 22

Susa, Persia

DRYPETIS

We remained in Susa for five weeks after the weddings and then embarked on the tedious procession toward Ecbatana, a journey that would take many months due to the sweltering summer heat and the impressive baggage train. Hephaestion and I learned to further appreciate each other's tastes both in and out of bed, and we stayed up long into the night arguing the merits of Greek writers, often reading to each other while naked over glasses of chilled wine and sweetmeats. I'd had plenty of practice with Greek literature after Stateira's moonings over Plato's droll treatises—dry enough to put even a dead man to sleep—but Hephaestion introduced me to the heady verses of Anacreon and especially Sappho.

> *Now my heart, paining my bosom,*
> *Pants with desire as a maenad*
> *Mad for the orgiac revel.*
>
> *Now under my skin run subtle*
> *Arrows of flame, and my body*
> *Quivers with surge of emotion.*

Those particular verses he'd murmured line by line while dropping kisses along my neck. I didn't care to think of what emotion I felt toward Hephaestion now, for it was easier to insult him than to ponder how my feelings were transforming. He did make me pant and quiver for him each night, and many mornings too, which was certainly something.

My evenings might have been spent enjoying Hephaestion's tutelage in bed-sport, but I soon spent my days in the dark interior of Stateira's traveling cart, as I tended to my sister and her mysterious new malady.

Stateira grew listless and her stomach gave her trouble several days after our departure from Susa, a fact that the camp greeted with secret smiles and conspiratorial whispers, believing that Alexander had so quickly fathered a child on her. Even he swaggered about like a man who had sired twenty boys in so many years.

And then Stateira's moon bloods came.

Still, her stomach remained sour and she struggled to keep down even ox broth. Then, after a few days, she would recover, and her cheeks would blossom with their rosy glow, only to succumb to the illness again.

"I wish our grandmother were here," I said one night as I spooned watery barley *ptisan* into Stateira's mouth. She swallowed obediently, no mean feat, as the gray sludge wasn't fit for feeding mules. "I hate seeing you suffer like this. If you were a broken chariot axle or winch line . . ."

"Then you'd already have mended me." Stateira gave a wan smile as I dabbed the corner of her lips with a clean cloth. "You're so smart, Drypetis, smarter than I'll ever be."

"Hush," I said, rolling my eyes. "I may be able to measure angles and mix tar, but I've always looked to you for guidance in everything else."

She flushed. "Then perhaps you should pretend I'm one of your machines. I weary of this illness."

I pursed my lips at her feeble complaint. I'd have been far more useful if my sister *had* been a splintered battering ram or a goat cart with a broken wheel that I could fix. Our grandmother Sisygambis would have known what to do, but she had remained in Susa, claiming that her old bones were too weary to traipse to the ends of the empire. I'd craned my neck as our wagons left for Babylon, watching through bleary eyes until the speck of our indomitable grandmother disappeared into nothingness, knowing it would likely be the last time I saw her. Now Stateira was left with only me to bathe her forehead with damp linens while moth-eaten physicians consulted one another.

"Queen Stateira suffers from *dyscrasia*, an imbalance in the four humors. Her first digestion is inhibited, thus prohibiting the second, third, and fourth digestions," the senior physician proclaimed that same night. Glaucus was as thin as the snake-entwined staff of Asclepius, the patron god of Greek physicians. "She possesses too much yellow bile, likely a result of the excitement of her marriage and the passion that ensued."

Stateira moaned in pain and mortification. Her tent was freshly erected but already smelled of stale sweat and bile despite the slave girl's having left to empty her befouled pail.

"The pain in her bowels comes from her overindulgences in hot foods," the fattest of the physicians added, his three chins wobbling as he spoke. "I recommend withholding food during the paroxysms and introducing a diet of cucumbers, cold chickpeas, and a well-watered *ptisan* of barley for at least a week once the disease gives way."

Another moan from Stateira. I couldn't blame her, for the idea of barley gruel made my gut churn.

Alexander delayed our procession several times to better accommodate his Queen of Queens, but it was impossible to halt the journey altogether. Despite Stateira's stubborn illness and our slow progress, we arrived in Ecbatana during the month *Ābān*, the time of waters or, according to the old calendar, the season of wolf killing.

It was there that the illness seemed to spread.

The city contained seven concentric walls all painted in different vivid hues and into those walls poured three thousand artists, actors, and singers from the greatest cities in Greece. Thus, Alexander plunged the entire army into an array of spectacles, each grown more extravagant than the next. Hephaestion dragged himself from his poetry and I from my schematics so we could be seen at bardic recitals and feats of sportsmanship. One night we returned from a display of Aristophanes' comedy *Lysistrata*, a performance that had made me laugh so many times I lost count as the Greek women—masked actors dressed as women, of course—attempted to strong-arm their men into surrender by withholding sex during the Archidamian war between Sparta and the Athenian Empire.

"Perhaps something can be learned from Aristophanes' little satire," I said on our way back from the theater, smiling to myself as I kicked a rock and watched its trajectory before it hit the city's third wall, painted the same scarlet as a whore's lips. Come to think of it, the shade was exactly the same color Roxana had recently taken to wearing.

From the third wall we still had to pass beneath the blue, orange, silver, and gold battlements in order to reach Ecbatana's palace and our new chambers. "If all the women of Persia had risen up, we might have stopped Alexander at the Gates of Ishtar. Of course, that would have also meant that the Persian women would have missed out on the joys of the Lioness on the Grater." I'd been reading Philaenis of Samos and her studies on sexual positions and aphrodisiacs—much to Hephaestion's delight—and the position mentioned in *Lysistrata* involved bending forward on all fours like a lioness crouched and ready to spring. I gave Hephaestion a sly smile. "Perhaps we should experience its joys ourselves tonight."

I expected him to chuckle or expound the virtues of the position, but his brows were knit together and his face was pale against the torchlight.

"I know Aristophanes isn't your favorite playwright," I said, nudging him in the ribs, "but surely *Lysistrata* wasn't so terrible."

"*Lysistrata* was palatable, although the women were worse rascals than even you," he said, but then he swayed on his feet. I yelped when he stumbled, halting his fall by grasping him around the waist. "I feel as if I've poured out all my blood on a battlefield."

He panted as I pressed my palm to his forehead and frowned at the fire burning there. "You're ill."

"I've never been ill a day in my life."

"There's a first time for everything. It's to bed with you as soon as we reach the palace."

He rubbed his temples with one hand and gave a weak smile. "It seems you're always trying to get me into bed."

At least he wasn't so ill he'd lost his sense of humor. I gave him an evil grin. "You've created a bit of a monster."

He pulled me close and nuzzled my hair. "Sadly, I fear the Lioness on the Grater may have to wait."

I let him lean on me for balance and gave a rather dramatic sigh. "I suppose I'll grant you a reprieve. At least until tomorrow morning."

Laughter rumbled in his chest and once we reached our new extravagant chambers in Ecbatana's citadel, I sent a eunuch to fetch a physician and helped Hephaestion into bed myself. The leather thongs beneath the feather-stuffed mattress groaned with his weight and I piled blankets on him to ward off his shivering.

"You poor beast," I said, tucking a fleece over my husband's chest. My meager skills at nursing had improved slightly with Stateira's recent bouts of illness, and I stoked the coals burning in the brazier to heat the room as Glaucus entered.

The aging physician made a great show of opening his portable medical box, an ingenious contraption with bronze doors and an immaculately organized collection of scalpels, ointments, drills, and hooks that I'd already riffled through once while he'd examined

Stateira. He palpated Hephaestion's chest and limbs, smelled his breath, and felt for his heartbeat, all the while ignoring my husband's bellows to leave the blankets on before he froze to death. Finally, he straightened.

"Your pulse is sluggish," he said to Hephaestion. "And you burn with a fever because you have too much yellow bile. You must drink an infusion of holly, partake in a diet of only cold foods, and consume plenty of *ptisan* until your temperature stabilizes."

This time it was me who groaned at the familiar diagnosis and treatment. Stateira's chambers smelled so of the foul barley sludge, I feared that all her silks would need to be burned and replaced. Now it was my room that would smell worse than a sickbed.

"I'll arrange a tray for you," I said, dropping a kiss on Hephaestion's still-flaming forehead.

"A perfect opportunity to poison me," Hephaestion muttered.

"How do you know I'm not already?" I asked, offering him my sweetest smile.

He gave a wry chuckle, then winced. "Because I'd wake with an ax of Damascus steel in my back if you were trying to kill me. Although it feels as you've already plunged it into my skull."

Glaucus pledged to return in the morning and an attendant entered with a tray of the prescribed and utterly tasteless foods. Hephaestion took one look and waved them away with a grimace. "I'd sooner starve," he said.

"Then starve you shall, husband," I said, kicking off my slippers and sidling into bed next to him. I'd sleep on one of the couches tonight to avoid the great oaf's fevered tossing all night, but for now, being next to him was the warmest place to ward off autumn's encroaching chill.

I retrieved a book from an inlaid walnut chest. Our belongings were beginning to merge, but it was a simple matter to locate the right one, as Hephaestion kept his books ordered by subject in a more stringent manner than Glaucus' medical box. "And while you starve," I said, "I shall read you to sleep."

He closed his eyes. "So long as it's not more drivel from Aristophanes."

"Even better," I said, dropping my head scarf to the ground and snuggling in closer to him. "Aristotle's *Metaphysics*. I'm particularly interested in his treatise on the Pythagorean theorem and how it can be applied to laying the corners of a rectangular building."

Hephaestion groaned as if he were truly dying. "Where's my sword?" he asked. "You may as well kill me now."

I thumped his chest with the book. "Cease your prattle," I said. "Or I'll shove Glaucus' chickpeas down your throat."

"Fine," he harrumphed. "But only because you have a lovely voice, when you're not droning at me, that is."

I read from Sappho instead of Aristotle that night, continuing until I was sure Hephaestion had drifted off to sleep. Yet as soon as I shifted, his fingers threaded through mine.

"My heart is tight, Drypetis."

He spoke not in Greek, but in flawless Aramaic. I stared hard at his profile in the dark, wondering if he knew what those words meant in my language.

Surely not . . .

"I'll send for the physician," I said, but his fingers didn't release mine.

"Not from the illness," he said. "From you."

"I don't think you understand what you're saying, at least not here in Persia."

"You still think I'm just a thick-skulled soldier, don't you?" He sighed, but squeezed my hand. "It means that I love you. And I do, much against my better judgment."

"That's the fever speaking," I protested weakly, but Hephaestion released my hand to retrieve something through the folds of his discarded *chiton*.

"This is for you," he said, revealing a thick gold chain that ended in a heavy pendant. "Icarus on one side of the bulla and his father, Daedalus, on the other. They were engineers, just like you."

"I know who they were," I said, my throat tight as I let him press the gift into my hand. I pushed the clasp and exclaimed as the pendant opened to reveal a hollow compartment.

Hephaestion chuckled, then winced. "I think most women would hide perfume in there. You could probably use it for a spot of axle grease or a spare nail or two."

I didn't know what to say. *Thank you* seemed so inadequate, yet I could scarcely form the words.

"I hate to disappoint you," I finally said, "for unlike Daedalus and Icarus, I have no intention of flying into the sun."

But Hephaestion only turned toward me and pulled me so my back fit against his chest.

"Don't argue with a sick man," he said, wrapping his arms loosely around me. "Wear your new bauble and go to sleep, wife."

His bold declaration of love had paralyzed me just as surely as a phalanx of soldiers bearing down on me with deadly *sarissas*. Still, I smiled at Hephaestion's warm breath on my neck and snuggled closer, for his love was an idea I could become accustomed to.

And so I fell asleep, the Icarus pendant around my neck, Hephaestion's arms around me, and his words of love in my mind.

H ephaestion was a man accustomed to being obeyed, and as such, he expected this inconvenient illness to follow his orders and depart immediately. Instead, he remained unable to rise from his bed for seven days, his limbs heavy with malaise and a strange spotted rash upon his chest that no compress of lavender or chamomile could chase away. There were no further words of love as his temper grew blacker until it would have been easier to please a bear dragged from its den in the height of winter than to please my ailing husband.

Alexander came to visit Hephaestion every day, often bringing gifts of new books. I remained in the shadows with a book or sketch to keep me busy, for although Alexander offered me the most polished of manners, he skirted me like the sea demon Charybdis, believing me to be unimportant but dangerous if provoked. However, as I cared little for the golden-haired conqueror, it suited me to remain in the periphery while he discussed the latest wrestling tournament or javelin contest with Hephaestion.

"Glaucus says you're improving," Alexander said on the seventh day, propping his heels up on a crate of freshly delivered Thessalian wine. "If you can rouse yourself, there will be a chariot race between Ptolemy and Seleucus tonight. I'd like you to award the olive wreath to the winner."

I frowned at Alexander's attempts to cajole Hephaestion from bed. Of course he didn't realize that Hephaestion hadn't even been able to dress himself today, despite Glaucus' optimism that he would soon rally. My husband's cheeks were sunken like those of a man twice his age and he'd lost at least a stone in weight over the past days, making me wonder whether Glaucus' promises were aimed only to save both Alexander and Hephaestion from browbeating him.

"I shall do my best to please you," Hephaestion said, struggling to sit, but Alexander waved away the attempt. I watched from the corner of my vision, ignoring the schematics in my lap and instead imagining the two men when they first marched out of Macedon, young and unscarred. The potent stab of jealousy made me feel petty and small. "By the way, congratulations about Roxana," Hephaestion fairly croaked.

I looked up sharply at that. I'd been so immersed in alternating between Hephaestion's sickbed and Stateira's during her recent bout of illness that I'd heard almost no news about anyone else. The entirety of the Persian Empire might have succumbed to an army of India's giant ants and I wouldn't have noticed.

"You heard?" Alexander asked, a grin breaking out upon his face even as my heart fell. There was only one type of news regarding the Bactrian harlot that could make him glow hotter than the sun.

Hephaestion gave a weak nod. "I have my sources."

Most likely he'd wrangled it from Glaucus when I was visiting Stateira. Hephaestion could persuade a rock to tell its secrets.

Alexander laughed. "I seem to recall a time when we did everything from your bed."

I glanced at the cypress rafters, wondering if Alexander even remembered I was here.

"Those were the days," Hephaestion said, glancing at me and wincing as he shifted in bed. "Still, it's about time you had your heir."

So the foulmouthed Bitch of Balkh—my nickname for Roxana, which never failed to tease a smile from Hephaestion—had finally conceived. If there were any justice in this world, she'd whelp a spotted desert jackal.

"With the blessings of the gods, by this time next year we might both have our heirs." Alexander's gaze strayed to me, but I became suddenly entranced with a sketch for a new type of battering ram. My monthly bloods had just ceased and Hephaestion had been too ill to attempt any seduction. "Did your spies tell you that Antipater is due to arrive any day?"

"I feel a headache coming on at the very thought," Hephaestion grumbled.

"He brings guests," Alexander said. "Arrhidaeus, Cynnane, and Thessalonike."

"Your brother and sisters," Hephaestion said. So the onslaught of unfamiliar Greek names heralded the advance of more of Alexander's ilk. Suddenly Roxana of Balkh seemed tame in comparison.

"You'll like Thessalonike," Hephaestion said to me, prompting

Alexander to purse his lips as if he were suddenly being ignored. "I suspect that the Fates spun you both from the same thread."

"I haven't seen Thessalonike since she was ten and falling out of oak trees," Alexander mused, shifting to block Hephaestion's vision of me. "She'll be a grown woman now."

I could scarcely reconcile the image of this mercurial conqueror laughing and shouting with his siblings, climbing trees or playing tag down palace corridors.

"It will be good to see them again," Hephaestion said, closing his eyes with a faint smile as if imagining just such a scene. "Like old times."

"Perhaps I'll skip the races so we can dine together like those days back in Aigai," Alexander said. "It's been too long since I've spent a night in your tent. There's roasted duck from my hunt this morning and plenty of wine."

I supposed I might sleep curled up at the foot of their bed, like a faithful dog. Despite his declarations of love, would Hephaestion accept Alexander's proposition? And what would I do if he did?

"A generous offer," Hephaestion said. "But unless I'm mistaken, tonight is the debut of your prologue for Python the Fat's new comedy."

"It is indeed." Alexander stood, his face lit with excitement as he gestured in the air as if outlining a battle map. "The stage is a marvel; there's a mausoleum to one side of the entrance to the underworld, hewn entirely from wood and paint, but to the faraway eye it appears as if chiseled from marble."

I doubted that very much, but thought to humor him. "What is the play about?"

Alexander smiled, his turn to indulge me. It was a delicate dance we played. "The chorus is made of magi from the East who summon the spirit of Harpalus' mistress from the underworld."

"So this comedy takes place in a tomb?" I asked, ignoring Hephaestion's look of warning. "It sounds more like a tragedy."

"The chorus japes at Athens throughout the play," Alexander said, his tone growing cold even as Hephaestion mimicked drawing a blade across his throat at me. "I assure you it's quite humorous."

I remained skeptical. Humor had never been one of Alexander's strongest traits.

"Athens is surely what I'd discuss if my mistress returned from the dead," Hephaestion said, flinching as he reached for his wine cup. I passed it to him and Alexander watched us both with eyes that missed nothing.

"It's no good, Hephaestion," he said, his tone bordering on a warning. "I've made up my mind to stay with you tonight and order Python the Fat to play tomorrow instead."

Hephaestion frowned. "I fear I'll be poor company."

"He threw a bowl of *ptisan* at me this morning," I said.

"I didn't throw it *at* you," he muttered. "Although I'm sure you'd have deserved it if I had."

I rolled my eyes. Only Ahura Mazda knew where he'd found the energy to hurl the bowl in the first place. His aim hadn't suffered during his illness, spattering me with *ptisan* while obliterating a treatise on Pythagorean hammers. I'd smacked him on the nose in retaliation.

"You won't come with me and you don't want me here," Alexander said, rising in a huff. "I know not how to make you happy, Hephaestion."

"Imagine me at your side in the theater as the actors speak your prologue. I'll hear the crowd roaring your name and will flush with pride from my sickbed," Hephaestion said, but he looked grayer than he had before Alexander had arrived, as if every word had sapped his remaining strength. Still, his praise worked its intended magic, for even I could see that Alexander yearned to sit upon his great marble platform alongside the stage and allow the theatergoers to chant his name in honor of the prologue he had written. And there was no doubt everyone would swoon with delight, even if the words stank worse than horse manure.

"I shall do as you ask, then," Alexander said, using the tip of his purple *chlamys* to polish the snarling lion pendant pinned at his shoulder, one in a vast collection that included the fearsome beasts in all manner of repose. "Is there anything else I can do?"

"Send real food, maybe even one of your roasted ducks. One more night abed and then I swear I'll join you tomorrow for the discus throwers, lest I go mad in here."

"It shall be done," Alexander said. He bent over Hephaestion and kissed him full on the mouth, a lingering kiss deeper than any *proskynesis*. A stew of uncomfortable emotions made me avert my eyes, so I saw only the hem of Alexander's purple robe when he finally strode from the tent.

"You should go to the theater," came Hephaestion's voice from bed. "There's no need for you to stay and risk me throwing more food at you. And you won't want to miss the announcement about Roxana."

"That would be worth missing," I said. "I'll stay, but I swear I'll hurl Alexander's entire goose at you if you throw anything else in my direction."

Or if he mentioned Alexander. It was easy to name the foul emotion squeezing my heart then, despite my rare acquaintance with jealousy.

"I'll replace the treatise on Pythagorean hammers." He chuckled and then squeezed his eyes hard, as if the light from the oil lamps was too bright. "I'll eat Alexander's duck and some wine too. I'll never regain my strength on Glaucus' foul gruel and water."

"Good," I said. "I want you chasing me around this bed on the morrow, not wasting away in it with fever."

He kissed me, his lips dry and still too warm. "I'm happy to oblige."

I helped Hephaestion sit, then arranged myself behind him so his head lay on my breast, massaging his temples in a vain attempt to ward off the constant ache in his skull. My stomach rumbled when the servants finally entered with Alexander's trays: baskets of pomegranates and persimmons, a mallard dressed in its own emerald feathers and stuffed with brown bread and onions, lamb stew with saffron and yogurt, and a full *amphora* of a rich, dark wine. My yellow dog had slipped in with the attendants and sat expectantly at my feet, his tail thumping in anticipation of the feast to come.

"Bring the platters here," Hephaestion said. "We shall feast from bed."

And so we did, although I forced Hephaestion to swallow down his medicinal *ptisan* first before we fed each other tiny bits of moist duck and spoonfuls of steaming stew until we could eat no more. I ate my fill of the season's first persimmons, known to the Greeks as the Wheat of Zeus, licking the juice from my fingers. Hephaestion ate slowly but steadily, as if each bite were a medicinal draft prescribed by his bevy of physicians. We washed it all down with wine, leaving the empty plates discarded on the ground for the dog to enjoy.

"Come closer, wife," Hephaestion said, letting me settle farther into the crook of his arm. "Thank you for your patience these past days."

I smiled as he dropped a kiss on the crown of my head. Hephaestion might bluster outside our rooms and I knew his hands were stained with the blood of countless men, but at his core he was a good man.

A man who loved me.

And so I gathered the courage to speak the words that I'd never thought to say, words that a few months ago might have marked me as a madwoman.

"I love you, Hephaestion."

"I know," he said, his eyes closed. "Loving me is a common enough malady."

"Are you sure your name isn't Narcissus?" I asked, hitting his chest so hard that he grunted.

"Don't abuse a convalescent. Asclepius might smite you with his snake staff."

"I'd smite him back," I growled, but calmed as I felt the rumble of laughter in his chest.

"I love you too, Drypetis," he said. "I suspect I always will."

I stayed with him a while longer, then moved and lit an oil lamp so I might read a collection of poems while he napped. My dog—*our* dog now, I supposed—glanced at me before availing himself of the empty foot of the bed, yawning once and then laying his head on his paws. Sometimes it was difficult to tell who snored louder, the dog or Hephaestion, but now both were silent. I reveled in the rare peace, my feet tucked under me with a book in one hand and a cup of wine in the other.

There was a rap at the door and I held my breath, hoping it hadn't roused Hephaestion, but he still slept. I opened the door to see Parizad standing in the open corridor, the palace's sprawling tiled courtyard behind him. He grimaced to see me, then dropped his eyes as he clutched a worn leather bag to his chest.

"What is it, Parizad?" I asked, trying to keep the exasperation from my voice. Roxana's twin had taken to lurking in the shadow of our traveling tent on our way to Ecbatana, and had tried to attach himself to my husband at every opportunity. I understood the pull that Hephaestion exerted on people, but Parizad's doggedness was vexing to witness. And I didn't trust him, especially considering that he'd shared a womb with the Bitch of Balkh.

"I brought herbs for Hephaestion's illness," he said, swallowing hard so the apple of his throat bobbed. "He should drink them brewed into a tincture tonight. I'd be happy to brew it myself—"

But I wasn't going to let Parizad wake Hephaestion, knowing

that we'd never be rid of him. Instead, I took the bag from him, startling him so his head jerked up.

"That's very sweet," I said. "But I can manage boiling water."

He opened his mouth to protest, but I silenced him with a kiss on the cheek. "Thank you, Parizad," I said. "You're very kind."

"You'll be sure to tell him I sent the herbs, won't you?" he called after me, but I only shut the door, dropping the bag onto a table. Hephaestion could drink them when he woke.

I curled on the couch again with Sappho's poetry in my lap, but my eyes grew heavy and soon I nodded off. When I woke, the setting sun cast the chamber in a muted orange haze and it took me a moment to recognize that Hephaestion was muttering to himself, as if trapped in some sort of nightmare. His head jerked from side to side and his fingers plucked the fleece blanket as if it were a lyre.

"Hush," I said, reaching into the basin of water to dampen a rag, dabbing it on his scalding forehead while I pressed a kiss against his temple. "Can't a woman get any rest these days?"

But his muttering continued, garbled and incoherent. I drew back the coverlet to find his body flushed all over, his abdomen strangely distended and as hard as wood under my hands. The dog roused too and jumped from the bed, a whine building in the back of his throat.

I hushed him and stumbled to the door, throwing it open to the setting sunshine. The open-air corridor was empty, but two figures strolled across the courtyard. "Wait!" I yelled, almost crying out with relief when they stopped and Ptolemy turned, a wide-eyed and tousle-haired attendant draped on his other arm. "Hephaestion requires a physician," I commanded him. "Find Glaucus and order him here immediately!"

"Glaucus will be at the celebration," he said, his eyes widening at my bare feet and state of disarray. "He may be at the theater or the games, but there are thousands of spectators. To find one man amongst the crowd would be impossible—"

"Find Alexander!" I yelled. "And find Glaucus or it will be your head that Alexander puts on display while Hephaestion travels across the river Styx!"

The general scuttled away and I ran back to the room, helpless in the face of Hephaestion's worsening symptoms. I fell to my knees at his bedside and felt for the pulse in his neck, fast and thready. His forehead burned hotter than the furnace of his divine namesake, and I bathed it with a cool towel, ineffective and useless as his breathing came fast and shallow. I knew that sound, for I had heard it before my mother was called to the netherworld.

Hades.

Ahriman.

Call him what you will, but that sound heralded the unmistakable arrival of the god of death.

"Go away," I muttered under my breath to the dark presence. "Hephaestion's of no use to you now. Come back for him when we're old and withered, once we've lived our lives."

My answer was a chill that raised gooseflesh on my arms, and I knew I'd find no help from that quarter.

Hephaestion had bested death countless times on the battlefield, and even in the Mieza cave with Alexander. He could do so again.

"Stay and fight," I whispered to Hephaestion, clutching his hand. "If you ever loved me, you must conquer this. Because I love you, and I won't let you leave me."

I willed him to open his eyes, to tell me that he'd fight and that he loved me.

But I'd never see his brown eyes sparkle or hear his laughing voice again.

Death is a sneaky and cowardly foe. In the end it wasn't a sword, a mace, or a *sarissa* on a field of battle that caught Hephaestion unawares. Instead, it was an ordinary fever—the death of a common man—that stole my uncommon husband from me.

He gave a great, final exhalation, akin to his heated sighs of frustration when I'd first taunted him at Issus, at Tyre, and at Gaugamela.

And then he was gone.

I stared at his flushed body, still burning hotter than the desert sun, and willed his chest to rise again. I pounded my fists against him and begged him to open his eyes as he lay motionless, his dark hair matted to his scalp and a day's worth of stubble on his jaw, his massive hand in mine for the final time. Our dog inched toward the bed, pressing his muzzle against Hephaestion's arm with a questioning whine.

I begged death to claim me then, for without Hephaestion, the brightest star in the sky had gone out, leaving me blind in its absence.

Stunned, I crawled into his arms, sobbing inconsolably as our dog laid his head on Hephaestion's chest. I refused to accept that my husband would never rise from our bed or tease me again for filling our room with more models than an engineer's desk, that I would never feel his lips on mine, or sit with him while we watched our children climb the trees in the Hanging Gardens.

Without him, nothing would ever be right again.

I know not how much time passed before Alexander burst into the chambers, only that Hephaestion's limbs had grown cold, although his broad chest still retained its warmth. I would cling to that warmth until it was gone, stealing the last trace of my husband's soul from me.

"I came as soon as I could," Alexander began, then stopped short as his gaze fell first on me, and then on Hephaestion. Abject horror spread across his face and he fell to his knees as if he'd received a mortal wound. "No," he moaned. "No, no, *no!*"

The last word was a shout that might have shaken the stars from their moorings. I sat up as Alexander crawled to Hephaestion's side, ignoring me as he threw himself over the body of his friend, companion, and lover.

"I should have stayed," he sobbed. "I should have stayed." Tears cut swaths down his handsome face as he howled and beat his fists against the mattress, his entire body shaking with the force of his grief. Tears poured freely down my cheeks then, grief for myself and for Hephaestion, and also for this man who had inspired Hephaestion's love and who so clearly still loved him.

"Leave us!" he screamed, hurling the copy of Sappho's poetry at me in a flurry of bone white pages. "Get out!"

And I did, the dog on my heels as I stumbled outside into my sister's waiting arms. "Oh, Drypetis," Stateira said, falling to her knees as I keened into her shoulder. "My poor, dear Drypetis. I'm so, so sorry."

And I sobbed then, releasing the torrent of grief for my lost husband within the strength of my sister's frail arms.

CHAPTER 23

Ecbatana, Persia

THESSALONIKE

We approached Ecbatana that autumn, a city known as the Place of Gathering for its location in the center of Persia, gleeful with anticipation at the fanfare and celebrations promised for Alexander's sister and brother. Our travels had been smooth, save for a fever that had overtaken our traveling party outside Babylon, affecting several soldiers, Cassander, and young Adea. Cassander hadn't pressed his suit with me since the night by the fire, but now he stayed behind in Babylon to recover, freeing me from glaring at him to make him keep his distance. Cynnane too remained with her feverish daughter in Babylon and would rejoin our party after Adea recuperated, but the rest of us pressed on with Antipater's entourage to Alexander, passing golden fields that promised a bountiful harvest and a pleasant year to come. But instead of fanfare, our entourage was greeted by a city swathed in black.

Ecbatana was built onto a hillside with rainbow-hued battlements clinging to its incline, first white, then black, red, blue, orange, silver, and gold with the gleaming stone palace atop the pinnacle itself.

"What's that?" Arrhidaeus pointed from his place in the chariot next to me, but I could only squint at the strange shape on the road that led to the main gate of the outer wall. I recoiled as we drew closer.

"Close your eyes," I barked at Arrhidaeus. "Now!"

I cringed myself and averted my gaze from the crucified corpse covered in a swarm of feasting flies. A crude wooden sign lay at his feet, a black scrawl in Greek that proclaimed his crime.

Here stands Glaucus, the man who killed Alexander's heart.

"Alexander," I gasped. Next to me, Arrhidaeus moaned and burrowed his face into my shoulder as if he could sense my panic. I squeezed him tight even as my heart thundered with fear for Alexander. A glance at Antipater's chariot revealed that he shared my shock.

I cracked the whip over our matched sorrel mares, making the chariot lurch over the rutted path.

"He can't have died," I murmured, clutching the chariot with one hand and Arrhidaeus' thick wrist with the other. "Not Alexander."

It had been more than ten years since I'd seen my brother, and I'd traveled nearly all the way across the empire to see his face again, to hear his battle stories, and to join him as he conquered the rest of the world.

Now the gods had stolen that opportunity from me.

I told myself that it couldn't be true, that nothing could kill my golden brother—but even a man who claimed Achilles and Heracles as his ancestors could not cheat death.

We approached the outer white gates and I threw our name and titles up to the silent guards, my mind still reeling. "Where is Alexander?" I asked the soldiers, and held my breath, fearing the answer. "Is he dead?"

"Not Alexander," one of them said, and my heart lightened, only to be ripped from my chest with his next words. "It is Hephaestion who has traveled to the river Styx."

The man who killed Alexander's heart.

Since they were boys, Hephaestion had been Alexander's companion, the Patroclus to his Achilles. Laughing, brilliant Hephaestion, now cold and dead so far from home.

The man I'd thought to marry.

My fingers stifled my moan and Arrhidaeus' hand grasped my elbow. "How?" I asked. "What enemy could have slain Hephaestion?"

"No enemy," the soldier answered. "'Twas a fever that laid him low, though some say it was poison that finally killed him. Some feared Alexander would follow him after the way he clung to the corpse for a whole day and a night. It took all his Companions to pull him from the bed."

"When did Hephaestion die?" I asked, scarcely able to croak out the words.

"Five days ago."

Five mere days. I felt a flutter of panic, wondering if Cynnane or Adea might have fallen too since we'd left them behind in Babylon.

But the guard continued. "Alexander threatened to have Hephaestion's wife killed if she laid a finger on her husband. It's not right, what Alexander's doing, keeping the body locked away."

Hephaestion's *wife*. We'd heard rumors of the massive weddings at Susa and that Alexander had taken two new wives, but there had been no mention of Hephaestion's marriage. I thought of the last time I'd seen him at the banquet in Pella and his letter urging me to seek out Cynnane, feeling a flush of guilt that we'd parted so poorly.

Hephaestion was gone now, but I prayed that he'd found happiness at Alexander's side these past years, and perhaps with his wife too.

I cracked the whip and we jerked forward toward the citadel, traveling through all the colored gates in silence. The residents of Ecbatana watched us with curiosity and many wore ashes in their hair and streaked on their foreheads to proclaim their state of mourning. The air was still, no music to herald our arrival, no children laughing as they played catch-and-find or ran with hoops down the streets. It was as if the city had been sieged and all those who remained were merely shades. We passed horses with their manes shorn off in a clear sign of mourning, and a temple that had been razed to the ground within the blue ramparts, incongruous with the otherwise splendid surroundings.

"Asclepius," I murmured, frowning at the ruined stone remnants dedicated to the god of healing, his snake staff broken and forgotten on the ground. So Alexander had thought to punish the god who forsook him, and crucified his healer too, presumably the physician charged with treating Hephaestion's fever.

Arrhidaeus disembarked first and lifted me down by the waist, thrusting one hand into mine. "I'm scared, Nike," he said. "I don't like death."

I pressed my lips against the back of his hand as we entered the palace. "No one does, my Titan."

Yet we each carried within our hearts the day that Hades would claim us. I prayed that the god of death would be gentle when he came for Arrhidaeus, stealing my brother white-haired and warm in his bed.

My sheathed sword bumped along my leg like an old friend as attendants directed us to Hephaestion's chambers. A dark-haired and disheveled young woman stood in the corridor, yelling at the contingent of guards posted outside. "I don't care if Ahura Mazda himself gave you the orders," she said, stomping her feet. "You will let me inside that room!"

The soldiers remained impassive, their spears and shields held at attention.

I approached just as the woman whirled around, her face ravaged from days of crying. Her features were too angular to ever be called beautiful, but her gold-flecked eyes flashed with intelligence.

And fury.

"Who are you?" she asked, her Greek accented with the rolled consonants I'd come to expect from the Persian nobility, at odds with the rumpled robe she wore.

"I am Thessalonike, Alexander's sister," I said. "And this is Arrhidaeus, his brother."

She stopped, as if my words had sapped some of her anger. "Hephaestion spoke often of you. . . ." Her voice trailed off and she rubbed her red, sore eyes before regaining control of herself. "I am Drypetis, daughter of King Darius and wife of Hephaestion."

If I'd had to guess which woman Hephaestion would one day wed, this woman would have been at the bottom of the heap. Still, there must be more to her than was evident at first glance if she dared now to berate Alexander.

"And Alexander?"

"Is within." Drypetis gestured toward the guards. "These brutes answer only to him, but perhaps you can make them see reason." She looked ready to gouge out their eyes, but then her lower lip quivered. "He's been in there with Hephaestion for five days. Hephaestion must be prepared—not even Alexander has the right to deny Hephaestion's funeral rites."

"Have there been funeral games?" I asked, but I knew the answer even before Drypetis shook her head.

"Only the order against music and the command that all horses be shorn," she said. "And Glaucus was crucified."

I shuddered at the remembrance of the physician's body. I'd see to it that the corpse was removed regardless of whether Alexander found his right mind again.

"Have there been any priests?"

Drypetis blinked and nodded, wrapping her arms around herself. "Both the priests of Ammon and Ahura Mazda, but Alexander ordered them away."

My brother truly had lost his mind to grief if he risked offending the gods or their officials. Perhaps that was the route to help him recover again.

"Find an oracle," I said. "And bring him here."

"An oracle?" she asked. "There are no oracles in Ecbatana."

"None at all?"

She shook her head. "You Greeks love your oracles, as do the Egyptians, but we Persians don't claim to read the future in Ahura Mazda's sacred flames."

I tapped an unsteady rhythm with my fingers against my sword, pacing as Cynnane often did, before suddenly halting. "I need parchment," I said to Drypetis.

"Parchment?" She slanted her brows at me.

"I've traveled all the way from Greece and along the way, I intercepted an important message from the oracle at . . ." I snapped my fingers, plucking a name from the air. "From Siwa. The oracle of Ammon foresaw the death of Hephaestion and has instructions from the god as to how the epic hero must be honored. Alexander answers to no mortal, so it will take a god to order him to live again."

Drypetis wiped her eyes with the back of her hand and drew a shuddering breath. "You know Alexander well. That sounds like a plan Hephaestion would have concocted."

"Hephaestion never stood for Alexander's tantrums."

"I know," Drypetis said, fingering the gold pendant at her throat, a hollow bulla depicting a winged Icarus on one side and what appeared to be Daedalus on the other. "I reminded Alexander of that through the door, but it didn't go over well."

I smiled, for I already liked this Persian princess, even if she *had* married Hephaestion.

Drypetis eyed my sword and greaves after she'd waved down a passing attendant and ordered the boy to find paper and pen. "I didn't realize the Greeks trained women to fight," she said.

"Only the Illyrians," I said. "And me."

She smiled at that, seemingly satisfied, but her fingers fluttered in her lap as if they itched to ply a loom or whet a blade, depending on what sort of woman she was.

"Hephaestion was like a brother to me," I said, which I now realized was true, despite my attempts to think of him as a possible husband. "The sort of brother that puts spiders in your bed, but still manages to make you love him."

"He did think himself Ahura Mazda's gift to this world," she said, dashing a sleeve across her eyes. "I thought it my duty to point out his many flaws lest he start demanding cups of ambrosia like a god."

I knew then that Hephaestion had won over this Persian princess in her rumpled silks, just as he'd won over every slave, merchant, courtier, and king he'd ever come across. I hoped they'd found some small shred of happiness together, however fleeting.

Finally, the pen and parchment arrived and the words of the oracle at Siwa took form. I blew on the ink once the missive was finished and gestured for the guards to stand aside.

"Ready a bier for Hephaestion," I murmured to one as we passed. "With any luck, we shall soon have need of it."

The sweet and sickly smell of decay hit me like a foul gust of wind as we entered Hephaestion's chambers, the wooden shutters drawn tight so thin shafts of sunlight shone through the cracks. A single oil lamp illuminated the interior, revealing Hephaestion's bloating body in repose on his bed. Drypetis choked back a sob from the shadows behind me, but I had eyes only for the man sitting at his lover's bedside.

"Get out!" Alexander's feral growl and the sound of his sword being unsheathed tested my resolve. His long curls had been roughly shorn—likely by the blade he held—and now littered the floor like clumps of freshly reaped hay. His eyes were blue bruises, his Persian robe surely hadn't been changed since Hephaestion's death, and a scruff of golden beard covered his jaw and neck.

My beautiful lion of a brother, now broken before me.

I forced myself to step closer, then threw open the shutters to chase away the stench of death. "I've traveled too far to turn back now, brother," I said, taking the chance of kneeling before him. I calculated a lunge to the left in case he decided to swing that sword at me. There was a significant chance I might lose my head if I didn't move fast enough.

Alexander stared at me a long moment, then blinked. "Thessalonike? What are you doing here?"

"Your mother ordered me to travel with Antipater, remember? We sent word ahead." I hoped to draw him into a discussion, although this wasn't the time to deliver Olympias' demands that Antipater be deposed, but Alexander shrank back.

"I care little for Antipater, Olympias, or anyone," he said, drawing a shuddering breath. "Not without Hephaestion at my side."

My poor, dear, battered brother. His every day had been full of a lust for life, but now he was forced to face the other side of living: grief and pain and suffering. And although my brother had forded rivers as wide as oceans, scaled walls taller than Mount Olympus, and bested impossible odds on the battlefield, I feared he might not be equal to this terrible new task.

"I wasn't here when he died." Alexander's face crumpled, giving me a glimpse of the child he'd once been. "I might have saved him if I'd been here, but instead he died without me. And now they want me to burn him, he who feared nothing in life except for fire."

"Not even you could slay Hades," I said. "But you can't leave Hephaestion as he is."

Alexander glowered at me and reached for his sword again, as if he might somehow banish his pain with that length of metal. "You're just like the rest of them, begging me to burn him. Leave me!"

"I won't," I said. "For I bring a message from your godly father Ammon," I said. "To tell you how to best honor Hephaestion."

He hesitated at that. "What does Ammon require?" Alexander finally demanded, for my brother was impatient even when dealing with the gods. "How may I honor Hephaestion so he might take his place among the gods?"

I cleared my throat and read the letter, hoping Alexander

wouldn't notice when my thumb smudged the fresh ink. "Ammon, the Great Cackler, acknowledges your grief for the shade of Hephaestion of Macedon," I read. "Hephaestion was only a man of sinew and bone while he walked this earth, but he can be honored so that his name is never forgotten."

Judging from the thunder that blackened Alexander's face, we might soon find ourselves greeting Hades if we weren't careful.

"Hephaestion was like a god to me," Alexander said, rising like a lion ready to claim its prey. "Is that not enough for my father Ammon?"

I held up a placating hand, improvising. "While Hephaestion lacked *ichor* in his veins and thus cannot be revered as an immortal god, Ammon recognizes the bravery and sacrifices of such a divine hero and demands that he be celebrated as such."

"A divine hero," Alexander murmured, resuming his place alongside the bed. The tension in the room dissipated at Alexander's nod and my shoulders slumped, accompanied by Drypetis' audible sigh of relief.

"Patroclus to your Achilles," Drypetis said to him, stepping farther into the room. "Celebrate him and proclaim his bravery so loudly that even your gods on Mount Olympus shall know his name."

"I will not expose him to vultures and dogs like you Persians do," Alexander growled, waving his sword at the parchment. "I've forbidden such barbaric practices."

Drypetis' hands curled into fists, but otherwise she held herself like a queen in the face of his insult. "Then give him a royal tomb instead, like the great kings of Babylon."

"You cannot leave him here in this room," I said to my brother, not allowing him a chance to answer Drypetis' demands with his sword. "Nothing will bring Hephaestion back, but perhaps his name can be sung alongside yours through the ages."

"Please," Drypetis said to him, gesturing to the letter I held. "Hephaestion would want you to do this."

And we waited with bated breath for my brother's answer.

"It shall take time to plan such a magnificent showing of games and competitions as Hephaestion deserved," Alexander finally said, speaking to himself although the madness seemed to have cleared from his eyes. "I shall do as Ammon decrees, but Ecbatana isn't fit to host such a spectacle, nor shall it have the honor of hosting his tomb for all eternity. We shall fete him in Babylon and then his body shall be sent home to Macedon."

He leaned over and pressed his lips to Hephaestion's forehead. "I shall erect a statue of a mighty lion here in Ecbatana in your memory," he whispered as if they were the only two in the room. "And you will be celebrated in Babylon with its great kings, for you deserve no less and yet so much more."

He straightened then and strode to the door, pausing to squeeze my shoulder as if suddenly remembering my presence. "It is good to have you here, sister," he said, once more the golden lion of my childhood, despite his ragged hair and the stink of death that clung to him. Then he was gone, leaving Drypetis and me alone with Hephaestion's body.

Drypetis fell to her knees. "Thank you," she said in a quavering voice, looking up at me with eyes that gleamed in the lamplight. "My sister, Stateira, will help me prepare his body, but I'd be pleased if you'd assist as well."

"I'd be honored," I answered.

I took Alexander's chair, its leather still bearing my brother's warmth. My brother had always burned with the heat of the sun, bringing heat but also the possibility of scalding all that he touched. Hephaestion had tempered him, like water cooling a blazing sword when it's forged, but now he was gone. I pressed my forehead to his, blinking hard as a pair of tears fell from my eyes.

"Good-bye, Hephaestion," I whispered. "Rest well."

Unbeknownst to us, Hephaestion's death was like my father's so many years ago, a shorn lifeline that whetted the voracious appetites of the sleeping Fates. In the days to come, their shears would usher countless souls to Hades in a bloodbath that the bards would sing of for generations to come.

I finally delivered Olympias' demands for Antipater's removal once the procession to Babylon was under way.

"My mother's voice has been loud in my ear since the day I left Pella," Alexander grumbled. "Now she wishes me to settle her complaints against Antipater while I attend to Hephaestion's funeral and make plans for our new navy." He sat atop a sleek brown horse. It jarred me to see him without Bucephalus, as if he'd been abandoned by all his friends of old. He sighed and ran a hand over his shorn hair. "My mother punishes me hard for the nine months she carried me."

I snorted. "I'm the one who's had to live with her these past twelve years. You're the lucky one who managed to run away."

Alexander chuckled then, the first bit of laughter I'd heard from him since my arrival. With patience, time would heal his grief.

Of course, Alexander had never been a patient man.

And this brother of mine was no longer the laughing youth who had marched out of Aigai but a hardened warrior. Before we left for Babylon, he'd ordered a skirmish against the Cossaeans and massacred every one of their men as an offering to Hephaestion. It was an eerie echo of Achilles' sacrifice of twelve highborn youths to Patroclus' funeral *pyra*.

Drypetis had raged against Alexander when she'd heard the news, howling that Hephaestion wouldn't have wished to have a whole tribe slaughtered in his name. It had taken both her wan-faced sister and me to persuade Alexander not to punish her for her presumption. I had no wish to see her crucified.

Alexander drove Hephaestion's funeral carriage halfway to Babylon, the shadows under his eyes growing ever darker as he drove by day and spent the evenings planning both a new navy to conquer Arabia and Hephaestion's magnificent funeral monument with Dinocrates, a renowned architect from Rhodes. The whip-thin man had been charged with engineering Hephaestion's seven-tiered *pyra*, a monument that would never be burned, but would instead stand outside Nebuchadnezzar's palace for the ages.

During the long weeks of travel I often sought out Drypetis and Stateira. They, along with Cynnane, were the only women in the empire who didn't make me want to stuff my ears with hot wax when I sat with them. Stateira was calm and always proper, but Drypetis reminded me of a more refined version of Cynnane, although I didn't doubt that if the Persians allowed their women swords, Drypetis would have been a warrior to make the Amazons drop their weapons and run screaming for the hills.

I looked forward to seeing Cynnane and Adea again, for we had word that Adea had recovered from her fever and awaited our arrival in Babylon. Sadly, Cassander had also survived Apollo's plague arrows, which was enough to make me doubt the sun god's wisdom and aim.

It took extra time to enter Babylon, for the priests of the temple of Esagila sent out messengers with word of a new prophecy that Ahura Mazda forbade Alexander to enter Babylon from the west, claiming that to do so would mean his sun was setting and his reign declining. Inconvenient marshes surrounded the city by all other sides, so Alexander scoffed at their warnings, declaring that the sun could never set on his glorious rule, and entered Babylon through the forbidden western gate. Regardless of the ill omen, the city welcomed him with full pomp, their conquering hero dressed in a well-draped Persian robe and the curled oxhorns of his godly father Ammon. We continued on to Nebuchadnezzar's palace to find the entire royal court assembled in all their finery. And at the forefront stood Cynnane and Adea.

And Cassander.

"I see you've recovered from your illness," I said to him in a cool voice after hugging Cynnane and Adea in a joyous reunion. Despite her illness, young Adea had grown in the month I'd been gone and after greeting Alexander with a graceful bow, she was now chatting gaily with Arrhidaeus. The tiled floors had been sprinkled with flower petals, and altars on both sides of the throne burned precious myrrh, so the entire room smelled like a heavily perfumed priestess. I wondered if it stung that Alexander hadn't acknowledged Cassander after their shared days at Aristotle's elbow, but my brother was already busy ordering a harbor to be dug at Babylon—the better to accommodate the navy he planned to sail for Arabia—and also issuing commands for Hephaestion's funeral games, which would begin on the morrow. Messengers had run from Ecbatana to Babylon and a staggering sum of twelve thousand talents of gold had been spent, thus ensuring that generations to come would revere these games long after we were all roaming the Fields of Asphodel. Hephaestion may not have been a god, but he was being laid to rest with enough honors to bury Zeus, and I was glad of it.

Cassander ignored my slight alongside Alexander's. "So it's true, then," he said. "Hephaestion is dead and Alexander has come untethered."

"I don't know what you mean," I lied, not allowing my gaze to stray to my brother.

"They say he can scarcely breathe without drinking a vat of wine each morning when he rises, and that he's more dead than alive without Hephaestion," Cassander murmured, even as Alexander called for a wine bearer. "I believe the decree now that I see him."

"What decree?" I was weary from our travels and in need of a bathing pavilion. I rarely had time for Cassander's riddles, but now I had even less patience for them.

"A few weeks ago, after we first arrived in Babylon, a priest from

Esagila sacrificed a spotted ox in Hephaestion's name and examined the entrails. The liver was found to be deformed, created smooth and without a lobe. The priest foretold that death would soon claim Hephaestion of Macedon."

"It's simple to prophesize the death of a soldier," I scoffed. "Death stalks armies and feeds on their men like starved carrion."

Cassander glanced at me. "That may be, but another ox was sacrificed for Alexander three days ago." His tone made a chill like the north wind run down my spine, yet he paused as if debating whether to continue the tale.

"And?" I asked.

"The same deformity was found," he said. "The people whisper that Alexander will never launch his campaign against Arabia, much less return to Macedon with a still-beating heart."

"A state of affairs which would suit you and your father," I said, glaring. I gestured to where the Persian women stood to the far side of Alexander's dais, demure and properly veiled, although Darius' daughters leaned away from preening Roxana as if she were rotting vermin. I'd already decided I didn't care for my brother's first wife, who constantly crowed about the babe she carried and insisted on being transported everywhere in a gilded litter. Fortunately for me, lofty Roxana had condescended to exchange with me only as many words as I had fingers and toes. "Roxana's womb holds Alexander's heir. My family's dynasty is secure."

"I hope you're right." Cassander straightened. "I just made an offering to Hephaestion's shade in remembrance of our days together at Mieza. I have no wish to do the same for your brother's shade." I waved a hand to silence him. The throne room was a veritable sea of Persian robes and men with beards of oiled ringlets, yet Cassander remained in his crisp military *chlamys* and tunic, a staunch Macedonian down to his unlaughing heart.

I watched as Ethiopians and Libyans, Scyths, and Persians filed in to genuflect and offer their condolences to my brother, bending so deeply that their foreheads brushed the ground as they kissed their fingertips, a gesture reserved only for the gods in Macedon. Next to me, Cassander gave a derisive snort. "The foreigners do worship Alexander, don't they?" he said. "Perhaps they'll build him a temple to rival Artemis' in Ephesus. They've already opened all their gates and treasuries to him to avoid being slaughtered, or, worse, burned to death like that singer he doused in naphtha."

Alexander swiveled toward us and glowered like an angry statue of Zeus. Then he stood and walked down the steps of the dais, coming to stand directly before Cassander. In one fluid motion suited to a battlefield maneuver, he lifted Cassander by the neck of his *chiton* and slammed him against the wall.

"Don't you ever insult my *satraps*," he growled, eliciting a collective gasp as he banged Cassander's head repeatedly against a fresco depicting a hunting scene. "You and your family are nothing save a lot of sniveling, grasping snakes and I'll see you all thrown into the pit of Tartarus before I'm through with you!"

"Dearest brother." I touched Alexander's arm, feeling everyone's attention heavy on my back. "I'll be the first to admit that Cassander is a terrible bore, but surely this fresco is too fine to ruin with his thick skull."

Alexander turned to me, his brow furrowing and the fury in his eyes clearing, only to be replaced with revulsion. "I have no qualms with my sister enjoying herself with the men of my court," he said. "But I'd have hoped you'd have had better taste than to spread your legs for the son of Antipater."

My cheeks flared and I recoiled at the very suggestion. Me, spread my legs for Cassander, when I might as well have pledged myself to the virgin goddess Artemis? "I've never taken any man between my legs, much less Cassander," I said in a stony voice. "And if you were anyone save my brother, I'd make you regret the very suggestion."

Alexander loosened his grip on Cassander, whose face had contorted and gone pale. "I knew you had better sense," my brother said, smiling and chucking me under the chin as if I were a girl of ten again and he hadn't just thoroughly denigrated me in front of his entire court.

"I believe you have yet to bow to me," he then said to Cassander, his countenance turning to ice again and making me wonder what had become of my golden brother who seemed to carry the sun under his skin. "Perhaps you seek to rectify your error."

And so Cassander bent his knees to my brother just as the Persians had done, although a vein in his jaw beat an angry tattoo as he kissed his fingertips.

"Welcome to my court, Cassander, son of Antipater," Alexander said, turning his back to greet some Persian noble, as if the entire episode had never happened.

"You'd do well not to anger him," I murmured to Cassander. "For I won't bare my neck for you again."

Especially as such an intercession might be construed as affection for Cassander and his ugly face.

"He'll pay for that," Cassander muttered under his breath, and I waited for him to prattle on about deformed livers again, yet he only clenched his fists. "The gods won't allow such hubris to go unpunished."

I sighed. "If I were an Olympian, I'd punish all the men who claimed to know my mind by causing exactly the opposite of whatever they'd prophesized for the future."

Cassander only frowned at me. "How do you know they don't already?"

He turned then and departed without another word, leaving me to remember the Pythia's prophecy that had echoed throughout Greece and followed Alexander since almost his earliest days of campaigning.

The lion of Macedon is invincible, as was Heracles before him.

Yet Heracles had died a brutal death, poisoned by the venom of the very Hydra he'd once slain.

And while Alexander claimed Zeus and Ammon as his fathers and Achilles and Heracles as his ancestors, at thirty-three years he'd already accomplished more than any god or hero. Surely he'd accomplish much more still before the gods granted him immortality in exchange for his labors spent conquering the earth.

I only hoped that the weight of my brother's labors wouldn't fell him as they had his ancestor Heracles.

CHAPTER 24

323 BCE
Babylon, Persia

ROXANA

I lay sated and wrapped in Alexander's arms, our flesh still damp as I traced the jagged line of an old scar on his neck. I'd tried counting all the faded pink marks with my lips earlier, but my husband's demanding hands had distracted me by the time I hit seven. Now those same demanding hands stroked the pale moon of my belly.

"My son," he said.

The babe beneath fluttered and I laughed, pressing Alexander's hand more firmly so he might feel the magic within my womb. "Did you feel that?" I asked. "He's eager to meet his father."

"And I him," Alexander answered. "I've ordered the finest sword smith in Babylon to forge a golden half blade with a half-sized helmet. My son's shield will be emblazoned with the sun of Macedon and the winged griffin of Persia."

Macedon and Persia united, just as Alexander and I had been only moments before in this very bed. The thought made me grow wet and eager for him again. The last time my husband had visited my bed had been on the night I'd conceived our son, a hurried groping after Alexander had guzzled a tub of wine to drive away the lingering pain from his many war injuries. He'd fumbled at me between belched wine fumes, but I'd moaned and let him take me from behind like a temple whore, feigning pleasure even as I clenched my thighs tight to claim the ultimate prize.

His spent seed had been sown deep in my womb, planting the babe that grew there now.

Tonight Alexander had come to me out of duty. I missed the pleasures of the early days of our marriage, when he had devoured me each night and left me quivering for more. While I'd guarded my battered heart from him, his lust for me had been more intoxicating than the sweetest of wines. How could it not be, coming from so godlike a man?

Hoping to recapture that passion, this evening I'd dressed in anticipation of his visit in a diaphanous robe pinned at my navel to reveal the swell of his child and the dark triangle of hair beneath. He'd protested that he didn't wish to harm the baby until I'd guided his hand from my belly to the warm wetness between my legs, moaning and parting my lips as I brought his other hand to my swollen breasts. He'd squeezed the tender mounds, pain mixed with pleasure as his tongue flicked a darkened nipple. Soon he'd been buried deep inside me, crying out his release as I clung to him.

"What shall you name him?" I asked, fairly purring with pleasure as Alexander's fingers painted transparent circles around my navel.

"My son by Barsine is called Heracles," he said, his hand stopping as he stared up at the drab painted ceiling depicting the flowers of Babylon's famed gardens, a ceiling that might have been studded with pearls and rubies had I commissioned it. My lips curled in distaste at the mention of Alexander's whore and her bastard son.

"But this child shall be your heir," I reminded him, keeping my voice as sweet as peach syrup as I sat up, baring my naked breasts, which Alexander had moaned into only moments earlier, worshipping their new ripeness. "Thus, he must have an even more magnificent name."

Alexander threaded his fingers through my hair, fanning out the strands. "And what would you name him?"

"There's only one name I'd allow," I said, looking at him through my sweep of lashes. "Alexander."

The grin that spread across his face almost banished his sallow skin and the shadows around his eyes. "Alexander it is, then," he said. I tried to curl into him, but he rose in one fluid motion, the muscles of his back and legs bulging as he slipped into the purple robe I'd so recently tugged over his head.

"Where are you going?" I tried to make my tone alluring, but it shrilled with desperation even to my own ears.

"I must visit Stateira this night," he said.

Stateira with her royal blood, her perfect graces, and the title she'd stolen from me.

"Surely Stateira and her sour stomach can wait until tomorrow," I said, rising and running a perfectly manicured finger up his arm in a way that should have induced gooseflesh. Yet my husband had already returned to a man chiseled from stone. "Stay with me tonight."

He clasped my wrist so hard that I gasped, but then released it to kiss my hand. "I cannot neglect Darius' daughter," he murmured, pressing my open palm to his lips.

"Yet you can neglect me, your first wife? Is that because I'm only the daughter of a *satrap*?"

And not even that, although Alexander would never learn the truth of my sire from my lips or Oxyartes of Balkh's. My marriage had brought Oxyartes sniffing for an appointment, blackmailing me with the truth of my parentage. It had been an easy thing in those early days to persuade Alexander to appoint him as the *satrap* of faraway Paropamisadae. It was a situation that benefited us both: Oxyartes received a lucrative position that allowed him to gamble away a kingdom's worth of gold, and I never had to hear from him again.

"I can neglect neither you nor Stateira," Alexander said with a sigh. "Especially as both your wombs carry my children."

A winter wind wrapped around my heart. "How is that possible?"

I gasped before I could stop myself. I'd bribed Stateira's slaves to grind Parizad's steady stream of mustard seeds, rue, and devil's snare into her food, keeping her stomach in knots. I'd presumed the never-ending, painful gas and stink of vomit would have kept Alexander from her bed, but it appeared that he was more determined to hammer her gates than I'd anticipated.

"Stateira has a weak constitution, but rallies to do her duty," he said.

"And what about Parysatis?" I asked. "Have you filled her womb as well?"

"Not yet," he said. "But soon."

I grimaced. "I'm not sure how you can bear to look at that mangled face of hers."

"I am an able farmer, sowing all my fields equally," he said, letting his fingers brush my belly. "Rest well, Roxana, and take care of my son."

I watched him go in silence until the door closed, then grabbed a discarded slipper and hurled it after him. It hit the wall and fell harmlessly to the floor.

"Piss and shit!" I yelled.

Parizad's herbs had failed to keep Alexander from Stateira's bed and now my husband plowed Parysatis, the traitor Bagoas, and the gods only knew whom else. Not for the first time, I thanked the dark god Ahriman for Hephaestion's death, which had removed at least one bed from Alexander's rotation.

There was no doubt that I'd resume my position as Queen of Queens if I bore Alexander's only son. I'd be wife to one king and mother to the next, my future secure.

But if I bore a girl or if this child died, or if Stateira bore a son, or even Parysatis . . .

Parysatis was easier to intimidate than a whipped puppy. And as for Stateira, surely I was more than a match for that dumb, obedient cow.

I would be queen. And I'd allow no one to stand in my way.

* * *

Parizad blanched when I told him what I wished, but wordlessly he ground a tea of milkweed root, crocus stamens, and balsam pear seeds for Stateira. So stricken had been my brother upon first hearing of Hephaestion's passing that he'd dared to accuse me of poisoning the great oaf. It had taken all my restraint not to lash out and instead convince him of the disappointing truth. For while I'd loathed Hephaestion, there were several others I'd have poisoned first, namely Darius' condescending daughters. I'd forgiven my brother's cruel words and wiped his tears all that night, stroking his hair as he alternated between apologizing to me and cursing the gods for stealing away his former bedmate.

Since then, my brother had become a shade of his former self, but I coddled him, secure in the knowledge that he loved only me now.

Once I was queen, I would swathe my twin in furs, send a steady stream of girl slaves to pleasure him, and build him an herb garden to rival Nebuchadnezzar's famed terraces.

But first I had to deal with Stateira and the sprat she now carried in her womb.

I bribed her attendants with a small fortune to brew the mixture for her each night, yet even that failed to cleanse her womb and instead her belly grew like a tumor before all our eyes. I railed against the unfairness of it all, and prayed that she'd catch the same mysterious fever that had felled Hephaestion so we might celebrate a double funeral here in Babylon.

All to no avail.

Instead, the entire population of Babylon had been subjected to weeks of funereal chariot competitions and footraces, including the ridiculous *hoplite* race where grown men ran around in the circles of a stadium dressed in greaves and helmets, carrying their heavy battle shields and often tripping over one another. Now the entire city waited dour-faced under ominous clouds that threatened a sudden spring downpour so we could pay homage to a dead man and the obscene monument erected in his honor, a *pyra* that would never be burned so that future generations would never be able to forget Alexander's faithful he-bitch. Would that I could have found a motley dog to devour Hephaestion's bones and save us all the expense.

I might have used the twelve thousand talents spent on Hephaestion's funeral to build a new palace for myself and my son, or at least a fine estate complete with vineyards and plenty of shepherds I might tax. Even a fraction of its cost could have kept me in a new wardrobe for the coming summer, a more fitting expense considering that Hephaestion couldn't witness Alexander mooning over him through the maggots in his moldering eyes.

"Two hundred and forty ships with golden prows adorn the base," Drypetis was droning on to her sister like the dullest of bees. I didn't think it fair that she should share the royal dais, but Alexander had refused to listen to my concerns, claiming that he didn't wish to upset Stateira in her delicate state.

"And on the topmost level?" Stateira asked, squinting at the pinnacle and sounding as if she actually cared.

"It's the sirens," Drypetis said quietly, sniffing and rubbing the bridge of her bent nose. "Singing their lament."

I rolled my eyes and feigned slitting my wrists to Parizad, who humored me with a weak smile. He hadn't wished to attend the funeral, but I'd begged him, hoping that seeing Hephaestion's *pyra* might allow my brother to forget the man who had turned him into a catamite.

The crowd quieted as Alexander stood and walked solemnly to the funeral *pyra*. My heart stopped for a moment and I almost cried out when he removed his dagger from its sheath and lifted it. I imagined him plunging the blade into his own heart in a fit of mourning, and I sagged with relief when he raised it and cropped off a lock of his already shorn hair. He laid the meager curl reverently on the *pyra* before beginning his address, some inane drivel about this being a monument fit for a hero to equal Patroclus.

"When I die, I want Alexander to spend twice this much on my funeral," I said to Parizad once Alexander finished and the Macedonians began filing past Hephaestion's bier. "My *pyra* will touch the sky and drip with gold from top to bottom."

Parizad's smile didn't reach his eyes. "You'll outlive all of us, railing against Ahura Mazda for your white hair and hunched back."

I wrinkled my nose at the revolting idea even as I laid my head on Parizad's shoulder. "Better to die an early death than grow into a wrinkled old crone." Hephaestion's one redeeming quality was that he'd possessed the good sense to die before he accumulated a belly like a sow and lost all his hair.

I tapped my foot in impatience until the last Companion made his obeisance and the entire assemblage bent one knee in Hephaestion's honor. The soldiers scooped handfuls of earth and rubbed it into the golden suns on their swords and shields, dedicating their arms to the memory of this so-called hero. Then Alexander did the unthinkable. He ordered in a booming voice that the Royal Fire in every temple of the empire be quenched, a sacred act that occurred only when the King of Kings had died. In fact, each fire should remain lit until Alexander's own death. But what did I care for heroes and eternal fires? My stomach itched and I longed for the jar of goose fat and the army of silent attendants who would slather it over my belly when all this was over.

"Your knee appears stiff, Roxana," Drypetis said to me, her voice loud enough to carry to Alexander. He turned in our direction. "Do you require assistance so you might honor Alexander's favored companion?"

I gave her a honeyed smile, although my eyes surely sparked with something less pleasant. "Of course not," I murmured. "I'm simply overcome with emotion at Hephaestion's passing."

I bowed then, deeper than was necessary beneath the weight of Alexander's gaze. I closed my eyes as if in prayer, then almost jumped out of my skin as the entire Greek army let out a bloodcurdling war cry, pounding on their shields like a violent thundercloud fallen to earth.

"Hephaestion's final farewell," Parizad assured me, squeezing my hand. "They'll spend the rest of the day and night drinking in his honor."

"Another banquet?"

It seemed all Alexander did these days and nights was plan out his next campaign and then drink himself into oblivion. I frowned, forcing myself not to furrow my brow and etch lines there. I'd thought myself fortunate with Hephaestion's death in that I now had fewer competitors for my husband's attentions, but here I was, still fighting for the stale crumbs of his time.

"Fine," I said. "Then I'll join them."

"Women aren't invited," my brother said slowly. "Certainly not any wives."

But I was more than just a wife. I was the Whore of Sogdian Rock, the Bitch of Balkh.

I smiled, tracing the sweep of my neckline. "Remember who I was before I became a wife, dear brother. I still have a few tricks tucked away somewhere."

In the meantime, I hoped Stateira spent the night retching into a chamber pot with only her bore of a sister to hold her hair back.

I'd never before seen so much wine in one place, great golden goblets full of it, guzzled by Alexander and his men until their voices boomed and the flagstones of Nebuchadnezzar's massive hall grew slick with crimson pools. Alexander's Companions lounged on silver-footed sofas, and slaves armed with terra-cotta *amphorae* and ram-headed drinking horns lined the walls. Alexander's own griffin-head *rhyton* was three times as large as the others and was kept full by Cassander, Antipater's thick-browed son, who had been relegated to the position as wine bearer after his outburst in Alexander's throne room. Antipater ignored his disgraced son and reclined on a far-flung couch, his *chiton* pristine and his white beard freshly combed.

Alexander raised his cup in three traditional Greek toasts, honoring first the gods, then fallen heroes—with a special salute for Hephaestion that made the gorge rise in my throat—and finally Zeus, the king of his gods. I waved away the endless platters of stewed plums and rabbit fetuses, boiled ostrich drizzled with a sweet date sauce, and sea urchins fried in the pungent oil of a tree fungus. Things had gone wrong from the moment I'd entered the hall, so that now I regretted coming.

Alexander had allowed my sweeping entrance and my impromptu placement near his throne, but I could tell that my unexpected appearance nettled him. He ignored me entirely, too engrossed with his talk of fresh conquests toward Arabia with Admiral Nearchus while Cassander dutifully kept his silver goblet from running dry. I consoled myself with the knowledge that Stateira and Parysatis remained in their chambers, out of Alexander's sight and therefore out of his bed.

Alexander's face tonight tended toward a florid red that matched the wine Cassander poured and his shorn golden curls were in need of a good washing and oiling. He stood and motioned to one of his Companions, leaving his throne vacant with nary a thought for my comfort while they discussed a bout of recent war games. Men scoffed at women for our gossip and pretty gowns, but then they played at war like boys with bruised fruit and wooden swords.

Bagoas was there and had made one attempt to approach me,

but I turned my back on him, refusing to ever speak to the traitor again. When I glanced back in his direction, it was to see that Alexander had flung an arm around my former eunuch's shoulder and fondled his beautiful curls while still engrossed in conversation with the Companion.

How *dare* Alexander favor that half man over me, his first wife and the mother to his heir.

I fumed in silence until a bent-backed man dressed in an unkempt slave's tunic emerged from the dining couches with a tray of cups filled with beer and bread. I waved him away—the mere sight of the foul Greek drink was enough to turn my stomach—but the slave continued to mount the dais. Then he did the unthinkable: He dared to sit his unworthy body on my husband's throne.

"Alexander!" I shrieked, leaping to my feet and backing away from the vermin. The tray wobbled in the slave's hand and the cups crashed to the ground, splashing beer and bread everywhere.

There was a collective gasp and Alexander turned from his conversation, his face contorting in outrage.

"What is the meaning of this?" he demanded, Bagoas and his curls suddenly forgotten in the face of this insult.

The man only shook his head with a blank stare, his disheveled beard dropping mites with the movement. I gathered my skirts closer to avoid contamination. "This seemed a perfectly good chair," he said, scratching his head. "So I thought I might rest a while in it."

Alexander stared so that I thought he might laugh at the madman. "It is treason to sit upon my throne," he said. "Remove yourself immediately."

But the foul creature didn't move.

Antipater cleared his throat from his couch. "There is an ancient festival here in Persia in which a slave would dress as a king and sit upon his throne for a hundred days. Mayhap the man takes his inspiration from there."

"That festival is in the autumn," I snapped, "while this is clearly summer. The imbecile must be dumb and mad to get the two confused. And he's certainly not dressed like any king I've ever known."

All eyes turned to Alexander, yet still the filthy man lounged on the throne.

"Flay the skin from his back," Alexander ordered. "Let this be a warning to all those who seek to amuse themselves at my expense."

The man didn't make a sound as he was dragged away, leaving a trail of nits and bewilderment in his wake. I squelched one of the tiny insects with my thumb, smearing a trace of blood across the gilded wood of Alexander's throne.

"You should have this scrubbed with vinegar," I said to Alexander as he threw himself into the chair. "What a foul creature."

But Antipater sang a different song. "This may be interpreted as an ill omen, especially as everyone has heard by now of Babylon's sacrifice for you of the ox with the deformed liver. Perhaps you should have allowed the flea-bitten mongrel to rule in your stead during the summer months."

"Livers without lobes and now this," Alexander muttered, his face still dark. "I've no patience for these ill omens or the whispers they cause." He raised a hand and snapped his fingers at Cassander. "This night calls for more wine and revelry," he said, thrusting out his goblet. "Much more."

The heat from all the bodies and the cup of wine I sipped made my eyelids heavy, but I dared not excuse myself as Alexander commanded everyone's attention so he might give a recitation. I preened to realize he was playacting Perseus fawning over Andromeda, chained to a rock by her father and waiting to be devoured by a sea monster. I recognized the guise, for I knew a thing about daughters being wronged by fathers, and raised a hand over my breast, making to stand and allow Alexander to adore me, even if it was in the guise of Andromeda.

That is, until Alexander bent his knee to Bagoas, praising *his* beauty above the silvery nymphs of the sea.

In that moment I wanted Bagoas to suffer as I've never wanted anything in my life, for a pox to disfigure his pretty face or for him to become a leper so his talented hands, which had taught me so much, would wither into worthless lumps of flesh like his lost prick.

I didn't hear another word of the performance over the roar in my ears, but at its end Alexander raised his massive *rhyton* and drank a toast to one illustrious guest after another until I ran out of fingers to count them.

Admiral Nearchus attempted to strike up a conversation with me, but I was ready to excuse myself—not that any of these barbarians would notice the departure of their queen—when there was a thud to my left and Alexander's great goblet clattered to the ground.

I whirled about, expecting to see him passed out drunk and itching to overturn my goblet of wine on his face, but he had fallen to his knees before his throne and clutched his abdomen as if there were a demon gnawing at him from inside. He cried out and curled into himself, but thankfully there was no blood, no weapon. Only a man who had drank too much.

Bagoas moved to help him, but I blocked his path. "Stay back," I snarled at the eunuch under my breath. "What is it?" I asked Alexander, kneeling at his side.

"It feels as if I've been shot in the liver with an arrow," he gasped. "Like in India."

My scar-riddled husband certainly knew pain, but surely this episode was only the result of overindulgence. After all, no man was meant to swill wine as he had tonight without being visited by a sour stomach.

A man cleared his throat and Antipater stood behind me, his spine straighter than if a spear had been run through it. "Perhaps my son and I might be of service in removing the king to his chambers," he said. "We've experience with this, especially after Alexander's recent debauchs since Hephaestion's death."

"Of course," I said, thinking fast. "I shall accompany you."

Alexander swayed unsteadily between them, his head lolling from side to side, and stumbled with every step. "I imbibed too much," he rasped, his fingers fluttering although his eyes remained screwed tightly shut. "Only Hephaestion could ever rein in my lust for life." I stiffened at the mention of his dead pederast, but he didn't notice.

We approached his chambers to find oil lamps left burning for his return. Antipater and his baboon of a son helped lay Alexander upon the bed, his limbs heavy and his pallor increased to a startling paleness.

"He needs to empty his stomach," I said to Cassander, but he only shrugged.

"This is the warrior who scaled Sogdian Rock and massacred all of Thebes. He won't allow a cup of fermented grapes to lay him low. He'll recover, though I doubt he'll have learned his lesson."

I dismissed the men with a curt nod, then settled stiffly onto the bed beside my snoring husband so that mine would be the first face he saw when he awoke.

I'd imagined my days as queen to be filled with entertaining elegant *satraps* who would flatter my beauty and wit while I chose which robes would best impress the envoys sent from all corners of the empire. The reality was far less glamorous, being insulted by my husband's bed companions, tromping through India with its mosquito-infested swamps and mountains, and now playing nursemaid to my sour-smelling husband.

Alexander moaned in his sleep and rolled over, throwing an arm over my chest, his foul breath like a wind of curdled wine.

He owed me an empire of cities named Roxania, all filled with towering statues of me in my golden glory.

And I would make him give them to me.

* * *

But Alexander was in no mood to grant boons, name new cities, or commission statues when he finally woke at sunset the next day.

He hobbled like a hunchbacked old man to a hammered copper basin to void his bladder, and I cringed at the acrid smell of his waters clanging against the metal. "What are you doing here?" he growled at me, raking a trembling hand through his lank hair. He looked like a band of dark-winged *daevas* might have stolen him in the night and tossed him between them in a child's game of keep-away.

"You required assistance yesterday evening," I said. "It appears you still do."

"Leave me, woman," he said as he stumbled across the floor. I was at his side in an instant, linking my arms around his waist to steady him. His entire body burned with fever, evidence that this was no simple case of overindulgence.

Fever might fell Hephaestion, but I vowed it would *not* claim Alexander.

"I won't leave," I said. "Not until you've rested and recovered."

"A king has no time to rest," he argued.

Despite his protests, I called for Parizad, not trusting the other physicians. My brother listened to Alexander's heart, smelled his breath, and felt his burning forehead until Alexander ordered him away. Ignoring Parizad's recommendation that he rest and eat only cool foods, that night Alexander insisted on traveling by boat across the Euphrates to Nebuchadnezzar's second summer palace, where he somehow managed to play dice and talk with his men. The next day, still wan and feverish, he deigned to be carried on a goatskin stretcher to make his customary sacrifices to Ammon and the other gods while planning the Arabian campaign from his sickbed.

"It would be a kindness to kill me," he wheezed as Ptolemy and

Admiral Nearchus filed from his room, both casting worried glances over their shoulders. "Or at least let me fall on my sword."

"Don't speak so," I snapped. "It isn't fitting for a king."

I expected him to rail against me for daring to reprimand him, but he only closed his eyes and turned onto his side, offering me his back in response. After that, I ordered all the weapons removed from his chambers.

To my growing horror, over the coming days he weakened as if every labored breath stole a piece of his vitality. Stateira and Parysatis visited, as did Thessalonike with her slack-twisted idiot of a brother and surly Amazon of a sister, but after they departed, I ordered the guards to keep them away, at sword point if necessary. The woman who received the credit for nursing him back to health would be me, not his lesser wives, unnatural warrior sisters, or other outcast siblings.

"He is young for this malady to linger so," Parizad whispered to me on the fourth night. The earthy scent of the chamomile and comfrey, yarrow, and thyme he mixed did little to mask the stink of Alexander's stale sweat as my husband tossed and turned in a fitful sleep. "I fear he may never recover fully, not after all the wounds he has sustained."

I shook my head, refusing to entertain such thoughts. "He *will* recover," I said. "And you will see that he does."

Worry flashed in Parizad's eyes before he bowed his head over his herbs, pouring them into a painted *hydria* depicting Heracles dragging Hector's corpse behind his chariot. "I will do my best."

"Is it possible this is something else?" I asked, my fingers tapping on my forearm as I paced the length of the chamber. "Perhaps he's being poisoned by someone who wishes to remove him from power?"

Parizad glanced up sharply from his tincture, nearly upsetting the cup. "To poison a god is no small crime," he said. "I can't imagine that any mortal would attempt such villainy."

But Alexander was no god, only a man. And smaller men had been killed for much less.

On the fifth night I awoke to utter silence and feared for a terrified moment that the destructive god Ahriman had claimed Alexander while I slept. Instead, his bed was empty. I ran to the open doorway on unsteady legs to find a lone guard with the first fuzz of manhood on his upper lip and a breastplate polished to near blinding brightness standing at attention.

"Where is Alexander?" I demanded.

The boy pointed down the corridor, averting his eyes from my disheveled state. "That way," he said. "He forbade me from following."

"And you listened to him?" I shrilled. "He might fall off the ramparts or expire in the hallway from his fever. If he does, I'll have you impaled on a stake outside the palace!"

The soldier snapped a salute, the only thing he knew how to do properly. "He said something about the river." Fresh panic made his eyes wide as moons. "And meeting Hephaestion."

I ran, clutching my swollen belly and gasping for breath.

Parizad had told me far too many tales of Greek idiot-heroes who preferred to end their lives rather than linger in dishonor, their wits and strength fleeing in the face of death. Foul Hephaestion sought to ruin me even from his grave, beckoning Alexander to the afterlife with promises of Elysium.

Alexander would *not* die. I wouldn't let him.

I found him on the banks of the river that ran through the Hanging Gardens, crouched on all fours at the water's edge as in the story of golden Narcissus, admiring not his reflection but the promise of a quick death.

"Alexander!" I screamed. Some benevolent god carried my voice to him and he turned, his face warped with anguish.

I closed the distance between us, falling beside him. "You poor, stupid idiot," I sobbed. "What are you doing?"

"You rob me of my glory, wife," he said through clenched teeth. I could only guess at the agony that had driven him here. "I thought to ease Hades' task."

"You fool," I said, hysterical tears running unchecked down my cheeks at how close he'd come to abandoning me. "Let Parizad wrap you in poultices and brew his herbs for you. You're a warrior; fight Hades with every last bit of strength you possess, if not for yourself or your empire, at least for your son."

Alexander managed a meager smile at that. "I fear it shall be a poor fight." He cast one last lingering glance at the water, but allowed me to help him slowly to his feet.

And so, for the second time in days, I helped Alexander back to his chambers and into bed. And I swore I wouldn't sleep until he was recovered.

Rumors of Alexander's illness raged faster and hotter than wildfire until whispers claimed that Hades had reaped his soul days ago and that I kept his corpse hidden away out of madness, as Alexander had done with Hephaestion.

"He still breathes," I snapped at Ptolemy, Antipater, and Cassander, flinging the door wide so they might see their king, his sweat-slicked face barely visible above the sheepskin throws that had been piled upon him in a vain attempt to keep him from shivering to death. It had been ten hellish days since the terrible banquet and my eyes stung from lack of sleep, my breath was stale, and the child within my womb kicked my ribs with a ferocity that made me wince. "Despite the vultures that hover about waiting for him to die."

"The men need proof," Antipater said, ignoring my insult to fold his hands serenely before him in the hallway. "Perhaps they might be allowed to see him with their own eyes?"

"What do you propose?" I asked. "That the entire army file past his sickbed?"

"That would be acceptable," Ptolemy said, glancing over my shoulder to where Alexander lay. "Seeing Alexander alive—even in this state—will instill much faith in his men."

"Fine," I said. "Gather the men. Alexander's chambers shall be opened at the twelfth hour so they may see that their true Queen of Queens has been nursing him, not hiding his dead body."

And so it was that I dressed in my finest silks, doused myself with spikenard water, and donned the queen's diadem, watching as Parizad propped up Alexander in bed. My husband's beard had grown in the week he'd been ill, the burnished gold making him appear even more haggard.

"Shave him," I commanded, then thought better of it. "Ready a ewer and a blade. I'll shave him myself."

"You have a gentle hand, wife," Alexander rasped when I lathered his cheeks with warmed almond oil and scraped the blade across his skin.

"I used to shave Oxyartes' whiskers as a girl," I said.

"I know so little of your past," Alexander said, closing his eyes even as his chest moved in what had become his customary shallow breaths, the only ones that didn't leave him gasping with pain. I finished shaving him and set the bowl and blade aside.

"All you needed was to ask," I said, tears stinging my eyes. Memories came to me unbidden then, of the lionlike man who watched me dance, winked at me over our marriage vows, and laughingly tumbled me into bed.

Perhaps things might have continued that way if I'd opened my bruised heart to him, or perhaps if he'd been a less complex man.

But then, he could be no less than Alexander, and as the Whore of Sogdian Rock, I knew better than to truly love any man.

"I'd like the stories of your childhood to usher me to my dreams tonight," he said, managing a wan smile.

Stories embellished to ignore our relative poverty and Oxyartes' whip.

Alexander reached up with a clawed hand to touch my hair. "You are so beautiful, Roxana. You shall make a good mother to my son."

He fell silent as the doors opened and his Companions and shield bearers, horse archers, and infantry began to file past. They paused to pour him libations from a flat bowl of glazed pottery stamped with my husband's royal portrait. Alexander raised a hand and waved silently to each one, but the effort cost him dear. By the end he was paler than milk and shaking like a man afflicted with the falling sickness.

I kept my promise then, banishing everyone from the room and sitting by his bedside, telling him of Parizad and me hiding in the stables to avoid my father, of pretending that we were the children of a great *satrap* who gifted us with new litters of puppies and kittens every day, and of Parizad singing me to sleep when thunderclouds rumbled overhead.

Then, as Alexander finally slept, I prayed that night as I'd never prayed before, beseeching Ahura Mazda and the shade of Alexander's father, Philip, and all of Alexander's immortal fathers to spare him. I was so desperate that I even begged Hephaestion's shade to shield Alexander from death, to spare not just the golden god but my husband and the father of my child, the man who had warmed me in bed.

Then I made plans just in case the fathers, the gods, and the false hero turned a deaf ear to my woman's pleas.

The gods gave Alexander eleven days after that fateful banquet. Then, without the fanfare, cheering crowds, and cascades of rose petals he so loved, Alexander the Great died quietly in the darkness of Nebuchadnezzar's palace, the dry rattle that had become his breath finally ceasing and leaving a roaring silence in its wake.

And so, the greatest conqueror the world had ever known died the most ordinary of deaths, a final cruelty inflicted by the fickle gods.

I closed Alexander's eyes and bent to kiss his warm, dry lips. "You've failed me, my lion," I whispered, my beringed thumb lingering on his lower lip. "And for that I can never forgive you."

Abandoned again, just as Bessus had abandoned me. But I was more than a grasping whore in a stone garrison this time. Yet I knew what had happened to the lesser wife of Alexander's father when he had died, and knew that it wouldn't be long before the vultures came for me, and for my unborn son.

I was Alexander's queen, and my son would be a king.

And I'd kill anyone who threatened otherwise.

❊ · CHAPTER 25 · ❊

Babylon, Persia

ᴅRYPETIS

A never-ending wail shattered my dream of Hephaestion into tiny fragments, leaving me disoriented as I returned unwilling to the land of the living. I'd dreamed that Hephaestion and I were arguing over whether the *Song of Ilium* or the Avesta was the more important work, each of my successful arguments for the Avesta earning me a tantalizing kiss, but now the remembrance of my husband's touch and the sound of his laughter faded into the harsh morning light.

I'd fallen asleep at the table where I'd sat polishing the precious Damascus ax he'd given me as a wedding present. I was lucky I hadn't shorn off my own ear; my cheeks were smeared with polishing sand and goose fat. The wail grew so loud I covered my ears, but then I leapt to my feet at the realization of what the sound must herald. I scrubbed my face with my palms, wincing as the stubborn flecks of sand scratched my cheeks until I finally gave up and splashed my face with stale water from a ewer, then rushed down the corridor.

Death had stalked us from Ecbatana to Babylon like a black-winged Harpy, circling overhead to finally land and prowl the walls of Nebuchadnezzar's ancient palace while Alexander wasted away before our eyes. He had been ill for days, and without him, the empire would plunge into chaos. Yet the sight that greeted me outside his chambers already heralded the tumult yet to come.

A crowd of Companions and *satraps*, slaves, and soldiers had gathered outside Alexander's apartments, but it was Cynnane who beckoned me.

"My brother is dead," she said. She shed no tears, but her gaze held steady where her daughter, Adea, stood across the way with Arrhidaeus, their heads bent together. I doubted whether either of them felt deep pangs of grief at Alexander's passing. Adea was too young to truly know her famous uncle, and the gift of Arrhidaeus' simpleness would protect him in the days to come from fully feeling the knives of grief.

I envied him that.

"Alexander died alone in the early hours of the morning," Cynnane said. "His body was already cold when fresh sentries came to relieve the night guards," she added, meeting my gaze for only the briefest moment. "Thessalonike sits with him, but I must stay here," she said, jutting her chin toward Adea and Arrhidaeus even as her hand tightened on the hilt of her sword.

I realized then why she'd taken up such a post, for as Alexander's nearest surviving relative, Arrhidaeus stood to gain an empire this day or become the target of someone who sought to succeed Alexander. "I'm sure my sister would be glad of your company," Cynnane added.

"Of course." I squeezed her arm and slipped past the guards. Alexander's chambers were filled with people, many still dressed in their night-robes and without their curled beards and eye paint. I pushed through the spectators to where Thessalonike sat vigil next to her brother. She might have been Alexander's twin, an Amazon warrior with a lion's mane of blond hair tamed into a braid. Antipater bent and placed a polished gold stater bearing the likeness of Bucephalus in Alexander's mouth to pay Charon, the ferryman who transported the dead across the river Styx, almost as if the regent had kept the coin ready for this very moment. His son Cassander stood apace, his gaze drawn to Thessalonike like iron filings to magnetite.

Antipater cleared his throat. "The great Alexander has left us as he journeys to the Fields of Elysium. The task of administering his empire now falls to us, his faithful subjects."

"To us?" Ptolemy shouted from across the room. "Or to you?"

And thus, the war for Alexander's throne began.

Had Hephaestion lived, he might have tempered this fight as he had so often done, or perhaps, with the army's support, he'd have seized Alexander's many crowns for himself, not because he wished to rule but merely out of duty to his dead friend.

Tears clawed at the back of my throat as they so often did when I thought of Hephaestion, but I blinked them back, staring at the ceiling until they cleared.

Without Hephaestion, anyone might claim the vast empire, especially while Alexander's heirs had yet to be born.

The babe growing in Stateira's womb was still a secret, but my sister and Parysatis were widows now, as was Roxana, although the former Queen of Queens was nowhere to be seen in the tumult of Alexander's chambers.

In a world turned upside down, Roxana's absence made no sense, for the Bitch of Balkh had barked and growled like a guard dog at anyone who'd dared to approach Alexander for the past eleven days. Why had she abandoned him at the moment of his death, unless she thought to protect herself and her unborn son by escaping the turmoil of the succession?

I wanted nothing more than to leave the crowded apartment full of men's shouts, reminding me as it did of another death chamber still fresh in my memory. Roxana's lingering spikenard perfume and the encroaching odor of death threatened to choke me, but I paused to touch Thessalonike's shoulder. "I'll be with Stateira," I murmured in her ear. "You're welcome to join us if you'd prefer some peace and quiet."

She gave a sad smile. "It's difficult to say good-bye to Alexander, much less think, with all these vultures hanging about."

"Order them to leave," I said. "They'll obey if you roar loud enough. After all, you're Alexander's sister."

I'd scarcely turned my back when Thessalonike's strong voice echoed off the stone walls, so that even the painted flowers overhead seemed to tremble. "Get out, all of you! Alexander's shade doesn't wish to listen to your arguing, and neither do I!"

I smiled to myself and hurried down the corridors to Stateira's sprawling apartments. At least I knew that Thessalonike would survive her grief.

And yet, I knew not how Stateira would handle Alexander's passing, whether this would lay her even lower than her illness and pregnancy had already done. We were two sisters who became brides on the same day, now two widows before the year was out.

We were all we had left.

Stateira's chambers were located in the farthest wing of the palace so she might benefit from the quiet rarely afforded those near the main courtyard, but I'd gone only halfway before I was met by a harried Bagoas, moving at twice his normal, controlled gait.

"Greetings, Princess Drypetis," he said to me, every word enunciated with crisp vowels despite his heaving chest. "Is it true? Is Alexander dead?"

"He is, claimed by a fever while he slept."

Bagoas' entire face contorted with panic and fear. "Then we must hurry."

I shivered suddenly, despite the morning's warmth. "What do you mean?"

"A messenger came before dawn," he said, his voice cracking. "He ordered me to wake Stateira and give her this letter from Alexander."

I nearly ripped the letter he retrieved from his hands. It was written in the Script of Nails, but in a hand that I didn't recognize.

My dearest Stateira,

I have rallied against Hades and long to gaze upon your sweet face and the swell of my son in your belly. I await your presence in the gardens.

Your king and husband,
Alexander

The letter was counterfeit, certainly not written by Alexander as he lay cold and dead just hallways from here, never having rallied this morning. My pulse thrummed and an acrid taste filled my mouth as I read and reread the first sentence.

The swell of my son in your belly.

Only Alexander, myself, Bagoas, and perhaps a few other trusted attendants knew of Stateira's pregnancy. And perhaps one other soul . . .

"Does Roxana know how to write?" I asked Bagoas, dreading the answer.

He shook his head. "She can scarcely use her fingers to count, but Parizad was tutored in the Script of Nails." A terrible understanding dawned in his eyes and his long fingers fluttered to his mouth. "And I've been intercepting herbs that Roxana bribed Stateira's attendants to sneak into her food. I didn't wish to worry Stateira in her condition—"

I crumpled the letter in my fist and raced for the gardens even as Bagoas sank to his knees, his cries at my back begging my forgiveness. It was the last I ever saw of him, for without Alexander's protection, he fled rather than face Mithra's justice.

My legs moved faster than they ever had before as I shoved past attendants in the corridors and finally burst into the famed Hanging Gardens. I darted within the same grove of trees where Hephaestion had once confronted me about fomenting rebellions against

Alexander, and screamed Stateira's name into air filled with the scent of damp earth and running river water, fragrant cedar bark and lush greenery.

But Stateira didn't answer.

Instead, another woman called my name.

"Drypetis?"

I turned toward the entrance to see Thessalonike, the last person I expected, as she should have been still mourning her brother.

"Bagoas came running for me," she said. "He said you needed help, something about Roxana and Stateira?"

"They're not here," I said. "I don't know where they are, but we need to find them, and fast—" My words and the beats of my thudding heart were interrupted by a woman's scream.

"Stateira!" I shouted, and sprinted into the corridor toward my sister's terrified voice, tearing around the corner to a tiny tiled courtyard shaded with potted cypress trees. In its corner was a wide well with an inlaid wooden cover, the source of fresh water for the palace's bathing pavilions.

Standing at its edge were Roxana and Parizad.

Beads of perspiration glistened at Parizad's temples and his robe was stained with a dark flower of what might have been scarlet were it not for the shadow of the cypress that fell upon him.

"Where is Stateira?" I demanded, hearing Thessalonike unsheathe her sword behind me.

We'd startled Roxana and her expression snagged between fear and fury, her glorious hair loose down her back and her swollen belly covered with orange silk embroidered with florid golden stars.

"It's done," Roxana said, her eyes wide as a wild grin erupted across her face. She was breathing hard as she wiped her hands down the front of her robe, leaving two smears of wetness.

"We must go, Roxana," Parizad said, clutching her wrist and pulling her toward the entrance.

But I blocked their path.

"I won't ask again," I said, my voice ringing out across the courtyard. "Where is my sister?"

My skin prickled at Roxana's hollow laugh, her brown eyes emptier than that terrible sound. "I'm afraid Stateira is rather indisposed at the moment."

And then her eyes darted toward the well.

And I knew.

I screamed and scrambled for the well even as Roxana and Parizad darted for the exit behind me. Thessalonike lunged after them, but I had eyes only for the well. The ground was slick with splashed water, but beyond the puddles, spatters of scarlet decorated the dry tiles like tiny rubies. I tore the wooden cover open and threw it aside.

And then I screamed.

Below the water's surface billowed one cloud of purple silk and another of pale yellow. Two women floated atop the other, their mouths and eyes half-open as if they were drifting off to sleep, the water around them pink with flags of crimson still seeping from the wounds to their necks.

Stateira. And Parysatis.

Their names in my throat were like the burning embers of a fire, and I screamed them over and over as I scrambled to pull their waterlogged bodies from the well. It took all my strength to heave them onto the tiles with violent splashes. Parysatis' limbs had already gone cold, but Stateira . . .

My beautiful sister might have been only napping, her body still warm with life. I felt for her pulse, but the blood in her veins had stopped save the graceful crimson rivulets that leaked in a steady stream down the gaping open wound at her throat. My poor sister, terrified of water since our brother's death, had been stabbed and then drowned in the very waters she feared.

It was the nightmare from my childhood all over again, watching as our brother was pulled from the Euphrates, his lips blue and his chest unmoving.

I wanted to die a thousand deaths as I tugged Stateira's body into my lap, hugging her in a fierce embrace as if I might trap her soul with me where it belonged. I rocked her like an infant and crooned into her wet hair, which still smelled of roses, begging her to stay with me.

The clash of weapons and a scream of pain overwhelmed the roar in my ears. I turned to see Thessalonike parry hard with Parizad at the edge of the courtyard, his sword coming down to slash the soft skin of her arm. She howled with fury and stumbled back as blood streamed from the wound. Parizad raised his sword for the deathblow, but Thessalonike feinted to the side, her sword arcing low to slice into his unprotected ribs. Her next thrust buried her sword into his belly so hard that the blade emerged out his back, slick with his blood and viscera. Parizad looked down, his gaze transfixed on the blade sheathed in his abdomen. Then he laughed, scarlet pouring in a torrent from his lips as his fingers fluttered at his bloody navel.

"Oh, Roxana," he said, his voice garbled with blood. "The things I've done for you . . ."

He fell to his knees as Thessalonike yanked her sword from his body, kicking him so he fell back to gaze with blind eyes at the rags of blue sky above us.

"Where's Roxana?" I cried, but the Bitch of Balkh was gone, escaped while her brother had fought and died for her.

"I'll find her," Thessalonike said, then tore from the courtyard in a storm of echoing footsteps. I sat by the well with my sister's head in my lap, staring at the placid water that had poached the last breath from her lungs.

I wished to keen then, to scream my grief and outrage at the gods and the world, but I was numb. I saw only death in Parysatis' calm face with its ruined lip that matched the gash in Stateira's neck and frail body, driftwood bones from her long illness beneath luminescent skin.

I know not how long I sat there, only that Thessalonike finally reentered, her bloodied sword hanging in her hand. "Roxana's disappeared," she said, her chest heaving and covered with Parizad's lifeblood. "I sent the guards to find her, but the palace is in chaos. She might have gone anywhere."

I pressed my sister's cool hand to my cheek, then stifled a sob as I closed her eyes and folded her arms across her belly, feeling my heart shatter into a million irreparable pieces as I remembered the unborn babe inside her womb. I choked to think of all I'd lost this day—this life—and sent an errant prayer to Hephaestion's shade to welcome them into the afterlife.

"Roxana will suffer for this," I whispered through my tears, making the promise to my sister, still beautiful even in death, and to poor, disfigured Parysatis. "I'll hunt her to the ends of the earth, until the day I watch her drown in her own blood."

Only then could I join my family and finally rest.

CHAPTER 26

Babylon, Persia

THESSALONIKE

The gold-plated laurel diadem placed upon Arrhidaeus' head was several sizes too small, akin to a child's plaything as my older brother grinned broadly at the assembled *satraps* and generals. My heart nearly broke then, for all my life I'd tried to shield Arrhidaeus from the horrors of politics and war, and now he'd been plunged into the midst of them. I wondered what Alexander would think to know that our bighearted, slow-witted brother was now king of his entire empire, a territory that Arrhidaeus could scarcely locate on a map much less govern.

Within hours of Alexander's last breath, arguments had erupted over who would become the new *basileus*. Some argued in favor of crowning Roxana's unborn son even as Barsine's bastard son, Heracles, was passed over, leaving me to wonder whether his mother would thank or curse the gods for his tender age and muddy lineage. Drypetis and I had informed the generals of Roxana's crimes, but Alexander's first wife had fled, whisking away her precious unborn son and any chance of immediate justice. There were whispers that she was heading to her father in Paropamisadae, but surely there was no shortage of *satraps* and petty rulers who would happily harbor the mother of Alexander's heir.

She would be found, and her son too, but right now the world cared only for who would rule in Alexander's place.

It had taken until Apollo roused himself the next dawn and drove his sun chariot across the sky for the generals to broach a fragile compromise. As our father's last surviving son and despite my many protests, Arrhidaeus was proclaimed king with the military's backing, to rule alongside Roxana's possible son. Still, no one expected either to be an active ruler; they were mere placeholders until the situation could be fully resolved. My hand on the hilt of my sword, I'd made the generals swear that Arrhidaeus would never come to harm, that when the time came, he would be gently set aside, not murdered. Until then, Antipater would serve as their regent.

Alexander had died, but his men and his empire still lived.

At least for now.

Rumors abounded regarding Alexander's final wishes, that he had ordered the siege in Arabia to continue, for the harbor in Babylon to be expanded to hold a thousand ships; that he'd whispered only the strongest should succeed him.

Worse still were the rumors about what had killed him, that Antipater and Cassander had poisoned his wine at the ill-fated banquet where a slave had sought to supplant him. It wasn't difficult to imagine the two men murdering my brother in retribution for their removal from power and Cassander's humiliation in Alexander's throne room.

And across the chamber from me, Cassander watched as Arrhidaeus fingered the diadem at his brow. Antipater stood behind him, whispering in his son's ear as they bent their knees to their new *basileus*.

Cassander's gaze caught mine for a moment, and I gave him a stony glare, wishing I could see into his heart.

"We must protect Arrhidaeus," Cynnane said, dispelling my dark thoughts as *satraps* and generals filed from the throne room after our brother's hasty coronation. "He's an easy target for anyone seeking a taste of power: Antipater, Olympias, even Ptolemy."

Our brother's empire would be better ruled by a pack of wolves than by a suspected poisoner, a cold-blooded murderer, or an ambitious and oiled courtier.

"They swore an oath—," I protested, but Cynnane waved her hand.

"Oaths are meaningless in times like these."

I rubbed my temples, willing away the ache gathering there. "What do you propose?"

"A wedding," she answered, and I almost laughed until I realized she was serious. "Arrhidaeus will marry Adea. And then you and I shall help them rule."

I scoffed. "Have you been inhaling Apollo's vapors?"

"Arrhidaeus is too vulnerable without us to help him. Surely you must see that."

I did, as I'd seen every threat to my sweet brother stretching back to the noblemen's sons who'd pelted him with insults and rocks. And I'd been my brother's protector since I was old enough to wield a slingshot.

I shook my head. "It's too dangerous, especially for Arrhidaeus and Adea. Antipater thinks to seize power for himself, not hand it over to the likes of two women."

"Antipater can dine on dirt for all I care. He may have been Alexander's regent, but he's no king. The military supports Arrhidaeus and thus, he and Adea will wed with every one of Alexander's soldiers at his side."

I frowned, feeling as if I were staring at a fresco with a gaping hole chiseled out of the center, unable to discern the final image. "And why would the military support such a match?"

"Because the Macedonian veterans here have longed to return home since before Alexander marched to India, and Arrhidaeus will happily grant their request when we leave to accompany Alexander's body to Macedon. The rest of our troops are Macedonians and Illyrians bred on tales of despotic Persian *barbaroi* who let long-legged vultures eat their dead. Any child born to Adea and Arrhidaeus will be fully Greek, not a half-blooded Persian, a heritage not even Roxana's sprat can boast."

I marveled to see my sister's fighting instincts transferred to politics. "I assume Antipater won't be invited to the wedding?"

She snorted. "Not if I can help it."

I grinned. "Have I ever told you what a genius you are?"

My gruff Amazon of a sister reached out to ruffle my hair as if I were six years old again, the way I'd wanted her to do a thousand times when I was a child. "Thanks, little sister," she said, making me beam still more at her. "I couldn't ask for a better partner at my side."

And so it was that we left the palace with Arrhidaeus and Adea later that afternoon, bound for the main encampment of soldiers along the Euphrates' banks. I'd invited Drypetis to join us, thinking she might benefit from time outside the palace, but she'd demurred, retreating into Babylon's Tower of Silence to lay her sister and her cousin to rest. The entire city mourned for my brother and his slain queens; women had shorn their hair and men smeared their foreheads with ashes, and courtiers and slaves alike scratched their cheeks so they might cry tears of blood for Alexander, conqueror of the greatest empire on earth.

For the first time in his life, Arrhidaeus was outfitted as a Macedonian soldier, a heroic cuirass depicting Macedon's eight-pointed sun creating well-defined muscles over his soft belly, a too-tight helmet set in place of his laurel crown, and Alexander's sun shield strapped to his forearm.

"It pinches, Nike," he whimpered to me, trying to shove his fingers beneath the brow of his helmet, but I only stood on tiptoes to kiss his nose, almost missing as our chariot lurched over a rock.

"You can hold it instead of wearing it if you promise to stand still during the ceremony," I said, patting his cheek. "Pretend that you're a tall tree waiting for a bird to land on your head while all the soldiers march past you."

Arrhidaeus wrenched the helm from his head and grinned, his hair sticking out in all directions. "I like birds."

"And I, brother," I said, smoothing his hair, "like you."

I recognized the cunning of Cynnane's plan as soon as I espied the army, and easily identified the Illyrian helmets from her mother's homeland at the forefront of the Macedonians. These were the troops freshly sent from Greece that would soon join the veterans of Alexander's remaining army from the Indian campaign. Their commanders stood at attention before the sea of men, and my hand tightened into a fist to see Cassander positioned next to Alcetas, one of the Macedonian commanders.

I trusted none of them.

Arrhidaeus fidgeted while the men newly placed under his command made the customary march between two halves of a disemboweled dog, its stomach now twin caverns gaping with white rib bones and bloody sinews. I'd seen the same scene of purification played out after my father's death before the army bent its knees to Alexander, and prayed to the four goddesses that this would be the last time I witnessed such a grim processional in my lifetime.

"Men of Macedon and Greece," Cynnane's voice rang out. She too was dressed in full battle armor, her unadorned Illyrian helm and menacing silver-studded Macedonian boots marking her as an equal to all the men present. "Today you dedicate yourself to Arrhidaeus, son of Philip and brother of your beloved *basileus*, Alexander of Macedon."

At this, the Macedonians banged fists upon their shields in a gesture of respect and mourning. Even in death, Alexander demanded their love and affection.

Cynnane gestured for young Adea to join her, and I hoped no one else could see the way her daughter's hands trembled. Thirteen-year-old Adea too wore a leather cuirass and greaves, but being so slight, she looked like a child playing dress-up in her mother's armor. "With your support, Arrhidaeus shall rule for many years," Cynnane continued. "To that end, you are also here to see your new *basileus* wed his fair niece Adea, Philip's granddaughter and Alexander's niece, ensuring the peaceful continuation of Alexander's empire for generations to come."

There was a moment of stunned silence, broken by Illyrian stomping that shook the earth as if a thousand giants strode across the plains. Of course Cynnane's countrymen would approve of such a match, setting a queen of their blood at Arrhidaeus' side.

I shrugged away my shock to see that the first officer to step forward and bend a knee was Cassander, prompting the rest of the men to fall into line behind him. Arrhidaeus began to mimic Cassander's bow until I touched his elbow. "They bow to you," I whispered as Cassander backed away and Alcetas, a second-rate general from Alexander's Indian campaign, filed past Cynnane. "You can nod to them, but a *basileus* never bows."

I resumed my position as Alcetas stepped forward, his eyes downcast as befitted a general paying homage to his ruler. His sword remained sheathed at his hip as he genuflected to my brother.

But he bowed too low, his hand darting for his boot and the weapon secreted there.

Acting on instinct, I shoved Arrhidaeus behind me, drawing my sword to protect him with the same fluid motion. But I misjudged Alcetas, for he sought a different target from my brother.

And in the days and years to come, I would never cease blaming myself for not guessing his murderous intent.

Alcetas' hidden dagger thrust up and to the right. The world slowed as I realized helplessly that the pale flesh of Cynnane's throat was completely exposed.

A warm spray of blood spattered my face and Adea screamed, one long ululating cry as her mother crumpled to the ground beside her in a burnished halo of wild hair and a heap of worthless armor. Alcetas lunged as if to slay Adea too, but this time I blocked his attack with a cry of rage and a wild parry that would have felled a smaller man.

"Run!" I yelled to Adea, but she clung to Cynnane and continued screaming even as my panic-stricken brother tried to pull her away.

Alcetas drew his sword and came at me hard then, but my fury was equal to his forceful assault and I deflected his every blow until our blades were clenched. My eyes bulged and the muscles of my arm screamed in protest as I tried to advance, intent on disarming him. I could see his death in my mind, how I would plunge my blade deep into his bowels, how he would drop his sword in horror just before my sword arched up to behead him.

But even that wouldn't bring back Cynnane.

Perhaps he sensed my weakness, for his free hand darted under my sword arm to scoop the hilt of my weapon and twist my wrist, disarming me in one quick motion. My blade slipped from my sweat-slicked palm and fell to the earth with a dull thud. His foot to my groin sent me flying back, landing so hard that all the air was knocked from my lungs. I lay on the earth, deaf and blind from the pain, unable to move and panicking as I struggled to draw air into my lungs, waiting for the deathblow.

And then my vision cleared and I stopped trying to breathe, for Cynnane lay scarcely an arm's length from me, her glazed eyes staring into mine as blood poured from the gash at her throat.

I had lost her. My idol, my protector, my sister, gone.

Because I'd failed to protect her.

My breath returned then in a strangled choke and the world roared with sound again, and I wanted nothing more than for Alcetas to kill me. But I'd take the foul traitor with me.

Through slitted eyes, I saw that a soldier had taken a position between Alcetas and me. Alcetas kept his sword pointed in my direction as he yelled to the men over the clamor of Adea's screams.

"Cynnane, the foul, conniving bitch from Illyria, sought to make a laughingstock of us by setting her daughter and herself above the regent and even your new *basileus*," he shouted, waving his sword at Arrhidaeus, huddled on the ground next to Adea. "First a simpleton set above us, and now we're to be ruled by two women? Alexander would curse us all the way from Elysium to know that we've allowed ourselves to be so cowed!"

I didn't care if he stabbed me and sent me to Hades, not so long as I could drag him to the river Styx with me. I struggled to my knees, my weapon lost, but prepared to fight with my bare hands, until the man between us spoke.

"Killing Cynnane was the act of a traitor." Cassander's deep voice bellowed so that it was clear he addressed neither Alcetas nor me, but the thousands of soldiers gathered before us. "You men pledged yourselves to Arrhidaeus and now you've witnessed his sister slaughtered before your very eyes. I swear on the twelve Olympians that there shall be no more blood spilled here today."

But the sound of hundreds of swords being drawn filled the air and I looked up to see the Illyrians' blades pointed in our direction, whether at Alcetas or the rest of us, I couldn't tell.

No one moved then, for not even the winds dared to breathe.

"Take King Arrhidaeus to his palace," Cassander commanded me as he hauled me to my feet. "Now."

Too late I realized that Cynnane had committed the same act of hubris as our father, shunning a contingent of personal guards who might have protected her today and leaving that critical job to someone woefully unprepared for any real battle.

Me.

Somehow, I pulled Adea from her mother's body and dragged

Arrhidaeus with us. I shoved them before me into the chariot and maneuvered the horses back toward the palace, whipping their flanks as if they might carry us all the way home to Macedon.

I half hoped they would.

I'd once boasted to Antipater that I'd ride halfway to Hades before I ever returned to Pella. Today I'd done more than that, visited the rocky depths of the pit of Tartarus and had my still-beating heart ripped from my chest.

Once back in the palace, I'd armed myself with a fresh sword and done my best to comfort Adea and Arrhidaeus as they howled in grief until I'd finally ordered them both dosed with poppy milk. I'd tripled the guards at their doors and windows while they slept, then taken up a position in the courtyard where Alexander's funeral carriage had been assembled. I stared blindly at his sarcophagus. The priests had embalmed my brother's body in a mixture of honey and spices, and now he lay entombed in a borrowed golden coffin that bore his armor and famed Trojan shield, all protected beneath a pillared canopy sewn with lustrous pearls and glittering jewels. There were paintings as well, hastily composed to depict Alexander in his prime: laying the first stone of Alexandria-in-Egypt, marching into India with his elephants, and accepting homage from his Macedonians and Persians.

And in the courtyard's shadows was a second sarcophagus hewn from a single block of Pentelic white marble, engraved with scenes of a lion hunt, Hephaestion's bones protected within its graceful walls.

I felt as if I too had died but been forbidden the comfort of the bleak Fields of Asphodel and instead sentenced to serve an eternity as a witless shadow in this fresh hell of a world.

I could hear Cynnane's voice in my mind, barking at me to stop wasting time crying over her death, her earlier words of praise echoing over and over.

I couldn't ask for a better partner at my side.

But I had failed her and now stood stiff before our brother's sarcophagus, numb and exhausted, trying to reconcile myself to the fact that she was truly gone.

While I grieved for Alexander and Hephaestion, the brothers I'd lost, it was Cynnane's death that had truly shattered me.

I reached out to trace a depiction of Alexander as he led his Companions into battle in a nondescript desert. "You may have been brave and beautiful, brother of mine," I said. "But I hope that Hephaestion and Cynnane are wringing your neck for the mess your death left behind."

I almost laughed then, for Alexander, Hephaestion, and Cynnane together would be a magnificent and terrifying thing to behold. I hoped that the god Hades had a strong constitution.

Cautious footsteps sounded at the courtyard's main entrance and I drew my sword to defend myself. But it was only Drypetis, still swathed in the same black raiment she'd worn when she disappeared into the Tower of Silence.

A lifetime ago.

"I heard what happened," she said, her face drawn as she paused to run a hand along the foot of Hephaestion's marble coffin. She looked at me with tear-filled eyes. "I'm so sorry, Thessalonike. I've come to help you in any way I can."

"But your sister's rites . . ." It was difficult to think through the fog of grief enveloping my mind. "I thought they took five days."

"I left early. Stateira wouldn't want you to be alone now; she'd understand." She hesitated, then pulled me into an embrace scented by the temple's sacred fire, a bold move considering the sword held tight in my hand.

Her simple touch splintered something in me and I dropped the sword, letting it clatter to the tiles. Unable to speak, I'd have fallen to my knees had it not been for Drypetis' strength. Instead, I sobbed into her shoulder, great, gasping, terrible sobs that threatened to tear me in two. And all the while she stroked my hair until her face was wet with her own tears, both of us cast adrift without our sisters.

The bleak horizon swallowed the sun like a soul welcomed into the afterlife before Cassander arrived at the palace. He lifted his hands, revealing that he'd left his weapons elsewhere. Unarmed, then, to put me at ease.

But I'd never be at ease again. Not until I was home in Macedon, and perhaps not even then.

Drypetis rose, smoothing the front of her black robe as the last light faded from the courtyard. Attendants entered as if on cue, lighting a few scattered oil torches. "I'll sit with Adea and Arrhidaeus for a bit," she said.

I nodded. "Thank you. And promise me you'll think about my request."

She smiled, a forlorn gesture as she glanced once again at Hephaestion's sarcophagus. "I will."

I watched her go, knowing how Atlas felt with the weight of the world on his shoulders.

Cassander waited until Drypetis disappeared before he spoke. "You asked her to come to Macedon, didn't you?"

I glanced sharply at him. "And if I did?"

He shrugged. "There's nothing left for her here. I'd guess it's a welcome invitation."

He sat next to me unbidden and I shifted to put more space between us. I caught a whiff of the lemon used to sweeten his linen, at odds with the crimson stain on his *chiton*, already darkening to brown.

Cynnane's blood.

How many times could a heart break in one day?

"Where is she?" I whispered, my eyes feeling as if they'd been scoured with sand from this day's tears. An eternity cursed with the oblivion of Asphodel's Fields would have been a kindness compared with this all-consuming grief that threatened to lay me low.

"She lies on her shield in the throne room, away from prying eyes," he answered. "Adea and Arrhidaeus can see her when they're ready."

"And Alcetas?"

"Gone," he said stonily. "The army denounced him today, but refused to act against him. I've set Ptolemy and the other generals to find him, but he'd as like fall on his own sword before allowing them to take him."

Thus denying me the satisfaction of watching him die a slow and painful death.

My hands curled into fists, my grief making me bold. "And was it your father who coerced him into killing Cynnane? Just as he convinced you to poison Alexander?"

I expected Cassander to sputter in anger and deny the accusations, but he only stared at me, his face settling into harsh lines. "What purpose would Alexander's death have served me?"

"He demoted your father. And he insulted you in his throne room."

Cassander gave a coarse chuff of laughter, but the sound was flat and empty. "You think I would kill a king because he insulted me? I'm constantly awed by your low opinion of me."

"So you don't admit to helping your father kill Alexander?"

"My father's power is an illusion," Cassander said, waving an impatient hand. "He's thrown his support behind Arrhidaeus, but everyone knows that Olympias will fight him. He won't live to see the end of this power struggle, regardless of his being named regent."

I scoffed. "Then let me guess what happens next: You take his place and rule as my brother once did."

Cassander shook his head. "No one could rule as Alexander did. But someone *shall* rule and it won't be Arrhidaeus or a babe yet to be born."

"It would have been Cynnane," I said, clasping the cold edges of my bench. "She'd have made a worthy successor to our brother, an Amazon to follow in his footsteps as she guided Arrhidaeus. But she wasn't given the chance."

"The men wish to carry out Cynnane's plans," Cassander said slowly. "The Illyrians spoke first, demanding that Arrhidaeus be allowed to marry Adea. The other regiments lent their voices to the order. They were much impressed with Cynnane, and don't wish for her to have died for nothing." He reached out as if to touch me, but his hand fell to his side. "Your sister was a rare woman."

Cassander's praise made it impossible to swallow over the lump in my throat. "Then they shall marry as soon as can be arranged," I said, turning my attention to Alexander's battle paintings so I might regain my composure. I'd always dismissed Cassander as a droning bore, but today, unasked and unbidden, he'd assumed Cynnane's responsibilities in protecting Adea and Arrhidaeus, perhaps even in protecting me. The realization left me both bewildered and grateful. Now it remained for me to help Adea and to honor Cynnane by seeing her plans to fruition.

"I'm sorry, Thessalonike," Cassander said. "I truly am." Then he looked at me with a grim twist to his mouth. "Olympias kept you locked away and Alexander allowed you to do as you pleased, but many in the coming days will view you as a priceless link to Alexander and his empire."

My skin went cold and I shivered.

"There's nothing I can do about that," I said.

"You can marry me."

I gaped at him, his face shrouded in shadows so I couldn't read his expression. "I'd have thought that you'd have waited at least until my brother and sister were in their tombs before launching another vile marriage proposal. I can see I was wrong."

He stood and kicked the base of the granite bench, hard enough I was surprised it didn't break his toes. "The battle for your brother's throne has only just begun, Thessalonike," he said, each word carefully uttered. "You'd sleep better knowing you didn't face the fight alone."

"I'm not alone," I said. "I have Arrhidaeus and Adea. And Drypetis."

Cassander stared at me a long moment, then spread his arms wide. "Then you have no need of me."

He stood and backed from my presence, leaving me alone in the courtyard surrounded by the sarcophagi of two dead warriors and the empty vault of sky overhead.

I'd grown weary of death as my constant companion, but it would be still longer before I could shake Hades from my side.

We purified Cynnane with olive oil and dressed her in her armor before placing her in a third sarcophagus to travel home to Macedon, then witnessed her daughter being wed to Arrhidaeus in a simple ceremony in full view of the army. Adea helped guide Arrhidaeus' hand as he cut the traditional loaf of rye bread and she blushed to offer him a fragrant yellow quince in the manner of Greek brides stretching back to the birth of the gods, while the soldier-spectators threw nuts and dried figs at the solemn couple. I prayed that Cynnane's shade saw her daughter's meager smile as Arrhidaeus fed her the sweet fruit, even as I swore I would do everything in my power to see them both safely delivered to their thrones in Macedon.

We were to travel with Ptolemy and his contingent of Egypt-bound troops overland to Tyre and there board ships for a sea journey that I looked forward to as much as I did having a rotten tooth pulled. A good portion of the army had been dispatched to quell a revolt in Cappadocia, the sole area of the Levant not conquered by my brother, leaving only a small contingent to guard Arrhidaeus, Adea, and the rest of the funeral cortege. Drypetis had decided to accompany Hephaestion's bones to his final resting place in Macedon, but we were still at a disadvantage when another of Alexander's generals sought to benefit from his death almost two months after our departure from Babylon.

We woke to a hue and cry at dawn one morning still several days outside Tyre, to discover Alexander's gaudy funeral carriage missing. Taken with it were my brother's body and his armor; left behind were only the lifelike paintings of him.

"What is the meaning of this?" I demanded, hands balled into fists on my hips as I stood in the exact place where the carriage had rested the night before, its wheel tracks now leading to the west. Drypetis stumbled from her tent, her hair in such disarray that for a moment I was reminded of Cynnane.

I pushed the thought away.

"Ptolemy has stolen Alexander's body," Antipater proclaimed, his polished facade ruined by the black curse he muttered under his breath. Cassander stood next to his father, scowling as he searched the horizon.

Ptolemy, the newly proclaimed *satrap* of Egypt, who dressed like a Greek, smelled like an Egyptian, and schemed like a Persian.

"And I assume you've already ordered men to recover Alexander's carriage?" I said.

Antipater straightened, the morning sun gleaming on his balding pate. "I have not."

I blinked. "Which would you prefer, to fall on your sword or enjoy a cup of chilled hemlock when you inform Olympias that you allowed a sneaky Egyptian *satrap* to steal her son's body, presumably to abandon him in some barren desert for the vultures to pick apart?"

"I assume Ptolemy will take the utmost care of Alexander's body and its raiment. At least in Egypt, Alexander's remains will be protected from the storm to come."

"What storm?" I demanded, my hand tightening on the hilt of my sword.

"You may soon have need of that blade," Cassander said. "But not against us."

"What do you mean?" I asked.

At a nod from his father, Cassander plucked a scroll from Antipater's saddlebag and handed it to me. "A message from Olympias. She has given Roxana refuge."

I heard Drypetis' sharp inhalation, felt the hatred roiling off her even with my back turned. "And her child?"

"A son."

If there were any justice in this world, Roxana would have died birthing the child.

"Olympias has raised thousands of men and even her own array of war elephants in Macedon," Antipater said. "In support of the sole claim of her grandson, Alexander the Fourth."

I scanned the remainder of the letter, written in Olympias' slanting hand. "She has denounced us," I said.

"She condemns Arrhidaeus and his family," Cassander said. "And the regent of Greece."

With one fell swoop of her pen, Olympias had plunged us all into civil war.

Suddenly, I understood Antipater's decision to allow Alexander to lie at rest in Egypt rather than to drag his remains across the world into what promised to be a bloody and prolonged conflict. I'd have preferred to have my brother forever in Macedon where I might one day visit his tomb with my children and grandchildren, but I also didn't wish to see him lost or, worse, destroyed in the fight to come.

"What do we do?" I asked.

"Roxana's infant cannot rule," Antipater said. "Macedon supports Olympias and Alexander's bloodline, but the rest of the army has declared for the established regency. There are revolts for independence already in Aetolia, Athens, and Thessaly."

My brother's empire was fracturing before us, and we were powerless to stop it.

Drypetis cleared her throat. "Perhaps Olympias might be persuaded to release Roxana. Surely she wouldn't harbor her if she knew of Roxana's crimes?"

But I only shook my head. "You don't know Olympias."

"There is an empire at stake," Cassander said. "Everyone plays only for themselves now, Olympias most of all."

"Not me," I said quietly, my voice almost a growl. "I play for Arrhidaeus. And for peace."

"We must put down the revolts first," Cassander said, as if I hadn't spoken. "And then deal with Olympias."

"And Arrhidaeus and Adea?" I asked.

"It is a regent's place to remain at the side of his king," Antipater answered. "Thus, Arrhidaeus and his queen shall enjoy my protection."

He turned then, barking out orders to speed our departure and hasten us to the brewing war. I could well imagine Ares and the other gods of Mount Olympus pricking their ears in our direction, for this fight promised to rival Homer's sagas of Paris and Helen, Achilles and Hector.

"If any harm comes to Arrhidaeus, I swear I'll gut you like a fish," I said to Cassander, low enough that only he could hear. "And I'll do it slowly, so you have the pleasure of watching me carve out your innards before I set them on fire."

Cassander exhaled with great control and looked toward the ripening skies, as if dealing with a petulant child. "Of course you will, Thessalonike."

I hesitated for a moment before facing southwest, toward Egypt and Alexander's resting place for all eternity.

"Good-bye, brother," I said for the final time. "Rest well."

The gods only knew if and when I'd see him again.

CHAPTER 27

Macedon

DRYPETIS

Mithra's eyes, what a terrible year that was. A gray and red year, the grayness of my unending misery and the red of blood that would never cease flowing. Blood as Antipater chased Olympias' men, blood as regiments of Epirean soldiers allied with Macedon to drive out Antipater, blood on my thumb where I cut myself on the Damascus edge of Hephaestion's ax while sharpening it, and wept all over again with the agony of losing him.

Blood on the edge of Thessalonike's sword as she came striding back grim-faced and lion-maned from yet another fight. Her sword was rarely sheathed that year, nor was she ever longer than a sword's length from the sides of Arrhidaeus and Adea. Their Amazon protector prowled light-footed and stony-eyed in their wake, more like Cynnane than even Cynnane had ever been, or so it seemed to me.

Yet I could still tempt a smile from Nike in the evenings when she walked with me, the only bright spot in my days as I taught myself to live again. No one would ever replace all those I had lost, but I knew that Stateira would have smiled to know that I'd found another sister to keep me from being utterly and hopelessly alone in this cruel world.

Gods, but I missed my sister too, her sweet smile and calming disposition. She might have brought some semblance of peace to all of us, but now I had to content myself with her dog-eared copy of Plato and an old sketch she'd once made of the two of us. I ignored the simple charcoal lines that made my profile and the bend in my nose, my finger hovering instead over the gentle curve of Stateira's cheekbones and the sweep of her arched brows. I dared not touch the paper and smudge the charcoal as I had the first time I'd seen the picture after ushering Stateira to the Tower of Silence.

I'd sobbed then, curled around the sketch while unable even to touch it.

The scrap of paper was as precious to me as the Icarus pendant that Hephaestion had given me. Small trinkets of another life irrevocably lost and yet revived each night in the hours before I slept; small trinkets that beckoned my loved ones to join me in my dreams. Sometimes my father was there too, his smile blossoming from beneath his beard as he hugged my mother and siblings, Hephaestion at my side.

Ahriman had stolen my mother and father, and Hephaestion too. But it was Roxana who had killed Stateira. And each evening as I put away the pendant and the portrait, Stateira's copy of Plato and Hephaestion's beloved volume of Pindar, I swore that I would live to see Roxana die.

One night Cassander ordered that we camp outside Mieza, for although Antipater was the official regent, it was his son who now directed the army while his father grew more and more infirm. Thessalonike and I walked in silence to the Shrine of the Nymphs, the forest where Aristotle had once taught Hephaestion and Alexander. There I sat in the cave where Hephaestion had escaped Alexander's fire, as I'd sought out so many of the places where my husband might have walked since we'd arrived in Macedon. The walls were dark in the falling twilight, so it was difficult to tell if the fire had left its mark, but I knelt on the ground, feeling the cold earth and imagining a younger Hephaestion asleep on his side there, an image so vivid I almost reached out to touch his dark curls.

"You really loved him, didn't you?"

I startled at Nike's voice, torn between a wish for privacy and thankfulness for her solid presence. She'd waited outside when I'd told her that Hephaestion had once camped here, but as always, Alexander's sister had a difficult time staying in one place for long.

"So very much," I murmured, straightening. "I hope you'll find happiness like ours one day."

"I'd have to marry for that," she said. She'd been using her knife to whittle a stick and tossed the wood to the ground, sheathing her blade. "I always thought I might marry one day, like Cynnane. . . ."

Her face crumpled and I reached out to squeeze her hand, giving her a moment to compose herself.

"You'll avenge her death," I said, a reassurance I'd repeated more times than I could count. This time Thessalonike's lips twisted, as if she'd just swallowed broken glass.

"Like you plan to do with Roxana?"

"I don't know what you mean—"

She snorted. "Anyone with eyes can guess that you fall asleep each night dreaming of new ways to kill the Bitch of Balkh. Sadly, I can't even do that much for Cynnane." She glanced at me through slitted eyes, but I tried not to let show my shock that my desires had been so transparent. "Cassander brought word today that Alcetas is dead, fallen on his own sword. I'd envisioned cutting his throat as he did to Cynnane. . . ." She sniffed and ran a ragged sleeve under her nose. "Most girls my age spend their days soothing their babes still at the breast and their nights pleasing their husbands. I spend my days dreaming of blood and iron. Broken, aren't I?" she asked with a shaky laugh.

I linked my arm through hers. "Perhaps," I said. "But I still like you."

But then, I supposed I was broken as well.

Nike chuckled and we stood that way for a moment, the darkened leaves of larch and mulberry rustling in the breeze as if the shrine's namesake nymphs flitted from behind the gnarled trunks in a child's game of hide-and-find. I could easily imagine Alexander and Hephaestion playing here as boys, and the image curdled my gut with fresh jealousy and grief.

"It's peaceful here," Thessalonike said, with a wry twist of her lips. "I'd forgotten how much I miss the calm."

But I knew the quiet to be an illusion, the stillness before the final storm.

"We're closer to Roxana," I said, broaching the earlier subject. Alcetas might be dead, but Roxana still breathed. For now. "And justice."

"But Olympias protects Roxana," Thessalonike said, glancing up to where the first stars of the night were beginning to spark to life. "We may as well be throwing pebbles at Scylla and Charybdis for all the impact we've had thus far."

But if perhaps the two women could be turned against each other . . .

"Surely there is someone who might be able to carry witness of what happened to my sister." The foul bastard Parizad might be dead, but I wouldn't rest until the Bitch of Balkh was rotting too for all she'd done. I'd thought to take out my revenge alone, but Thessalonike was a natural ally. "If Roxana's reputation could be shredded so thoroughly that no one could support her, not even Olympias . . ."

Then we could get to her. And then we could kill her.

Nike and even Cassander believed I had joined them here in Macedon to see Hephaestion's bones to his tomb. While that was true, my desire for revenge burned even hotter than my need to see my husband laid to rest.

"You shred the bitch's reputation." Thessalonike stretched like a panther, frowning at yet another half-healed sword cut on her forearm before she linked arms with me again. "I'll chase her down and shred her foul throat."

It was then that I told her of the babe Stateira had carried, of the precious niece or nephew I had lost to Roxana's ruthlessness. And she hugged me as I shed fresh tears, and shed a few of her own, for the child would have shared her blood too.

"We'd have been aunts together," she said. "And ruined the child thoroughly when we taught her to wield a sword and build battering rams."

I laughed through my tears then, which felt good, for I was heartily sick of crying.

Nike might smile for me on those soft evenings, but otherwise she had a mind for nothing but sword-clang and vengeance. I saw her the next morning sparring in a circle of guards, spitting at them to come at her two, three, four at a time, and she looked so like Alexander that for a moment I saw him as he had been at Issus and Tyre and Gaugamela. Cassander watched Thessalonike too, his blunt face stony as she surged and clashed and spat curses against the guards.

I set down the rag I'd been using to polish a set of training swords and brushed the sand from my hands as I stood beside Cassander. "Do you really think you and your father can win against Olympias?" I asked.

Cassander glanced at me from the corners of his dark eyes. His heavy features rendered him far from handsome, but I liked to think my own brother might have grown up to resemble him: strong, intelligent, and steadfast.

Such simple traits to make a good man, yet so rare.

Cassander nodded toward Nike as her sword crashed against another soldier's, neatly disarming him before she whirled on the next unfortunate guard. "We'd win in a week if all our men fought like her."

Yet Thessalonike alone couldn't win the war. And Cassander knew it.

He rubbed his jaw, his face haggard. "Our best hope is to entice Olympias' Macedonian troops and Thracian mercenaries to turn against her. If they come to our side, we might win the war by the time the year is out."

But it was a terrible year, with the worst yet to come—news that turned Cassander's face gray, followed by even darker tidings.

Oh, my poor Nike. I rested my cheek against my Damascus ax and wept.

CHAPTER 28

Amphipolis, Macedon

ROXANA

Olympias' womb had never carried me, but I knew we were meant to be together as mother and daughter from the moment I was ushered into her solar in Amphipolis, begging for refuge from those who sought to kill me.

It was a refuge that she happily granted even as she lifted little Alexander Aegus from my arms like the most precious treasure, my son so freshly fallen from my womb that the black nub of his cord had yet to come away from his belly.

If my crimes against Stateira and Parysatis had truly been wrong, the gods would have cursed me with a girl or let me die in childbirth. Instead, they'd given me a perfect son as a sign of their favor.

And so it was that I sat in the palace's converted aviary on a winter's day several months later, ignoring the lethargic snakes in the dovecotes as I struggled to spin coarse brown wool into usable yarn before ordering it dyed a vibrant purple and darned into tiny socks for my son. The nursemaid would bring Alexander Aegus to me after the midday meal, for I insisted on feeding my own son despite Olympias' offer to secure a wet nurse. I'd have demanded at least three wet nurses to guarantee my son's health had I sat upon the Eagle Throne alongside my husband, Alexander, but feeding his son with my own breasts was one way to prove myself demure and unassuming, dispelling the rumors of murder that had followed me from Babylon.

"Roxana, dearest, I don't think I gave you a proper gift to celebrate little Alexander's birth, now, did I?" Olympias asked me, stroking the scaly skull of the mottled orange and black viper that she'd finished milking. She enjoyed instructing me on how to best handle the serpents while she milked their venom, but the snakes and their beady eyes made my skin crawl. Still, I dared not show Olympias such weakness. Fortunately I was saved from the task as slaves entered with wine and trays of crusty brown bread, goat cheese flecked with rosemary and wild chives, and an assortment of olives for the midday meal. The food served in the past weeks had been common fare in response to the recent skirmishes between Antipater's and Olympias' forces, which had ruined countless fields and threatened the harvest. So it was with great glee that I spied a bowl piled high with rare late-season pomegranates, each fruit sliced open to reveal seeds like polished garnets.

I reached for one of the decadent fruits, but Olympias pushed the bowl from my reach. "Pomegranates might sour your milk, my pet."

I resumed my needlework with a dainty sniff. "No, I don't recall any gifts."

She pursed her lips in what might have been a smile and tapped the fresh vial of poison on the table. "It's a bit late, but I have a gift for you. Two, in fact."

"Truly?" The last gift I'd received for anything had been a handful of wilted wildflowers that Parizad had gathered and presented with a kiss to my forehead and a whisper that he couldn't wait to meet his niece or nephew. That was before Alexander had died and before I'd enticed Stateira and Parysatis to the well in Babylon.

I willed away the memory of my brother's careless laugh and the earthy scent of herbs that had clung to his hair. I spoke to him every night as if he were still here with me, so that now the slaves thought I spoke to myself. They muttered chants against evil spirits each time they saw me.

Stupid wart-faced hop-frogs, the lot of them.

"I received news this morning that Antipater has died of illness," Olympias said, gesturing to a parchment on the table. "I hope the Hydra in Tartarus relishes the taste of traitors."

I tried to summon some sliver of excitement, but a dead gray-beard scarcely made an enticing gift, despite the war he had waged against Olympias. "Good news indeed," I said, hoping her next offering involved something that shimmered in firelight, perhaps a new bolt of black silk I could cut to hide the bulge of my belly that remained after Alexander Aegus' birth. I might be mother of the *basileus*, but I felt like a milk cow with deflated udders each night when I undressed and prodded the slack skin across my hips.

"Now we have only Antipater's ambitious sprat Cassander to contend with," Olympias said, more to herself than me. I wondered what terrible fate she was planning for the bore I'd often seen hovering around Thessalonike. "And now your second gift."

At her signal a contingent of guards marched into the aviary with a mockery of a man stumbling between them. The oaf was dressed in a poorly arranged *chiton* with a purple cape that set my teeth on edge.

"Piss and shit!" I cursed before I could stop myself, my spindle falling to the floor in a heap of tangled wool as I glowered at Alexander's half-wit brother, Arrhidaeus. My son should not have to suffer the indignity of sharing his birthright with a beast better suited to mummery or goat herding. His mother might have spared the lot of us by ordering him abandoned on a dung heap as soon as he fell from her body. "What is *he* doing here?"

The imbecile cocked his head. "They took us," he said simply, as if *I* were the simpleton.

"Immediately after his father's demise, Cassander attempted to entice my Macedonian troops and Thracian mercenaries to turn against me," Olympias answered, stroking the sardonyx pendant bearing both her and Alexander's likenesses. "He didn't anticipate their refusal or that they'd move against his allies. Sadly, Arrhidaeus and his wife were forced to flee. Fortunately, they didn't get very far."

"You captured the Cyclops?" I asked Olympias. Parizad had recited to me the story of Odysseus' encounter with Polyphemus the Cyclops, filched as it was from Hephaestion's ridiculous collection of outlandish Greek tales. Pluck out one of Arrhidaeus' eyes and he was exactly as I'd imagined the giant monster.

"And his wife," Olympias confirmed. "Fragile Adea is enjoying my hospitality elsewhere in the palace while she recovers from the fright of facing several regiments of armed Macedonians."

In truth, Arrhidaeus' capture was a pleasing gift, as it meant that Alexander Aegus would no longer share his throne with a half-wit. But the capture of him and his wife paled in comparison with the woman who next entered the aviary, several guards prodding her with spears while she hurled insults at them.

Thessalonike looked like a crass joke of the gods in her silver-studded greaves and polished breastplate. Her expression curdled still further when her gaze fell on me.

"I might have known you'd give refuge to a known murderer," she said, gesturing to me. "Do you two sit around the hearth fire at night and swap stories over the best way to kill your rivals?"

"Stateira and Parysatis sought to murder me," I lied through gritted teeth, rising from my chair before she could say more. "I dispatched them to protect Alexander's son."

It was the story I'd first told to Olympias, recited each night until

I almost believed it myself. I'd never told her about the child in Stateira's belly, nor did I ever plan to.

Some secrets beg to be told, others must be kept until the right moment, and still others swallowed until we forget they existed. The death of Stateira's whelp was only one of the secrets I'd choked down. *It was her child or mine.*

Thessalonike's eyes devoured me. "I killed your brother and I'll put a sword through you too."

I might have killed her then, for some irrational part of me clung to the belief that Parizad still lived, that I hadn't led him to his death. My knees threatened to crumble to dust beneath me, but I reached out a hand to the snake cages to keep myself upright, digging my fingernails into the wood even as the serpents darted away from my sudden motion.

"Enough!" Olympias' voice rang out and she studied me for a moment, then patted the bench next to her. "Come and sit, Arrhidaeus. I ordered a tray of pomegranates for you."

"No!" Thessalonike screamed, but Olympias' guards held the captive back, their hands clamped tight across her mouth as they dragged her toward the door. I bristled as the Cyclops stepped closer, chewing on the tip of his thumb as he glanced first at the snakes in the dovecote and then at Olympias, as if wondering which serpent was safer.

"Pomegranates are my favorite," the beast finally said. He sat at the table with a loud thump and shoveled the garnet-hued seeds into his mouth like a starving, overgrown, ugly ape.

A full helmet should always cover a face like his, the better to save terrifying children and small animals. Especially when he ate.

"Enjoy," Olympias said to him. "They're all for you."

"You show Alexander's brother great benevolence," I said with a genuine smile for Thessalonike, who remained restrained by the guards while tears poured down her cheeks.

"His bastard *half* brother, sown from a common dancing girl who could barely dance," Olympias said, breaking a crust of bread and eating a dainty bite even as her eyes devoured the Cyclops' every movement. He made short work of the pomegranates, their scarlet blood staining his fingers, cheeks, and lips. "And I am indeed benevolent, considering the many Thracian mercenaries I lost during the slaughter of Cassander's supporters."

But I knew Olympias' mind and almost clapped my hands with glee. This would indeed be the best gift I'd ever received.

It didn't take long before the Cyclops frowned and stomped his feet. "Legs feel funny," he said. "They hurt."

Only then did the guards release Thessalonike. She ran to Arrhidaeus and fell to her knees at his side. "Your joints are swelling." She whirled on Olympias and me. "What poison did you give him?"

Olympias continued eating, cutting a sliver of cheese even as her lips curled into a shade of a smile. In the meantime, Thessalonike implored the beast to bend his legs, but to no avail.

"It's cold," he slurred as if his tongue had gone numb. He wrapped his arms around himself and rubbed them, but his fingers seemed frozen into misshapen claws. "Want to lie down."

"He needs a physician," Thessalonike said to us, trying unsuccessfully to wedge herself into the pit of his arm to help him stand. Instead, Arrhidaeus slumped from his chair and fell to the tiles. "Fetch someone!" Thessalonike ordered.

"There shall be no physician," Olympias said, finally setting down the cheese. She lifted the vial of fresh snake venom toward the sun to admire the cloudy liquid. "The milk of the valley viper will soon render Philip's last surviving son immobile. It shall be a quick death and relatively painless. As I said, I am nothing if not benevolent."

"You are a foul, murdering bitch!" Thessalonike reached for her sword, but her belt was empty. I laughed then, a high-pitched trill of delight. Thessalonike's blade had stolen my brother's life; now Mithra's justice would be served as she watched her own brother die before her very eyes.

"Restrain yourself or I shall have you removed," Olympias commanded her calmly. "Then your bastard brother will die alone."

"And little Alexander Aegus shall rule alone," I said to myself, a warm feeling spreading to *my* fingers and toes. "As he was meant to."

But Arrhidaeus ruined my moment of exultation with his blubbering.

"I don't want to die," Cyclops said, his fat lower lip trembling. "I want to stay with you, Nike, you and Adea. I love Adea."

"Arrhidaeus!" Thessalonike fell to her knees next to her brother, tears pouring down her cheeks in a touching display.

"My legs won't move," he said, his mouth opening and closing like an ugly fish's. "Why is it so cold?"

"Give him a blanket!" Thessalonike yelled, swallowing her sobs as she pushed shaggy curls away from his face.

"Here," Olympias said, unpinning the snake brooch at her shoulder and removing her linen *himation*. She let it fall to the tiles in a puddle of fabric. "You may use this."

Thessalonike yanked it up and wrapped it around her brother. The thin fabric scarcely covered his heaving chest.

"The venom will soon reach his heart," Olympias informed her as if commenting on the movement of the clouds outside. "Then he will be gone."

"I'm scared, Nike," Cyclops said. A vein throbbed in his neck, like a tiny snake trapped beneath the skin.

"You're so brave," Thessalonike told him, her tears splashing his face. "Just like Heracles. Would you like me to tell you the story of Heracles and the lion? It's still your favorite, isn't it?"

Thankfully, it didn't take long for the venom to do its work, although we were forced to listen to Thessalonike blubber her way through the story of Heracles and the Nemean Lion. Still, it was the clean and easy death that Olympias had promised, more than the man-child deserved.

"Remove the body," Olympias commanded to the waiting soldiers. "Arrhidaeus shall be buried alongside his father."

"Don't touch him!" Thessalonike shrieked as the guards moved closer, the sound sending the snakes slithering to the corners of their cages. "How could you? Arrhidaeus was no threat to anyone!"

"Surely even your feeble mind can understand that so long as your brother lived, he was a rallying point for Cassander's faction," Olympias said. "And now you shall remain with us here in Amphipolis, lest Cassander decide to wed you and strengthen his supposed claim to the regency."

"The gods shall curse you for this," Thessalonike roared. "Both of you shall writhe in the abyss of Tartarus for all eternity."

"Seize her," Olympias directed the waiting guards, a look of smug satisfaction settling on her features as Alexander's sister struggled helplessly against the soldiers. "I have no need to listen to you or your worthless prattle."

Thessalonike continued crying as she was dragged away behind her brother's body, leaving a blessed peace in her place. Slaves removed the tray of pomegranate husks and shuffled off. To any outsider, this might have been an ordinary day spent among women, no hint of execution by poison.

This wouldn't be the last time that Olympias awed me with her cunning.

"An impressive gift," I said to her.

"Ah, here we are." Olympias smiled as a messenger arrived wearing a staid expression. "Now we shall find out what fate young Adea has chosen for herself."

"Will you keep her imprisoned here?" I asked.

"Not precisely," Olympias answered, crossing one ankle over the other in the posture of a perfect queen. "I left three gifts for Adea in her chamber: a noose of silken rope, a vial of hemlock, and one of her mother's old swords." Olympias folded her hands in her lap as she addressed the messenger. "Which did she choose?"

The man cleared his throat. "The lady Adea thanked you for your generosity, but said that she preferred none of them."

"Perhaps you didn't understand my orders," Olympias said, her eyes narrowing to slits. "You were not to come to me until the scheming sow breathed her last."

"As she has," the man hurried to amend. "Adea, daughter of Cynnane and Amyntas, breathes no more. She hanged herself with her own girdle instead."

Olympias stared for a moment, then gave a little chortle. "She inherited her mother's stubborn streak. It's unfortunate she didn't put the trait to better use."

It was my turn to smile, a gesture mixed with awe and appreciation. "Several moves well played."

Olympias shrugged and sipped her wine. "Adea and Arrhidaeus were very small players upon a very large stage."

Then she turned and issued orders for poached red snapper to be served that evening, commanding extra garlic and preserved lemon to flavor the fish. Slaves armed with buckets of hot water and horsehair brushes entered to wash the pomegranates' scarlet stains from the mosaic floor; the crimson marks would require enough scrubbing to strip the skin from their work-hardened hands.

And while Olympias' back was turned, I palmed the vial of fresh viper milk and tucked it into my girdle.

I might learn much from Olympias of Macedon. And guard myself against her while I was at it.

* * *

The deaths of Arrhidaeus and Adea prompted Cassander to besiege us with renewed vigor, so that Thessalonike crowed with vengeful delight from the confines of her chamber until I considered slitting her throat myself just so I wouldn't hear her cackles echoing down the corridors. Months passed until Cassander's relentless siege forced Olympias' household to move from Amphipolis to the drab little village of Pydna-on-the-Sea, a far cry from the palace I'd envisioned as my new residence when I first set out for Macedon. I told myself to be patient, but the chipped mosaics of the drunken god Dionysus underfoot cut the delicate skin of my feet, the drafty rooms made me shiver, and the frescoes of frolicking satyrs might have been painted by a bare-bottomed child still shitting himself. I refused to succumb to such travails and daydreamed during the siege reports of ordering a barrage of slaves to stitch me a wardrobe of different silk robes for each day of the year, all while planning to enlarge my own entourage to befit a woman of my station. Until then, I would cultivate patience here in miserable little Pydna. Olympias claimed it to be a better vantage point from which to best Cassander at his game of cat and mouse, yet she confided to me in private the true purpose of the move.

"As to be expected, Cassander is enraged at Arrhidaeus' death," she said. "He plans to attack us, to make a final stand and end this once and for all."

"Naturally," I said, clapping as little Alexander crawled away from his nervous nursemaid and toward me, his head held proudly as his bottom bounced in the air. I picked him up and rubbed my nose to his. "You don't need ugly Cassander to help you rule when you have your mother and grandmother to do it for you, now, do you, my little lion cub?"

Olympias afforded us a tight smile and handed me a fresh parchment, its seal recently broken. "He sees the futility of this engagement and turns to pen and ink instead of swords."

I continued to bounce Alexander, but scarcely glanced at the letter with its indecipherable scribbles. "And what does he say?"

I didn't care to parade my total ignorance of Greek—or any written language—before Olympias, lest she think me too dim-witted to help my son rule.

She refolded the message, then held it over a burning candle of twisted rag and sheep fat. "He offers me protection if I surrender. Yet he makes no mention of you or my grandson."

I fingered the golden necklace at my throat, her words a rope around my neck. "And will you accept?"

"I don't think that's necessary, do you?" she answered.

And so it was in far-flung Pydna-on-the-Sea that Cassander surrounded us with both his ships and his infantry. Olympias mustered all her available resources against him, even the war elephants that Alexander had sent from Persia before his campaign into India. The gray animals trumpeted and threw their gleaming tusks into the air as they were led out to fight. They returned relatively unscathed, but fewer and fewer of Olympias' Macedonians and Thracian mercenaries survived. I'd never learned to do figures, but as the months dragged on, even I could tell that we'd lost too many men. No food came into the city and Cassander's men scavenged our fields, leaving us to starve.

There was no grain for the elephants and so they were fed on sawdust. Then they were butchered, and the beleaguered villa was heavy with the smell of boiling elephant, without even an onion or a head of garlic to season the chewy meat. I cried tears of salt when Olympias thrust my bowl at me that first night, the gray at her temples starting to show through without the regular washes of wood ash and goat tallow.

"Cease your sniveling," she snapped as a slave approached and fell on one knee, the hollows beneath her cheeks turning her face skeletal in the quivering lamplight. She wore a red *peplos* with Macedon's customary eight-pointed suns along the bottom, but the stark shade leached her complexion of its color. "What is it?" Olympias demanded of the slave.

"A messenger from Cassander's camp requests an audience."

"I've endured far too much whining this night," Olympias said, waving a hand at the slave while casting me a withering glance. "I refuse to hear Cassander's latest terms for my surrender, not when we may well have to flee from him come high tide."

The slave's eyes darted to me and back in a way I didn't relish. "The messenger swore that she had information you would wish to hear, especially regarding the mother of Alexander Aegus."

Olympias followed his gaze to me and her eyes narrowed. "Do you know about this?"

My mind raced and my hands went clammy under her stare, akin to a freshly sharpened blade against my throat, but I only shook my head. "Not at all."

And I had no idea which of my secrets this messenger claimed to know: my true parentage, the depravities I'd committed as the Whore of Sogdian Rock, or the truth of Stateira's murder.

Olympias scowled, then rose and followed after the scurrying slave. And so I set down my portion of elephant and watched Olympias go, feeling as if a horned *daeva* was clawing my stomach. I sniffed, then bashed a girl slave about the ears as she tried to refill my wine cup.

I would not be cowed by Olympias, for *I* was mother to Alexander's only legitimate son, regardless of the crimes I'd committed. Little Alexander was my treasure, my jewel that I would never part with.

And without Alexander Aegus, Olympias was nothing more than an old woman who had once tasted power and lost it. I'd see that she didn't forget it.

* * *

I awoke the next morning with breasts aching and hard with milk, for Alexander Aegus hadn't woken during the night and demanded to suckle. I'd fallen asleep to the sound of his even breathing after much tossing and turning, finally resolving to demand that Olympias move Alexander Aegus and me to Pella, where we might live in some semblance of comfort. But when I went to pick up my son from the twisted willow branch cradle, I found it empty, not even his goat-shaped clay rattle left behind.

I screamed then and ran into the deserted corridor, grabbing the nearest slave by the neck. "Where is Olympias?"

"She is gone," she blubbered, scratching at my hands. "So is everyone else."

I released her, my palms falling open at my sides. "What do you mean?"

"She left before dawn." She dragged her bare arm across her nose, hiccuping between her words.

The tides had turned before dawn. Olympias had fled, and taken my son with her.

She'd left me behind.

I screamed in impotent rage, shaking the slave girl so hard that her neck threatened to crack until she managed to shake me off. She ran down the corridor, blustering like a simpleton without sparing me even a final glance.

Olympias had escaped and taken my son—my shield—but there was one woman that I wouldn't allow to elude me, the unnatural harridan who might give me the leverage I needed to sway Cassander to my side.

But Thessalonike's apartments were emptier than a tomb.

I overturned a polished mahogany gaming table, sending the abandoned glass playing pieces scattering across the floor mosaic.

"Piss and shit!" I yelled, letting my voice echo as I fell to my knees and pounded the floor with my fists until the knuckles bled.

I didn't have long to wait before Cassander's men came for me.

My nerves screeched louder than the long-legged vultures in a Tower of Silence when the set of perfectly matched military footsteps finally approached. I'd returned to my chamber and dressed for the occasion, trying in vain to ease my swollen breasts before robing myself in turquoise silk embroidered with peacock feathers. Alexander's gold lion brooch was pinned at my shoulder and a head scarf sewn with tiny bells fell like a waterfall to my waist.

"Roxana of Balkh," called out a thick-necked soldier while his companions—at least ten of them, all armed with swords and Macedon's golden sun shields—filed into my chambers. "We have been ordered to seize you and bring you to justice before Cassander, *basileus* of Macedon."

My throat tightened with panic as they bound my wrists with iron manacles streaked with fingers of rust and what might have been dried blood. I followed the guards, spewing curses with every step and expecting a gloating Cassander outside the dilapidated villa, but the soldiers prodded me off the grounds to Pydna's decrepit market square, its cobbles emptied of merchants hawking toasted melon seeds, hide-wrapped cheeses, and copper bowls so tarnished that not even a two-obol streetwalker would piss in them.

Cassander stood in the center of the square surrounded by his many supporters, their assorted shield sigils claiming the entirety of Greece and Persia. Yet there were those other than soldiers assembled: men who appeared from their dress to be merchants or artisans, old men missing half their teeth, and even a scattering of women. I had eyes for none of the faceless crowd, only for the two women who flanked Cassander, one clad in mud brown silk and the other outfitted like an unnatural soldier.

I knew not how they had done it, but there was no doubt that they had somehow betrayed me to Olympias.

I snarled at Alexander's sister and Darius' younger daughter, wishing I could claw out their eyes, but they only stood like twin statues.

"Roxana of Balkh," Cassander said, and I winced at the absence of all my lofty titles, leaving me as defenseless as if I stood naked in the square. "You have been brought here to stand trial for your crimes. But you are not the only one who faces the scales of the goddess Dike's divine justice today."

To my shock and triumph, Olympias was marched from the back of the crowd to stand beside me, her wrists shackled in fetters identical to my own. She wore the same rumpled red *peplos* from the prior evening, its border of tarnished Macedonian suns embroidered by her own hand along the hem, and the sardonyx pendant of Alexander and herself. The crowd seethed at the sight of her, hurling angry epithets and shouting so not even Cassander could calm them.

"You foul, conniving bitch." I threw the words at her as she assumed her typical rigid posture. "Where is my son?"

"Yours wasn't the only womb my son filled before he died," Olympias said, scarcely deigning to look at me. "You slew the babe in Stateira's belly, my second grandson."

She must have read my unspoken question, for she only tipped her chin toward the women next to Cassander. "Drypetis informed me last night, in the same breath with which she demanded my surrender and Thessalonike's release."

"Stateira's and her child's murder were an idea I stole from your sordid history," I said, struggling to keep my voice level as everything unraveled around me. "Or don't you recall doing the same to Eurydice and her son? We are similar, you and I, both queens seeking to protect our sons."

My eyes scanned the crowd for my child, but the crowd was too thick to see him.

Olympias ignored me.

"You promised me safety if I surrendered and released Thessalonike," she said to Cassander in a voice that brooked no argument, raising her wrists in a silent command of release. The mob stilled at the sound, but there was no mistaking the fury that shimmered in the air as they glowered at her.

"Safety in that I didn't set fire to the ship beneath your feet and watch you jump burning into the sea," Cassander answered. "I fear you mistook my promise."

So Olympias had sought to flee with my son. My eyes darted in and around the crowd again, searching for Alexander Aegus and my lone chance at survival, but there were no babes in arms to be seen.

"You have ushered countless undeserving souls to Hades, most recently Arrhidaeus and Adea." Cassander continued his tirade against Olympias, his voice ringing out over everyone's heads. "Do you deny your role in their murders?"

"I do not," Olympias said. "They were criminals who threatened my son's legacy and the legitimacy of my grandson's rule."

"Arrhidaeus was no criminal!" Thessalonike shouted even as Drypetis held her back. "He was Alexander's brother!"

"He was a simpleton," Olympias retorted in a cool tone. "And unfit to rule."

"Olympias, wife of Philip II and mother of Alexander," Cassander droned on in the monotone voice I had already come to loathe. "You have been tried and found guilty of the erstwhile execution of Eurydice and her infant son, as well as of the recent murders of Arrhidaeus and Adea. You are also responsible for the deaths of hundreds of my supporters in Pydna's recent siege and their families bear witness to this trial. The only acceptable penalty for such crimes is death."

I suddenly understood the furious crowd: a whole mob of enraged families seeking revenge.

Olympias tilted her head as the grieving horde stomped its feet in a terrible drumbeat like a thousand angry hearts. This time they fell silent at Cassander's upraised palms.

"You must die this day," he said to Olympias, "but I would allow you the option of honorable suicide."

There was no doubt that he'd already planned this, seeking to cast himself as a magnanimous while still just ruler. The blood roared in my ears as I wondered if I too would soon face the choice of an execution or suicide. I almost laughed aloud; would Cassander be so charitable as to offer Olympias the three options she'd given Adea?

A slow smile spread across Olympias' face. "Coward," she accused him. "Only a weakling would be unwilling to sully his hands with my blood." She spread her arms then, like a supplicant to the gods. "If you wish me dead, you'll have to kill me yourself."

Soldiers yanked me away from her as the crowd stirred. "I think not," Cassander said, giving them a nod.

I expected the bereaved family members to fall upon Olympias like a pack of rabid wolves, tearing at her hair and brandishing all manner of blades and cudgels. Instead, they revealed cruel smiles alongside countless bags of rocks tied to belts and larger stones pulled from pockets. The more ambitious among them wielded crude slingshots, like children's playthings.

Olympias would be stoned to death.

Even formidable Olympias couldn't hold in her terror against the dark face of Ahriman. She screamed as the violent volley began and tried to shield her face. Then came the hail of wet thuds and the sickening crunch of bone. I covered my eyes with my arm, tasting the blood as I bit my cheek and cowered, willing the sound away and waiting for the mob of ravening beasts to turn upon me.

Eventually, an appalling silence fell and the seething tide of stones receded.

I peered through eyes screwed tightly shut to see Thessalonike kneeling over Olympias' broken body, arranging her bloodied arms over a chest brutalized by at least a thousand stones. "Good-bye," she whispered. "May you fall forever into the abyss of Tartarus."

"Roxana, daughter of Oxyartes of Balkh and wife of Alexander." Cassander's voice made me flinch. "You have been found guilty of the murders of Stateira, daughter of King Darius, and Parysatis, daughter of King Artaxerxes. As such, you too must die this day."

"But we will allow you a kindness you denied my sister," Drypetis said, motioning to someone at the fringe of the crowd. A plain-faced woman stepped forward with a bundle in her arms.

I knew even before the child cried that it was my son she held.

"You may say good-bye to Alexander Aegus," Drypetis said.

Some in the crowd tossed their remaining stones in eager hands even as I clutched my son tighter. The iron shackles were cold against his soft skin and he cried, flailing his tiny fists as his face turned redder than blood. My breasts leaked milk in response to his wails, and I knew then how he might yet save me.

The soldiers eyed me warily as I fumbled with my husband's lion clasp that pinned together my Greek *peplos*, baring the hard mound of one of my milk-filled breasts. My son grunted and latched on to the dark nipple, his cheeks working hard as his blue eyes met mine in a sort of understanding.

He and I would face the world together.

I stood before Cassander not as a murderer or even as Alexander's wife, but as the revered mother of the future king.

"I do not claim to be free from evil, and there is no doubt that I've sometimes followed the lure of the dark god Ahriman," I said, allowing my voice to quaver even as I blinked back false tears, my heart racing so I thought it might break my ribs. "But I committed no murders, although the whispers from the East claim otherwise. I throw myself upon your mercy, for I am a mother still nursing her firstborn son. I allow myself to be guided by Hera now, your goddess of the hearth and home."

I cared little for Cassander's reaction, for I'd made my plea to the mob, locking eyes with as many of them as I could.

"Killing a mother would incur Hera's wrath," a man called out. "We have no quarrel with Alexander's wife, only with Olympias."

In that moment, their bloodlust banked, replaced by a growing murmur of assent. Only then did I dare glance at Drypetis, triumph coursing through me even as I fell to my knees and bowed my head to Cassander.

"I seek your mercy," I said to him. "And swear to be your loyal subject from this day forward."

"You cannot let her live," Drypetis said to Cassander. "You know her guilt as well as I."

But the crowd said otherwise, growing agitated and calling for my release.

"Seize Roxana and her son," Cassander ordered his soldiers. "They shall be taken to Amphipolis for confinement, so as not to elude us again."

Drypetis turned purple-faced with anger as soldiers swarmed over me like wasps, the spoiled bitch's glare so murderous that it might have pierced the strongest armor.

Yet I only grinned, wanting to crow my victory to the heavens.

Against all odds, I had survived.

My dour chamber in Amphipolis echoed just as had Sogdian Rock, both prisons built of stone to keep me trapped within. As the months passed, a great mounded tomb began to take shape nearby, hewn from Amphipolis' hillside by an army of stonemasons and mosaic masters. Lifelike marble female caryatids disappeared within and workmen set fearsome lion statues with ribs straining against their stone hides to guarding the entrance. I knew not for whom the tomb was intended, nor did I care.

So long as it wasn't my name being chiseled onto its walls.

Cassander solidified his base of support within Greece and kept me so heavily guarded that I couldn't breathe without inhaling the acrid stench of his soldiers' sweat. Yet nothing in Amphipolis escaped my notice as I bided my time until I could flee with my son.

My little Alexander, who would never abandon or betray me as even his father and my own brother had done.

After months of the guards' ignoring me, several new sentries joined their ranks. I watched their every move and listened from behind closed doors as they traded news of the recent maneuverings of Cassander, Ptolemy, Seleucus, and Lysimachus—Alexander's generals were a busy lot these days, tromping all over the world— and bragged about the whores they'd buried their pricks into in Amphipolis' brothel. It was tiresome work, but one day I was finally rewarded for my vigilance.

A new guard, an unimpressive youth whose voice still cracked when he spoke, sat in the meager excuse of a courtyard, a piece of cheap parchment spread across his lap as he scratched painstaking letters onto it with a broken stylus.

"What are you writing?" I asked.

He leapt to his feet, the letter clutched tight in his hand. "Do you require something?" he asked, staring determinedly at my feet. "If so, I can fetch your slave girl."

"I require your name," I said.

"L-Leander," he stuttered, twisting the parchment as if it were a goose he meant to strangle. "It means strong, like a lion."

I almost laughed then, for this poor boy was a scrawny cub compared to the Macedonian lion I'd once had.

"It's so dull here, Leander," I said, stepping so close that my breasts touched his arm as I took his seat, forcing him to step back. "I was just curious who you were writing to." I gave him my most alluring smile, letting my finger trace the neckline of my robe. "Who is she?"

His flush, turning his cheeks the color of a ripe peach, was all the answer I needed. A peach mottled with the red eruptions of youth, but a peach nonetheless.

"Her name is Helen."

"And is her love magic to make the sanest man go mad?" I'd listened to Alexander recite the convoluted *Song of Ilium* enough times to remember the line. Helen was the only character I'd cared for out of the entire dreary tale, mostly because her beauty might have rivaled my own.

"I think she's magical, and beautiful," he said. This time his eyes flicked to mine. "Not as beautiful as you, of course . . ."

It was a simple matter after that to lead Leander back to my chambers and let him take me against the wall there. It wasn't long before he'd forgotten his Helen and I'd convinced him to write letters on my behalf to Olympias' cousin the king of Epirus. The dear boy even taught me how to sign my name, fondling my breasts with an eager hand while I struggled to form each imperfect letter. So while I remained caged in Amphipolis, my whispers flew on the wind, for I was unwilling to die in this forsaken village, stoned to death like Olympias or poisoned like Arrhidaeus.

Or worse. Forgotten.

Now that the message had been sent, I'd put Leander off with the excuse of my women's bloods and settled in to play with little Alexander. My son was walking now in stunted little steps and he was often irritable from the tiny white teeth breaking through his gums. He pulled himself to sitting and shoved his clay rattle shaped like a goat into his mouth, gnawing it like he might devour it while a slick of spittle oozed down his chin.

There was a commotion in the courtyard, but I'd long ago grown accustomed to the self-important comings and goings of the many guards. Yet the clamor outside my chambers this morning was louder than usual. I hefted my son onto my hip and carried him to the window, wincing as he shook the pebble-filled rattle at my ear.

And then I swayed on my feet, for this was no ordinary change of sentries or delivery of fresh ox meat for the kitchens. Instead, Cassander dismounted his horse among his entourage of salute-snapping soldiers. He paused to assist two women robed in costly silks from their sedans and then marched toward my chambers.

Whereas once I'd had perfumed attendants to announce every supplicant and visitor to my traveling tent, now my door was flung open without ceremony and Cassander stormed into my room, his purple *chlamys* fluttering behind him.

The purple he'd stolen from my son, and from me.

"Cassander," I said, holding my son before me as I bent my knee and kissed my fingers in a flawless *proskynesis* before I remembered the way he'd scoffed at the Persians for heralding Alexander as a god.

"Rise, Roxana," he commanded.

There was only one reason Cassander would visit me now, especially accompanied by his she-bitches and a contingent of men armed with swords and pikes. But perhaps I might persuade him to see another, more elegant solution that would benefit him, and save my own head.

"I understand your position as regent is quite secure now," I said. "I pray every morning that your able hand shall usher in an era of peace and prosperity for my late husband's empire."

Perhaps the praise was a bit heavy-handed, but surely a thick-browed ape like Cassander enjoyed hearing a woman's praise now and again.

"There shall be no peace and prosperity in Macedon, much less in the remainder of the empire, while you still live," Cassander said.

"We intercepted the letter you sent to Epirus," Thessalonike said, waving the tattered parchment between her thumb and forefinger.

"The one where you offered him your bed and your son's claim to the crown in exchange for his marching on Amphipolis?"

"I can neither read nor write," I scoffed, pressing little Alexander's head to my chest in a vain attempt to still my pounding heart. "Surely you don't believe I wrote such treason."

"We intercepted a soldier named Leander as he came from your villa earlier today," Drypetis said calmly. "He admitted to composing the letter at your behest. You've finally lost this time, Roxana."

I tasted the metallic tang of panic then, like a fighting cock backed into a corner. I calmed as my thumb caressed the reassuring bulge I'd kept tucked into my girdle since the day of Arrhidaeus' death even as my son looked at me with trusting blue eyes inherited from his father. I wanted to scream against the injustice of all the years I'd spent clawing my way from the bottom of life's dung heap, first against Oxyartes and then Bessus, at Sogdian Rock and now in Macedon.

So once again, I was to fight for my life.

I ignored Thessalonike and Drypetis to address Cassander as if only he and I occupied the room. "A king needs a queen. Ally yourself with me, become the new Alexander with his first wife as your Queen of Queens."

"A daring proposal," Cassander mused. "Yet I've already proclaimed myself king of Macedon and I have no desire to spend my rule sniffing out your machinations to maneuver your son onto my throne. I'm through with your schemes and betrayals, Roxana, but your son shall be raised at my hands, so no harm shall ever come to him."

Behind Cassander, both Thessalonike and Drypetis smiled like cheetahs as little Alexander began to fuss, giving me an opportunity to remove the tiny treasure from my girdle.

"He's teething," I said, removing the lid from the vial and rubbing its liquid onto his gums. "Poppy milk soothes the pain."

Now all I needed was time. . . .

"If you're to kill me now, you may as well know the truth about

Hephaestion," I said calmly, rubbing my fingers over little Alexander's swollen gums. For a glorious moment I delighted to see the blood drain from Drypetis' face. She might have her revenge on me for her sister's death, but my next words would haunt her until the end of her days. "Don't tell me that you never puzzled out how your precious husband died after he humiliated my brother," I said to her. "He cast Parizad aside like an unwanted toy after he'd married you. It took me until we arrived in Ecbatana to find a cook who was willing to add wolfsbane to Hephaestion's *ptisan* without asking questions, in exchange for some of my favorite Indian jewels."

"You lie," Drypetis whispered, but I only cackled with glee, my words coming fast and reckless as the dark lord Ahriman himself cleaved my face with a wild grin.

"I even sent Parizad with a purgative the night that Hephaestion died to ensure that no suspicion would fall on him," I lied, for not even Ahura Mazda himself could have stopped my brother from fawning over his dying lover. And much as I wished I'd had a hand in Hephaestion's death, the gods had rendered that bit of justice on their own. "And no one ever suspected either of us, now, did they?"

In one deft movement, Drypetis stole Cassander's iron sword from his belt and pointed it at my throat. Alexander's sister unsheathed a bronze blade aimed at my belly.

I saw the end, yet it didn't matter. Not anymore . . .

"Lower your weapons," Cassander commanded the women, but they ignored him.

"Set down your son," Drypetis ordered me, her voice trembling with emotion. "For unlike you, I won't harm an innocent child."

I would die before I lost my beauty, and my son would die before he could betray me, as had all the other men in my life: my father in selling me, Bessus in using me, Alexander by dying, my brother in his love for Hephaestion, Bagoas in going from my bed to my husband's. . . .

I laughed then, a strangled sound as I repositioned Alexander on my hip, his head lolling to one side and his open eyes blank. I held out a hand, Olympias' empty vial still clasped in my palm.

"You think I'd let you have my son?" I asked, my breath coming in desperate gasps. "The venom of a valley viper guaranteed you'd never steal him from me, never turn him against me."

I howled still harder as Thessalonike and Drypetis lunged toward me with faces like terrible *daevas*. I cackled to think of all the men I'd manipulated through my life and the strange twist now that it was two women who would bring me down.

I'd never been any good with women. . . .

And I choked back a sob of rage as they plunged their cold swords into me with a rush of red, wet pain.

CHAPTER 29

Thessalonike

"Let it be known that I've executed Roxana and her son," Cassander ordered as he finally restrained Drypetis and me both back from the business of Roxana's murder. Drypetis gasped and dropped her bloodied blade to the tiles with an earth-rending clatter. I continued to clutch my sword, staring at the raw wounds in Roxana's bloody carcass. I looked away, reminded too much of Cynnane's murder even as Drypetis fell to her knees, her entire body shaking. Cassander removed his purple *chlamys* and wrapped it around her heaving shoulders.

Royal purple and the crimson of freshly spilled blood. Were the two ever inseparable?

A glance at the unmoving child in Roxana's lap confirmed that young Alexander Aegus was truly gone, an innocent pawn in his mother's twisted game.

Yet I balked at Cassander shouldering the blame for both of these two new murders, not only because his hands were clean, but also because the world should know what sort of monster Roxana had become.

"It will be easier for me to take the blame," he said softly as if reading my thoughts, kneeling to chafe Drypetis' arms as her teeth started to chatter. "Everyone expected that I would order their executions."

Drypetis stirred, blinking hard. "Roxana was a demon from the deepest abyss of *Duzakh*. She deserved to die." She glanced at the broken vial on the tiles and shuddered. "But her son did not."

With the cutting of Roxana's tangled lifestring and Alexander's tiny thread, the three crones of Fate grew weary of my family's saga and finally let fall their rusted shears. There was no one left who wished us harm, no one left to challenge Cassander's rule.

"The people won't believe that Roxana poisoned her own child," Cassander said, bending down to close her eyes with a rough hand. "Olympias shouted to the heavens that I poisoned Alexander. This shall be a small slander to bear compared to that."

And Cassander had proved himself to be loyal and true time and again since Alexander's death. While the men might not follow him blindly, they *would* follow him.

We watched silently as soldiers removed the bodies, little Alexander Aegus destined for a well-placed tomb near that of Cynnane, Arrhidaeus, and Adea, as Cassander commanded that they be buried together in a sumptuous mausoleum befitting their sacrifices. I cared little for what happened to Roxana's body; feeding her to sharp-toothed rats would be more than she deserved.

"I need fresh air," Drypetis said. She thrust Cassander his *chlamys* and rushed outside to the courtyard's rainwater cistern. I motioned for Cassander to remain behind, following as she thrust her befouled hands into the sun-dappled water. The blood dissipated as if it had never been, but she continued to scrub as if she meant to flay the flesh from her bones. I forced her to turn and look at Amphipolis' sprawling vista until her breathing calmed, at the river Strymon surrounding us like a brown snake, hugging the hill beneath our feet.

She wrapped her arms around herself and I wondered then how much misery one soul could bear before it buckled and became permanently warped from the burden. My own arrival into the world had killed my mother, and since then my sister, my brothers, and the only mother I'd known had bowed a knee to Hades. Yet Drypetis had watched her parents, siblings, and husband die, and today her blade had joined mine to slay Roxana. I knew not what could fill the dark void that her life had become.

"What will you do now?" I asked her, drawing a hand around her waist and pressing my temple against hers. "You can always stay in Macedon."

She stared east, toward the lands of spices and silks. "I was born in a king's traveling pavilion as my father moved us from Babylon to Persepolis. Perhaps one day I'll stop moving. . . ." Her voice trailed off, as if she was trying out the words in her mind before speaking them aloud. "For now I want to see the world as Hephaestion and I once planned."

"Hephaestion would like that." I smiled, for it was a dream I'd once shared, although my dream had involved swords, shields, and the grime of battle. I could do without swords after all the recent bloodshed.

"Do you think what Roxana said was true?" I asked. "That she killed Hephaestion?"

Drypetis hesitated, then shook her head. "Wolfsbane induces vomiting and kills instantly. Hephaestion was felled by fever, not poison."

I was grateful for that at least. Roxana had done enough damage to Drypetis' life without having killed Hephaestion too. It was a sign of her depravity that she had used her last words to boast and lie about still another murder.

"I wish you well while you travel the world," I said to Drypetis, "but you must promise to visit Pella every so often."

"Is that where you'll go?"

"It's home," I said. "Right now I want nothing so much as to walk Pella's golden hills with a dog at my heels, to come home and kick my muddy feet onto a table surrounded by a menagerie of animals."

Drypetis drew me into a long embrace scented with cassia and our shared grief but also infused with a heady dose of hope. "I pray you'll be happy there," she said. "I wish you a long life of peace and contentment, my sister."

"Ours is a strange friendship," I said. And it was, forged and strengthened by Hades' touch.

"One that will end only when we're dead," she said, echoing my sentiments, and I thought of myself and Arrhidaeus, Cynnane and Adea, Hephaestion and Alexander.

I smiled, a bittersweet gesture. "Then we shall tell our story backward. Everything from this moment shall be sunshine and happiness."

Drypetis looked over my shoulder and a knowing smile tugged at her lips. "I believe there is much joy to be had in your future, Thessalonike of Macedon, if only you'll allow it to catch you."

"I don't know what you mean," I started to say, then glanced behind me to see Cassander, his soldiers and guards dismissed and his *chlamys* tossed carelessly over his forearm, its hem flapping in the wind.

"Let him catch you," Drypetis whispered, squeezing my arm. "Happiness often finds you when you least expect it. Seize it while you still can."

She left me in the courtyard then, but paused in front of Cassander. "I would take my leave from your court, King of Kings, for now at least."

"You need no permission, Drypetis of Persia, but you shall be missed among us."

She bowed to him and kissed her fingertips, but spared a glance and a smile for me.

Then, just as abruptly as she'd entered my life, Drypetis ascended her litter and was gone, merely a pale hand waving to me from the open window of her sedan.

I clutched the hem of my cursed *peplos* that threatened to trip me with every step and followed her out of the villa, waving wildly until she disappeared from view. Cassander approached slowly, standing beside me, so close that our arms brushed.

"You'll proclaim yourself the *basileus* of all of Greece now, won't you?" I asked him, staring out at the river and hills to avoid looking at him.

"I will," he said.

"Don't think I'm going to bow and scrape to you," I said. "You're still just Cassander, and I could still beat you with a sword if it came to it."

"A fact I can never forget due to your constant reminders."

The heavy silence that followed was punctuated by the call of a hawk in the distance. I startled when Cassander's hesitant hand clasped my own, yet I didn't pull away. His was a strong hand, scattered with dark hairs that gleamed in the sunshine, which hinted at the courage and stability of the man.

"You once claimed that you didn't need me, Thessalonike, but *I* need you," he said, his voice gruff with emotion. "So I'll ask you again. Marry me and be my queen."

"I swore as a child with the heat of Eurydice's pyre on my face that I'd never let the queen's diadem touch my head," I said. "Lest I become like Olympias."

Yet I'd plunged my blade into Parizad's belly and helped to slay Roxana.

Perhaps I had already become Olympias.

"You are nothing like Olympias," Cassander argued. "Alexander's mother was single-minded about her son's power, and her own. You've never sought to gain power or to control others."

No, but as queen I'd possess both.

I scoffed. "You only wish to marry Alexander's last surviving sister, to make me your queen in order to solidify your claim to his throne."

"Of course I do," he said simply. "I'm weary of fighting. I'm just a common bore who's spent too much time memorizing rules and looking down my nose at you, but if you marry me, I swear I'll be the most dutiful of husbands."

I opened my mouth to lambaste the echo of his first proposal, but the glint of laughter in his eyes stopped me. Funny, but I'd never noticed how warm his eyes could be, when he wasn't droning on about duty and Greek values.

Instead, I turned up my nose. "I want—I *deserve*—a husband who will worship the earth beneath my feet until the day he carries me to my tomb."

Cassander smiled, a rare gesture that transformed him even as he looked shyly away. "Then I have a confession to make. I've been enamored of you since the night of the Dionysian revels, when you were debauched with wine and spouting nonsense from that pert little mouth of yours, and you hurled your fists at anything that moved."

I snorted in disbelief even as something warm fluttered in my heart and I recalled his prior proposals, his tenderness at Athens' Acropolis. "How could you have been so *enamored* when you've since lectured me about the impropriety of everything I've ever done?"

"The feeling wasn't by choice, I can assure you," he said, his lips still curled in a smile. "I couldn't keep my thoughts from turning to such an improper little beast." He looked to the horizon but leaned sideways to whisper, "It's part of your allure."

"Is this your way of professing your love?"

He grew stern then. "Yes, Thessalonike. Against my better judgment, I *do* love you."

I quashed a grin even as my heart threatened to burst from my chest. This wasn't quite how I'd envisioned receiving my first declaration of love, drenched in another woman's blood, but then, my life had rarely followed convention. "Despite the fact that I'll make the world's most terrible wife?"

He shrugged. "There's no denying that I'll be a wretched husband. It seems fitting that we not punish any other undeserving souls by forcing them to marry us instead."

I'd never sought out marriage, but had always accepted that one day I'd be a wife and mother. Cassander claimed that he'd be a dutiful husband, but it was more than that. I had a duty to my brother, not to ensure that his blood continued to rule Macedon and beyond, but that the best man rule in his stead.

The best man was Cassander.

Cassander *was* ambitious and driven, but he was also loyal, dedicated, and honest. And if he was to be believed, he loved me despite the fact that it went against everything that was right and sane in this world.

I rose on tiptoes and brushed my lips against his. "Yes," I whispered, tasting the mint on his breath.

"Yes, what?" he asked, appearing for all the world like he was negotiating a peace treaty with some fearsome tribe of *barbaroi*, even as his dark eyes sparked deep.

"Yes, I'll marry you," I said. "On one condition."

"And what might that be?"

"That you let me continue to be an improper beast. After all, I don't intend to change now."

Cassander tapped his chin and gave me a hard stare. The flutter of nerves in my stomach surprised me, for against all odds, I *wanted* a future filled with Cassander's black stares and philosophical screeds. "I accept your condition," he said. "In fact, I demand it."

I wrapped my arms around him then, Drypetis' advice echoing in my mind as he caught me up in an exuberant embrace.

And I was delighted to let him do it.

DRYPETIS

A tomb hewn of cold stone now sufficed to house the lion of a man for whom the world had not been enough.

It had been fifteen years since Alexander had breathed his last, but I'd waited until nightfall to approach his tomb, its grounds littered with trampled rose petals and the walls stacked with towers of bread and coins, all offerings to the man who was now revered as a god. The spiced tendrils of an Egyptian breeze still tugged at the hem of my Persian robe as I stepped inside the sanctuary.

Alexander's tomb was a gaudy monstrosity of thick-veined marble attended by stark and silent columns. A geometric mosaic underfoot made my head whirl if my eyes lingered on it too long, and led visitors to a raised porphyry platform bearing a sarcophagus of hammered gold. The stone walls were a testament to Alexander's empire, the flickering torches illuminating Macedonian sun symbols and images of Zeus and Ammon, along with inscriptions written mostly in Greek and Egyptian hieroglyphs, but also in Persian and Indian, recounting tales of elephant charges, of scaling the colossal wall at Sogdian Rock, and of the celebrations of the Susa weddings.

This tomb was a graveyard of dusty dreams and tarnished triumphs.

Yet it was also a monument to all that Alexander had accomplished, his joining of two massive nations to become the largest empire on earth and his melding of their cultures, languages, and gods. Alexander had always believed that the gods' golden *ichor* flowed in his veins and he had proved it with his actions in this life, guaranteeing that his deeds would be sung for eternity while he celebrated in the afterlife.

My own name was absent from the list of revels, which I preferred, but I let my thumb linger on Hephaestion's name, slowly tracing the same Greek letters that I'd carved into sand and wood and parchment, all left behind at the pyramids of Gizeh and the Temple of Artemis at Ephesus, the Mausoleum at Halicarnassus, and the Colossus of Rhodes. My husband would have commented about the folly of wasting such manpower on the pyramids and mocked Artemis for the cacophony of egg-shaped breasts on her statue, but still, I liked to think that perhaps he'd seen all those wonders and more through my eyes.

My time with him was the greatest treasure of my life, each day a glittering jewel atop the pile of memories I kept of Stateira and my brother, my mother, father, and grandmother.

And while Alexander had caused great tumult in my life—in so many people's lives—without him, I never would have met Hephaestion. I knew not whether Alexander's strivings had been worth the cost, but I had long ago made peace with the reality. Everything was as it was, and there was nothing I could do to change it.

"I didn't think you'd come," a woman's too-loud voice sounded behind me. "I waited all day, and finally decided you'd washed your hands of us."

I turned and grinned, for although many years had passed since I'd laid eyes on Alexander's sister, Thessalonike looked the same, save for the bulge of her obviously pregnant belly. "I wouldn't have missed all this—or you—for anything."

"Is Hephaestion's tomb as grand as this?" she asked, gesturing to the surrounding decadence even as she toyed with the gold collar around her neck, a tangle of acorn and lotus pendants intermingled with several Dionysian heads.

"Almost," I answered, for I'd been at Hephaestion's tomb mere months ago with a spotted dog at my heels, the descendant of the four-eyed mongrel Hephaestion had given me in Tyre. I'd left my husband an offering of a fine vintage of Lesbos wine and some newly penned Greek poetry he'd have abhorred. It had been more than fifteen years since I'd seen him in the flesh, but that didn't mean I couldn't still tease him on occasion.

I hugged her, then stepped away to marvel at the swell of her belly. "Cassander certainly keeps you in swords and babies, doesn't he?"

She smiled broadly and waved an absent hand at her queen's retinue, causing the flock of rainbow-colored geese to fall back. "This will be our fourth. I'm hoping for a girl to give her brothers complete and utter hell."

"And how fare young Philip, Alexander, and Antipater?"

"They fight like demons, just as their namesakes once did," she said, but her eyes sparkled with pride. Motherhood sat well upon her, had tempered her. We had both found our peace in this world, mine by tramping over it and drinking in its sights as Hephaestion and I might have done, and she by settling down with her unlikely husband.

"Cassander must be a proud papa," I said.

"He can barely look at them without bursting at the seams." She laughed. I felt a pang as she linked her arm through mine as my sister had once done. Time had softened that pain too, to a dull throb.

"And I believe he's proud of you as well," I said. "I heard from little Greek birds that your husband just renamed a city in your honor."

She waved off the accolade. "The city of Therma was built on a mosquito-infested swamp. I'm not sure how its residents feel about now being citizens of Thessaloniki, although surely it's an improvement over living in a city named for malarial fever."

I chuckled as she bumped my hip with her own, a movement that made her look like an off-balance hippopotamus, albeit a beaming one. "You should stop there someday," she said. "On your way to visit us in Macedon."

"I'd like that very much."

She stopped and clasped my wrist with a hand covered in gold rings, some shaped like snakes or twined laurel leaves, and each studded with a king's ransom in pearls and gemstones. "Really?"

"I'd stay in Pella with you for a while—if you'd have me, that is."

Regardless of the sanctity of her brother's mausoleum and its air of solemnity, Thessalonike's screech of excitement sent the pigeons flapping from the rafters, even as she grabbed me in a hug so tight that my ribs creaked. "My home is your home," she said, pressing a kiss to my cheek. "Forever and always."

Together we approached Alexander's sarcophagus, gleaming gold and hammered into the shape of a man. We knelt amid fresh piles of offerings—balls of frankincense and myrrh, Bucephalus coins and silver bangles—and I waited as Thessalonike whispered a prayer to her brother's shade in Elysium. I had no doubt that Hephaestion was at his elbow there, sharing a glass of wine with the likes of Pindar and Socrates, and laughing as in old times.

It was Alexander who had brought us all together, the golden lion of a warrior who carved out an empire from Macedon's shores all the way to India's rocky hills, from the barren mountains of northern Persia to Egypt's vast deserts. He had transformed the world and our small lives forever.

I both hated him and loved him for it, yet I refused to dwell on what my life—what any of our lives—might have been without him. After all, we cannot choose the lives the gods give us, only how we face them.

Thessalonike and I had been left behind to face this life and live after all the others had died. And we *had* lived, had laughed and cried, had bled and savored each moment. And one day we would greet all of those who'd gone before us to the afterlife and regale them with stories of all that we'd seen.

And Alexander would be there too, lifting a cup in our honor.

CAST OF CHARACTERS

denotes a historical figure

The Court of Macedon

*Philip II, king of Macedon and Alexander's father
*Olympias, Philip's first wife and Alexander's mother
 *Alexander, Philip's heir
*Eurydice, Philip's seventh, and youngest, wife
 *Cynnane, Philip's eldest legitimate daughter and Amyntas' widow
 *Adea, Cynnane's daughter
 *Arrhidaeus, son of Philip and an Illyrian dancing girl
 *Thessalonike, legitimate daughter of Philip, raised by Olympias
*Hephaestion, Alexander's companion
*Antipater, regent of Macedon
 *Cassander, son of Antipater and former student of Aristotle

The Persian Royal Family

*Darius III, King of Kings
*Stateira I, Darius' queen
 *Stateira II, elder daughter of Darius
 *Drypetis, second daughter of Darius
*Sisygambis, mother of Darius
*Parysatis, daughter of King Cyrus, cousin to Stateira and Drypetis

The Persian Nobility

*Bessus, *satrap* of Bactria
*Oxyartes of Balkh, minor noble
   *Roxana, daughter of Oxyartes
   *Alexander Aegus, Roxana's son
   Parizad, Oxyartes' son and Roxana's twin brother
*Mazaeus, *satrap* of Babylon
*Ariamazes, rebel leader at Sogdian Rock

Others

Adurnarseh, Greek singer
*Alcetas, Alexander's general
*Bagoas, eunuch and lover to Darius III
*Barsine, Alexander's mistress
*Heracles, Barsine's son
*Glaucus, physician
*Nearchus, Alexander's admiral
*Ptolemy, Alexander's general

AUTHOR'S NOTE

Although Alexander the Great (in typical, pompous Alexander fashion) reputedly bemoaned the fact that he had no Homer to record his triumphs in the annals of history, that's likely due to the fact that he had his appointed historian, Callisthenes, convicted of treason and imprisoned for criticizing Alexander's adoption of Persian customs. However, several of Alexander's contemporaries—including Ptolemy and Nearchus—did write of his various campaigns. Sadly, their works have all been lost and thus, we are left with the often conflicting accounts from Plutarch, Arrian, and Quintus Curtius Rufus, all of whom lived roughly four hundred years after Alexander's death. This sketchy historical record gave me the rare and wonderful benefit of being able to choose which historian's account would best accommodate my story arc during various events. That said, I still took a few liberties regarding certain characters. For example, Cassander's character is combined with that of his brother Iollus, who served as Alexander's wine bearer in Persia and was rumored to have poisoned the great conqueror. Ariamazes is a mixture of the historical Ariamazes, commander of Sogdian Rock, but also that of Spitamenes, a Sogdian warlord whose wife reputedly cut off his head and sent it as a peace offering to Alexander. Also, while there is no mention of Alexander's sister Thessalonike becoming a warrior, it is well documented that both

Cynnane and her daughter, Adea, were trained in the art of war as befitted noble Illyrian women. It didn't seem too far a stretch to believe that Thessalonike would yearn for the same training as she grew up with two warrior siblings. I also tweaked history to have Hephaestion take the place of two other documented soldiers, Peucestes and Limnaeus, atop the Mallian wall where Alexander was wounded. Finally, ancient historians disagree on the manner of Bessus' execution, so I combined pieces of Plutarch's and Arrian's versions, giving the torture a decidedly Persian twist.

In order to keep this tale from becoming a thousand-page saga, certain events and the overall timeline were condensed, especially toward the end of the book. According to history, the fire in Persepolis occurred weeks after Alexander entered the city and received the citizens' gold, although sources do speculate whether the ancient city was burned at the recommendation of the courtesan Thais or whether the fire was ordered by Alexander as vengeance for the Persian War. The gruesome and never-ending string of murders that took place from Alexander's death until Roxana's execution took roughly thirteen years and many more men served as regent until only one man was left standing in Macedon: Cassander. I decided against making Cassander a villain, since the historians writing about him hundreds of years later seemed blinded by their awe of Alexander; it is easy to see why they cast suspicion on the role Cassander played in Alexander's death.

Both ancient and modern historians continue to debate the real cause of Alexander the Great's premature death, with theories including typhoid fever, malaria, alcoholism, and poisoning. Lacking a time machine and the ability to definitively prove what felled the great conqueror, I chose to combine several factors: namely, his grief at Hephaestion's death, his overindulgence in alcohol, and a possible infectious disease. Hephaestion's death also remains a mystery; it was possibly caused by poisoning or typhoid compounded by an ulcerated intestine. It is unlikely that we'll ever know the true cause of either of these deaths, so given the existing evidence, I chose what could be considered plausible for both men.

After Alexander's death, the main players on the stage really did drop like unlucky flies. It's believed that Roxana colluded with one of Alexander's generals, Perdiccas, who became regent after his death; Roxana's real aim was to murder Stateira. In a book with a weighty list of characters, I replaced Perdiccas with Roxana's fictional brother, Parizad. There is also debate as to whether Parysatis or Drypetis was killed alongside Stateira, but after being forced to kill off so many of my favorite characters, I decided to let Drypetis live.

If I could, I would name several ancient cities after a number of people who were instrumental in shaping this book. I owe Kate Quinn a lifetime's supply of swan fat beauty cream (or perhaps just a bottle of really great merlot) for her hilarious comments regarding severed heads and her talent for hashing out appropriate curse words for my leading ladies. Jade Timms makes Alexander's achievements pale in comparison with her ability to critique my manuscript immediately after giving birth and while wrangling two very small children. Renee Yancy and Amalia Dillin both helped make this book readable in its infancy, a feat akin to storming fortified cities in the ancient world. My agent extraordinaire, Marlene Stringer, gave me the encouragement I needed when she insisted that readers want to read about ancient history's infamous women. Thank you also to Jenn Fischer, for ushering this book through the final hurdles toward publication. And a seaside palace should be erected in honor of Ellen Edwards, my exceptional editor, who once pondered whether I'd consider writing a book about Persian women. (I just happened to throw in a few Greeks for fun!)

Finally, I am forever indebted to my friends and family, without whom this whole business of writing books would be a long and lonely enterprise. To the usual suspects—Cindy Davis, Eugenia Merrifield,

Kristi Senden, Claire Torbensen, and Megan Williams—for insisting that I get out to run and hike instead of living with my laptop. To my parents, Tim and Daine Crowley, for being the best and most persistent cheerleaders a girl could ask for, and to my sister, Hollie Dunn, for always asking about my latest book.

Most of all, to Stephen and Isabella, who scarcely bat an eye anymore as I drag drafts and revisions to Hawaii, Peru, Disneyland, and everywhere in between. I'd rename Alexandria after both of you, but seeing as I lack that power (and StephenIsabellia is quite a mouthful), I'll settle for saying thank you.

And I love you.

FURTHER READING ON
THE EMPIRE OF ALEXANDER THE GREAT

NONFICTION

Arrian. *The Campaigns of Alexander.* Translated by Aubrey de Selincourt. New York: Penguin Classics, 1958.

Carney, Elizabeth Donnelly. *Women and Monarchy in Macedonia.* Norman: University of Oklahoma Press, 2000.

Dalby, Andrew, and Sally Grainger. *The Classical Cookbook.* Los Angeles: J. Paul Getty Museum, 1996.

Foreman, Laura. *Alexander the Conqueror: The Epic Story of the Warrior King.* Cambridge, MA: Da Capo Press, 2004.

Fox, Robin Lane. *Alexander the Great.* New York: Penguin, 1973.

Mayor, Adrienne. *Greek Fire, Poison Arrows, and Scorpion Bombs: Biological and Chemical Warfare in the Ancient World.* New York: Overlook Press, 2003.

Plutarch. *The Life of Alexander the Great.* Translated by John Dryden. New York: Modern Library Paperback Edition, 2004.

Sappho. *The Poems of Sappho.* Translated by John Myers O'Hara. Portland, ME: Smith and Sale, 1910.

Stoneman, Richard, translator. *The Greek Alexander Romance.* London: Penguin Classics, 1991.

Wood, Michael. *In the Footsteps of Alexander the Great.* Berkeley: University of California Press, 1997.

FICTION

Renault, Mary. *Fire from Heaven*. New York: Vintage, 1969.

———. *Funeral Games*. New York: Vintage, 1981.

———. *The Persian Boy*. New York: Vintage, 1972

THE
CONQUEROR'S
WIFE

A Novel of Alexander the Great

STEPHANIE
THORNTON

A CONVERSATION WITH
STEPHANIE THORNTON

Q. In your previous three novels, you've written about many forgotten women of ancient history. What inspired you to turn to the women associated with Alexander the Great?

A. I had just finished writing *The Tiger Queens*, a novel about Genghis Khan's wife and daughters, when my editor suggested that I might focus next on an ancient Persian woman. I stumbled upon Roxana while I was researching and discovered that, as with Genghis Khan, incredibly strong women also supported Alexander. It was a natural jump to go from writing about one conqueror's women to the next!

Q. Alexander was highly educated for the time—by the great Aristotle no less—yet he chose a path of violent conquest that included the slaughter of thousands upon thousands of people. As a Macedonian, did he have an unconscious need to prove his superiority to the Greeks, who tended to think very highly of themselves? What do you think drove his quest for power and heroic stature?

A. Alexander's driving force for his conquests was quite likely his father's earlier subjugation of Greece. Philip II of Macedon consolidated his rule over virtually the entire Peloponnese, to the point where Alexander once commented that there would be nothing left for him to conquer. Of course, Alexander wouldn't tolerate the many rebellions in Greece after Philip's death, and seeking to subdue the Achaemenid Empire was likely a natural inclination after the Persian War. From there it's no great leap to consider vanquishing India and thus becoming the conqueror of the largest empire the world had ever known.

Q. *You suggest that many of Alexander's military tactics were truly inventive. Can you tell us more about that?*

A. It's impossible to argue that Alexander wasn't a tactical genius. He inherited a well-trained army from his father, but shaped them into a truly formidable, and creative, fighting machine. For example, Alexander really did order the building of a mile-long mole, or causeway, in order to better position his siege weaponry at Tyre and he also scaled what was believed to be an impassable wall in order to reach Sogdian Rock. (Which may well have been to spite the commander of the fortress after he taunted Alexander that he'd need men with wings to take the rock.) He was often willing to chance the impossible, and was rewarded for his daring.

Q. *You also suggest that Hephaestion played an essential role in both assisting Alexander's conquests and tempering his excesses. What does the historical record tell us about Hephaestion and their relationship?*

A. Hephaestion served as Alexander's second-in-command, and both ancient and modern sources compare the men's relationship to that of Achilles and Patroclus during the Trojan War. Their closeness seems to have been public knowledge, considering that Aristotle claimed they shared one soul abiding in two bodies and the historian Curtius wrote that Hephaestion was Alexander's "sharer of secrets." Most telling is perhaps Alexander's reaction to Hephaestion's death, in which he flung himself on the body and ordered a period of mourning for the entire empire. The temple's sacred fire was extinguished and a massive funeral pyre built, followed by an extravagant show of funeral games. One modern estimate places the cost of Hephaestion's funeral at more than two billion dollars by today's standards. I'd say that means Alexander and Hephaestion were fairly close!

Q. I love Drypetis' interest in how things work. How unusual would her interest in engineering have been for a woman of her time? Can you expand on what the historical record tells us about her?

A. Very little is known about Drypetis, only that she was captured at Issus along with the rest of her family and traveled with Alexander until he left her in Susa. She did marry Hephaestion at the massive Susa weddings, and some sources claim that Roxana murdered her alongside Stateira. However, it's likely that Plutarch misidentified Drypetis as her cousin Parysatis in reporting Roxana's victims.

As for Drypetis' love of tinkering, I know of no documentation of ancient women with a similar hobby, but there were a number of intriguing Greek and Persian inventions near this time, including the Baghdad Battery and the Antikythera Mechanism. Obviously people were experimenting with many new ideas, and it didn't seem a far stretch that a Persian princess with time on her hands would mind getting those same hands dirty in the name of knowledge.

Q. Thessalonike's antipathy for Cassander is an entertaining refrain throughout the book. Do we know if their marriage was ultimately a happy one? How long did they rule together?

A. I assumed that their union was mostly happy, considering that Cassander did rename the ancient city of Therma in her honor, but sadly, the two didn't have long to enjoy their marriage. Cassander died of edema in 297 BCE, only eight years after proclaiming himself king of Macedon. Much like the events after Alexander the Great's death, a fight for Macedon's throne broke out once again, this time among Cassander's sons. Thessalonike supported her third son, Alexander, a choice that led her eldest son, Antipater, to eventually order her put to death.

Q. How typical a queen was Olympias, especially with regard to her ruthless support of Alexander? How did her membership in the cult of Dionysus shape her moral code? Or can you tell us more about the mysterious cult of Dionysus?

A. Olympias was definitely not a typical queen, especially considering that Greek wives were expected to live out their lives in the women's quarters. There's no doubt that she was ambitious, and as sister to one king, wife to another, and mother to a third, she was in a unique position to wield her power. That said, as with many formidable ancient women, such ambition spawned stories that she copulated with snakes and possibly even arranged her husband's assassination.

The cult of Dionysus is still shrouded in mystery, but we do know that women were welcomed into its ranks and allowed to shed society's expectations during the rites: drinking, fighting, and engaging in orgiastic revels. One can only guess whether initiation into such a group might have shaped Olympias' beliefs, but I suspect her ambition for herself and her son was the main motivating force in the brutalities she committed.

Q. The Greeks and Persians fought each other off and on over many centuries, in wars that have come down to us in epic poems and ancient histories. Alexander is described as adopting many Persian ways, and being criticized for it by his own men. Can you expand on the relationship between the Greeks/Macedonians and Persians?

A. The Greeks and the Persians fought against each other in the Persian Wars and again during Alexander's conquests. And while Alexander did torch Persepolis and fight several bloody battles against Darius, he spared many other cities, adopted the *proskynesis* and Persian dress, and allowed thousands of Persian youths to join his army. Perhaps the most telling example of Alexander's aims toward Persia is his benevolent treatment of Darius' female family members after their capture and his later marriages to Stateira and Parysatis. While he had subdued Persia's lands, he sought to assimilate its people into his new empire.

Q. Do we know what happened to Barsine? Was her son by Alexander, Heracles, his only surviving offspring?

A. According to several ancient accounts, Barsine and her son managed to escape the worst of the initial bloodshed after Alexander's death, only for both to be put to death by Cassander's orders in 309 BCE. Thus, Alexander would have had no known surviving offspring; a child with his blood would have been too dangerous a contender for any other man trying to secure one of Alexander's many thrones.

Q. What do scholars now consider to have been Alexander's lasting legacy? Who was most responsible for shaping that legacy?

A. Alexander conquered roughly three thousand square miles in only thirteen years, but his legacy was most assuredly his spreading of Hellenistic culture beyond Greece's borders. His destruction of the Achaemenid Empire and conquest of the known world meant that it was Greek customs, philosophy, and language that influenced later

Rome, Byzantium, and much of the Western world. Alexander has the rare honor of being one of the few people who truly changed history and he did it mostly through his military innovations and the force of his own personality.

Q. Was there any material that you wanted to include, but ended up cutting?

A. There were actually several battle scenes that were trimmed away, including one after Susa where the wily Persians catapulted boulders into a ravine on top of the Greeks, complete with exposed brains and all sorts of other gore. However, in a book fraught with battle scenes, not all of them made it into the final manuscript!

Q. Your author bio says you've been obsessed with the women of ancient history since the age of twelve. What happened to get you hooked?

A. My junior high social studies teacher assigned research reports on famous people in history and since I'd always been a huge fan of ancient Egypt (what kid isn't?), I raced to sign up for Cleopatra. Sadly, she was already taken, but I found an encyclopedia entry for Hatshepsut—a lone, meager paragraph—and knew there was more to her story. Since then I've found all sorts of ancient women whose lives have been relegated to historical footnotes, and have decided that their stories need to be told.

Q. You travel extensively during school vacations. Do you travel to the places where your novels are set? How do your trips enrich your work, and inspire new ideas?

A. I've been fortunate to have traveled to Turkey, Egypt, and Greece for three of my four novels. Being able to immerse myself in the culture and history of those countries certainly helps me infuse into my writing more accurate details about daily life as it might have been lived thousands of years ago: seeing animal-hide-wrapped cheeses for sale in the Grand Bazaar, children splashing in the Nile, or a herd of shaggy goats in Crete. However, sometimes I travel just to travel!

Q. *Do you have a new writing project lined up?*

A. I've actually made a time jump and am currently doing my own tinkering on a novel set in twentieth-century America. I've got a bit of a soft spot for a certain presidential family and one of its wild-child daughters in particular!

QUESTIONS FOR
DISCUSSION

1. Which characters did you most like and which did you dislike? Whom will you remember?

2. At first glance the title, *The Conqueror's Wife*, seems to belong to Roxana, but several characters could actually lay claim to such a title. Who do you think is best described as "the conqueror's wife"?

3. Many of the main characters—Roxana, Drypetis, and Thessalonike—have siblings who support them in various ways, while Hephaestion and Alexander consider themselves as close as brothers. Discuss how these siblings both support and hinder one another throughout the novel.

4. Alexander's character is associated with fire throughout much of the story. Discuss who and what temper that fire, and to what extent they also fan his flames.

5. Were you familiar with the history before reading the book? What did you find particularly interesting or surprising about it?

6. What do you think of Roxana and Olympias, two women who kill to get what they want? Do you find them sympathetic? How do they differ from each other?

7. Alexander conquers the world with the expectation that he'll become heroic and live forever in memory, song, and lore. Compare ancient and modern understandings of immortality, and how it can be achieved. Is Alexander like someone today who commits mass murder with the intention of becoming famous?

8. Many of the characters suffer gruesome deaths. Discuss ancient and modern capacities for violence.

9. What are some of the strategies the women characters use to stay one step ahead of events that threaten to turn against them?

10. Discuss Hephaestion's comment: "After a battle, you bed a woman to forget what has happened. You bed a man because he knows exactly what you're trying to forget."

11. What do you consider to be Alexander's lasting legacy?

READY FOR MORE
FROM STEPHANIE THORNTON?
READ ON FOR A LOOK AT

THE SECRET HISTORY

A Novel of Empress Theodora

AVAILABLE FROM
NEW AMERICAN LIBRARY

Twenty-sixth year of
the reign of Emperor Anastasius

My life began the night death visited our house.

I lay on the straw pallet with my sisters and listened to Comito grinding her teeth and Anastasia breathing evenly in the dark. An animal snorted in the distance—probably the scraggly new bear Father had acquired to train for the Greens, a beast scarcely fit for the spectacle of the Hippodrome. I scratched my stomach and poked Comito, none too gently. The fleas were bad tonight, and Constantinople's sticky heat made the stench of the nearby garbage heap especially pungent. I missed our old home in Cyprus, the salty smell of the Mediterranean, and the cicadas buzzing amidst the olive trees. Our ramshackle house near Constantinople's amphitheater could hardly compare.

There was a shuffle in the dark—possibly a rat—but then my father grunted.

"Quiet, Acacius." My mother giggled. "You'll wake the girls."

She gave a little moan as I snuggled into Anastasia's bare back, hoping for more dreams like last night's fantasy of roasted goat with mint yogurt. Comito claimed I had made cow eyes at the butcher's son when Mother sent us to collect our monthly grain ration earlier today, but in truth I was more impressed with the fresh leg of goat hanging from his stall than the cut of his calves under his tunica. It seemed like years since we'd had meat.

"Acacius." My mother's voice woke me, the same tone she used when my father came home after too much wine at the Boar's Eye. There was another sound, a thud like a sack of flour hitting the ground. "Acacius!"

"Mama?" I opened my eyes. My father was facedown on their pallet, arms crumpled like twigs under his bulk.

My mother struggled to move him. "Help me, Theodora."

The chipped mosaic blossoms scraped my knee as I helped shove him to his back. Anastasia whimpered in the moonlight.

Cold sweat covered my father's skin as he opened and closed his mouth like a mackerel freshly pulled from the Bosphorus, fingers plucking the neck of his tunica. My mother clutched his hand to her chest. "You stay right here, Acacius."

She rifled through a little cedar box with her free hand, the one with our scant supply of spices and medicines. Willow bark and chamomile filled my nose as Comito rubbed her eyes and Anastasia crawled into my lap, thumb in her mouth and her wooden doll tucked tight under her arm. It squinted at me through its charcoal smudge of an eye. My father looked from me to Mama to my sisters, and his tongue lurched in his mouth, as if he were trying to speak. Death has many sounds, the shrieks of men crushed by a chariot in the Hippodrome, the final rattle of ancient lungs, or the gentle sigh of a child ravaged by creeping sickness. My giant of a father only gurgled like an infant and then went still.

We sat in silence for a moment. Then my mother screamed and pummeled my father with tiny fists, dusting his chest with the yellow ash of crushed herbs. "No!" Tears streamed down her face. "No! Get up!"

She collapsed to his chest, golden curls covering him like a burial shroud as her body heaved with sobs. Departing this life in the throes of passion is as good a way to go as any, but I could not fathom my father greeting Saint Peter now. I clung to Anastasia as my tears fell into her hair.

"Don't be sad, Dora." She traced my cheeks with fingers still sticky from the honeyed *kopton* we'd eaten before bed, but her chin wobbled as my mother wailed louder. My little sister slid from my lap and touched Mama's shoulder, but she jerked back as Comito added her voice to the howls.

I pulled Anastasia to me and tucked us into the crook of my father's arm, savoring his fleeting warmth.

My father was dead.

Never again would he carry Anastasia on his shoulders to see the zebras before a show, or tease Comito until the tips of her ears turned red. He would never wrap me in an elephant hug that smelled of the wild rosemary he constantly chewed and the ever-present animal musk that clung to his skin, even after he'd just come home from the baths.

I don't know how long we listened to one another's tears, but his body grew stiff and clammy before I could rouse myself. He would have to be buried soon, before his flesh began to decay.

I touched my mother's back, but she jerked away as if stung, still draped over my father. "The sun will rise soon." I rubbed my eyes with the back of my hand. "We have to purify him."

She stumbled to her feet, hair veiling her eyes. "No. I won't." Her hands fluttered in the air. "I can't."

She slammed the door behind her, followed by a surly thump on our ceiling from the Syrian neighbors above. Raucous laughter from a nearby taverna floated to our apartment, the high trill of a woman and throaty baritone of the man who had likely paid for her services for the night. I stared at the shaft of silvery light that had swallowed my mother, torn between the urge to follow her or stay with my father's body.

"What should we do?" Comito wiped her puffy eyes. She was older than me by two years but looked far younger in the moonlight. Anastasia sucked her thumb and reached out to touch our father's cheek with her little hand. It was more than I could bear.

"Go. Gather flowers."

"It's dark out." Comito hated the dark—she still liked to fall asleep with an olive oil lamp burning, although she claimed it was for Anastasia.

I pressed a frayed basket to her hand as Anastasia whimpered. "The lion will eat us if we go outside," she said, her eyes big as plums.

I would have laughed—my father had been telling Anastasia myths from the Golden Age, most recently acting out the story of the Nemean Lion falling from the full moon—but instead I blinked hard and tweaked her nose. "Silly goose, Heracles slew the lion. You'll be perfectly safe." I bent down to whisper in her ear. "And you're much scarier than any lion when you growl."

She bared her teeth and made claws with her hands, her little mouth opening in an adorable roar. I swallowed hard and dropped a kiss on her head. "Help Comito pick a pretty posy. And find Uncle Asterius." My voice quavered as I spoke to Comito. "He needs to bring a priest."

They left and I was alone. I shouldn't have been alone—this was my mother's job. I didn't know how to prepare a body, how to purify my father so he could pass to the afterlife. But there was no one else.

My hands trembled as I struck the flame for our oil lamp and rummaged through our lone trunk, past my father's ivory backgammon set with its missing piece and the worn codex of Homer's *Song of Ilium*. I tossed out Mother's saffron wedding veil before I finally found what I was looking for—a single bottle of olive oil pressed from our own trees in Cyprus. I tried not to cry but had to set the bottle down to wipe the stream of snot and tears from my face. Once started, I couldn't seem to stop.

I didn't hear my mother return until she gathered me into her arms, the hot smell of wine on her breath as she pressed her lips to my forehead. Together we readied my father—she washed his body and redressed him in his green tunica, and my uneven stitches sewed him into his brown cloak until only his face and the splayed toes of his feet showed, the better to allow the angels to examine him and determine his fitness for paradise. He looked asleep, and I prayed that he might sit up and roar with laughter because we'd fallen for another of his jokes. Yet God was deaf to my prayers.

Myrrh choked the air and the sun had almost heaved itself over the horizon when Comito arrived with a priest and Uncle Asterius, Anastasia asleep in his arms with her thumb tucked in her mouth. He wasn't really our uncle, but our father's boss. As leader of the Green faction, he was also one of Constantinople's most powerful politicians. He draped an arm around my mother. "You have my deepest condolences, Zenobia." He crooned something in her ear that made her blanch white, but then she looked at us and gave a terse nod.

Uncle Asterius swept me into a hug that smelled of the lavender used to sweeten his linen. "Poor child," he said. "Everything is going to be all right."

Even then, I knew that to be a lie.

The funeral began in the thin morning light as Uncle Asterius' bleary-eyed slaves hefted the greenwood coffin onto their shoulders, my father's circus whip and pitchfork nestled beside him. Yawning shopkeepers crossed themselves as we made our way to the cedar-lined path that led to the cemetery outside the Gate of Charisios. The air stunk like rotting fish, compliments of the nearby *garos* factories, forced outside the city walls with their vats of fermenting fish sauce. The flowers my sisters had picked on the banks of the Lycus River—daisies, blue crocuses, violets, and scraggly yellow poppies—had already begun to wilt over the sides of the box, and the calm hymns of the lone priest battled with the mournful dirges sung by a professional mourner paid for by Uncle Asterius. We recited a truncated version of the Divine Liturgy and each kissed the rough wooden cross the priest held over the coffin before accepting a square of dry bread and a sip of *phouska*, the watery, sour wine only the poor would drink. My mother's hands trembled violently as she struggled to cut a lock of my father's hair, and the tears ran unchecked down her cheeks. I took the knife from her.

I stared at the blade and ran my thumb down its edge, transfixed by the pearl of blood that dropped onto my father's rough brown shroud. One swift cut and I could join him, free myself from grief's jagged teeth.

Two dark eyes stopped me. Anastasia wiped her nose on her sleeve and took my hand in her little one, kissing the tip of my thumb above the blood. "You hurt yourself, Dora. Are you going to die, too?"

I shook my head, the words tangled in my throat. It would be cowardly to abandon my family. I had many faults—Comito was always quick to point out my temper and snitch on me when I lied—but I wasn't a coward. Family was all we had.

I managed to cut a lock of my father's dark hair, identical to my own, and folded it into my palm, mingling my blood with the black strands. My mother fell to her knees and refused to rise long after the slaves tucked him into the red earth. We were alone in Constantinople—no money squirreled away under a pallet and no way to provide for ourselves.

I'd have promised God anything then to have our old lives back. Unfortunately, our new lives were just beginning.

Photo by Katherine Schmeling Photography

Stephanie Thornton is a writer and history teacher who has been obsessed with infamous women from ancient history since she was twelve. She lives with her husband and daughter in Alaska, where she is at work on her next novel.